ANOTHER NEGRO

for my

PLANTATION

Written by **Andre Linoge**

Originally published by Linoge Book Company LLC
First Published July 2022

Copyright © Andre Linoge 2022

Printed in the United States of America
10 9 8 7 6 5 4 3 2 1

ISBN: 978-1-7363538-2-0

ACKNOWLEDGEMENT

This manuscript was written in the light of hope that all will take the positive and influential message contained herein. The title is guaranteed not only to open your eyes, but to open your mind, ears, and truths within all human beings. It is intended to be a source of encouragement rather than despair.

Inspired by the life of Mr. Charleston White, who has positively influenced many people and black communities, I give thanks. Through his works, lectures, and teachings, I have been greatly affected by his words. I am forever grateful to him for overcoming negative situations and circumstances, and believing that all people can change for the positive. He has been a role model to me.

Andre Linoge

ANOTHER NEGRO

for my

PLANTATION

PROLOGUE

"Yes?" he asked, as John heard his boss call his name when he stuck his head outside the trailer.

"Can you come inside for a moment?" he had asked.

"Shit, what have I done now?" John thought as he walked from his car across the gravel parking lot to the construction foreman's trailer parked inside the chain linked fence. There were three squad cars pulled up by it. If there had been anymore John would have thought someone had died. But, only three cars - that was nothing for neighborhoods near his hood.

The Boodie Boyz had flipped his hood upside down before he was even born, but the pains of their reign still lingered to this day. The master was Kenneth "Boodie" Cole. He dominated the streets and built an empire worth over a hundred million dollars. That was a lot of dough for some street boys from Carol City, Florida. The only problem was that he wasn't Kenneth Cole who built his fashion empire from the ground up. He paraded around, from the stories told, wearing KC swags, but he wasn't the real KC. He was the most likable kid from the hood. Even John's gramma liked him. She had been his third grade teacher.

Boodie swagged up and down the streets, bought his first Cadillac at nineteen, and then something changed him. By the time he reached his late twenties, he and his gang heated up the table saw by lining over a hundred wooden coffins. The number of bullet holes left in the nearby houses, trees, cars, signs, and human tissue is still unknown. Their pixie dust was flying off the shelves. And, even if you didn't want any, he made you buy some anyway.

"John Bramble, Jr?" an officer asked when John stepped foot inside.

"Yea," John said, looking down at the dirt covering the floor of the old trailer.

"What have I always told you?" Warren Laikin asked John when he saw the young man look away from the officer.

"Yes, sir," John said again looking into the eyes of the police officer. If the boys on John's street had heard him call an officer sir, they would have jumped him right then and there. According to them, officers should never be given respect.

John knew exactly what Warren was talking about. He told John to always look people in the eyes when talking to them. No matter who they are, you must always look straight into their eyes and use proper English.

"We just have a few questions for you, John," the other officer said. "Have you seen or heard from Alvaro Hernandez since Friday?"

"No. Last I saw him, he was waiting to get on the bus over there," John said as he pointed to the corner stop. "It was about four-thirty on Friday when we got off work."

"Did he mention anything at all to you as to where he might be going?" the first officer asked.

"We don't talk much about our personal lives here at work," John said, trying to figure out why they were questioning him. "He didn't say a thing. Why are you asking?"

"As you probably know, Mr. Hernandez did not show up for work yesterday, and apparently he hasn't been seen by anyone since he left work on Friday afternoon," the officer replied.

Alvaro had only been working about six months for Laikin Construction Company. He was on the framing crew, so John didn't see him that much. Warren had been John's boss for three years now and was teaching him how to become a successful job foreman and businessman. John hit it off with him the first day he stepped foot onto the job site near Surfside. Warren told John time and time again, *Your skin may be black, son, but you don't talk like the other black kids around here. You are different.* John didn't know if he was being prejudiced or not, but he was giving John a chance to learn hands-on.

"What's that have to do with me?" John then asked, a bit annoyed.

"We know you live near him and went to high school with him. We were hoping you could shed some light onto his disappearance," the other officer said. "Did he say anything at all to you on Friday that seemed a bit odd?"

John looked at Warren and then looked down to the ground, thinking to himself and pondering the questions. He didn't even realize that Alvaro was missing. "No," he said after a brief moment of silence. "He was singing that Ricky Rose song that helped put the Carol City cartel on the news, 'This shit about to get deeper than rap,' he said. That's the last thing I heard come out of his mouth when he walked away. I stayed for a few minutes to chat with Mr. Laikin," John said looking at Warren.

"That's true," Warren told the officers.

One of the officers jotted something down in a little black book.

"Alvaro listens to that kind of stuff all the time," John added.

"Thanks kid," the older officer said, as they stepped down from the trailer and headed back to their car. The other officers were standing there waiting for them. Maybe they had talked to other workers or even checked out the job site. John really didn't know.

Once the officers had left, Warren asked John if Alvaro really had been rapping that song. "Why?" he asked.

"Somebody painted those exact words on the roof of my new building," Warren said, as he looked up towards the top floor of the building next to the trailer. "A local news helicopter spotted it this morning when they were doing their morning traffic update."

"Damn," John said looking into the eyes of his boss. "Do you think that has anything to do with Alvaro being missing?" he asked.

"I have no idea," Warren replied. "His mom called me yesterday to see if he had shown up to work. She said that she had not seen him all weekend. The officers stopped over after the news channel reported their findings to them."

For the most part, the rest of John's day at the job site seemed typical, with one exception. John threw on a tool belt, pounded some nails with the guys and met with several of the crew foremen to review the electrical plans. All of the elevator towers had been built, and all the concrete had been poured. They were ready to begin the next phase of this multi-building project at Hialeah Flats.

"Hey, John boy," Ralph called out, "who fried up all that bacon?" he continued. Ralph was a weathered Floridian who rubbed John the wrong way. He always had a smart remark to make and a half smoked

Newport dangling off the side of his yellow tooth smile. "I'd seen ya walk out of the trailer after they left. You gotta know somethin."

"Not really," John said. "Apparently, Alvaro is missing. He didn't show up to work yesterday or today."

"That's it boy?" Ralph persisted. "I could a tol' ya that." The rest of the crew laughed when John started to walk away.

"I don't hang out with him, so I have no idea what he's up to," John claimed.

There was chatter the rest of the morning about Alvaro, but it soon died down when the roofers showed up to clean the paint off the roof. None of the men knew that they had some graffiti above their heads. Before the roofers arrived, John ran over to the corner hardware store to buy two one-hundred foot hoses for them. With a power washer and some special cleaning agent, they were able to spray the fresh paint off the white clay tile. Fortunately, the remedy was a minor cost to Warren. He was more concerned with the message and his missing employee.

Warren wanted Hialeah Flats to be the best housing development north of the airport. Each unit would have its own washer and dryer, high end appliances, large walk-in closets, and balconies. The large fitness room that overlooked the pool which was centered in the middle of the complex had every feature imaginable including a climbing wall. A pool table, bowling alley and golf range would round out the clubhouse amenities upon completion. A modern exterior and contemporary interior would upscale this property and hopefully begin the revitalization needed in Hialeah.

Everything was up to code with a wind-resistant design according to the new building laws that had been established in Florida back in 2002. After Hurricane Andrew created havoc down there, building codes changed. Hialeah had become the fastest growing city in Miami-Dade County with Laiken Construction Company leading the way.

Life was good. Warren had placed John in an apprenticeship program where he was learning skills that he never knew existed. John took one evening class every Wednesday night and worked side by side with him. Warren treated John as if he were his long lost son, but he wasn't. Warren was white, and John was clearly black. John's parents were happily married and had been for many years. Warren was right in his evaluation of John. He was not like the other African-American boys in this town.

"Junior," John heard his gramma Shanice call the moment he first stepped through the front door of their old wood framed ranch home that once shimmered with bright white paint. Years of neglect and the brutal heat had changed its glow to a dull pale-yellow. The roof had a mix match of orange terra cotta tile from hurricane repairs over the years. "You come in here and give me a hug and kiss," she demanded before John even had time to take off his shoes.

She had been gone for the past seven days visiting her sister up in Ellerton, on the other coast, north of Sarasota. "Gonna tell me bout that trip of yours?" John asked her.

"No, not until you first sit down and tell me why I came home to a bunch of cop cars down yonder at the Hernandez home," she said.

"Why does everyone think I know something about Alvaro Hernandez?" John asked his gramma.

"I'm not everyone, and I didn't ask about Alvaro, but you obviously must have something to say about him," she said, giving John that grandmotherly look that she had perfected over the past twenty years. "And, just because I have been gone a week doesn't mean you can slip back using street language," she continued, demanding that John use proper pronunciation of words.

"All I know is that he didn't show up for work yesterday or today. Last I saw him, he was at the bus stop on Friday afternoon, headed home I suppose."

"So then," she continued, "why is Hialeah Flats all over the news tonight?" she pondered.

"What?" John said in disbelief. He then walked into the living room and turned their new smart television to channel 9, WMIA Miami. Sure enough the roof of their building was on the local news, painted with the words of their local rapper, 'This shit about to get deeper than rap.' Thankfully, the news did not mention the name of the building. Instead they stated that it was a new construction site in Hialeah.

"That is it," John said, returning to the kitchen where his gramma was sitting at the table. "I have no idea, Gramma. I just know when I got to work this morning, the police were there waiting to question me. You know that I don't really like Alvaro so I try to avoid him whenever I can. I see him enough at work and really don't want to become friends with him now, especially after what happened in high school," John reminded his gramma. "I'm telling you what I told them. He was waiting at the bus stop around four thirty on Friday afternoon after he got off work. That's the last time I saw him. I waited around to talk to Mr. Laikin after work."

"Okay, you be sure to tell me if you hear anything else, Son," John's gramma added. "You know I don't want to be left out in the dark," she said. "Please take my bags to my room before your ma and pa get home too. You know I need a strong young man like you to help me out these days," she said with a smile.

John walked back to the front door and picked up her bags and started to head down the hallway, when she stopped him again. "Junior," she said, "I'll tell you about my trip around the dinner table tonight when your parents are home to hear as well. There is one thing I can tell you now about my trip though. You know that property you sold up there on University Parkway?"

"Yes, ma'am, I do," John politely replied.

"Your auntie and I drove by there two days ago. They are building a Culver's on that little piece of land."

John smiled and carried his gramma's bags to her room. He had done something right. Warren Laiken had given him a small investment loan two and a half years ago. He was teaching him how to invest in real estate. As much as he knew John's dad loved him and wanted the best for him, he also knew that his parents didn't have the finances to invest in his future. Warren was giving John a once-in-a-life-time opportunity, and John did not want to fail him or himself. John had bought and sold three pieces of land, all commercial properties. This one grossed his largest profits to date, providing enough to pay back the initial loan and invest in more property.

John recently made two purchases with his profits. He bought another piece of commercial property just north of University Parkway in Lakewood Ranch, a growing community northeast of Sarasota. His second purchase was a large chunk of land near a preserve. He had not told anyone about his latest purchase. He set it up through his new business which was being funded through a new trust fund from an offshore account. Warren had told John that a lot of wealthy people use offshore accounts for investments. He told him early on that smart people are not just people who receive a college education. Some of the brightest men in history did not have college educations. If you can not afford college or do not have the patience to sit around in a boring lecture hall, then you can still educate yourself. That is exactly what John had been doing the past two years.

When John brought home a fifty-inch smart tv for his family, news spread throughout their neighborhood like a wildfire. Alvaro had seen him carrying the box up to their front door. Even last week, Alvaro continued to taunt John at work with the claim that he's a rich boy now. Not that it matters what he says. Alvaro had been the star tight end on their high school football team and was recruited to play for the University of Florida. His life as a Gator didn't last long. Two short seasons and he was booted off the team for possession of marijuana.

John never understood why Alvaro thought owning a smart tv made him a rich boy. With all the liquor and smoke sales around their hood and school, everyone in this part of Miami could have purchased ten televisions with the money they had wasted over the years. Instead, they find a way to complain, be nosy, lazy, and pull the race card.

When John started following Warren's advice, he knew he had to keep some secrets to himself. No way did he want Alvaro, or anyone else, sniffing around his business. John loves his family way too much for targets to be put on their backs due to his success. They have been working hard and trying their best for years, and they have been failed time and time again by friends, co-workers, and people living with excuses. Anytime someone tries to succeed in this hood, they are shot down by young black folks taunting them for their success. Somehow they believe that hard work does not equate to success. They are ignorant and would rather live in poverty and under the influence of government programs for the rest of their lives. They think the world owes them a pot of gold. John thinks the world owes them a lesson or two about life, but he doesn't want to be the one teaching them that lesson. Nor will he be bragging to anyone about his recent purchase.

John's gramma, Shanice Bramble, was a school teacher for many years, working right there at their local elementary school until she retired. Working for an inner city school with multi-racial students is not an easy job, nor is it high paying. Yet his gramma was diligent in her job, caring for each and every student, regardless of their flaws.

John's momma, Ebony, had been working at the local deli ever since John went into first grade. She started at minimum wage and receives a yearly salary increase of fifteen to twenty cents per hour. That means her income has only increased a few hundred dollars each year. She has made numerous attempts to find a better paying job, but complications always seem to find her. The deli always worked well with her schedule. She would go into work early and be home in time to care for John after school. After all these years on the job, she still only receives fifteen days of vacation. John has never heard her complain, not even once. She's just thankful that she has a steady job.

John's dad, John Bramble, Sr., has been laid off more times than he can count. He's a hard worker, but every time the economy dips so does his job. Years ago, he worked as a baggage handler for Eastern Airlines until they went out of business. Then he switched to the other Miami based airline, Pan Am. That job didn't last long either when they filed bankruptcy in December of 1991 just before Christmas. He then switched over to retail, unloading trucks for Jefferson Stores and Richards until both of them went defunct.

John, Sr. has worked multiple jobs making and delivering pizzas as well, and he even worked security for the Miami Heat games. He liked the security job, but discovered that he wasn't making a lot of money after taxes, parking fees and gas for his car. He was bringing home only five dollars an hour. He knew he would have to make another change. Warren offered him a job, but it required manual labor, something John's dad was too old to start now. Too many years of loading luggage and unloading trucks had taken a toll on his body. After six attempts, John's dad finally landed a job as a mailroom clerk at the largest law firm around. He's been working there for the past year and a half now and loves his job.

After dropping off the bags in his gramma's room, John showered and laid down on his bed with his towel wrapped around his waist. He had only planned to rest his feet for a few minutes before dinner, but he must have dozed off because the next thing he knew, his gramma was shouting, "How many times do I have to call for you, Junior? Dinner is on the table."

John quickly jumped out of bed, threw on some shorts and a t-shirt and headed to the small dining room that was only big enough to seat four people. A black veneer speckled table with black metal legs had hosted their family dinners as long as John could remember.

CHAPTER ONE

"Has anyone seen Davon lately?" Nia asked the guys sitting next to her. They all shook their heads no, not thinking much about it. "Last week Davon said he was planning to come today because he didn't want to miss out on the church potluck afterwards."

"It's still early. He might show up," John remarked with the others nodding in agreement.

No sooner had the words come out of John's mouth when Davon's younger brother, Jamal, came running into the sanctuary breathing heavily.

"Slow down, pal," John said.

"Anyone seen Davon?" he asked, paying little attention to the choir director who had taken her place at the front of the church. The disturbance caused everyone in the church to turn around and look at Jamal.

The minister, standing nearby and seeing the commotion, stopped the music director before she began. Walking up to Jamal and putting his hand on Jamal's shoulder, he asked, "Son, tell me what's going on? Is Davon okay?"

"See, that's the problem preacher, we haven't seen him in four days. My mom thought he would have come home by now, but he ain't home. She sent me down here to see if any of ya seen him?"

The silence of the church was temporarily broken when everyone mumbled among themselves. Nobody in the congregation had seen Davon since last Sunday. "Why don't you come with me," the preacher added as he nodded to the choir to begin. Nia stood up and walked out with them.

Nia Abara, dressed in a short skirt with a sleeveless magnolia print shirt, had sat in the back row of the Carol City Community Church next to the only guy she ever cared about, yet he didn't even know it. She had dated many guys over the years, but never once did John Bramble Jr. think that Nia liked him. He wasn't like many African-

Americans his age. He dressed more conservatively than most, never wore baggy pants down to his knees, and typically wore collared shirts. Today, he had strolled into church wearing a cranberry Ralph Polo shirt with milky white shorts. He sat down next to Nia, as he had done every Sunday for years.

John really didn't have any close friends, and the few from church that he had over the years always found a way to annoy him. He and Nia had been friends since ninth grade when they both started attending youth group together on Saturday nights. They had shared a few secrets along the way, including the fact that they always bought designer clothes at second-hand stores or the outlet malls. Neither could afford the luxury of new clothes, let alone expensive ones. He had increasingly become more introverted since graduation from high school, believing that everyone around him was content living in poverty and sin. He and Nia had drifted apart as well.

John had been attending church with his gramma since he was three years old. His parents came whenever they were off work, but sometimes it would be months before they could all attend as a family. Today was an exception. His parents sat in the third row on the padded wooden seats with Shanice while he sat with Nia and a few other church friends. Outside of church functions, he rarely saw anyone from the youth group anymore. The youth group days were long over, and everyone had gone on to other things, mainly working part-time jobs trying to find their niche in life. Not a single one from their small group had gone on to college.

Jamal's unexpected appearance was not sitting well with John. He went through the motions of participating with the congregation, but clearly was not engaged in the singing or sermon. His mind kept wondering about the guy who used to be his friend. They had stuck together all four years of high school, hanging with each other, laughing together, and going to youth group together. But, their friendship came crashing down in a single moment.

John remembered the event vividly as if it were yesterday. It was one o'clock in the afternoon on a Saturday in July, just a month after high school graduation. Davon had been playing hoops with the boys in the park. Being so hot on a July afternoon, the game ended earlier than usual. According to Davon, he accidentally left his backpack under the park bench. He made up some excuse that he couldn't get it and texted John to see if he would stop to pick it up and drop it off at his apartment. It was exactly where Davon had said it would be.

As John was getting back onto his old worn-down bicycle, three guys, all dressed in blue jeans and grey hoodies, jumped him. He wished he had seen them coming because no one was wearing jeans and hoodies on that excessively hot summer day. He had immediately fallen to the ground and blood rushed out of his nose as he struggled to stand up. Then a blow came to his stomach. The pain was excruciating. As he doubled over to protect his stomach, one of the guys tried to grab the backpack off his back. Trying to stand, John fell again onto his knees to the ground. The blood was gushing into his mouth, causing him to choke. The profanity was endless as the punches and kicks kept him face down.

"All that. Give us what's ours, you fuckin n*gg*," one of them said. He then took a banger and cut the straps right off John's back, intentionally dragging the blade along John's flesh, leaving two large cut wounds underneath both of his shoulders. His flesh ripped open, and the pain of his bloody face and stomach lessened as the pain in his back overwhelmed him. He could feel the warm oozing blood rush down his back into his shorts. "You otta be thankin' us," the guy continued as they ran away.

A hood rat stood under a tree on the opposite side of the court waiting for another streetball game to end, but as soon as everyone saw the jack, their kicks took off in every direction. No one wanted to be around when the jakes showed up. John just knelt there on his knees in too much pain to move.

Blood covered his face, hands, and both sides of his shirt. It seemed like an eternity, but it was likely only a few minutes before he heard the sirens coming closer. His head was spinning, and he remembered falling over onto his side before his world turned black. He doesn't recall if the seconds were minutes or the minutes were seconds, but a sniff of smelling salts brought him back to reality.

When his gramma picked him up from the emergency room five hours later, she only had one thing to say, "It's a good thing that banger wasn't a biscuit." John wasn't sure if he was in more shock hearing his gramma use slang for the first time ever in his life, or that he had eighteen stitches under his left shoulder and twenty-four under his right one.

According to the doctor, John was fortunate. The backpack straps had actually saved his muscles from being cut in half. The cuts weren't deep, but it still took about four weeks for John to recover. Davon never said a word to John about that day. John knew that Davon had set him up to take the blow. When you steal someone's coke, they will track you down.

John didn't even realize the sermon had ended until he saw everyone stand up in front of him for the final prayer. He didn't close his eyes or bow his head like he had done hundreds of times before. On this day, he thought to himself, *"So what if Davon is missing, he probably deserves it."*

John filled his paper plate with pulled barbecue pork, Cajun-style baked beans, and sliced cucumber vinaigrette salad which came straight from the kitchen of his gramma's friend, Carolee. Everyone around him was chatting about Davon.

"I see you like my salad," Carolee said to John when he added another spoonful.

"Yes, ma'am, I do," he said, as politely as possible. John didn't want to talk to anyone. He wanted to eat the good home-cooked food that all the ladies in the church prepared along with the men who smoked the meat and fried the chicken. The food was always top-notch and nobody ever wanted to miss a potluck.

"That was something to hear about that friend of yours this morning," Carolee told John as he picked up a fresh piece of cherry pie set out on the dessert table. She was an older woman from church that John had known his entire life. She thought she could hear the gossip straight from John, not realizing that there was no gossip to share.

"Yes, I was as surprised as everyone else," John responded to her.

"Oh, so you didn't know anything about it?" she inquired, as if he should somehow know.

"No, ma'am, I didn't. I heard the news for the first time just like everyone else," John replied. He quickly walked away hoping she would not follow. Instead of sitting at one of the long tables like everyone else, he snuck off to a different part of the building away from people. He did not want to talk about Davon. Fortunately, no one followed. He enjoyed every last bite of his meal before heading back to gather his folks and gramma.

"Can we go now?" he quietly said to his dad, knowing his gramma would stay and chat as long as possible.

The five-minute ride home was rather quiet. Gramma made a comment about the fried chicken, but that was it. They all knew that Davon had gotten himself into trouble again, and John didn't want to talk about him ever.

CHAPTER TWO

Sitting at the end of the bar in the House of Ale, Regi Taylor surveyed the restaurant patrons coming and going from his favorite college dive in Orlando. He had never paid much attention before to the crown moulding that lined the walls just beneath the ceiling, nor the dark golden oak countertops that had countless layers of lacquer. The place was old and dirty and certainly had seen better days, but for Regi it was the crowd that he missed. His college buddies and girl friends would come here several times a week, being loud and obnoxious, and occasionally being asked to leave. He reminisced about the good old days when he didn't have a care in the world, other than finishing an assignment on time or winning a game. He had lived for the parties, his friends, and his basketball team.

Regi was a five-ten guard who had played basketball all his life. Unlike most college players, his dream was never to play pro ball. Instead, he wanted to coach. He loved being in high school and always thought it would be sweet to coach for his alma mater. Instead, he ended up in Carol City for four seasons.

Initially, he hated being there. It was a tired community, and the school was old and dirty. He didn't like his students, and his players were lazy. Yet, he knew if he didn't make a good impression with his boys during his first season that things would never work out for him. He put all his time and energy into coaching his first ever varsity team. He didn't even know how he got the coaching job because most schools would have chosen someone with experience. The position had likely been turned down by other qualified coaches, and he was their only option. He was a rookie teacher and a rookie coach. He was hoping his basketball skills would translate into coaching.

Since he loved playing, he decided he would teach and coach his players by participating alongside them. Even though it wasn't the typical coaching method, he thought he had everything to gain and nothing to lose in an effort to get his players invested.

Shockingly, his strategy worked. He took the basketball team from a 3-15 record the previous season to a 9-9 record his first year. His team took second in the league in both his second and third seasons with a 15-3 record. And, this past season, his team not only won the league championship, but they also won districts and took second in the state finals. He had made a name for himself in four short seasons and was eagerly awaiting a new contract from the school.

"Mr. Taylor," the school administrator had said, "You have some unique skills, and this district will forever be grateful for your tenure," he remembered clearly. "But, we can't renew your contract."

"What?" Regi said. "You've got to be kidding me?" He snickered. "I just led this team to a league title, a district title, and a second place finish in the state. This is how you are going to treat me? I thought you called me here to give me a raise with a new contract?"

"Well, we had hoped to be doing that very thing," the administrator continued. "But, it has been brought to our attention that you have been dating a student."

"Former student," Regi protested. "She graduated a year ago."

"Well, that may be true, but according to our sources, you began dating her while she was still a senior in high school. You know that is entirely unacceptable. We have evidence that will likely stand up in court. You know how school districts hate to be sued, don't you?" he continued.

Regi nodded his head in agreement.

"It doesn't matter how poor this district is, we don't want to be the headlines on every paper and news channel in the state, let alone the country with a teacher and winning coach having sexual relations with a student. We appreciate everything you have done for this school and our basketball program. We are giving you an opportunity to resign rather than be fired. The choice is up to you. If you choose to be fired, we will indicate a breach of contract, due to moral misconduct."

The words of that evening were ringing in Regi's mind as he sat drinking his classic ginger beer while eating an all-nighter burger. The last time he had set foot in this bar was four years ago after graduation. He and his buddies came in for their last drink, ringing in a new era in their lives. He sat on the same bar stool, but this time he sat alone with only his memories to cheer him on, or taunt him as they were doing now.

"Who would have thought?" he said to himself. Three bites into his burger, still feeling depressed and confused, he couldn't believe he had taken a position at Niceville Senior High School in the panhandle of Florida, leaving his girlfriend back in Miami. She was the reason he had to leave his head coaching position for a secondary role as a junior varsity coach. The school he was headed to was actually a prestigious school, and they had a really strong basketball program. The only problem was he had taken a step backwards in his career goals, and it was very likely that he wouldn't be able to play basketball with the boys as he had in his previous job. Niceville was the team that had beaten his Carol City boys in the state finals just a few months earlier.

"You're looking a little blue," a young lady said, as she sat next to Regi. Her hair was long and blond, and her skin tan from the obvious hours she spent in the sun. "Aren't you Regi Taylor?" she asked. I remember seeing you play basketball in college. You haven't changed a bit."

Regi was stunned that somebody from Orlando would actually remember him, let alone step foot into this college dive. He had seen plenty of alumni come back through these doors over the years, but he wasn't expecting to see any tonight. He was only there because he was traveling to a place he didn't want to go.

He was three and a half hours into his hike from Miami to the panhandle. With a late afternoon departure, he knew he wouldn't make his destination tonight. Instead of rolling into town late, he decided to stop off at his old stomping grounds to spend the night. A few beers and a good night sleep would take him the remaining six and a half hours into Niceville.

"Yeah, I'm him," Regi responded. "I'm surprised anyone around here would even know my name."

"Well, I do. I'm MacKenzie," she said. "But, you can call me Mac."

As the two talked, Mac discovered that Regi was not excited about his new adventure. He had come so close to winning the state championship, but now he was settling for a junior varsity position. He was even more frustrated that he had not had a single offer for a head coaching job. Maybe the school administrators had not been up front with him when they claimed they would give him good references for future employment.

"What brings you here tonight?" Regi inquired of his new beautiful friend.

"I'm traveling like yourself," she said. "Except, I'm heading much further than Niceville. I have a great opportunity to work out west so I'm going. It will be an adventure. I've never been out west before," she continued.

"I've traveled a little," Regi noted. "But, I was never a tourist. I've only traveled outside of Florida to play basketball."

"Well, you oughta ditch your plans for Niceville and come with me," Mac encouraged. "You wouldn't be drowning in your beers right now if you wanted to go."

Regi knew that Mac was right. He hadn't gulped down so many beers since he was in college. And, Mac was super hot. A guy had to be crazy if he didn't want to tag along with someone like her. Before Regi was even sober enough to realize it, Mac had coerced him into going with her. He was too drunk to drive and hadn't even booked a hotel room yet.

"Hey, I have to use the restroom before we leave," Regi told his friend. "Can you grab my bag out of my car?" he asked, handing her his fob. It's the red Impala sitting out front. The moving truck was supposed to meet Regi in two days. He packed light, knowing the rest of his belongings would be coming shortly.

"Sure," she said as she walked away. Once outside, Mac realized that Regi's car probably shouldn't be left at the first spot closest to the bar's entrance. She pulled it around back to an empty lot where overflow cars often parked for nights when the town was hopping. When she came back around, she found Regi standing outside.

"Hey, I thought you had left me," he shouted.

"Nope," she explained. "I just pulled your car around back so it will be out of the way for now. Here's your bag."

Regi grabbed his belongings and thanked Mac.

"Let's get going," she then said while she led him to her car. She was driving a Ford convertible mustang.

"You've got some sweet wheels," he said as he tossed his Nike bag into the back seat. He stumbled into the car and immediately put his seat back into the reclining position. Before they even made it to the highway, Regi had passed out.

Mac, on the other hand, was wired to go. A hamburger, caffeine, and a full tank of gas was all she needed to drive through the night. Her wireless headphones carried her favorite jams too. She was headed to freedom. The roads would be clear for the most part, and they would be hours away from Orlando by the time Regi would wake up.

Little did he know that they weren't headed out west. Mac had other plans.

"Junior," John heard his gramma call for him when she walked through the front door.

Every Saturday morning for years, the two of them would join Cheryl Stadder and Mary Lou Jenkins for coffee. If John was fortunate to be home, he became the fifth ring in the gossip ladder as he listened to story after story for a half hour or so. Once his gramma spoke her piece, John was good to go for the rest of the day. She always needed someone to vent to, and usually it was John. The only difference was the gossip ladder stopped with John. He didn't have anyone to share the stories with, nor would he want to, until today maybe.

"I don't have a clue what you are talking about," John said to his gramma as they walked into the living room.

"Well," she said, "Laurelyn heard from Mr. Parker, you remember the athletic director, don't you, John?" his gramma then asked.

"I do," John responded back to her, shaking his head up and down while rolling his eyes and licking the jam off his fingers. For some reason, his gramma seems to think that John doesn't remember people from high school. He has only been out a few years, and she thinks he has lost all memory of everyone since he doesn't hang out with them.

"Why, of course you remember him," she then added. "Well, Mr. Parker told Laurelyn that Regi Taylor never made it to Niceville. He had taken a new position at the high school there and was traveling that way. The athletic director from Niceville had called Mr. Parker to see if he knew the whereabouts of Regi. He was supposed to arrive there on Tuesday, but never showed up. Apparently, the police found his car in Orlando parked in an empty lot behind a bar. According to Mr. Parker, the bartender told the police that a young man fitting Regi's description had come in several nights earlier and had a few beers along with a burger. A young lady approached him, but she left, and he left by himself about ten minutes later.

"Man, that's strange," John said to his gramma. John hadn't heard anyone talk about Regi at all.

"You know, son," his gramma added. "That's the third person in two months that you know who has gone missing."

"That's really weird," John said.

"Yes it is," she agreed. "If I were the police, I would be looking for some kind of connection between them. Those of us who live in this neighborhood, go to church together, and have or had children in the same high school would all have a connection. Yet, the police might not be able to connect those dots without the help of an outsider."

"I guess when you put it that way, you're right," John said to Shanice. "You know me. When I'm not working, I'm usually studying on my computer. I should be ready to take the test for my builder's license by the end of the year," he added.

"And, your point, Junior?" she asked.

"Well, I guess I was trying to say that I don't ever hear much gossip unless it's from you because I really don't have many friends," he explained. "I'm working hard trying to get ahead, and the first step for me is getting my license. I plan to stay with Laikin Construction because I'm learning too much to walk away right now."

"I know you're trying," his gramma said. "And, I'm really proud of you."

"Thanks," John said in return as he gave her a hug. "One of these days, I'll be able to build my own house in a nice neighborhood and forget about the unpleasantness of this hood."

"Oh, that would be foolish for you to forget, my dear," she said. "You never want to forget your past. You remember it to help you never go back to it when it's not worth going back. It's your landmark of triumph. If you forget, then your accomplishments won't seem so grand."

"Oh, Gramma," he said. "You always have such good advice, even though I never want to hear your lectures."

"I do have a few years on you," she said with a smile.

"You do, but sometimes it's hard to notice," John said. "As far as Alvaro, Davon, and now Regi are concerned, I haven't heard or seen anything that would be helpful to the police. I feel bad for their families, but there really isn't anything I can do to help."

"Yes, I know dear," his gramma then said. "If you do, please let me know."

The moment John turned to walk back to his room, both his gramma and John jumped as a rock came crashing through their front window narrowly missing his gramma. The glass shattered everywhere and knocked a vase of garden flowers from the coffee table onto the tile floor. The rock landed on the sofa next to Gramma.

"What on earth was that?" John asked, confused by the invasion. "Are you okay, Gramma?"

"Oh no," gramma said as she looked out the front window. "I'm going to be fine. I just need to shake this glass off my lap without splattering my ketchup everywhere."

John opened the door to see EZ squeal his tires turning the corner in his 2000 Camaro. Not only did the whole neighborhood know when EZ was around, but so did the entire Carol City community. His souped up car was bright blue with two black racing stripes painted down the middle of the front hood. His hubcaps had been changed out to black, and his muffler was louder than most speakers.

"Oh that boy is never going to learn, is he?" his gramma commented.

Without the need to answer her question, he opened a hand-written note tied around the large rock and began to read it out loud.

"Ya betta tell ya pigs to get off my back or ya gonna see more than tis rock in ur winder."

"And you said you don't know anything about those disappearances?" his gramma asked again.

"I really don't, Gramma. The police probably questioned EZ about the graffiti up on the roof, and now that Regi is missing maybe they suspect Boodie's clan to be involved somehow."

EZ was the nephew of Kenneth Cole. His real name was Elijah Jackson. John had never liked him. Unlike his uncle, he's never been nice to anyone. Back in high school, when they were freshmen, he put a bag of marijuna in John's locker at school when John turned his back to talk to another student. Two hours later the police dogs were sniffing lockers, trying to nail kids. John got busted. He was furious. He knew that he didn't put any weed in his locker, but when he heard that his locker had been searched he was afraid that his homework assignment would be snatched.

The suspension hurt his grades, yet he was fortunate that no charges were pressed since it was his first offense. In this neighborhood they gave everyone at least one chance and sometimes even more. The police were tired of booking kids all the time. They wanted the big deals like Boodie and his boys, not the small stuff. Everyone got off the hook on their first offense.

From that day on, EZ had been a pain in John's side. He mocked him for going to church and not having a girlfriend. He always had a new name to call him too. He wanted everyone to know that he was the new gangsta in the hood whom everyone should fear. Most people just laughed at him because he's more mouth than anything, but he had been known to key cars. He did it to the neighbor's car across the street because she yelled at him for driving over her newly planted flowers. Unfortunately for the neighbor, she couldn't prove that EZ actually committed the act.

"You better get your ears unplugged and find out what's grinding that boy," his gramma said.

"The only thing I know is that he's the one guy in this hood that everyone wishes was missing." Gramma wanted to laugh when John spoke those words, but she knew he had spoken the truth.

John grabbed the broom and dustpan from the front closet and began cleaning up the mess."I'll get the window fixed as soon as I can get the glass cut," John continued. "I've only glazed a window once, but hopefully it will withhold any hurricane winds."

"Just do your best to get it done quickly," Shanice replied. "This house is so old that any new glass is better than the old."

John and his gramma then took duct tape and a piece of plastic that John had in his car and cut it to fit the window.

"That will do for now," Shanice nodded in approval of John's work.

"It will at least keep the bugs out," John agreed.

CHAPTER THREE

It had been several weeks since Nia had comforted Davon's younger brother, Jamal, at church. She had spoken with Jamal and Davon's mother at length and came to the conclusion that Davon may have gotten involved with some drug dealers. Now she was second-guessing her conclusion and wished she had not upset his mother with that premise.

"Where are you taking me?" Nia asked her boss.

"Just walk with that smile of yours smacked on your face as if everything is normal. If you dare twitch, a bullet will penetrate your spinal cord making it impossible for you to ever walk again," her so-called friend said.

Nia was confused. She had just spent the afternoon with two co-workers at Haulover Beach. The three of them had been working closely with one another at a local boutique for the past two years. The last several months they seemed inseparable as they all loved the sandy beaches of South Florida.

They had spent a good portion of the day being whistled and eyed by the college boys, trying to be noticed in their barely visible swimsuits as they walked along the shoreline and down the pier. It wasn't difficult for them to pick up guys. They actually had beers earlier with two guys they met on the pier, only to find out that the one talked only about his ex-girlfriend. That was a red flag in their eyes.

Unsuccessful in their luring attempts at that moment, they spent most of the afternoon soaking up the rays, taking selfies, and posting pictures on their Instagram pages. When their stomachs began rumbling, they made their way to the Beach Bar for dinner where their thirst and hunger could be satisfied. There they continued their laughter while eating and drinking strawberry daiquiris and mojitos, forgetting about their concerns for a while.

A local band had already begun its nightly gig, drawing more patrons to the bar and restaurant. Nia was content. They had already played a crowd favorite, "Margaritaville," and she had danced to "Kokomo" on her way to the ladies' room. Tonya and Nia had just left Simone at the table to pay the bill as they headed to the restroom, but instead of going there Nia was now walking out the side door onto the beach.

The hostess was seating a table, and there was no one nearby to even notice their existence. Everyone was facing the direction of the water, paying little or no attention to the patrons at the restaurant. Both ladies had their beach bags flung over their shoulders, and Nia thought there was a gun pointed in her back.

The sun was still high enough in the sky that they instinctively put on their designer sunglasses the moment they stepped foot outside. Nia's hair was pulled up in a bun now, making her even more unrecognizable.

"We are going for a little ride," the voice behind Nia proclaimed.

"Just keep walking and don't do anything stupid," she heard. They walked about two blocks along the beach before cutting through a path to a nearby hotel parking lot where a car was parked. Nia had driven to the beach with Simone where they had met their friend.

"I really need to use a restroom," Nia protested.

"I guess it's your lucky day," her boss proclaimed as she pointed to the public shower that beachgoers use to rinse the sand off their bodies. "You'll have to take off your shorts and pretend that you just came back up from the beach, which you did. No one can see the difference between running water and urine."

"You have got to be kidding?" Nia again protested.

"Well, try me, if you don't believe me."

Nia looked around hoping to see someone in the parking lot who could help, but no one was entering or leaving at that very moment. There were two young boys building a sand castle about fifty yards away. Their mom was reading a book nearby. A few more families were down closer to the water, but the crashing waves and wind would make it nearly impossible for them to hear a cry for help. Nia's options looked slim. She had a split second to make up her mind. The thought of being shot was even more terrifying.

She placed her beach bag on the nearby bench and grabbed her towel, as she stripped down to her bathing suit. She turned on the faucet with one hand letting the cold water stream down her dry body. She stood motionless for a few seconds before rinsing off again. Mission accomplished.

"That wasn't so bad now was it?" she heard her newest enemy say.

She dried off and put her shorts and t-shirt back on. "*Dear, God, please help me,*" she prayed to herself as she got into the back seat of her boss's car.

"Now, I have one last thing you need to do before we go on our ride," she remembered hearing before she passed out. It was too late. The roofie that had been slipped into Nia's drink at the restaurant by her friend was taking full effect now. Nia opened and closed her eyes trying to stay awake as she sat down in the back seat.

"Wha wer ya sayin?" Nia slurred as her body slumped over in the seat. It was too late. Nia was out cold. She was buckled into the back seat with her legs sprawled to the other side of the car as her friend quickly picked up a silver band from beneath the seat and placed it around Nia's neck. Nia had never liked the choker collar trend. This one she would hate even more.

The police were in the parking lot again when John showed up for work on a Wednesday morning. This time they didn't bother to talk to him. They had gone straight inside the trailer where Mr. Laikin presumably had been working.

The sun was up early this time of year, so the crew was required to be there by six o'clock in the morning. John usually showed up at five thirty, but today he dropped his mother off at the deli before coming into work. She usually walked to work, but her feet had been really sore, and she didn't want to add any more miles to them if she could help it.

The interior walls were all up at the job site now, and the paint crew was finishing up the first floor of the second building. John was responsible for making sure the crew did the required work using the correct colors. He had already put together a paint schedule listing the general wall color for each room, the door and trim color, along with the hallway color. In other apartment complexes that John had worked with Laikin Construction, the wall color was the same throughout each room.

Mr. Laikin had decided it was best to distinguish this apartment as high-end living so he made the amenities nicer. One of those amenities included each of the bathrooms to be painted a different color from the general wall color. John had chosen a very neutral and pale green. It wasn't too feminine, but added a splash of life to the walls. It actually complemented the seafoam green glass tile being used for the kitchen backsplashes.

"Hey, John, what do you think of the bathroom?" Kyle asked when John entered apartment one twelve. Kyle was the paint foreman, and they were now painting each of the bathrooms.

"I love it," John said with enthusiasm. This was the first time that John had a say in any of the colors or materials being used on site. In the past, Mr. Laikin had used an interior designer, but for this project he decided only to use a designer for the main common areas. "I did okay, didn't I?" John asked as he held the tile sample up to the painted wall.

"A near perfect match," Kyle responded. "Congrats on all this, kid," he said. "You did a good job."Thanks," John responded. He sat in a few meetings this past year with the interior designer and listened to her reasons for making selections, so he was hopeful that he was on the right track.

The general wall color was called Swiss Coffee. It was actually off-white with a tint of mocha. John chose Cup o' Java, a soft chocolate brown for the doors, trim, and baseboards. He was grinning ear to ear when Mr. Laikin walked into the apartment.

"I like it, John. I like it," he said smiling. "You've come a long way these past few months. I'm proud of your accomplishments."

"Thank you," John said looking into his boss's eyes. "I appreciate the compliment."

John spent the rest of the day going through each apartment placing a piece of blue painter's tape everywhere that needed touch up. Kyle had told John that it was his responsibility to do a walk-through prior to John, but John decided he couldn't learn if he wasn't actually doing the job himself. Kyle had walked through the first building on his own, and John had noticed some touch ups that got missed. He decided it was better for him to do the job himself. If anything was missed he couldn't blame anyone but himself this time.

The following day, John had met with the flooring installers down on the first floor of the second building. They had completed the first building and were ready to begin the next round of apartments. Kyle's crew had already finished the touchup on the first two floors, making it possible for the flooring crew to start. The luxury plank flooring they were installing was hardcore and scratch-resistant, allowing apartment dwellers to be pet owners as well.

"Let me know if you need anything," John told the installers. "I'll be upstairs on the third, fourth, and maybe fifth floors today."

"You got it," one of the installers replied.

John walked upstairs and into the first apartment where he began looking for mistakes made by the paint crew. He found a few places that needed another coat on the trim, but for the most part, he was pleased with the job done. He then proceeded to walk through each of the apartments, sticking a few pieces of tape on any area that needed to be touched up.

When he arrived in the last apartment on the floor, he noticed two police cars pulled up outside the trailer again. "*Now what?*" he thought to himself. "*Has Mr. Laikin got himself into trouble? Or, maybe one of the guys?*" John continued to make his way through each apartment, heading upstairs to the fourth floor.

The task was becoming monotonous, but John continued to do the work knowing that it needed to be done. As he walked out of the bedroom of apartment five seventeen, he heard a knock on the slightly opened front door. "Are you in here?" Warren called out. Mr. Laikin and three officers then proceeded to walk into the room and closed the door behind them.

"These officers have a few more questions for you," Warren offered. "I'm sure it won't take too long. Do you want me to stick around?" he asked.

"Sure, that will be fine," John said as everyone walked into the kitchen area. John leaned against the countertop and folded his arms. He knew better than to put his hands in his pockets. Officers never liked that. "What can I do for you today?" he offered.

Officer McDuff had his name plate just below his badge. He was an older gentleman, probably in his fifties, with a tint of gray hair along his sideburns and just above his ears. He was African-American. Officer Ortez was easy to identify. John had seen him in his hood countless times over the past five years. He was in his late twenties now. The third officer was a white man, likely in his thirties. John couldn't see his tag, but noticed that he was a little stockier than the other two men.

"Are you John Bramble, Jr.?" Officer McDuff asked.

"I am," John told the men.

"Have you heard from Nia Abara in the past two weeks?" he continued.

"No," John said. "Why?"

"The minister down at your church told us that you might know of her whereabouts. He said that you two sit next to each other almost every Sunday in church," McDuff continued.

"Her whereabouts?" John asked.

"Yes, her whereabouts," Officer Ortez piped in.

"I don't know. Isn't she at home or work?" John then asked.

"Kid, she's been missing for almost two weeks now," McDuff said.

"You didn't know that?" Ortez then asked.

"No, how could I?" John replied. "I see her at church every Sunday, and that's about it. We used to be close friends in high school, but she got busy with her job, and I've been busy trying to get my builder's license, so I don't really socialize with her any more. I see her at church on Sundays, and that's it."

"So, you didn't think anything of it when she didn't show up for church this past Sunday?" McDuff asked.

"No. I slept in on Sunday, and my dad dropped off my gramma at church before heading to work. I arrived so late that I only heard a few minutes of the tail end of the sermon. I waited in the back to pick up my gramma. I never saw any of my friends so I had no idea that Nia wasn't there."

"You don't ever text or talk on the phone?" McDuff asked.

"No, we don't," John told the officers as he pulled out his phone to show the men his phone history. "It's probably been two months since either of us have texted one another."

Sure enough, the officers could see that John was telling the truth. He had last texted Nia on May twenty-fifth to see if she had plans for Memorial Day. She responded that she would meet him at church to watch the parade, and then they could go to the fair together with the others. That was the last time he did anything with Nia.

"Nia met me and two other guys from church there," John explained. He then showed the officers the other text messages from the other two guys.

McDuff scrolled through John's phone for a minute. "It looks like you text your parents more than anybody," he said. "With the exception of a few other calls, it looks like Mr. Laikin is your main caller too."

"That's true," John agreed.

"So, you're telling us that you didn't even know that Nia was missing?" McDuff confirmed.

"Yes, that's what I am saying," John said.

"You do realize that two of your church friends are now missing, plus a co-worker?" Ortez asked.

"Does that mean I might be next on the list?" John responded, fearful of what was unfolding before his very own eyes.

"Not necessarily, but you do need to be cautious at this point," McDuff said. "Do you know your whereabouts for the past two weeks?"

"Yes. My life is rather simple. Sundays are family days so I always spend Sundays with my gramma and parents, if they aren't working. I work every day from six in the morning until four-thirty in the afternoon. Mr. Laikin can vouch for that."

"He's always here," Warren confirmed.

"On Mondays, I drive home, shower, eat dinner with my gramma and take her to her women's Bible study. She doesn't drive any longer, so I am her driver on most days. I usually go grocery shopping while she's at Bible study, so I don't have to drive home and back twice. I'm sure the grocery mart has me on film to confirm that. On Tuesdays, I come home from work and study. My folks and gramma can vouch for that. On Wednesdays, I go to class down at the community college. I'm getting my builder's license right now. On Thursdays after work,

I usually study some more. I didn't leave the house on either of those evenings the past two weeks after I came home from work."

The officers looked at one another, but John continued to speak.

"You can ask Mrs. DeWitt, who lives one house down and across the street from us. Ever since Elijah Jackson tore up her flower garden she keeps an eye out the window all the time. I'm sure she can vouch that I never stepped foot outside of my house and that my car was in the driveway each of those days. She's become the neighborhood watchdog. She has nothing better to do with her time. On days that it's not too hot, you'll even see her sitting in her lawn chair out front or working in her garden."

"That leaves Friday two weeks ago," Ortez commented. "Can you account for that day too?"

"I had dinner with Mr. Laikin at Fish and Shrimp down on the water. He was telling me about a new construction project that we will be starting next spring. I'm sure his credit card and the restaurant manager can vouch for us."

The officers then looked over at Mr. Laikin who was still standing near the closed door. "Yes, that's true," he told the men. "I'll be happy to provide evidence if you need it."

"The next day was the Fourth of July. I took my gramma to the parade, and then we went to church for a potluck. The reverend can vouch for me there. We came home for a few hours, and I studied some more. I'm sure my computer history can attest to that as well. And, then my folks, gramma, and I went to South Beach to watch the fireworks. I treated everyone to an early dinner at Havana 1957." John then pulled his wallet out of his front pocket to find the receipt which he had left in it.

"You're alibi is squeaky clean, kid," McDuff then said.

"This past Friday, I went to the movies with Mr. Laikin's daughter at Starr Theater. We got ice cream afterwards down the street at Miami Ice Kream." Again, John pulled out his receipts to show the officers. "This past Saturday, I took my gramma and mom to Vizcaya Museum and Gardens. My ticket stub is out in my car, if you want to see it," John told the men.

"No, we believe you," McDuff said, "but, don't throw it away. You just might need these receipts later."

"Are you implying that I am a suspect?" John then asked.

"No, that's not what I meant," McDuff corrected himself. "I'm just saying that there have been some rather bizarre things happening around this area the past few months, and the more we know about the whereabouts of people who have known connections with the missing persons, the sooner we might be able to solve the cases."

"For example, there are a lot of people at your church who know both Davon Williams and Nia Abara," Officer Ortez explained. "There are a lot of other people from school who know both Alvaro Hernandez and Regi Taylor, but you are the only kid from church your age who knows all of these people. It may be coincidental or it may be that you become the next target. We are just trying to watch your back so you don't become the next victim."

"At first I thought you were implying that I was the culprit, not the victim," John replied.

"No, you seem to have evidence of your whereabouts. We just prefer that you don't do anything alone and become the next missing person," McDuff said. "I guess that's all for now. If we have any other questions later, we'll let you know."

The officers walked out of the apartment while Mr. Laikin followed behind them. John sat down on the floor beneath the counter against the cabinet door. He began to shake. He had no idea that Nia was missing. That was four people that he knew, and all he knew fairly well too. Nia was the only one who was important to him. Yes, they had fallen away from each other in recent months, but she still knew his secrets and interests. She was the only one of the four who ever cared anything about John. Davon had used John like a puppy dog.

Alvaro thought he was better than John because he was more athletic. Mr. Taylor mocked John because he seemed more "white" than "black" as he once told the class. Nia and John had been great friends, but she always wanted to date other guys. Never once did she seem interested in dating him. Initially, it didn't bother John because he spent more time with her than the guys she was dating. Over time he realized that maybe he cared more than he was willing to admit.

John sat on the dusty floor for about ten minutes until he heard a soft knock on the door, and Mr. Laikin came back in. "Are you okay?" he asked John.

"I think I will be," John said. "I didn't even know that Nia was missing. Her mom never called me, and I didn't hear anything about it at church. This is just too strange."

"The next time the police want to question you, if there is a next time, I think you need to have an attorney present," Mr. Laikin told John. "I'll call my attorney and fill him in on the latest just in case he has any other advice to give you now. His name is Jonathan Trieger. He's a good guy. He handles all of my business and personal assets, but his firm has defense lawyers as well. Matter of fact, we are going to review my contract for the next property I plan to purchase, the one we talked about last week at dinner. We plan to go for lunch on Friday. Just plan to join us."

"Okay," John said as he stood up to shake the dust off his pants.

"Do I need to wear something nicer than jeans and a t-shirt?" John asked.

"No, just put on a collar shirt instead, and you should be good," Mr. Laikin said. "I will probably send you over to your mom's deli to pick up sandwiches for us, and we can eat in the conference room. It's completely finished, and the table will be delivered this afternoon. No one will think anything of it to see you in a meeting with my attorney if we stay here."

"Okay, just let me know if you have a preference on sandwiches," John said.

"Just get a variety. I will eat anything you choose." Mr. Laikin then pulled a fifty dollar bill out of his pocket and placed it on the countertop. "Keep a receipt for me too," he said with a smirk. "I just might need it."

John gathered his thoughts before he continued on to the next apartment. He wanted to stop right there and call Nia's mom, but it had already been two weeks since she disappeared. "*Maybe she thinks it's my fault,*" John thought. For the next two hours as he finished posting little pieces of blue tape in each apartment and along the halls in building two, he couldn't stop thinking about Nia and her mom. "*Maybe her mom doesn't have my phone number?*" he thought. "*Couldn't she have stopped by church on Sunday to look for me too?*" he questioned again.

John's stomach began to growl when he realized that he had skipped lunch unintentionally. He walked back down to the first floor to see that the installers had completely finished four of the apartments.

Each building had twelve to fourteen apartments on each floor, depending on the size of the apartments. The bathrooms, kitchen, and living areas all had the vinyl luxury tile. Another team from the same flooring company would install the carpet in the bedrooms.

The first floor was unique because the bedrooms would all have vinyl tile as well. Flooding in South Florida was always a concern during hurricane season, so they were erring on the side of caution by using tile instead of carpet on the main floor. Kyle told John that it would take at least one month for his crew of twenty to complete building two. By the time they were finished, building three would be ready for them to conquer.

Most of the workers were heading to their cars when John left building two. He saw Ralph and two other men in the parking lot on his way out today.

"Them pigs still questioning you about Ricky Rose lyrics?" Ralph teased. "You gotta know more than you're sharing, boy."

"That's the problem. I don't know a thing," John responded back.

"Tomorrow I want you guys to start placing the shoe moulding on level one of building two. Four of the apartments are already done so we can begin the shoe. The kitchen back splashes will be starting tomorrow in those same apartments as well. Just don't be rude to any of those installers, please."

"Aye, aye Captain," Ralph sneered as he blew a fresh puff of smoke into John's face. "We'll be here bright and early like we always are," he said before slamming his car door shut.

Ralph continued to rub John the wrong way. He was nice to everyone except the kid who was trying to better educate himself. John didn't know what he had done to deserve this disrespect.

CHAPTER FOUR

"Junior, Junior, Junior, what have you done now?" Shanice said to her grandson when he hobbled through the door.

John was mad. He didn't want to talk to his gramma. "Everytime I turn around someone is trying to mess with me," John spouted as he limped down the hall to his room. He slammed the door shut and laid down on his bed staring up at his ceiling

Shanice saw the hospital tag dangling around John's wrist when he came home. He was an hour later than usual, and she knew by the looks of the bandage that his day on the job site had not gone well.

She finished preparing dinner about the same time Ebony got home. "How is everybody this afternoon?" Ebony asked her mother-in-law when she arrived.

"Junior had a rough day," Shanice said. "He hasn't come out of his room since he's been home. It looks like he had a little visit to the ER too," Shanice reported. "He wouldn't talk about it though."

"Oh no. Is he okay?" John's mom inquired.

"He appears to be, but his leg is all bandaged up."

Ebony walked into the other room and down the hall where she quietly knocked on her son's door.

"What?" John said.

"It's your momma. Can I come in for a few minutes?" she asked.

"Yes. I guess so."

"Your gramma says that you had a rough day, dear. Do you want to tell me about it?"

He didn't want to talk about it, but he also knew he couldn't live under the same roof without sharing the facts. John proceeded to tell his mom the events of the day. He arrived at work a little before six as he did every morning.

The day before he had told Ralph and a few other guys to start on the baseboard in the apartments that were already painted. When he walked in to check on their progress, Ralph attacked him with a nail gun. If only he had shot him in the foot, his steel toe boots probably would have protected him.

"I could see the evil in his eyes when he looked at me," John told his mom. "Before I knew it, he started laughing then aimed the nail gun right at my leg. Of course, I stumbled to the floor, and when the other guys who were working with him came out of the guest room into the living room, Ralph told them that I tripped on the hose, and he 'accidently' shot me."

"That's rotten of him," Ebony said to her son.

"The worst part is that the other men believed him. When I tried to tell them the truth, they just told me to sit still while they ran for the first aid kit, like it would do any good. Ralph told them that he would stay with me."

"I'm so sorry, John," Ebony said, trying to comfort her son.

The whole time John waited for help, Ralph just laughed at him and said that it was his word against John's. There was absolutely no evidence to prove otherwise.

"He kept snickering and even said, 'I gotcha ya good, boy, didn't I?' " John explained. "Momma, I just wanted to beat the living daylights out of that man. If I didn't have three nails buried deep into my leg, I might have just tried it too."

"How did you get to the hospital?"

"Warren Laikin drove me, but he didn't stay. He told me to call when I was done, and he would pick me up. He was going to get one of the guys to drop off my car here at the house so I wouldn't have to go back for it later."

"Well, honey, what did the doctor say?"

"Oh, he gave me six stitches after digging out the nails. That's nothing for me," John said with a slight smile. "The shot to numb my leg was worse than the stiches. The doc said that I need to be careful that I don't get an infection."

"It looks like you might be sore for a few days, but hopefully your leg will heal just fine," Ebony said, trying to make her son feel better. "You know it could have been worse, so count your blessings, dear."

"Yeah, Momma, I know, but it's hard to count your blessings when this kind of shit happens."

"Dinner is ready so why don't you come out to the table and join us. I know you will feel better after you get some of your gramma's cooking in you."

While they were talking, Senior came home from work so they all sat down to eat as a family. The swiss steak, mash potatoes, gravy and green beans tasted better than Junior imagined. He retold the story to his dad and gramma, and none of them were too happy about the incident.

During their meal, John received a phone call. "May I take this call?" he asked. "It's Warren Laikin."

"You may take it right here at the table," Senior replied.

The family rule was no phone calls at the table. John, Sr. must have been feeling rather bad for his son to allow the rule to be broken.

"What do you mean?" John said as he jumped up from the table. "You've got to be kidding me?"

His parents and gramma looked at one another trying to gauge what Mr. Laikin had just told John.

"It must be about his car," Ebony said. "Warren was going to drop it off at the house, but it wasn't here when I came home."

"No, it's not here," Senior replied in return.

John then hung up the phone.

"Spit it out, Son" Gramma said, anxious to hear the details.

"When Warren got back from the hospital, he pulled into our dirt lot to find that all the tires on my car had been slashed, and my car had been keyed."

"Oh, boy," Shanice replied. "That could have been EZ or Ralph's doing."

Senior and Ebony looked at one another, surprised that Shanice thought EZ might have had a hand in it. Their encounter with EZ's rock could make him a prime target, but the nail gun incident was current.

"Warren had the car towed to a body shop. He told me he would pay to have the tires replaced and the car painted," John explained.

"Well, the good news, if there is any," Senior said, "is that you are getting fresh paint on your car. Down here in this Florida heat that's always a good thing."

"Yeah, you're right Dad when you put it that way."

"Did Warren say anything about Ralph?" Ebony asked.

"That's the other thing," John shared, "Ralph was gone when Warren got back and never returned to work."

"Did the other workers say anything about him?" Shanice inquired.

"They were all tongue-tied. No one said a word.

The rest of the evening in the Bramble household was uneventful until nine o'clock when a loud knock was heard on the front door. Gramma was in her room reading a book, and Ebony had already settled down for the night. Senior was watching a fishing show, and Junior was messing with stuff on his computer.

"What a surprise," Senior said when he answered the front door.

"Can we come in," the officer asked Mr. Bramble.

"No, you can't," he said. "Are you here to talk with John about the vandalism earlier today?"

"No," the officer said. "I'm not sure what you are talking about."

"His car and the nails he took to his leg at work," Mr. Bramble stated.

John could hear the talking from his bedroom. He hobbled down the hall to see what was happening. He remembered the words that Warren Laikin had told him previously. "*Do not talk to an officer again, unless your attorney is present.*"

"Hi, John," Officer Ortez said when John approached the men. The officer who had been with him the other day was there too. This time John could read his name tag clearly. He was Michael Longwell.

"Hello Officers Ortez and Longwell," John responded.

"Do you have a few minutes to talk?" Officer Ortez asked John.

"My leg hurts so I'm not going to talk right now. I haven't pressed charges against Ralph Lorenzo so there's probably no need for us to talk anyway," John replied.

"We're not sure what you are talking about," Officer Ortez began, "but we wanted to talk to you about Lorenzo for another reason."

"Do you have a warrant?" John asked.

"No," the men said in unison.

"Then you'll have to wait. I'm not talking to anyone without an attorney," John informed the men.

John, Sr. then told the gentlemen goodbye and closed the door.

They both started to walk away when the officers knocked again.

"Look, John," Officer Longwell said when they opened the door for the second time. "We don't know what you are talking about, but we just wanted to know if you knew anything about Ralph Lorenzo's whereabouts."

"You're asking me?" John said in disgust. "He put me in the ER today. Hardly would I know where he went after I left for the hospital. I sat in an exam room waiting to get nails pulled out of my flesh. I'm tired. It's late. I'm not saying another word."

"We found his car submerged in water out towards Bal Harbor earlier this afternoon. He wasn't in the car, and the dive team did not find a body. The men at Laikin Construction said that you were the last person to see him," Ortez said.

"I don't care," John said as he closed the door for a second time.

CHAPTER FIVE

"I thought Warren gave you some time off?" Shanice questioned John the next morning after breakfast.

"He did," John admitted. "That doesn't mean I need to stay at home."

"You can't be walking around on that leg until it heals a bit," Shanice said. "Plus, you don't have a vehicle to drive anyway," she reminded him.

"I know, Gramma. I called Warren's daughter to see if she could drive me over to Nia's house. I have some questions, and I'm hoping Nia's mom has some answers. I don't know what's going on, but I seem to be the center of everyone's attention these days," he said with a determination to find out what was happening.

Warren Laikin only had one daughter. She had graduated from the University of Central Florida in the spring and would be starting her dream job in the fall. She was spending the summer squandering her daddy's money, cruising up and down the Intercoastal on his fifty-three foot yacht while enjoying her last summer of freedom before joining the ranks of adulthood. She knew her dad really liked John and was prepping him to take over the business someday. "*Why John?*" she often thought. She knew that she would eventually own the business, but it wasn't the type of business she dreamed of operating hands-on. John never knew that he was being groomed to take over Laikin Construction either. He just thought Warren was giving a poor kid a chance to learn the construction business because he was an intelligent young man.

"Mrs. Abara," John greeted when Nia's mother came to the door, "can we talk?"

Rose Abara opened the door for him to enter.

"I'm really sorry that I didn't know that Nia was missing. I can't imagine what the past two and a half weeks have been like for you," John continued. "I know you have probably told the police and all your friends every detail of what took place, but you never even called me."

"You're right, John, I should have called you. Nia had mentioned just a few days prior to her disappearance that you and she rarely talk anymore. I made the assumption that you weren't really friends anymore."

"I guess that's fair to assume," John replied after a moment. "But, she's missing, and you still should have called."

"You're right, I should have called you. It's been a nightmare. Complete hell," she explained. "I did call her boyfriend, but he has never answered either."

"Her boyfriend?" John questioned.

"Yes, you know him. That basketball player from Carol City, Regi Taylor," she explained.

"You think he's a basketball player?" John questioned again.

"That's what they told me, and he also talked about his games when he was over," Mrs. Abara continued. "Why are you so angry?" she then asked John.

John was more than angry. He was outraged. Nia had lied to him and was lying to her mother as well. He tried to constrain himself, but his blood was boiling. He took several deep breaths trying to overcome the shock of hearing the truth.

"That's not quite the truth," John began. "Regi Taylor was the basketball coach at Carol City, not a player. He taught classes too. He was one of our teachers. Nia and I had class together with him."

Mrs. Abara was even more upset now. "Let me get us both a glass of ice tea," she said between her tears. "Feel free to sit down, and I'll be right back." She then headed into the kitchen where John heard her cry some more.

John took a seat in the front living room, with one eye on the door and window and the other on Mrs. Abara. He knew he was no longer in a position to trust anyone. While he waited, he sent a text message to Warren's daughter saying it would likely be an hour before he would need a ride back. He figured that would give him enough time to probe into this scenario more. Mr. Abara had died in an auto accident before Nia and John had met so it was just the two of them at the house right now.

Nia's aunt and cousins had been very active in her life so John wouldn't be surprised if any of them showed up. He was glad that he was alone with Mrs. Abara right now. John heard Mrs. Abara's phone ring, but she told the caller she would need to call back later at a more convenient time.

"Well, John, I don't even know where to begin," she told him as she handed him a glass of ice tea on her return into the room. "I had no idea he was your teacher," she continued.

"Let's start at the beginning and tell me everything you know," John proceeded to nudge, hoping she would not leave out any details. "Where and when did you realize that Nia was missing?"

With tissue in hand, Mrs. Abara began, "It happened on Friday the fourteenth. Nia had gone out with some friends. I believe her friend, Simone, was driving. They were headed to Haulover Beach. Tonya was going to meet them there." Rose Abara wiped the tears from her eyes as she recalled the events of that day.

John had met Simone, Nia's co-worker, a few times, but he had never heard of Tonya before. "Who is Tonya?" he inquired.

"That was Nia's boss," Mrs. Abara explained. "She is just a year or two older than you guys. She seems really nice."

"What happened?" John then asked.

The girls were going to the beach for a last rendezvous with Tonya before she moved. She had accepted a new job in one of the Carolinas. Nia texted me around four o'clock to say that they were going to the Beach Bar at the pier, and she would be home around seven o'clock. When she still wasn't home by eight o'clock, I texted her. She did not respond. I began to worry because she had told me that she wouldn't be out late since she was working the early shift the next morning. I checked her location on her phone, and it indicated that she was still at the Beach Bar."

"It's likely that her battery died and that was her last known location," John replied.

"We know it was her last known location," Mrs. Abara continued.

"Around nine o'clock I received a call from Simone asking if Nia was back home yet. When I told her 'no,' Simone went on to explain that her dad was with her now at the Beach Bar. He came when Simone realized her two friends were gone. Her dad notified the police on his way to the restaurant because Simone was hysterical at the time. She had waited at their table while Nia and Tonya used the restroom. They never returned to the table. The police were not concerned one bit when they arrived. They told Simone and her dad that people leave the beach all the time with other friends and fail to tell the people who drive them."

"So, the police thought they had ditched Simone, right?" John asked.

"Basically, that's what they were saying to her. But, Simone claims they would never have done that to her. They had a great time all day and didn't want the day to end. Of course, I knew Nia would never have left Simone there, so I called the police after I spoke with Simone and filed a missing person report immediately."

"Did Tonya's parents file a report too?" John asked.

"That's the tricky part," Mrs. Abara explained. "Her parents live in Virginia and claim that she's not missing. The police actually went to their house last week, and she was with them."

"Do you think that someone was pretending to be Tonya, but was really someone different?" John then inquired.

"I don't know. She's a really sweet girl. I have met her multiple times. She certainly wouldn't have a reason to work at a retail store for two years, then set someone up while pretending to be someone different. It just doesn't make any sense."

"No, it doesn't," John agreed. His anger towards Mrs. Abara for failing to call him when Nia disappeared subsided. He now felt sorrow for her. She had been lied to just like him.

"Did anyone look for Nia and Tonya at the beach?" John inquired.

"According to Simone's dad, he and Simone searched the restaurant multiple times, and they walked up and down the beach. Simone asked everyone around if they had seen the girls. Since it's a beach bar and people are in and out all day long, no one seemed to notice either of them."

Rose then reached for her phone and pulled up a picture of the three girls at the beach from earlier in the day. "Simone sent this picture to me. She said that someone at the beach took it for them. That's the picture she showed everyone when she was looking for her."

"Did the police confirm that Tonya from this picture is the same

Tonya they met in Virginia?" John asked.

"They claim it's the same young lady," Mrs. Abara answered, "but you never know if they are telling the truth or not."

John was puzzled. Five people that he knew were now missing. "Did you hear that Regi Taylor is actually missing too?" John asked after Mrs. Abara had explained everything to him about her own daughter. "Of course, you didn't," John continued after realizing that she would have said something by now if she had known.

John spent the next thirty minutes recapping the events he had heard from his gramma about Mr. Taylor, and he proceeded to tell her about the events in his life regarding the disappearances of Alvaro, Davon, and now Ralph. Mrs. Abara was motionless by the time John was done talking. She didn't even know how to respond. She was already numb from her own turmoil and pain, and now to hear about the others made her situation even more difficult.

"Nia told me about Davon, but thought he had gotten mixed up with some drug dealers," Rose Abara finally said after remaining silent the entire time John had spoken.

John then went on to say how upset he was with the police for continuing to question him, even when he was in the hospital yesterday. "That's when I decided to come to you to hear for myself what happened to Nia. I suppose they might be questioning others, but it seems like I am the only connection between any of these people, and my connection is simply that I know everyone," John said in bewilderment.

"They questioned Simone too," Mrs. Abara remarked, "but it wasn't until Monday when they realized that I had filed the missing person report."

John was a thinker. He pondered the details explained to him, but was still puzzled by the number of people whom he knew that disappeared without anyone seeing any perpetrators. He also wondered if he was supposed to be a victim.

"I don't even know how to move forward with my life," Mrs. Abara said as she cried some more. "Nia was my life. She's been my life for all these years since her father died."

"I'm truly sorry, Mrs. Abara," John said quietly. "I wish I had a better answer for you, but I don't. I know you don't want to hear this, but it could be likely that Regi and Nia ran off together. Maybe a parent got wind of Mr. Taylor dating a student. That would give him every reason to skip going to Niceville."

"Why couldn't she just tell me?" Mrs. Abara asked.

John could speculate a number of reasons, but thought it was best to leave that question unanswered. There was some silence before John asked another question. "Did you go out to Haulover Beach yourself?"

"The next morning, my sister and her family took me to the beach. My niece immediately printed photos of Nia with a contact number to call if anyone had any information on her disappearance. We placed them at every shop and restaurant and the public parking lots in that area."

"Have you gotten any response?"

"My sister received a few phone calls that people had seen her with two other girls. They described the girls, and they were Simone and Tonya. No one saw them leave the restaurant though."

John was not a social media fan, yet he knew that would be the first place to go for anyone wishing to find a missing person these days. "Did anyone in your family post anything on social media?" John inquired.

Rose explained that her niece who was now a senior in high school had posted on every social media outlet the picture of the girls that Rose had shown John. She had cropped the picture so that only Nia and Tonya were shown. Since Simone was not missing, they didn't want her photo to go viral. They got a lot of people responding that they would pray for the girls and their families, but no one has seen or heard from either of them.

When John noticed his ride was back, he politely thanked Rose Abara once again for taking the time to explain Nia's disappearance to him. He gave her a hug and walked out the door. "I'll keep you posted if I hear anything," he said.

As he was walking to the other side of the street, a car slowly pulled into Mrs. Abara's driveway. John felt uncomfortable not knowing if he was being targeted now. He stood frozen waiting to see who it might be when Nia's cousin shouted, "Hey John, is that you?"

John limped back down the driveway and spoke with her for a few minutes before going back to the car. He was relieved that she wasn't a stalker. He felt sorry for her too. It had already been over two weeks, and John could tell that Nia's cousin was still grieving her loss. Her eyes were bloodshot from days worth of crying, and her cheeks were as pale as a ghost. The beautiful young high school senior looked like death had won its battle.

Warren's daughter didn't say much to John on their way back to his house. John turned up the volume on the radio indicating he didn't have much to say either. He was hurt and angry. The only girl he had ever truly liked skipped town and didn't even say good-bye.

"Did you find the answers you were looking for?" she finally asked when they were almost back.

"Yes," John replied, "and then some. I got answers to questions I never knew I needed to ask."

CHAPTER SIX

"I was running around doing the jobs of two people again today," Ebony said as she plopped herself down on the faded sofa that had seen nicer days. "Ryan didn't show up for work again today."

"He's the twenty year old punk you don't like, right Momma?" John asked as he sat down in the chair next to his mom in the living room.

"Yes, that's him. Ryan Smith. He used to work fast food, but started working here nine months ago because he gets paid a dollar more an hour. That's what he claimed anyway. I think he got fired for missing too much work."

Momma never complained about her job. She never complained about anything until Ryan started working with her. He thought being fifty-five meant you were old. Instead of calling Ebony by name, he called her "Old Eb." That didn't go over well with Ebony Bramble.

He regularly told her how to do her job and would complain when he was asked to clean the slicers. He came into work late on a daily basis with every excuse imaginable. One time he even told Ebony that his dog ate the note paper that he had written his schedule down on, as if she would believe him.

"You just can't worry about that guy," John told his mother. "You should be happy he's not around to grumble about your every move now," John said encouragingly.

"You know me, John. I'm trying not to complain." Ebony then turned on the news to see the latest weather report. As she was flipping through the channels to get her local news, the image of Ryan glared her in the face.

"That's Ryan," Ebony shouted, as if John couldn't hear.

"Ryan Smith becomes the eighth missing person in Miami-Dade County in the past six weeks," the local Fox News anchor reported. "Twenty year old Smith, a black male from Miami Gardens, was last seen exiting an Uber car at the Miami International Airport."

A photo of Ryan stepping out of a black sedan was then shown on the news with the license plate blocked out.

"Officials have told Fox News that the Uber driver has cooperated with law enforcement and is not a suspect at this time. His identity is being withheld for his own safety," the anchor continued. "We have reliable sources that claim Smith did not get on a plane nor was he seen entering any other vehicles. The police have asked anyone with information regarding the disappearance of any of these people to call Silent Observer."

Fox News then showed photos of each person with their names bolded in black underneath their photos. Alvaro Hernandez, Davon Williams, Regi Taylor, Jaheem Jones, Nia Abara, Ralph Lorenzo, Frank Millerson and Ryan Smith were on the list.

"Frank Millerson?" Ebony asked when she looked at the names. "He used to work with your father. Your dad never liked that man. He was a mean one."

"Jaheem Jones is on the list too," John pointed out.

"Who is he?" Ebony asked her son.

"Remember the kid who punched me in the face when I was in fifth grade because we were playing basketball at recess, and I stole the ball from him to shoot a layup?" John asked his momma. "When I punched him back he went and told the playground monitor that I punched him," John continued. "I got in trouble for starting a fight by stealing the ball. Of course, the principal didn't care that the game of basketball actually involves stealing the ball from the opponent."

"I remember the event, but I had forgotten who the kid was," Ebony said.

"Well, that was Jaheem. Three months later, when we were playing football at recess, he threw a football and hit me in the back of the head because I intercepted a pass thrown to him, and I went down the field to score."

"I remember that too," Ebony said.

"Well, I punched him in the face after he did that and racked up another detention. Gramma took me to lunch that day for sticking up for myself," John remembered just like it was yesterday. "I never got along with him from that time on. He started hanging with the wrong crowd and blaming me for trouble that came his way."

"Was that the kid you were talking to in the hallway when EZ put that marijuna in your locker?" my momma then asked.

"Yes, he's the one. I haven't spoken with him since that day," John explained.

"That was years ago," Ebony recalled. "Is he still hanging with EZ these days?"

"I really don't know," John replied. "I hear he spends a lot of time at the gym. He's grown about four sizes since high school. One of the guys at work said his son ran into him there, and he thinks he must be using steroids. I have kept my distance from both of those guys."

John took the remote and flipped to the other local stations hoping to find more information on the disappearances of the people mentioned on the Fox report.

"I'm going to look on-line to see if I can find any more information about the people who disappeared," John told his mom. "I was hoping the anchor would share how Ryan disappeared."

John grabbed his laptop from his bedroom and headed back to the living room to sit with his momma. After browsing the internet, he closed his computer. The other channels were vague in their reporting as well. "No news," John told his mom. "You would think someone would know something."

"People are too busy fighting their own fires or having their noses buried in their cell phones these days that they don't pay attention to things going on around them anymore," Ebony expressed.

"You said that dad used to work with Frank?" John then asked his mom.

"Yes, he actually worked with him at a number of different jobs over the years."

"Why is he so mean?" John inquired.

"When you were young, your papa used to work with him as a baggage handler. He ran into him a while back at the arena when your papa worked security. He was pushing a mop, cleaning up beer spills. When he saw your papa he took the handle of his mop and jammed it into your papa's gut, leaving a goose egg-size mark. He claims your papa wasn't paying any attention and ran into his mop stick. Your papa's side hurt for weeks. It's a wonder your papa didn't split his kidneys. He told him he deserved it for getting a better job than him at the arena."

"So, what does that mean?" John asked his momma. "Did he apply for a security position and didn't get it?"

"We will never know, son, but he has never been nice to your papa. Your papa tried to talk to him a number of times years ago. He thinks living on food stamps is the way to go. The few times that he held a job, he only held it long enough to say that he was hired. Within weeks, he would always find a way to get fired."

"Why would he not like Papa?" John continued to inquire.

"Your papa was trying to be a big brother to him. He helped him sign up for a checking account at the local bank and tried to teach him the meaning of responsibility. He had four children with four different women and never paid a dime to any of those mothers. He lived in the projects here in town. Your papa explained how to keep a budget and that being a real man required owning up to his children and providing for them. He believed his only true son was Jack Daniel's."

"So, he cared more about drinking than being a father?" John asked.

"I don't think it's even that," his momma replied. "He was never sober long enough to even think about caring. He held on to that bottle as if it were his child."

"Does he have any other family?" John then wondered.

"No, Son. They gave up on him years ago. This was a choice he made. He had plenty of opportunities to get help, but chose this path. He would come into the deli on occasion trying to get us to give him extra chopped ham because he was poor and used green stamps. He would intentionally get arrested just to spend a night or two in jail too."

"That's crazy."

"It is, but some people's brains don't work properly. Or, they simply have given up on all hope."

Dinner was on the table and the Bramble family was enjoying gramma's chicken dumplings when they heard pounding on their front door. Senior answered the door to find EZ's mom and a man with her.

"We need to talk to your son," she told John, Sr.

"May I ask what this is all about?" John's dad responded.

"It's about all the news tonight," she responded.

"We are in the middle of dinner right now. If you would like to come back in a half hour, I'm sure he'll be available to talk."

"We don't f**kin want to wait," she exclaimed.

"Ms. Jasmine, that's your name, correct?" he asked.

"Yeah, I'm EZ's mom," she said.

"I haven't seen you in years so I wanted to make sure I was calling you by the correct name. If you want to come back in a half hour, we can all sit outside and talk, but my food is getting cold so I am going back inside now," Senior told the neighbor.

The man with Jasmine agreed they would come back even though Jasmine was not happy about it. John, Sr. went back inside to finish his meal as the neighbors turned to walk away. "We'll just wait right here," Jasmine blurted out as John was shutting the door.

The Bramble family took their time eating and finished up with Gramma's home-baked key lime pie. It was John's favorite pie so he savored every bite. They discussed why EZ's mom might be at their front door as well. It was then that Gramma confessed that EZ had been the one who broke their window earlier. John told his parents that they didn't want them to worry about something that they had no control over. With everything happening now, there was no better time than the present to share EZ's threat to them.

A few minutes later John returned to the kitchen table with EZ's note in hand. After reading it to his parents, they pondered the question even more as to why his mom would be outside their door.

"Maybe she is stopping by to pay for the window and apologize," John suggested.

"Well, Son," John, Sr. began, "if she doesn't know that he broke the window, she could blame you for starting a fight with her son. I think we need to keep the broken window and EZ's note private for now."

"I definitely agree," Shanice said. "We don't need a bigger battle than the one already here," she added.

Gramma and Ebony stayed inside cleaning the kitchen when both Johns headed back outdoors to see what was aggravating Jasmine.

"Hello, Mrs. Jackson," John said as he stepped outside.

"Hello," she responded, "but I'm not Mrs. Jackson anymore. I'm now Mrs. Jarvis. This is my new husband, Jarod."

"Nice to meet you," Senior said as he reached out to shake Jarod's hand.

Both father and son then grabbed the fold up campfire chairs which were under the front window. "Feel free to sit down," Senior told their guests.

"We want to know about all the missin people that was reported on the news tonight," Jasmine said. "You gotta know somethin, boy," she said looking at John.

"I don't know anything more than EZ would know," John responded. "Every few days it seems like someone else is missing."

"Well, I saw them cops down here the other day, so I figured you knew somethin," she said.

"Why does everyone think I know something?" John then asked.

"What does EZ think?"

"You see," Jarod finally spoke, "Jasmine and I just got married three weeks ago. We went on a ten-day Caribbean cruise. Elijah was staying at the house alone. When we got back the place was trashed, and we could see that he had a party there. Beer bottles, pizza boxes and stuff were left everywhere, but we haven't heard from Elijah at all. His car is gone, and his phone charger was in his room, so we know that his phone battery must have died days ago.

John knew what he wanted to say to EZ's mom. Maybe if she had cared about him when he was younger and raised him better he wouldn't be messed up with drugs and drug dealers today. Yet, he knew that wouldn't get him anywhere right now.

"Did you report him missing to the police?" Mr. Bramble asked.

"No, that's the thing," Jasmine began. "We know that EZ has done some things he shouldn't have done. And, we all know that he's dealing drugs too, just like his uncle. We're afraid that the police will put him behind bars if they find him. If we report him missing, then they actually have to look for him, and I don't want them in my house. They just may find some drugs or something that shouldn't be there."

"Did he take any clothes with him," Senior asked.

"It's hard to say," Jarod explained. "His room is always a mess. We just keep his door closed."

"We noticed on the news that Alvaro is gone too," Jasmine said.

"Do you think they are messed up with the wrong dealer or maybe a new gang?" John then asked.

Jarod stood up and put his hands on his bride's shoulders. "That's what we thought initially. We were hoping he would come home, but then when we saw the news tonight we knew there must be something else wrong," Jarod concluded.

"Has Alvaro been hanging out with EZ lately?" John asked.

"I had told Elijah that things needed to change after we got back from our honeymoon. I wasn't going to let him run around creating havoc at our place anymore. I was really young when I had him. I was still just a kid myself, and I messed up big time," Jasmine said looking down at the ground in embarrassment. "I'm tired of living in fear. I don't want to go through hell and back like we did for his uncle, ya know. So, I told him he needed to shape up and get a job. He promised me that he would, but he was angry about somethin.'"

"There were a number of kids who kept showing up around here," Jarod explained. "Their visits were always short, and they were constantly covering their heads with those damn hooded sweatshirts. So we don't know for sure. Alvaro definitely was one, but then he stopped coming."

"I don't know a thing other than what I've heard on the news and from people talking. It sounds to me that everybody's disappearances are very different from one another. Alvaro was last seen at a bus stop. Mr. Taylor was driving north when his car was found outside a local bar in Orlando. Nia was last seen at a restaurant on the beach. Davon never returned home like he told his mom that he would. And, now you don't know why EZ hasn't come home. I'm not sure about the others, but there's no pattern to any of their disappearances. It sounds to me like EZ, Davon and Alvaro may have been dealing with the wrong crowd, but I really have no idea," John told the neighbors.

He wasn't going to divulge that Nia had been dating Mr. Taylor. Some things he thought were best left untold.

"Have you checked with your neighbors next door?" Senior then asked.

"Everyone has pretty much said the same thing. They are all afraid of

EZ and try to avoid him at all costs. When he's around they don't look out their windows, and they keep their doors locked," Jarod answered.

"I don't fear him one bit," John then responded. "I avoid him because I just don't like him. He's been a bully my entire life."

Jasmine didn't know what to say. Her mood had changed drastically from the moment she first arrived until now. The Brambles had been frank and blunt with her, verbalizing truths about her son that most people would not want to hear.

"I guess there are several ways to look at it," Senior finally said after a brief silence. "You can hope and pray that something drastic happens to Elijah that will force him to change his ways. You can go to the police knowing the risk that he might end up in jail if he is found. Or, you can continue to seek answers on your own knowing that most people in this neighborhood don't like your son and really don't respect you either. If you can show them that you are a changed person maybe they will give you the benefit of the doubt. You might be able to piece together who he was with the night he left home and the specific night he had the party."

"I see," Jasmine said.

Senior continued. "If they had pizza, it's likely someone at the restaurant will remember which night the boys bought the pizza. That would at least be a start for you. And, if I were you, I would also begin by cleaning up his room to make sure there isn't any unwanted substance in there. You would hate for someone to hurt you trying to get drugs out of the house that he had hidden."

"We appreciate ya talkin to us," Jasmine finally said. "Ya have given me some thins to think about too. I'm tired of the drugs bein around. Jarod taught me that even poor people have better ways to make money than dealin."

Jarod again shook Senior's hand and Junior's and said it was nice meeting both of them. He definitely seemed better than the other men that Jasmine had around the house in years past.

"Congrats on your wedding, Mrs. Jarvis," John told his nemesis' mom.

"Thanks," she said as the couple walked away.

"Hey, Papa," John said as they walked into their living room, "I'm so glad you didn't mention anything to her about the rock that EZ threw at our window."

"That would only make her suspicious of you," Senior replied. "We don't need that happening, now do we?"

CHAPTER SEVEN

"Whoa, bro, where the hell am I?" EZ asked when he awoke from what he thought was a bad dream. "And, who the hell are all ya? And, why y'all staring at me?" he asked as he sat up on his cot.

"Welcome to your new home," an older man said to him with a smirk

"This ain't my home," EZ protested. "I ain't staying here. Nobody can make me do anythin."

The man laughed. "You'll learn soon enough."

EZ then grabbed the metal plate strapped around his neck, tugging and trying to pull it off. "What the hell is this?" he asked. The half-inch band was permanently attached around his neck resembling a choker collar. "What the hell is this?" he screamed.

EZ then looked around the room and noticed that everyone was wearing identical collars. He spotted a familiar face. "Is that yo bro Mr. T?" he asked Regi.

"Yes, EZ, it's me," he said with a look of disgust.

Before EZ had a chance to say anything else, Alvaro walked into the room. "Alvaro! What the hell are you doin here too?" he shouted. At this point the other guys all knew that there was some connection, but still very unclear as to why any of them were there.

"So, where the hell are we?" EZ continued to question. He wanted answers, and he wanted them now.

"Just chill," Alvaro said. "You gonna want to save all your energy for later."

EZ wasn't buying the bullshit. He stood up and kicked over his cot and the one next to him. Every possible cuss word imaginable started pouring out of his mouth. His tongue was so tainted you would have thought he was a chow chow with a black tongue. Like any Chow that is born with a pink tongue, EZ's tongue changed over time, and it wasn't pretty. "Nobody gonna tell me what to do," he continued.

All of the guys in the room started laughing. "Just wait and see," the older man said. "Now get these cots put back up before you regret it even more," he told him.

"I ain't doin anythin," EZ said again.

Charlie spoke once more, "Like I said earlier, you'll learn soon enough. That collar of yours is a necklace right now, but if you keep up the attitude it will become your worst enemy. Now clean this mess up now."

EZ looked around the room and noticed several of the guys shaking their heads in agreement with Charlie. Without saying another word, EZ obeyed the order

Three minutes later, Nia appeared at the door with another young lady named Tonya. "Breakfast is ready," she said.

The men followed the two women down the hall to what appeared to be the kitchen. There was an oven, stove, and refrigerator with a few pots and pans hanging from some hooks over the island. The room was void of all furniture, including tables and chairs. There were three windows about nine feet high that allowed sunlight to filter in. There were four can lights in the ceiling as well, with two additional can lights over the work station where the ladies prepared the food.

The men stood in line as the women gave each of them a bowl of oatmeal with one piece of cold toast. Tonya then handed a metal cup to EZ and said, "Don't lose it. Scratch your initials in it with a rock or your fork so you know it's yours. It's also your responsibility to wash it. There's water behind me at the sink. You only get one set of utensils as well. If you lose them or get them stolen, don't come looking for more."

"What kind of place is this?" EZ groaned as he took the cup.

"Just sit over here against the wall with me," Alvaro said to him.

"Stick by my side, and I'll tell ya what I know so far when I can. Trust me. Ya betta off keepin that mouth of yours shut."

"Can ya at least tell your bro where the hell we at?" EZ asked.

"We're on a plantation. That's all any of us know for now."

"This taste like shit," EZ complained as he took another bite of mush.

"Yea, but it's betta than the alternative," Alvaro reminded him. "Just eat the damn food."

"Bro, you callin this shit food? What's wrong with ya all?" EZ continued.

"We got two minutes left to eat. Finish it up, cuz you ain't gettin anymore any time soon."

With that EZ finally stopped talking and finished his last bite of oatmeal just in time. A bell rang from outside. It sounded like an old fashioned school bell. EZ envisioned the liberty bell that he had seen in a history book way back in middle school. He had never seen any bell like it before, so only imagined that it might have sounded like the bell that he was hearing now. With the sound of the bell, everyone stood up and walked by the kitchen sink to wash their spoons, bowls, and cups. Nobody said another word as they all washed their dishes.

"What the hell is wrong with all of ya?" EZ yelled as he filled his cup with water and flung the water across the room, just missing the guys who stood in line behind him. "You bros all acting like ya in some jail or somethin."

"EZ," Alvaro warned. "Keep that damn mouth of yours shut or you'll be regretting it." He then shoved EZ forward so the line would keep moving. "We're headed out to the fields now," he said.

When they walked outside, the sun was just rising over the hilltop. There was dew on the little bit of grass surrounding the house. It was made of concrete with windows high off the ground. A slightly pitched roof with brown shingles had a layer of dew at the far end where large oak tree branches hung high above the house preventing direct sunlight from hitting the roof. This old building housed the former slaves who had once lived on the plantation years ago.

A white two-story Southern Plantation home with floor to ceiling columns was hidden two miles down the road, out of view of the current plantation occupants. No one, except Henry, knew the much larger and nicer home existed. It would be a long time before any of them would see it.

"Hey, those are my wheels," EZ shouted out as the group turned the corner and started walking towards the fields.

"Yeah, we know," Regi said. "You drove here last night, don't you remember? We all saw you pull in when we were coming back from the fields."

"I knew it was you," Alvaro said. "I could hear ya comin from a mile down the road. Everybody in Carol City knows when you're around. Plus, everybody knows your car. It's one of a kind."

"I have no idea how I got here. I don't remember drivin here at all," EZ said.

"How can that be?" Regi asked. "You pulled right in grinning ear to ear."

"Do the rest of ya know how ya all got here?" EZ then asked.

"Some of us have ideas," Alvaro said, "but none of us drove our cars like you."

"And, then there are some of us, like me, who have no idea," Charlie added. "Hell, I didn't know anyone when I first arrived. At least you know some of these guys."

"Yeah, but that don't mean shit," EZ said. "Mr. T there was a prick of a teacher. He was always flirting with the chicks at school thinkin he was hot shit. Then he thought he was a better b-ball player than the boys on the team. He thought it was cool to play with the boys rather than coach em."

"You're just jealous EZ cuz you didn't have the balls to even try out for the team," Regi argued back.

"Hey, boys, just calm down. Fighting isn't going to get you any-where," Charlie said like any father might.

"Well, I'm leavin. I'm taking my car and gettin the hell outta here," EZ announced.

"Trust me," Charlie then said, "You don't want to do that."

"Hell, I don't even need my keys to start this car. Just watch," he said as he took off running towards his car.

He only got about forty yards away when he stopped still in his tracks. He screamed and reached up to his collar with both hands try-ing to tug on it and pull it off. "*Well, maybe I should just walk up to my car,*" EZ thought to himself, not saying another word to the guys watching. After turning his neck from side to side trying to ease the pain, he started walking towards his car.

He was only five feet away, when Alvaro yelled at him. "Stop EZ. Don't go any further. You'll regret it."

EZ turned around and looked at Alvaro and the others. They were all still standing in the same line waiting to see how EZ would react. They knew the consequences. "Don't do it," Alvaro shouted again.

EZ then looked back at his car and took a step towards it. Before he had a chance to go any further, he screamed an even bloodier scream than the first one. This time he fell to his knees grabbing his neck again in a feeble attempt to yank the collar off. It was permanently attached similar to an ankle bracelet that probos had the keys to unlock.

His body shook in pain as EZ's neck moved back and forth as he fell into the dirt. When he brought his hands down he could see the blood covering his finger tips. He laid on the ground cursing for a few minutes before he wiped them on his shorts as he slowly walked back towards the others.

"I thought I was havin a nightmare last night," EZ said when he finally rejoined the group. "I dream dat somebody put a gun to my head and forced me to drive. I didn't know where I was goin, and I remember pulling up to a buildin. That's it. I don't remember nothin more. I thought it was a bad dream."

"It is a bad dream," Regi agreed. "But, the dream is real."

"Just so ya know," Charlie added. "That was your first warning. You don't get any more. If you try to leave again, that little bit of blood on your neck will be pouring down your neck like raindrops from a torrential downpour. It's going to last a very long, long time. You'll be screaming and crying in agony, wishing you had never been born. Minutes will seem like hours as your body flails on the ground trying to gasp for air when the pain is so great you think you'll choke."

"Who the hell is doin this to us?" EZ asked in a bitter tone.

Alvaro looked him in the eyes and said, "We don't know. We're trying to find the connection between all of us, but so far nothing makes sense. You gotta trust us when we tell you to shut up and do as you're told."

"So, we're somebody's..." EZ started to say when he was interrupted.

"Biatch," Ryan said shly.

"You fuckin scared to say bitch?" EZ said to the only fair-skinned black guy in the group.

Ryan was shy and never said much to anyone. He knew he was the outcast being in the minority with this group. He was the only mixed guy in the bunch, but he had been raised in a white home.

"No," Ryan responded quietly as the others laughed. "I just don't like to cuss."

"Oh, so ya Yankee think ya too good for us n*gg**?" EZ snickered.

Ryan didn't even respond. He knew that no matter what came out of his mouth, he would not get the support of many of the guys. He decided right then and there that he would keep his mouth shut unless someone spoke directly to him. It would be safer for him to keep his opinions to himself. Ryan had only lived in Florida a few short years. He was a simple-minded guy who would rather avoid confrontation than engage in it. The last thing he wanted was to have a conversation about racism.

"**Y**ou boys are late," Henry pointed out when the group finally made it out to the field. "And, I can see why. Elijah Jackson, get over here now," he shouted.

Hesitantly, EZ walked out of line while pulling up his pants which had slid down once again, and stood three feet from Henry. He kept his eyes on the only white guy around, never looking back at the group fearful that Henry might try to hurt him some more.

"It's real simple, boy," Henry said with a loud, deep voice. Henry stood at six feet tall, sported dark curly hair, and flaunted muscles that made every one of them look weak. "You do as you are told. You keep your smart-ass mouth shut. And, you never try to take off again. Ever. On foot or by car. That nice pretty necklace of yours was given to you as a gift. I don't think you want to see what it can really do to a person. You understand me?"

"Yeah," EZ said quietly, looking down towards the ground.

"I don't think everyone could hear you, boy," Henry said with a smirk.

"Yeah, man," EZ said in a louder voice.

"Man? You think I'm your man?" Henry mocked. "You better think again, boy. I will never be your man. I actually don't think you will ever be anybody's man," he said now laughing.

The rest of the men held back their grins, laughs, and smiles hoping Henry wouldn't look at them and notice the comedy they just encountered watching the scene unfold before them.

"Yes, sir," EZ said, still looking down towards the ground.

"One last thing. That nice pretty car that used to be yours, now belongs to me. I appreciate the gift. Thank you."

Everyone could see the steam rolling off EZ when he heard that the car no longer belonged to him. EZ wanted to pounce on Henry even though Henry stood over him by six inches, and his arms were at least three times bigger. For once in EZ's life he made the right decision. He kept his mouth shut and waited for Henry to tell him to go back into line with the others.

"It's your lucky day, boy," Henry told EZ. You get to work longer and harder than everybody else. That way you might think twice before you decide to make everyone late again. "We're just beginning harvest season, and we have lots of cotton to be picked. The others will show you what to do. Enjoy the picking."

EZ had been walking the streets of Carol City for years now, believing that he owned the place. He wasn't like his uncle who treated the locals he knew with respect. Instead, EZ just walked around with his pants down to his knees thinking he was cooler than everyone else. Unlike his uncle, he only had a few followers.

Most young kids grew up hearing stories about the Boodie Boyz and didn't want to end up in prison like them. They smoked pot like most of America did these days and drank whiskey straight from the bottle. It was a lot easier to sneak liquor into school than a can of beer, so they became wiser in creating mischief.

Simply stated, EZ was rude to everyone he met. Even his own mother tried to avoid him when possible. She had given up on him when he was only eight, so it seemed.

"Strap this around your waist," Charlie said as he handed a large burlap bag to EZ. All the other men had picked up their bags and began strapping them around their waists too. "It's real simple boy. We are all going to line up along the front of this row, about six feet apart, and we are going to start picking all these cotton balls off of the plants. Put the cotton in your bag."

"Don't they have machines to do this bullshit?" EZ asked.

"Yeah," Alvaro said as he began picking. "See that green thing way over in the other field? That's a John Deere picker. It reminds me of a Zamboni on steroids with large tractor tires and large yellow front teeth."

"Yeah, whatever," EZ said, not having a clue what a Zamboni does.

Davon who was standing next to Regi then whispered, "That kid is as dumb as the rumors I've heard." Davon had kept his mouth shut all morning too, like most of the men. He was angry, frustrated and having a difficult time accepting his new reality.

Regi chuckled, but didn't say a word.

"Some people call them strippers," Charlie added.

"I could use a stripper right now," EZ said laughing.

"Quit being a dumbass," Alvaro responded as EZ continued to laugh at his own joke. "That machine can do everything we're doing in about twenty minutes that takes all of us to do in a full day."

"Why the hell are we doing this then?" EZ asked.

"Henry told us we are here to learn a lesson or two," Charlie responded. "But Henry doesn't know who's behind this. He's getting paid a lot of money to make sure we work. When we're done picking this field, the picker is going to come through here and clean up our mess and grab anything we missed. Basically, it's a slap in the face," Charlie told the young EZ. "You won't be laughing when you see that happen. Instead, you're going to be boiling inside, full of anger and wishing you could kill somebody."

"Who gets to drive that baby?" EZ then asked.

"One of us older guys," Charlie responded. "Trust me. You're going to be jealous too when you see us climb into it, cuz it beats bending over all day."

Most of the men worked diligently keeping their thoughts to themselves. They had all done their complaining in the first few days after they had arrived. They knew there was nothing they could do now except work and accept the conditions they were in.

"This if f**kin slavery," EZ blurted out about an hour into his new job.

"You are just figuring this out now?" Regi responded. "We all knew that the moment we woke up with collars strapped around our necks. It's the twenty-first century, and we've gone back about a hundred years in time."

Charlie, who had definitely taken on the role of team leader, then said to EZ, "Boy, you can continue to complain all you want, but it's only going to get you twelve angry men tired of hearing you scream and holler like a baby. You have to grow up, kid, and you can start by keeping that dirty mouth of yours closed. We are all tired of hearing the cursing and complaining. It's not going to change the situation you are in."

"But my back hurts," EZ complained again.

"We know. All of our backs hurt," Regi said.

"And, look at my fingers. They are all bleeding and hurt so bad," EZ continued.

"You'll learn soon enough," Charlie said, "the best way to pick without cutting up all your fingers. You can't just grab the plant with your whole hand."

"And, if you don't learn soon enough," Alvaro said, "we don't want to hear about it. Learn to keep that big mouth of yours closed."

The men continued to work as the hot sun rose above them. The heat was overwhelming now and nearly eighty-eight degrees as the sweat poured off each of their foreheads. When they didn't think they could handle it any more, they saw an old pickup truck pull up in the field behind them.

Nia and Tonya jumped out of the truck and opened the back tailgate. They pulled a large orange ten gallon Gatorade container to the edge of the tailgate. Unlike the other men who were grateful to be drinking water to quench their long overdue thirst, EZ complained once again

"This ain't even Gatorade?" he said. "The container says it's Gatorade."

Jaheem Jones, the largest one of the bunch, then walked up to EZ. "Look, ya punk, we are all tired of hearing that mouth of yours rattle. If you open your mouth one more time while we are out in the field, I am personally going to knock your lights out. It will take one punch only, I promise. So, stand silently and wait your turn to get your food, then go sit down and shut up. It's that simple."

The others cheered on the Jamaican when they heard his little speech. They were all tired of the young punk kid from Carol City.

Tonya, then spoke up, "We are having peanut butter and jelly today. You can each have two sandwiches and an apple. We are making something special for you for dinner tonight, so you better get a lot of work done this afternoon."

Both Davon and Regi sat down by Nia as she grabbed a sandwich and cup of water as well. "How are you guys doing?" she asked them.

"This totally sucks," Davon said before taking another bite of his sandwich.

"Yea, it does," Regi agreed, but at least we get to see you every day. "That helps me get through the day, knowing you're the one making our meals."

Davon had no idea that Nia was the girl that Regi had secretly dated while she was still in high school. He just knew that Regi had been Nia's teacher. Regi knew that Davon and Nia had gone to church together for a long time, but he didn't have any idea that they both had been best friends with John.

They finished their sandwiches and threw their apple cores across the field.

"Thanks, Nia," both men said when they stood up.

"I'll see you tonight," she responded.

Regi and Davon then walked to the back of the truck and lifted the Gatorade cooler off the back. They would at least have water for the rest of the day.

CHAPTER EIGHT

"Who is this?" John asked the caller on the landline.

"It's your auntie, you know Auntie Anna," the voice declared. "Is your momma home?" she then asked.

"No, but I can have her call you back," John responded.

"Well, I need to talk to her right now," John's aunt announced. "It's really important."

"She's not home," John said again.

"Well, then give me her cell phone number," the lady demanded.

"I can't do that Ma'am," John politely replied. "I never give out anyone's phone number, but my own."

"I'm your uncle's wife, and I need to talk to your momma right away," she said again.

John didn't know if he should ask questions to find out the problem or if he should hang up and let his aunt figure out the solution on her own. He knew his mom hadn't spoken with her brother for nearly ten years. He couldn't imagine anything so important that he would need to give out her phone number, especially to the wife of a person his mom was choosing to ignore.

"Junior," she said loudly, "didn't you hear a word I just said? I need to talk to your momma immediately."

"Yes, I realize that, but as I just told you, she is not home," he reiterated.

Expecting to hear that his uncle was in the hospital or had even passed away, John then said, "Is there anything specific you would like me to tell her?"

"You damn fool. You aren't even going to give me her cell number?" she said, annoyed that her nephew refused to pass on his mother's number.

"No, as I said before, I am not giving you or anyone my mother's number. I will pass on a message to her as soon as possible, and she can call you back at her convenience," John then told his auntie.

It was a Tuesday evening, and John's parents had walked down to the park after dinner. Occasionally, they would go together for ice cream. There was a little Whippy Dip shop attached to the gas station about three blocks away. The park was a block away from the gas station. They liked to buy ice cream cones and then head over to the park to talk. John was not about to interrupt their walk and together time.

"You are stubborn and just like your mother," she said. "Tell her to call me ASAP. Her brother is missing."

Anna never gave John a chance to respond. The receiver clicked with a bang as his auntie hung up the phone.

"Who was that?" Shanice asked when she walked into the kitchen.

"That was Auntie Anna," John told his gramma. "She wants to talk to Momma immediately. She got really mad at me when I refused to give Momma's cell number to her too."

"I know your momma doesn't want your auntie or uncle to have her cell number," Gramma agreed.

"She said that Uncle Charlie is missing," John then told his gramma.

"Oh brother," Gramma responded. "What's that make? Eleven now?" she asked.

"Well, it's really ten, unless we include Nia's boss, Tonya," John said.

"And everyone lived in South Florida, except your Uncle Charlie Rivers?" Gramma asked.

"I guess you could say that, except Tonya's parents claim she's from Virginia, and she told everyone at work that she was relocating to the Carolinas. Her parents never confirmed that with the police though," John recalled.

"I was in elementary school when things fell apart between Momma and her brother," John explained. "I have never asked Momma about it because she told me that she never wanted to talk about it again."

"It was a sad, sad day," Gramma said.

"So, what really happened?" John inquired.

The two walked into the living room to sit down to talk. "Hopefully, we won't have any rocks flying through the window again," Gramma said as she sat in her comfy spot on the sofa.

"Let's hope not. I think that problem is gone for a while anyway," John said.

"Your momma and her brother had always gotten along just fine, until your other gramma passed away," Shanice began. "Your grandparents didn't have a lot, but your granddad had managed to save enough to buy a condominium up in Broward County."

"I loved going to their place," John recalled. "Granddad always had a bowl of jelly beans waiting for me when I was younger."

"Well, after your gramma passed away both your momma and Charlie were supposed to split the profits from the sale of the condo. Being the eldest, Charlie was the executor of her estate. Instead of dividing the profits 50/50 like your gramma's will read, Charlie decided to charge the estate for his services. He ended up stealing all of your momma's profits."

"That's what their quarrel was all about?" John questioned.

"That's the simple version, Junior," Gramma said. "Charlie had moved up to Jacksonville when he finished college and opened a used car dealership. He became successful and expanded his business to new cars as well. He made a good name for himself, and his business grew."

"So, he got to go to college, but Momma didn't?" John asked.

Gramma shook her head. "Unfortunately, your granddad got sick just about the time your momma was ready to go to college. Their medical bills prevented her from going. She stayed home and helped your granddad and gramma. When your granddad was well enough to work again, they sold their house and bought a condo. That's about the time your papa and momma met. Your papa didn't care if your momma had a degree or not. They were happy and got married."

John knew there had been a rift between his momma and uncle, but had no idea it was over money. "In other words, Uncle Charlie, who is wealthy, refused to help Momma, knowing she could have used that money?" John asked.

"That's about it," Shaniced remarked. "Your momma and papa have always struggled, and your auntie and uncle have held it over their heads, acting as if they aren't good enough for them."

"Your momma told him that she would never speak with him again, if he didn't give her the portion that was due her."

"What about Gramma's belongings?" John then asked.

"You've seen a few nicknacks around the house that belonged to your gramma," Shanice said pointing to some glass figurines on the shelf. And, your momma has some Christmas decorations that once belonged to your gramma."

"What about everything else?" John inquired again.

"Charlie had an estate sale and claims that there was no money raised after paying the auction house for their services. We both know that can't be true," Shanice said.

"Wow!" John said. "Wow!"

As Shanice was finishing her story to John, Ebony and Senior walked through the front door. "A little gramma and grandson bonding time?" Senior asked.

"I wouldn't quite call it that," John told his parents. "Auntie Anna called a while ago," John announced. "She said it's really important that you call her back immediately. She's actually mad that I refused to give her your cell phone number," John explained.

"Did she say what it's about?" Ebony inquired.

"Yes. She said that Uncle Charlie is missing."

Both Senior and Ebony looked at one another. "You need to call her back, dear," John said as he placed his arms around his wife.

"I know, but I really don't want to," she said.

Junior walked into the kitchen to retrieve the landline. Fortunately, it was a portable phone that could be taken from room to room. "Here's the phone Mom. Do you want us to leave you alone right now?"

"No," she replied. "I would rather put the phone on speaker so everyone can hear. I won't have to repeat anything. I really thought I was done with him," she added. "In my mind, I wrote him off as dead. I mourned the first year that we didn't speak, but kept reminding myself, "*Charlie stole from me. He doesn't care about me or my family, and he only wants to get richer. What kind of brother is that?*"

"Yes, I know dear," Senior said, trying to comfort his wife. "Let's get this call over with now."

Ebony took the phone and pushed the call back button assuming no one had used the phone since that call came in. She then pressed the speaker button, and everyone could hear the phone ring. "Well, it's about time you called me back," Anna said when she answered the call.

"Hello to you too," Ebony responded with a grudge.

"That son of yours wouldn't give me your cell number. Can you believe that?" she then proclaimed.

"That son of mine has a name, Anna. His name is John just like his father. He has done exactly what I have asked him to do, and that is to keep my cell number private. If you have something else to say, other than complaining about my son, please say it now."

Junior was surprised to hear his momma talk back to his auntie with such guts and authority. He was downright proud of her.

"Your brother is missing," she then blurted out. "We went out for dinner on Saturday evening with our friends. We went to Ruth's Chris Steakhouse down on the water. I'm sure you have never eaten there before. It's just too nice for your taste and budget. I had a lobster tail with a six ounce petite filet and your brother ate a Tomahawk Ribeye," she began. "I couldn't make up my mind between a glass of pinot noir to go with my lobster or a merlot to go with."

"Stop it," Ebony yelled through the phone before Anna could finish her sentence. "I don't care one bit about what you ate, nor should you. Tell me about Charlie."

"Well, how rude to cut me off like that," Anna proclaimed.

Junior and Senior were both rolling their eyes and having a hard time remaining silent. The lady's husband is missing, and she only cares about bragging rights for the food they ate.

"After we finished eating a lovely meal, we strolled down the river walk with our friends. The sunset was beautiful, and we even saw a manatee and her calf. It was the perfect ending of a perfect evening, until we walked back to our car. You know how it is?" she explained. "We never know which car we are going to drive. Charlie gets to choose from the top line fleet. We thought we had driven the Mercedes, but Charlie had forgotten that he switched vehicles at the last moment. We actually came in the Audi instead. We had walked right past it not even realizing it was the car that we had driven. We were all laughing and giggling and having a good time so we walked our friends back to their car. When we arrived back at our car the sun had already set, and the street light was out, making it dark to see. I remember hearing Charlie press the fob to open the doors because the car buzzed, and the lights flashed. The next thing I knew, I woke up in a hospital bed."

"What about Charlie?" Ebony finally asked when Anna was done spewing her words.

"Don't you understand? He wasn't there."

"Do you mean that he wasn't home when you arrived back home, or he wasn't in the hospital with you?" Ebony inquired.

"Neither," Anna said with a loud sound of exasperation.

"Was the Audi still parked where you left it?" Ebony inquired some more.

"Why yes, dear," she said again, annoyed by her sister-in-law's questions.

"Did the police stop by the hospital or call you?" Ebony then asked.

It was clear to the entire Bramble family that Anna had probably been drinking again, and the mental stress of telling her story was becoming burdensome to her.

"Yes, they stopped by the hospital and told me that a young couple found me lying by the car with the fob in my hand. They figured I had passed out from drinking too much and hit my head on the concrete when I fell. But, I am so fortunate. They said that no charges were being pressed since I had not been driving."

"Well, that's good news," Ebony said with a hint of sarcasm. "What about Charlie then?"

"That's the problem. He hasn't come home, and he hasn't answered any of his phone calls. I've tried both of his cell phones, and the staff at the dealership hasn't seen him either," Anna explained.

"So, why are you calling me? Is there something you want me to do?" Ebony asked.

"I was hoping you were going to tell me that he snuck down there to see you, even though I've told him for years that you no longer need to be a part of his life ever again."

Junior's eyes just about popped out of his sockets when he heard his auntie talk so mean.

"I'm glad to hear that you hate me that much, Anna. To answer your question, he's not here either."

"Oh, it's not that I hate you or John," she continued. "You guys are just way too poor for my black blood. I don't even know how you can live in that filth of a place you call a home," she added.

"Thanks for calling," Ebony then replied. "Hopefully, if I'm lucky, I will never hear from you ever again."

"Wait! What? You're not going to help me find your brother?" she then asked.

"I'm sure you and the kids can hire a private detective to find him," Ebony suggested.

"Why that would require spending money," Anna replied, sounding even more drunk now than she did when she first called.

"Yes, hiring a detective will cost money. Perhaps, Charlie left you for a reason. Maybe he's not missing at all," Ebony belittled her disgraceful sister-in-law.

"Oh, he would never do that," she insisted. "He loves me too much."

"Yes, he might, but you love his money more than you love him from the sounds of it," Ebony rebutted.

"Oh, don't be silly. There's a reason I have never liked you," she then said.

Without even saying another word, Ebony hung the phone up on the dreadful woman who had married her brother. Tears streamed down her eyes. She never wanted this to be the ending of her relationship with her brother. Even though she hadn't talked with him in years, she had dreamed of someday seeing him again.

"It's amazing what a little alcohol can bring out of a person," Senior said as he tried to comfort his wife again.

"Let me brew up some hot blackberry tea for you," Gramma suggested as she left the room.

"I always thought she brought out the devil in Charlie," Ebony responded. "I surely doubt that Charlie is missing. It sounds to me like he left her intentionally."

"Are you going to try to help find him?" Junior then asked.

"No, Son, I'm not. Everyone makes choices in life. Some choices are good, some are bad, some are neutral, and some have everlasting consequences. Charlie made a choice long ago with everlasting consequences. Now he has to pay the price for it. For him it was losing his sister. Now he may be losing his wife and children too. Regardless, everyone is responsible for their own decisions."

John stood up and walked over to the chair where his momma was sitting. "Momma, I love you," he said as he reached down to hug her and give her a kiss on the cheek. "I had no idea until tonight why things had ended with your brother. I understand now."

"Thanks, Son," she said as she hugged him back.

John left his parents sitting in the living room as he headed to his room. His mind was churning as he added another person to his list. It was unlikely that the Carol City police or Miami detectives would even associate Charlie Rivers' disappearance with any of the others down in South Florida. And, unlike the others who John knew, Charlie was the only person related to him.

The tea kettle blew as John walked by the kitchen. Gramma turned and winked at him, indicating that everything would be okay. She then picked up the steaming kettle and began pouring a cup of tea. John wasn't so sure if his gramma was right this time around. It seemed like he might be the next target.

CHAPTER NINE

Some of the men had already been on the plantation for nearly eight weeks. Each week another man or two would arrive during the middle of the night. With each new arrival the instructions were minimal, but only one was crucial. Henry told everyone that if you run away or try to escape, you will be zapped by your collar. Each person was given one warning and one warning only. A second attempt to leave would be fatal. Those who had arrived earlier saw first-hand the attempt EZ made when he thought he could drive away in his car.

The days were simmering hot and dry. The once-moist land was now hard. Even the bugs looked for a cooler place to nestle as the temperatures soared each day. The heavy, humid air made it difficult to breathe especially with cotton sticking to anything and everything that came near it. It was summer, and the cotton needed to be picked.

The men had talked among themselves, but never as a group or at length to see more specifically how each of them came to be at this place at this time. They were so exhausted at night that they did very little talking. They had varying opinions as to their whereabouts. Some thought they were in Texas. One thought Oklahoma seemed like the better choice. Others thought they might be in Louisiana, Mississippi, or Alabama. South Carolina also received a vote or two.

"Shit," Davon shouted loud enough for Alvaro and Jaheem to hear. "Guys," he said hesitantly. "There's a snake."

He was exhausted and sweat rolled down his cheeks. He was guessing by the placement of the sun in the sky that it must be nearing two o-clock. His bag was almost full and needed to be emptied again.

Everyone of these men were city folk. They could all tell you about geckos, lizards and alligators, but snakes that crawled around in the fields were far different from the ones found in the Everglades and low lying wetlands of Florida.

"Should I stand here or move? What should I do?" Davon said as he slowly stepped backwards out of harm's way.

"Who knows anything about snakes?" Alvaro shouted out for the others to hear.

No one answered. They all stood around looking at each other, hoping someone knew something about snakes. After a moment when no one replied, Marble Rye finally spoke up. Ryan Smith, the only mixed guy in the group, had been given the nickname Marble Rye, after the bread. It didn't matter if he liked it or not, the men called him that regardless.

"I know a little, but there are thousands of snakes. I'm not sure I can help at all," he said. He unstrapped his bag and walked over to where Davon was standing. Davon pointed to an orange and yellow snake that had slithered between a couple of plants. It was about two feet long. "I'm not sure what it is," Ryan said, "but if you walk around it and move up past those couple of plants, you should be okay. From the looks of him, he's probably as much afraid of you as you are of him."

"Ok, thanks," Davon replied.

"Keep your eyes open. When there's one, there are usually more," Davon said as he walked away. "We all need to keep our eyes open."

Davon dragged his bag as far away from the snake as he possibly could before emptying his fill into the large wooden box fifty yards up the field. Davon was now behind everyone else in his picking. He knew he would need to catch up before the end of the day. He didn't want to be like EZ.

In the first week that EZ had arrived, he was so far behind that he took a couple of days off. His body was in shock as it acclimated from a state of being buzzed and high every day to being brutalized from the physical pain of picking. He collapsed right in the field on his third day.

He got that gatorade he wanted, but it cost him. They put him in a room called *SPIRIT*. It was there that he detoxed. It had a cot, pillow, blanket, Bible, and a bathroom. The only good thing was that he could vomit in private. His food was delivered to him. He had no contact with any of the workers for three days. He hated it, but was too sick to notice. He was still working two hours longer than anyone else every day to catch up for the work he missed.

With an empty bag Davon ran back to where he left off, hoping the snake would be gone. He looked everywhere, but could not find it. He knew his fingers would be hurting now. Speed would be critical as he tried to catch up. His fingers would get the brunt of his pain as he couldn't be as diligent in picking. "*Grab n go*," he kept saying to himself.

When EZ arrived back from the field later that day, everyone was sitting outside fixing their burlap bags. They would routinely get holes in them from dragging them across the fields. No one was talking, as they were hustling to fix them while waiting for dinner to be served.

Those facing the field watched as EZ slowly walked back towards the house. He was limping now. "Here comes trouble," Regi warned.

EZ didn't bother to respond or say a word. He walked straight to the spigot with an attached forest green garden hose at the other end of the house.

The hose ran to a rocky drain about thirty yards from the house. This was their shower. If you were first in line, you would get a hot shower from the water left in the hose line. Most showers only lasted a minute or two. Twice a week, the men were given shampoo and soap, straight off the shelves of the Dollar Shop. While some men complained, others were thankful that they got any at all.

EZ stripped down to the bare bone, not caring anymore who was there to mock his skinny frame. He danced around as the hot water drenched his body until it became a more pleasant temperature. No soap was available today so he rinsed off and then drank from the hose to quench his thirst. The water never tasted as good as the water from inside the house, but he didn't care. When his two minutes were up, he stood in the sun to dry off. He put his boxers back on just long enough to head into the house to retrieve some cleaner shorts and a shirt.

He then limped his way down to the watering hole where the men were allowed to wash their clothes. It was a concrete basin that used to be an old trough that filled with rain on some days. EZ only had two sets of clothes with him, so he found himself down there often rinsing the sweat and cotton off as best he could. For those lucky enough to have more clothes with them, they didn't have to go so often. The trough was under the shade of two elm trees. The men had broken off the scraggly branches to make a clothes line. It was there that their clothes hung to dry.

There was another rule that the men abided by without complaining. There would be no stealing of personal items or food. The men were allowed to barter and trade whatever personal things they had in their possession, but stealing was strictly prohibited. Everyone of the men knew that stealing was wrong, but everyone had stolen something valuable from someone in their lifetime.

"We gotta figure out who's behind all this," Ralph said when EZ approached them. "If we each tell our stories, maybe you smart guys can figure out what's happening. Someone gotta know somethin."

"EZ you start," Alvaro suggested. "We wanna know why the bro is limpin too."

"Aight," he said as he sat down on a log. "That damn snake came out from hidin again," he said. "It's scared the f**k out of me. I twisted my ankle when I landed in a rut nearby. It hurts, but as ya all know there ain't a thin I kin do bout it."

"That sucks," Alvaro admitted.

"I missed how you got here, kid," Ralph said. "Tell us about it."

"Yea ya did. If you weren't in the detox tank you would of known," he smarted back. "I ain't tellin the story for you. I'm telling it for Frank," EZ said, looking over to the newcomer.

"You're an idiot," Ralph responded.

"Yea, but you're an old idiot," EZ smarted back trying to have the last word.

The teacher in the group could not refrain from talking. "Are we in grade school again?" Regi remarked. "Seriously, you guys sound like you're in first grade."

"Just tell your story," Alvaro added.

"Ya know my momma got hitched, and when she was on that honeymoon of hers, I got the whole damn place to myself. It was like heaven. I was partyin with my boys, smokin shit, selling drugs and makin some racks. I didn't know what time of day it was, and I didn't even care. Every night them girls were hot. I don't remember much other than I woke up when the stars were still hanging and some bro was slapping a biscuit around. Told me to get in my car and drive. I never saw his ugly son-of-a-b**ch face ya know. I don't even rememba him bein in ma wheels, except that muffled voice of his. Next thin I know, I woke up to all you mother f**k**s."

"So, that's it? You f**kin drove here?" Ralph said. "Who was it? Dragon Danger or Star Lad? You know darn well those drug lords are out for ya."

"Naw, man, I'm tellin ya the truth," EZ protested. "It wasn't any of them comin for me. Hell, they could have popped me right there in my ma's hous. I didn't owe anybody anythin."

"You may be here for selling drugs, but most of us aren't," Charlie said. "I've never smoked anything more than a cigar," he continued. "So, if you two knuckleheads think it's because of drugs, you are both wrong." Charlie was tired of hearing from EZ. "You know kid, you're a poor dumb a** punk who never even deserved a breath of fresh air. From now on, you just keep that big mouth of yours closed. I have deep pockets, and my new friend, Jaheem, will keep you in line. Unless one of us asks you a question, you don't speak. You get it?"

Fearful of saying anything more, EZ nodded his head in agreement although he was wondering to himself, "*How on earth could Charlie access any money from here?*"

Charlie then pointed to Ryan, "Can you tell me how on earth you ended up at an airport without getting on your flight?" he asked. He had heard mumblings about Marble Rye, but didn't know the full story.

"I took an Uber to the airport to go back home. I've been living with my grandmother in Florida ever since my mom died. I was sixteen, but the courts would not allow me to live alone and finish school since I was still under age. I moved down here to finish school and have been working part-time."

"Where are you from?" Regi asked.

"I'm from Allentown, Pennsylvania," he responded. "My friends still live there and my cousins. I wanted to live with them, but my mom's last request was for me to live with my grandmother because she doesn't have anyone to help her. I agreed to help."

"That's pretty nice of you, Ryan, to help your gramma," Regi admitted.

"Anyway, I was already running about twenty minutes late when I got out of the car and tried to check in. I knew it would be a close call, but didn't have any luggage other than a carry-on bag. That's when I realized I left my wallet on the backseat of the Uber. I immediately called the company who notified the driver that I had left my wallet. The driver called me back to say that my wallet wasn't there. I know I had it with me because I had used my card to pay a bill on my way to the airport."

"I walked outside looking around where I had been dropped off, but didn't see a thing. It was getting dark now and looked like a storm was moving in. I then walked back inside knowing that I couldn't get on the plane without proper identification when I heard my name on the intercom. I was being paged to the security counter. I kept looking at my phone because the minutes to board the plane were dwindling down. When I arrived at security, they said someone found my wallet, and I needed to call a phone number which they gave me to retrieve my wallet."

"That's crazy that someone found it and actually called you," Ralph said. "I sure wouldn't have bothered to give it back."

"Yea, I wouldn't have either. I would have stolen your cash and dumped the wallet," Alvaro agreed.

"Maybe that's why you guys are here," Jaheem piped in, "because you are thieves."

"I've stolen a lot more than some kid's wallet," Ralph bragged.

"You better not steal anything here," Charlie reminded Ralph.

"What's there to steal?" Frank asked.

"Did you come bearing gifts?" Ralph asked.

"What do you mean?" Frank asked as the group laughed.

Regi went on to explain the importance of not stealing. "Some of us came with a backpack, duffle bag, or even a suitcase full of clothes and personal items. Those items are ours, and no one is allowed to take them from us. If anyone tries, he will be zapped. You can barter your items, but it has to be done in front of the group so everyone knows who is giving and who is receiving."

"That's pretty harsh," Frank said.

"Yes, but it's supposed to teach the knuckleheads not to steal simply because they want something," Charlie added. The men laughed again as they all turned their heads towards Ryan.

"Finish your story," Charlie urged.

"Instead of handing my wallet to security outside the terminal, the man who found it thought it was his and drove away. When he realized it wasn't his, he called the airport to have me paged to see if I was still there. When I spoke with him, he said he was turning around and would meet me outside the terminal. I walked back outside, and the storm had already moved in. It was black outside, and the rain was pelting down hard. It was a typical South Florida storm that came roaring in without warning. I knew if I hadn't already missed my flight that it would be delayed at this point. I looked everywhere trying to find the car, and then the man called me to say that he had pulled into short-term parking. Security was directing vehicles away from the terminal because too many cars were parking there afraid to leave in the storm."

"I imagine you had thought by now that you had missed your flight," Regi said.

"I really didn't know. It either snuck out early to miss the storm or it was parked on the tarmac waiting in line with the other planes. At that point, I was more concerned about getting my wallet. I continued to walk through the parking lot, down to the far end where the man said he was parked. When I got to his car, he opened the car door, and at that very moment there was a huge lightning strike, and the lights flickered for about five seconds. I thought the flickering lights were from the storm, but my lights must have flickered too because when I woke up, I was sitting on the edge of the fields about a mile down where the dirt roads cross each other. I had a lump on the back of my head, a pounding headache and my carry on. It was pitch dark outside, and the only light I could see were the ones here at the house."

"You thought you were walking down here to get help?" Frank asked.

"I did," Ryan said. "My head hurt so bad that I didn't even realize that I had a collar around my neck. "When I knocked on the door, Tonya greeted me and said she had a cot I could use for the night. She led me down to the *SPIRIT*."

"Why would she put you there," Alvaro asked, "if you didn't need detox?"

"I don't know. Maybe she didn't want to wake up the others. Maybe I needed extra time for the tranquilizer to leave my system. I just don't know," Ryan concluded.

The only question that Ralph had swimming around in the swampy head of his was whether Ryan got his wallet back or not.

"Kid, did you get your wallet after all that?" he finally asked.

"I actually did," he said, pulling it out of his front pocket.

The men wanted to sit around all night to hear each other's stories, but they knew it would probably take a few more days to learn about everyone. The sun was still beating down on them when Tonya popped her head outside the door.

"We are letting you eat dinner outside tonight," Tonya said as she motioned for the men to come in. "Everyone come in to get your food, and then come back out here. We have a surprise for you."

Most meals served so far had been simple meals. Breakfast consisted of oatmeal and toast, grits and toast, or scrambled eggs and toast. Lunch was peanut butter and jelly with fruit, grilled cheese sandwiches with carrots and celery, or sloppy joes with chips. Several times Nia and Tonya boiled a big pot of pasta and served it with butter and toast too.

Dinners were a little more heartier, and not because the men deserved it, Tonya claimed. "If you work hard in the fields each day, we will treat you to a nice warm meal each night," she said on multiple occasions. "We aren't feeding you because you deserve it. We are feeding you so you will work hard again the next day, and the day after that, and again the next day after that."

At this point in time, dinner was the main reason the men continued to work hard. Biscuits and gravy, chicken fajitas, beef stew, and chili with cornbread had been some of their favorite meals. This was the only meal that did not include white bread either. On rare occasions, they would even include some honey or jam with the biscuits.

The men were gleaming this particular night when they walked back outside with their plates full of country fried chicken, mashed potatoes and gravy, green beans, and chocolate cake. They were each carrying a can of cola as well. It was the first time they had received anything to drink other than water or ice tea with the rare exception of Gatorade for those who were detoxing. Country fried chicken was a favorite for most of them. EZ would have been satisfied with a pepperoni pizza, but he was thrilled to find a cold drink in his hand.

"Is the cola and chicken the surprise?" Davon asked Alvaro after they both licked their fingers while pulling the meat from the bones.

"Naw, I doubt it. Tonya was too excited for soda to be the surprise," Alvaro responded.

"We found an old movie projector. If you continue to work hard and obey the rules, Henry gave us permission to watch a movie this Saturday night," Nia told them.

"How about it guys?" Tonya followed up immediately when Nia was done speaking. "Aren't you excited about that?" she said.

"Is it a horror flick or Disney movie?" Ralph asked.

"Does it matter?" Davon responded back.

"Maybe," Ralph replied. "Aren't we living our own horror flick right now?"

Jaheem looked around at the expressions on each of the men's faces. He could tell most men were excited to hear that they would get to see a movie. "It could be worse," Jaheem told the men. "Have you ever been without food for three days in a row? Have you ever seen a family member shot in cold blood right before your very own eyes? Have you ever crawled to the roof of your house, only to see your grandmother washed away in the hurricane floods? Have you ever been homeless?"

"You're sh*tt** us," EZ said as he broke his silence.

"Why would I lie to you?" Jaheem responded back. "You think you know me, but you really don't. I don't have a good enough reason to lie to any of you."

Tonya wasn't expecting the conversation to become so serious. "We don't know the movie yet," she explained. Finish up your dinners, clean your dishes, and head back inside. Tomorrow is supposed to be another hot day."

As the men dozed off to sleep that night, Regi patiently waited to hear or see the truck drive away. That was his cue. Initially, it was infrequent, but lately Tonya had been driving away after dark and returning around midnight or so. If any of the men were still awake, he would tell them that he needed to use the john. As quietly as possible he would sneak to the other end of the house to find Nia. She and Tonya had dorm room styled beds. She would place her mattress on the floor to keep the bed from squealing. Nothing had really changed for her and

Regi. They were living even closer together now, under the very same roof, and they were still sneaking around pretending not to be sleeping together. The only problem this time was that Regi was running out of condoms.

"Oh shit," Regi said as he jumped to his feet pulling up his shorts. Somebody was in the house, and it wasn't Tonya returning from her rendezvous. Heavy boots could be heard of a man walking down the hall. Nia pulled her shorts up as well and threw her blanket over her body pretending to be asleep when she heard the knock on her door. There was nowhere for Regi to hide. He slipped under the covers in Tonya's bed hoping he wouldn't be seen.

"Who is it?" Nia asked, scared of whom she might find.

"It's Henry. Let me in," he said.

"You scared the hell out of me," Nia told him as she opened the door. A dim light from the hall lit a strip of floor in the room. "I just want you to know that Tonya isn't coming back tonight.

"What's wrong?" Nia immediately asked, assuming something terrible had happened.

Regi was trying his best not to breathe in fear that Henry would hear him. The light was just three feet from Tonya's bed. If it were any closer, Henry would have seen someone in the bed.

Henry chose his words wisely. He looked deeply into Nia's eyes, then said, "She'll be fine. She'll be staying at my place for a few days."

"And, where is that?" Nia blurted out, forgetting that she was a prisoner like everyone else.

"You know I can't tell you that," he said.

"How am I going to lift the water on the truck to take it to the field?" she then asked.

"That's another problem," Henry explained. "In the morning during breakfast pick three men to hike three miles down the road to fix the creek bridge. The truck got a flat when it hit a loose tie rod on the wooden bridge. There is a spare tire and lug wrench in the back of the truck to replace the slashed one. I don't care who goes, but make sure they are back before lunch or the men in the field won't be getting lunch. Here are the keys to the truck. Also, remind the men that their collars are working, and they will be killed immediately if they don't head back here."

"Anything else?" Nia asked.

"Yes. Hey Regi. I know you are here. Just don't let the other guys know you come down here and don't say a word about Tonya either. I will make your life miserable if you say anything."

Without saying another word, Henry strolled back down the hallway and out the door. Afraid the others might have awakened due to the loud muffler of EZ's old wheels, Regi stayed a bit longer.

"How did he know that I was in here?" Regi asked Nia. "Did you tell Tonya?"

"I promise you, I haven't said a thing to anyone, Tonya or even Davon," Nia whispered as the two stood in the darkness of the room.

"What does Davon have to do with us?" Regi asked, confused that Nia would even mention him.

"You know. I'm friends with him. We went to youth group together all through high school. I don't want him knowing that I'm not being a 'good' girl'," she explained.

"Why would he care? From the sounds of it, he was dealing drugs. Isn't that a bigger sin than us messing around?"

Just then the door opened to the room down the hall where the men slept. Instead of pretending to be asleep, Nia stepped out into the hallway, leaving her door open.

"What are you doing up this late?" She asked EZ, trying to distract him to give Regi a chance to return to the room.

"I thought I was dreamin and heard my car," EZ stated half asleep.

No, it wasn't a dream," Nia explained. "I just got a visit from Henry. He needed to tell me something really important. I'll tell all of you about it in the morning. Why don't we go to the kitchen to get a drink of water?"

Nia knew EZ didn't have his cup with him, but Nia needed to find a way to get EZ out of the hall so Regi could sneak back into the room. She was also hopeful that Regi would get the clue without anyone else waking up.

EZ agreed to a drink. "Shit," he said when they walked into the kitchen.

"What's wrong now?" Nia inquired.

"I forgot my cup," EZ responded, still dazed by his state of unrest.

"Don't tell anyone, but I have an extra cup," Nia fibbed as she grabbed Tonya's cup out of the cabinet. When they were done drinking, Nia slowly washed the cups by hand trying to add a few more seconds of time to their midnight encounter. "I'll see you in the morning."

"Yea," EZ softly muttered.

When Nia arrived back in her room, Regi was gone. She could only hope that he made it back without incident too.

CHAPTER TEN

"Look at that Son," Senior said to John when he pulled into the dirt lot to drop off John for work.

"What?" John responded.

The sun was still trying to sneak around a building, and the early morning came too soon for John today. He stayed up late, much too late, to be at work by six in the morning. He needed some caffeine, if only he were a coffee drinker. Senior was kind enough to drive his son because he had already missed the morning bus.

"Your car," Senior responded.

"I don't see my car," Junior muffled through his yawn.

Warren Laikin had told John the day before that his car would be waiting for him this morning. John had been taking the bus back and forth from work the past couple of weeks while he waited for his car to be finished. He drove an older style sedan that had seen better days. The once shining black top had turned into a dull dark muddy gray from the sun beating down on it relentlessly. The dust and dirt from the construction site always found its way to the side doors, leaving them tarnished and dirty every day.

Shiny and clean, a white sedan was parked in the corner of the lot. "I think that's your car over there in the corner," Senior told his son.

"Are you sure? It's white," John said when he spotted it.

Senior parked in an empty space nearby so they both could get out to verify that the car was really John's car. Sure enough, John's cross necklace dangled down from the rearview mirror barely visible in the morning light.

"Wow! Look at this," John exclaimed to his father. "I can not believe how much nicer it looks. He even replaced the rims."

The faded black Dodge Charger looked brand new now. John gave his father a quick hug before heading into the trailer to see Mr. Laikin. "Thank you so much," John said the moment he laid eyes on his boss.

"You are welcome," Mr. Laikin said in return.

"I wasn't expecting a white car, but I like it," John continued.

I was going to ask if you mind a change, but decided to surprise you instead," Warren explained. "White is so much easier with this summer sun. The paint doesn't fade like darker colors, and the dirt is actually less noticeable. I hope you like it."

"Oh, I do. Thank you so much." John was appreciative of everything his boss was doing to help him. This gesture was no exception.

"Are we still planning to interview for the management positions today?" John asked.

"My secretary scheduled all the appointments which will start at eight o'clock this morning. I have copied all of the resumes for your review prior to the first interview. I plan to lead the first round, and then I would like you to do the last ones. There's no better time than now to learn how to interview people." Warren handed John a handful of resumes attached to an interview sheet with specific questions that he would be asking everyone.

"I'm glad they are still on schedule because I forgot to bring my work clothes," John chuckled. He came dressed for interviewing, something he had never done before.

"We'll be holding interviews all day with a break for lunch," Warren informed his protege. "We are interviewing five people for each of the positions."

"Property manager, assistant property manager, and leasing agent, correct?" John asked.

"Yes. I'm planning to select the manager positions, but I would like to see if you can handle the leasing agent on your own. I'll make all final decisions, but would like to hear your input on all of them."

"Are we holding the interviews in the conference room?" John inquired.

"We are. Please make sure we have some cold beverages in the refrigerator there."

John took the stack of paper that he had just received and headed past the second building to the main facility where the rental offices and front entrance were located. Not only did Warren Laikin own a construction company, but he also owned multiple businesses including Laikin Properties. This was the company that facilitated all residential and commercial leases for him. With the first building near completion, they were ready to hire their team to begin filling the empty apartments.

John walked into the conference room to find that bottled water with the private label of Hialeah Flats was already chilled in the refrigerator. The live-edge solid walnut table was stunning. He sat down in a brown leather chair and leaned back for a few minutes to ponder the moment before diving into his work. He needed to make multiple phone calls to suppliers and contractors before reviewing each of the resumes. He couldn't believe he was sitting in such a wonderful room. As he looked around, he realized that the room was actually bigger than his family's living room. The conference table alone probably cost more than all their furniture combined. He then opened a bottle of water and savored the tasteless wetness as it trickled down his throat. He wasn't thirsty, but he wanted the full experience of holding a private label water bottle in his own hand for the first time ever.

With that moment etched in his head now, John began his phone calls checking off each item on his to-do list as he completed them. He then spent the next hour reviewing fourteen resumes, highlighting things he felt were important, and making notes or jotting down questions. He was shocked to find one resume at the bottom of the pile, Amber James. Of course, Warren Laikin would have no idea that this young gal would get negative reviews right from the start from John. Her resume was the least impressive of all, but something must have caught Mr. Laikin's attention to even include her in the first round of interviews.

John actually knew Amber rather well. He sat next to her in math class their senior year. He had known her all through high school, having had several other classes with her too. She wasn't popular, but she still got along with everyone. That was one of the things she and John had in common. They knew how to get along with people. They were neither jock nor dweeb.

Early on in the semester, Amber had hinted multiple times that she would like John to ask her to prom. Being their senior year, he decided to ask her to go, but he made it clear to her that they would be going as friends. He knew things could get awkward, and he didn't want to ruin any friendship by dating her.

The evening came and went, and everything was perfect until the very end of the evening. They went to dinner with several other friends, went to the dance, and then headed over to Amber's best friend's house for the after party. Amber was planning to spend the night with her friend, which was fine with John. Ten other couples had joined them, and they spent most of the time eating snack foods and watching television. The night would have been just fine except that the parents of Amber's friend turned a blind eye when a couple guys left the party, only to return with alcohol. It wasn't like other parties with kegs, but Amber got her hands on enough vodka to ruin her night and John's forever. The drunker she got, the more ditzy she became.

John knew the exact moment it was time for him to leave - when he refused to go with Amber into her friend's bedroom. John wasn't like the other guys. He had morals and values and had no desire to ruin a friendship over a one-night stand. What he hadn't planned was the backlash he would receive at school the following week. By the time he stepped foot into school on Monday morning, it seemed like the entire student body knew that he refused to sleep with Amber. There wasn't a soul who didn't laugh at him when he walked by. To make matters worse, Amber even told him that she enjoyed every moment she spent with John's friend, Daniel Roberts. In class, she warned the other girls that they should avoid John, if they wanted a "real" man. Amber eventually apologized to John, but the damage was done. Their friendship was over.

By the time John read over her resume, he needed to clear his mind. He couldn't go into the interviews with the thought of prom night lingering on his mind. He stepped out of the room and walked around the pool deck a few times. The sun was getting hot already, and the water looked refreshing. "*Too bad I'll likely never have a chance to swim in this pool,*" he thought.

Not wanting to sweat through his shirt before the meetings began, he walked back into the conference room. Warren was there waiting for him. They briefly discussed the first round of candidates before the first one arrived. As previously discussed, Warren led this round of interviews. They had planned to have a second interview with the finalists, but one man stood out among the others.

"John," Warren said, "I've been doing this a very long time, and I am a rather good judge of character. I don't think we need a second round of interviews for this position. Jacob Waters was most impressive by far. I want you to check out his references. Once you have a chance to talk with them, schedule Jacob to come back at the end of the week. Let him think he's coming in for a second interview. We will actually be hiring him for the job. If he accepts the position, he can start immediately."

"Well, that was easy enough," John said to his boss.

"It's not always this simple," Warren reminded his young employee. "Often candidates have strengths in one area and weaknesses in another. Deciding which strength is more important and which weakness will be the most insignificant can be challenging."

"Oh, I never thought of it like that," John replied.

The assistant manager position was next on the docket. They interviewed three candidates before lunch and two others after their break. Mr. Laikin again led these interviews, teaching and pointing things out to John along the way.

"I have it narrowed down to two candidates," Warren said at the end of the final interview. "What are your thoughts?"

John explained the strengths and weaknesses he saw in each candidate. He thought three of them had stronger personalities than the other two. The three he had selected were all on Warren's short list.

"Not bad for your first evaluation," Warren praised John. "I am going to eliminate one of the three. I just don't think he has the technical skills needed for this job."

"Okay," John replied.

"Again, I would like you to check their references. If they both seem good, plan on scheduling them to come back at the beginning of next week. If Jacob accepts the manager position, he can interview them along with you next week. There's nothing better than a manager who has some input in his or her right-hand assistant."

"Consider it done," John agreed.

As promised, Warren allowed John to conduct the next round of interviews for the leasing agent. After the first three interviews, John was expecting to find Amber waiting in the lobby when he turned the corner. He was glad that she would be last on the calendar today. He took a deep breath as he turned to call her into the conference room.

"Mom! What are you doing here?" John said.

"I didn't want to say anything to you, but after hearing you talk about the leasing agent position at the dinner table the other night, I decided that I might like this job," his mother explained.

By now Warren Laikin had walked out of the conference room behind John.

"It's okay," Warren said. "Your mother called me, and we decided she should come in for an interview."

"That's great Mom. I'm just a bit surprised," John said as he welcomed her into the room. "Can I get you any water?" he then asked as he pulled out a fresh bottle from the refrigerator.

"I didn't want you getting all anxious or concerned if you knew that your mother would be coming," Warren iterated. "Personally, I think she can use some of the very same skills she's been using at the deli here at Hialeah Flats. We are going to ask her the same questions that we have been asking everyone all day."

John shook his head in agreement while his mom sat across from him smiling.

"John, you can start by explaining the job responsibilities so your mother has a better idea of the expectations," Warren said.

John was relieved when the interview was over. His mother was probably just as relieved as well. "I just have one question," John stated to Warren as his mom was standing up to leave. "Isn't it a conflict of interest if my mom should work here too?"

"I suppose it could be," Warren replied. "But, your mom is not working for Laikin Construction Company, as you are. She will be working for my affiliate company, if she is offered the job. Once the construction site is finished, you won't be back here again."

"I never thought of that," John replied. "Thank you for the clarification. And, Mom, thanks for coming in. I'll see you at home later."

Warren and John talked about the final candidates for this position as they waited for Amber to come. She was the last interview of the day. Ten minutes passed, and she still had not arrived.

"I guess we have one less candidate," Warren said as he began packing his briefcase to leave.

The men then heard the front door open. "That must be her," John said, wishing that Amber had not shown up.

"Malaika, what are you doing here?" John questioned when he saw Amber's best friend in the lobby.

"John, what are you doing here?" she said in reply.

"I actually work here," John answered. "Mr. Laikin and I are conducting interviews today. Amber was supposed to be here at four o'clock, but she hasn't shown up yet."

"Yeah, I know," Malaika said. "That's the problem."

Again, Warren Laikin walked out of the conference room into the lobby. "What is the problem?" he asked upon hearing Malaika.

"Mr. Laikin. This is Malaika Adams, Amber James' best friend. Malaika, this is Mr. Laikin, the owner of this new development."

"So, you guys know each other?" Warren asked.

"Yes, the three of us went to high school together," John answered.

"Why would you show up for Amber's interview?" Mr. Laikin then inquired.

"That's the problem I am trying to explain," Malaika answered. "You see, Amber has been talking about this interview all week. She was super excited that she would even get a chance to come."

"Why isn't she here then?" John asked.

"That's the problem. Today is her birthday, and we wanted to do something fun together. We decided to go to the beach, knowing she would have time to get showered and cleaned up before the interview. We went over to Ski Jet Rental hoping to take a jet ski out for an hour. I don't know what we were thinking. We didn't have reservations, and who would have known it would be so busy on a Monday."

"Malaika, get to the point," John interrupted.

"I'm trying. You see Amber is missing."

"What?" John asked.

"How do you go from trying to rent jet skis to the fact that she's missing?" John asked.

"That's the whole point," Malaika tried to explain. "We couldn't rent any because they were already sold out for the day."

"Then how did Miss James go missing?" Warren asked.

"We are just so stupid. A couple of guys who were there said that they would take us out on the water. Of course, we said yes.'"

"Did you know these guys?" John then asked.

"What do you think?" Malaikah asked, annoyed that John would even ask the question. "No, we didn't know them," she said in a sassy tone of voice.

"The guy I was with came back after an hour because the rental was due back. The guy Amber was with took off up the coast. I waited around for two more hours, but they still never showed back up."

"Did you talk to any lifeguards to see if there was a reported accident further up the beach?" John asked.

"No, I didn't think to do that," Maliakah said.

"What about the guy you were with? Couldn't he just call his friend?" Mr. Laikin asked.

"That's the other problem. We just assumed that the guys knew each other. They didn't. The one was with some other guys. When the one dude offered, the guy I was with thought '*why not?*' so he offered too, thinking we would only be out on the water for an hour."

"Didn't the other guy need to return the rental too?" John asked.

"That's what I thought, but when I talked to the rental people they said that all their rentals were there. Apparently, he wasn't renting one of them."

"Have you been to Amber's home to see if she is there?" Warren asked.

"I stopped over, but no one was home."

John's mind was spinning, and Warren knew it. Instead of continuing the conversation, Mr. Laikin decided to end it before John got too emotionally involved.

"Maliakah, I know you are upset. You wouldn't be here if you didn't believe your friend wasn't coming. Unfortunately, there isn't anything that we can do to help. Your best bet is to get in touch with Amber's parents, and then together you can file a police report. I realize you are adults, and the urgency isn't the same as it is when a child is missing.

In light of the recent news about all the missing people around South Florida, I urge you to find her parents immediately. The other possibility is that she decided she was having too much fun, and the interview became less important to her," Mr. Laikin explained.

"I just have a gut feeling, and I don't like it," Maliakah assured Warren. "Hopefully, you're right though. Maybe she did skip the interview intentionally."

"**M**omma, how bad do you want this job?" John asked his mother when he arrived home from work with his new rims and freshly painted car. "You know that I never expected to see you today."

"Son, I've been working hard my entire life. Not once have I been late to work. I am efficient, friendly with customers, and am very knowledgeable about business management. I have never considered a career change, but when you talked about the criteria you were looking for in a leasing agent, I sat right across the dinner table from you thinking to myself that I have all the qualities you are looking for in that employee. As you know, I have never been given a break in life nor received any worthy raise. I have worked very hard for the little I have received in return. I went to bed praying, and when I woke up the next morning I had all the confidence in the world that I needed to make a phone call to Warren Laikin. Now, if you have a candidate who is better qualified than me, I encourage you to hire that person instead. I will always love you. I will never hold this over your head."

John didn't respond to his mother. Instead, he hugged her and walked straight to his room. He spent the entire hour there before dinner pondering over the resumes and the final four candidates for the leasing agent position. He tried to envision each candidate and how they would relate to the countless types of people coming from different walks of life. John had seen his mother at work many times over the years. She always jubilated with a smile on her face, and many of the customers knew her by name. Even when customers didn't know exactly what type of meat they wanted, she always seemed to provide helpful suggestions that made their decisions easier. Down deep in his heart, he knew his momma was the right candidate for the position.

"I have made a decision," John announced to his family at the dinner table. "As you are probably all aware, I was shocked to see Momma walk into the interview today. It never occurred to me that she would be a candidate for the leasing agent position. Yet, when I reviewed her skills compared to the other candidates, I was impressed."

John looked across the table from his momma and saw a smile light up her face as his papa gently placed his hand across the top of his momma's hand. One of the candidates who I think could be really good at the position is not available to start in the time frame that we need. Another candidate has experience as a leasing agent, but took several years off to raise her children. Even though she wants to rejoin the workforce, she informed us that she would need some time off for maternity leave in five months. Her mother is able to watch her children now, so that will not be a problem for her down the road. I actually like her honesty and truthfulness because many women probably would have waited until after they were hired to share this information. I am eliminating both of those women from the pool. So, Momma, that leaves you and one other candidate."

"Well, that's exciting Ebony," Shanice said to her daughter-in-law.

"Even though Mr. Laikin told me that I can hire any candidate, I am not comfortable hiring you, Momma. It is not right for me to hire you, nor is it fair to you. I know many people would hire a family member without even questioning the circumstances, but I'm not that person."

Ebony's smile quickly faded when John spoke. "I understand, Son," she said. "It was still fun going into your workplace and seeing you in action. The community center is beautiful, and anyone who works there will have an exciting future. I never thought you would be involved in the interviewing process when I spoke with Mr. Laikin. I apologize for putting you in this awkward position."

"If you will excuse me, I would like to phone Mr. Laikin right now," John said as he rose from the table.

John explained his rationale about each candidate to his boss. Warren was glad that John had come to the same conclusions that he had already surmised. After John spoke his piece, thinking that he would be making a phone call to the other candidate in the morning, Warren asked if Ebony was available to speak with him.

"Yes, she's home," John said. "I'll get her on the line for you."

"Momma," John called as he walked into the kitchen where his gramma and her were washing dishes. Mr. Laikin is on the phone and would like to speak with you."

Ebony dried her hands on a kitchen towel before lifting John's phone to her ear.

"Hello Warren," she said, "Yes, I'm fine, thank you."

John could hear his boss mumble words, but could not make out what was being spoken. His momma answered, "Yes" on several occasions and once said, "Oh."

When the conversation was over, Ebony handed the phone back to John.

"I'm so sorry, Momma," John said, anticipating that Mr. Laikin had reiterated John's concerns to her.

"No need to be sorry, Son," she responded back. "I'm submitting my two week notice in the morning," she said.

"What?" John asked. "Did Mr. Laikin hire you?"

"Yes, he did," Ebony said, smiling ear to ear. "I still think you made the right decision about me, John."

"What about the other candidate?" John asked. "Did Mr. Laikin say anything at all about him?"

"Matter of fact, he did. The other candidate called Warren after the interview to withdraw his application. He was offered another position closer to his home, which he accepted."

John was relieved. He wanted his mother to get this position, but did not want to compromise his conscience in hiring her. He was more than happy to hear that she would be working for Hialeah Flats.

"Oh, I almost forgot to tell you guys," John told his family after they all congratulated his mother. "The other candidate who did not show up for her interview was my prom date, Amber James. Apparently, she took off with some guy at the beach today when she and her friend went jet skiing. Her friend stopped by looking for her at the interview thinking she may have been there. She thinks Amber is missing."

CHAPTER ELEVEN

The men could tell it was going to be a blistering hot day when they woke the next morning. EZ had mentioned that Nia needed to talk with everyone after breakfast, but nothing was said about Regi sneaking back into the room. For the time being, both Nia and Regi felt their little secret was protected.

After serving pancakes with blueberries, Nia told the men to meet her outside before heading out to the field. The men anxiously awaited her appearance. Most of them had already asked about Tonya, but Nia didn't have any news to share about her.

"Listen up guys," she began. "In case any of you did not already hear, I don't know anything about Tonya, other than she won't be with us for a few days."

There was some rumbling among the men, and Ralph stayed true to his character when he shouted out, "Hey, is that all you wanted to tell us? Cuz, if it is, you're wasting our time."

"Just shut up," Charlie told the older man.

"Hey, Charlie, you should be agreein with me cuz us olda men ought to be stickin together," he shouted back.

"Ralph, we just want to hear what Nia has to say so we can get our day going, that's all."

"Everyone," Nia said in a louder than normal voice. "I need three of you to walk about three miles down the road to change a flat tire on the truck. If it doesn't get fixed by lunch time, then everyone else out in the field will be missing lunch today. I'm choosing the three that get to go. Before I make my selection, I want to know if any of you know how to change a flat?" she asked.

She looked around trying to gauge their reactions. She had already surmised that Davon, Alvaro, Jaheem, and Ryan were probably too young to have much experience, if any at all, in changing tires. Jaheem, however, was the strongest of the bunch so Nia had already decided that he would be chosen. And, she had every intention of giving Regi a break from the fields. Little did the men know that there was only one spot truly up for grabs.

"I know how," EZ piped up.

"Yea, right kid," Ralph smarted back. "You are barely old enough to have a driver's license," he remarked. "I know how. I've been around the block more than any of ya," Ralph continued.

"That may be true, but you just smarted off to me a moment ago," Nia fired back at him. "Why should I let you go when you cut me down?"

"Eww," EZ gloated. "She got ya there."

"From the looks of your car, or maybe I should say your former car, I bet you have some knowledge of automobiles, EZ," Nia commented. "The decision is final. EZ, Jaheem, and Regi can go. The spare tire and lug wrench are in the pickup truck. I encourage everyone to fill their cups with water and take them with you today."

Not everyone was happy with Nia's decision, but she walked back inside knowing that she didn't want to listen to their grumblings. The men all grabbed their cups, filled them to the brim, and most of them grabbed an extra t-shirt which they drenched with water to use as a head covering.

"Do we need any other tools?" Regi asked EZ.

"Yea, we need a jack," he said.

Regi knew that a jack was there too just from hearing Nia's conversation with Henry the night before. "Let me run in and ask Nia if she knows anything about a jack being there," Regi insisted as he hustled inside to track down Nia.

"I'm supposed to be asking if there is a car jack," Regi snickered as he leaned down to kiss his girlfriend.

"You already know the answer to that question," Nia giggled as she kissed Regi back.

"I know. I just wanted to kiss you this morning," Regi said as he smooched her again while holding her tight to his side. "Until tonight," he said. Then he let go and hustled back to the two guys waiting for him outside.

"All the tools are supposed to be in the truck," Regi said trying to hide the smirk on his face. "Oh, Nia also said that we need to fix the tie rod on the bridge that caused the flat tire." Regi knew that Nia hadn't said a word about that, but he remembered it from the night before. "Let's go."

The three men hiked down the road kicking up dirt and pebbles as they walked.

"How long is this gonna take us?" EZ asked.

"Nia said it was about three miles down the road. If that's true, it should take about an hour to get there. We've already been walking for thirty minutes," Regi commented as he looked down at his watch. He was one of only two men to have watches. Charlie was the other. He didn't even like watches, but Nia had given it to him as a Christmas gift. He was more than grateful to have it now. It wasn't expensive like Charlie's watch, but it did the trick.

Jaheem didn't say much as they walked along the road. "Why aint' ya talkin today?" EZ finally asked him. "What ya been thinkin?"

"I've been looking at all these fields with a tree here and there. As far as the eye can see, there are only cotton fields. It reminds me of the ocean and home," Jaheem remarked. "If anyone were to try to run away, I don't think they would get very far."

"Well, if ya wanna run, this is ya chance," EZ commented back.

"Are you crazy?" Regi asked EZ. "We need to be patient. We need to keep collecting information, and hopefully we can put the pieces of the puzzle together. Plus, you already know how that collar works."

Forty minutes had passed, and there was still no sign of the truck. The men could see a few rolling hills ahead of them. "I bet it's down beyond the hills," EZ said, pointing several hundred yards ahead of them. They continued to walk as the hot sun continued to rise above them. Sweat was already pouring down their faces, and they hadn't even done any work. There wasn't a breeze like the one they often felt while living in Florida either. The air was humid and muggy.

"There it is," Jaheem said as they reached the brim of the hill. Another few hundred yards further down the road was a small wooden bridge made from railroad ties, and just beyond it was the old truck leaning towards the passenger side.

The first thing the men did when they reached the bridge was climb down the small embankment to the edge of the tiniest of streams. It was flowing from west to east, but they didn't pay much attention to the direction of the water. All three of them bent down to splash water in their faces to cool off. They already drank the water they brought with them on the walk itself. After enjoying the moment of refreshment, they walked back up onto the road.

It was easy to see the big spike sticking out from the railroad tie. It would cause a flat tire on any vehicle that drove directly over it. "Jaheem, try to find a rock down along the stream to pound that spike back down. EZ, if you could get the truck jacked up and start untightening the lug nuts," Regi began before he was interrupted by EZ.

"Hey, who made ya the boss? This ain't the classroom any ma, teacha," EZ snickered.

"Just chill, EZ. You know you are here to change the tire. Don't make things more difficult than they need to be."

"So, where does that leave ya, watchin?" EZ chimed back.

"No. I'm going to make mud patties," Regi responded.

"What the hell are mud patties?" EZ asked.

"It's the yucky mud at the bottom of the stream. I'll mix it with some cotton to fill the tops of the tie rods. Once it dries it will harden like cement to help hold the tie rods down to keep this from happening again," Regi explained. "You see, I actually use my brain to think. This is a very old bridge, and the tie rods are loose."

"That's actually a great idea," Jaheem agreed.

Jaheem climbed back down the six-foot embankment to the stream and looked around to find the biggest rock his large hands could handle. He also grabbed a smaller stone which he placed on top of each rod to pound it below the surface of the bridge itself. He wanted some space for the mud to dry and harden inside the railroad ties. If he only pounded the rod down to surface level, they would just pop back up. He wanted space for the mud to set on top of the rods and still be below the bridge surface.

Once Jaheem climbed back up the gravel embankment to the bridge, he started pounding. With a loud clunk the rock banged against the metal rod, slowly lowering it back down into the wood. The sound deafened quickly as it had no wind or large hills to echo off. Jaheem noticed other loose rods too. He hammered all of them down one by one. He scanned the fifteen feet long bridge a second time to make sure he didn't miss any loose rods.

"I'm ready for your mud," he told Regi after pounding for fifteen minutes. Regi had made multiple trips up and down the bank scooping up handfuls of mud to use as cement. After rinsing his hands off again in the stream, he picked some cotton from a nearby plant. There were cotton plants scattered throughout the fields from days gone by. The men could tell that this had been a cotton plantation years ago. It wasn't like the fields they were working in now, but there was still plenty of cotton for Regi to make his paste.

"Hey, Jaheem, I could use ya help," EZ hollered. EZ had gotten the car jacked up and most of the lug nuts off, but he couldn't budge the final lug nut. "I need some additional muscle," EZ said as he pointed to the last lug nut.

Jaheem gave it his best shot three different times, but the lug nut still didn't dislodge. "The only other thing I can think to do is to use weight as gravity against it," Jaheem finally said. "If you and Regi hold onto the truck and support me while I jump down onto the lug wrench, hopefully it will loosen enough to get off. My only concern is that I don't want to sprain my ankle."

"I guess we can try it that way. I sure ain't doin it. My ankle still hurts," EZ stated.

"I'll be with you in just a minute or two," Regi shouted from the bridge. "I have a couple more holes to fill, and then I need to rinse off my hands." As quickly as he could, he finished the mud patties and washed his hands in the stream.

Both Regi and Jaheem strategized as they decided on the best approach to loosen the final lug nut. Jaheem suggested using the same rock he had used to pound the metal rods down, but in the end they decided his weight would probably be the best solution. EZ didn't give any suggestions. He just stood around agreeing with everything they had to say. He either had no solution in mind or his mind was drifting with other thoughts.

Regi stood to the left of Jaheem while EZ took his right side. Jaheem carefully stepped up onto the wrench while holding onto the truck. On the count of three, he put the entire weight of his body down on the wrench, budging it just enough for it to loosen. He fell backwards, but Regi and EZ were able to catch him before falling down. The mission was a success. It took another moment to unscrew the final nut.

EZ replaced the tire with a spare while Jaheem tightened the lug nuts back on again. Regi threw the flat tire into the bed of the pickup truck. The truck was ready to go. Regi checked his watch again. They had twenty minutes to drive back to the house.

"Let's wash our hands down at the stream again," EZ said as all three headed back towards the bridge.

"I'll volunteer any day to do this type of work," Jaheem said. "It beats bending over in the fields."

"Ya got that right," EZ agreed.

While Jaheem and Regi went back down to the water one last time, EZ admired the work done on the bridge. "I get it now," he said looking down on each spot filled with mud. "You'll need to be careful when driving back over them," EZ warned. "You won't wanna touch 'em until they are dry."

Jaheem and Regi were already down at the stream when EZ made his last comments. Not paying any attention to him, both men splashed water onto their faces trying to cool off when suddenly they heard the roar of the truck.

They immediately stood up to see that EZ was not with them. They ran back up the bank to see the truck driving away. "Shit," Regi called out. Both men were athletic and had a good kick to their stride. Without even hesitating, they took off after the truck thinking they would be able to catch up to it. Their lungs were burning in the heat, as dust mushroomed behind the truck, covering them head to toe.

"Stop EZ, stop!" Both men shouted when they realized their attempt to catch him was futile.

EZ kept on driving as the truck pulled further away from Regi and Jaheem. Knowing they would not be able to catch up to it, both men stopped running, bending over trying to catch their breath. They couldn't believe that EZ would actually attempt another get away.

About fifty yards ahead of them, the truck came to an abrupt stop. The men could see the driver door open, and EZ rolled out of the truck onto the ground as if he were dead. They ran towards him again, but he didn't move. Regi was a full stride and a half ahead of Jaheem and about ten feet away from EZ when he also abruptly stopped. "Stop," he yelled at Jaheem while putting his arm out to stop Jaheem from getting closer.

"What is it?" Jaheem asked panting from the sprint.

"There's… a… snake," Regi said between each breath. "I think it might have bitten EZ."

Sticking its head out the door with its large body still on the driver's seat was a cottonmouth snake. The whites of its mouth could clearly be seen. The men didn't know if they should try to pull EZ away from the truck or wait for the snake to leave.

"That's a big water moccasin," Jaheem said, looking intently at the hissing snake. "He's mad too." Jaheem then motioned for Regi to step back. "We are too close to him."

The men could see a large welt on EZ's arm below his elbow along with blood spooling down EZ's neck. "Are you okay, EZ?" Jaheem asked. EZ did not respond.

"The snake is too close to EZ. We must wait for him to leave before we can help," Jaheem calmly stated while he slowly walked his six-foot four-inch frame to the passenger side of the truck. "I don't see any other snakes," Jaheem said as he peered into the closed window.

Regi had backed far enough away that the snake didn't have a chance to reach him. "I think EZ is still breathing," Regi finally said after a few moments. "His chest rises just a little bit."

Jaheem then walked back to where Regi was standing. "As soon as the snake is out of our way, we can check," he said.

The five minutes that passed seemed like thirty, but the frightened snake finally stopped hissing. It slowly lowered its head down onto the ground.

"I think it's going to move on," Jaheem said.

"Will it bite EZ again?" Regi asked.

"No. I've never heard of snakes biting someone twice," Jaheem said. "EZ scared him, but he's not afraid of him any longer."

The water moccasin which likely crawled into the truck while it was parked by the stream overnight, slowly lowered its body down out of the truck. It crawled over EZ's foot as it headed back towards the field.

"It will probably hide in the fields and make its way back to the stream," Jaheem said quietly as the two men watched while the snake crawled across the dirt road away from them and the truck. Once the snake was far enough away, Jaheem and Regi approached EZ.

Regi leaned over EZ to see if he had a pulse. "He's still breathing," Regi confirmed. "We need to get him back to the house immediately," he said as EZ's body began to shake in shock. "We have to get him back," Regi stated again.

We can lift him into the bed of the truck," Jaheem insisted, "but not until I check for more snakes. I doubt that there's a second one, but I still want to look."

Regi then grabbed EZ and lifted him high enough that he could drag him away from the door towards the back of the truck. "I don't want you tripping over him, if you are frightened by another snake," Regi stated.

Jaheem spotted a stick a few yards down the road. "Hey, I've got a stick," he said when he came back with it. The three feet long stick was better than nothing at all. With his long reach, Jaheem prowled around under the seat with the stick. "Nothing on this side," he said with assurance.

"Okay, check the other side too," Regi suggested.

"I will," Jaheem agreed as he walked around to the passenger side. Still startled by the first snake, Jaheem was almost afraid to open the door, but he knew it needed to be done. He slowly opened it and jumped back about two feet.

"Shit," he screamed. "There's another one."

A smaller snake stuck it's head out from beneath the seat just as Jaheem started to reach under it with the stick. It looked just like the first cottonmouth snake, but this one was smaller and not so frightening. It's mouth was closed as it slithered out from under the seat onto the front floorboard where it stopped.

"I was just a second away from probing under the seat with this stick. It's a good thing, I didn't poke him," Jaheem told Regi as he walked back around to the other side. "I'm going to throw some pebbles inside the truck. Maybe that will get him moving," Jaheem decided as he ran back to the stream where he got some smaller rocks and the large one that he had used earlier.

As quickly as he could he approached the truck again. The snake had lowered his head back down to the floor of the truck. In the meantime, Regi had dragged EZ further away from the truck out of the way of the snake in case he came crawling out the driver's door.

From the driver's side, Jaheem was going to throw the pebbles. The large rock would only be used in an emergency. "Go to the other side to see where he goes when I throw a handful of pebbles at him," Jaheem told Regi. When Regi was ready to keep an eye on the snake, Jaheem bombarded the snake with a handful of stones.

The snake didn't like that one bit. He jumped up immediately while hissing and leaped out the passenger door into the field next to the truck where he disappeared in a few short seconds. "We should be good," Jaheem said, "as long as there are no others under the seat."

"Oh great," Regi said as he bent over trying to peer under the driver's seat, standing ten feet away from the truck. He had no intention of putting his face anywhere close to the seat itself. "I don't see anything."

Both men walked around the truck watching fiercely to make sure they didn't see anything else move while listening intently. Neither man had seen each other afraid before, but if there was ever a time, this was it. Jaheem cautiously approached the truck again and stuck the stick under the seat as he had done on the other side. After moving it around for a few seconds, he decided they were in the clear.

"I think we are good to go now," Jaheem said, trying to assure himself of no other hidden treasures.

"Do you want to drive?" Regi asked Jaheem, hoping he would agree. "Nope," he said.

Regi and Jaheem then lifted EZ into the back of the truck after moving the tire out of the way.

"I don't think there is anything else we can do right now. He's still breathing so we need to see if there is any medication in the house to help," Regi said, not knowing if EZ would live or die.

"Okay," Jaheem said. "I'll just stay back here," he told Regi. "I can have a better eye on the front seat in case another friend shows up, and I can keep an eye out on EZ"

The ride back to the house seemed long even though it only lasted about seven minutes.

"What took you...," Nia started to say when she noticed the men carrying EZ into the house.

"Open the detox room, quickly," Regi shouted.

Nia ran and got the keys to unlock the door. The men carefully placed EZ on the bed while they briefly explained to Nia what took place. They placed three pillows underneath EZ's head to prop him up. The swelling was moving up EZ's arm. They needed to keep it below his heart.

"We need to see if there is any antivenom around here," Jaheem said.

They searched all the cabinets, but didn't find anything other than some ibuprofen, benadryl, over the counter meds, penicillin, and benzodiazepine. There was only one cabinet left that needed to be checked.

Regi pulled hard, but the door was locked. "Why keep this door locked?" Regi asked without expecting Nia or Jaheem to answer.

"Do you have any more keys?" he asked Nia.

"There are a few keys hidden in a secret place, but we have no idea where they go," Nia said as she raced down the hall into the kitchen.

Within a minute she was back fumbling through the keys trying to unlock what looked to be a medicine cabinet. The first three keys she tried didn't work, but with the last key the door squeaked open. There were about fifteen old bottles with medicines lining the two top shelves. Nia quickly took them out by the handfuls and placed them on the floor for her and Regi to see. The names on the bottles were faded and most were unfamiliar to either of them.

"Nothing," Regi said in disappointment when he looked at the final label. "Is there anything else in there?" he then asked Nia.

The bottom shelf was lined with gauze and ointment. She pulled out all of the supplies, and in the very back beneath all of the gauze were three more bottles. "Antivenom" was labeled on each.

"Yes," Regi yelled.

"How do we give it to him?" Nia asked.

"Nowadays it would probably be given through an IV," Regi said.

"I have no idea. Jaheem, what do you think?"

"Let me smell it?" Jaheem asked as Nia handed him the bottle.

"It's bitter," he said. "In the ideal setting, we would give it intravenously, but this isn't ideal. And, I don't think we have any way to give it properly anyway."

"I agree. Let's just pour it down his throat and hope for the best," Regi insisted.

Jaheem then walked behind EZ and held him up from the back with his head tilted towards the ceiling to open his mouth. Nia opened the bottle, wiping the dust off onto her shirt. Regi then opened EZ's jaw with his hand, holding his chin down while he slowly poured the liquid into the back of EZ's throat. It took about a minute, but he was able to pour it all down. EZ coughed a few times as he choked on the unsolicited liquid.

EZ was clearly dazed. "Where am I?" he said as he drifted back into an unconscious state.

"I think you need to stay here with EZ while Jaheem and I drive lunch out to the men," Regi said after a few moments looking at EZ.

"There's nothing more we can do."

"What about the benadryl? Won't that help?" Nia then asked.

"I don't know if it will help, but it certainly won't hurt," Jaheem said.

"It's to help keep swelling down so we should probably give him some," Regi explained.

Nia grabbed the pills and took them out of their individually sealed packages. "How many should we give him?" she then asked.

"Let's start with two," Regi insisted, "and we can give him more later, if needed."

Jaheem then grabbed EZ's cup which was dangling from his belt loop. He ran to the kitchen to fill it with drinking water and returned as soon as possible. He again held onto the back of EZ trying to help keep his esophagus open. Regi took the cup from Jaheem's hand and spilled a little into EZ's mouth to moisten his tongue. Nia dropped two pills in the back of his throat while Regi poured water down.

EZ choked again and was quickly awakened from his sleep.

"What's goin on?" he said again, confused by his whereabouts.

"You were bitten by a snake," Jaheem said. "Just lay down and rest."

EZ's alertness only lasted a few seconds when he dozed off again.

"What's taking them so long?" Ralph complained. "I'm starving."

"Just keep working," Charlie ordered. "They will show up. If we stop working now, we will only have more work to do later."

The men were tired and thirsty. They had finished their water long ago, and their wet t-shirts were completely dry.

"But I'm thirsty," Ralph mumbled again. He had repeatedly told himself that he was thirsty for the past hour and a half. Everyone was tired of listening to him now.

"If you don't work, you'll be crawling on all fours trying to get your work done later," Charlie continued. "Stop complaining and only focus on your next bush. The guys should be coming soon." Charlie had no idea why the men would be so late, but he knew they wouldn't give up on them either. With little reason to hope, he was believing in them today.

Another fifteen minutes passed when Davon was the first to notice dust shooting down the road. "It's the truck," he shouted.

At that very moment everyone stopped picking and took their bags directly to the drop off pile. They were more than ready to have a break. They walked over to the road where the truck had stopped. The men couldn't get water fast enough from the Gatorade cooler. As they stood in line, Regi and Jaheem jumped out of the truck and immediately started handing out peanut butter and jelly sandwiches. Nia wasn't sure when the guys would be back so she played it safe. She knew the sandwiches would last a while. Each man was given two sandwiches, an apple, and a bag of potato chips.

"Where's Nia?" Frank asked.

"And where's EZ?" Alvaro questioned before anyone had a chance to respond to Frank's question.

"Nia's back at the house with EZ," Regi began to explain. "He got bit by a cottonmouth snake."

"That's a water moccasin," Jaheem added for clarification.

"We found some old antivenom at the house which we gave him, but he's going in and out of consciousness," Regi continued. Regi and Jaheem then looked at one another. They had decided on the ride out to the field that they would not tell anyone that EZ had tried to escape. They didn't want to stir up any more commotion for one day.

"Shit," Alvaro responded. "How did that even happen?"

"The snake was hiding in the cab of the truck. None of us saw it, and EZ was the first to jump in after we replaced the tire," Jaheem explained. "It was a monster of a snake too."

"That's crazy," Davon then said. "Is he going to be okay?"

"We don't know," Regi said without going into any further explanation.

"Nia is staying with him now to help out," Jaheem added.

"Jaheem found a second snake hiding where the first one had been. It took awhile for the snake to leave the truck."

"Man that sucks," Davon insisted. "Sure glad I wasn't the one to find it. I still have nightmares from the one I found out here in the field."

"The only other thing Nia told us to tell you guys is that we are having pasta tonight. It's the easiest thing for her to make. Dinner will be an hour late though because she'll be getting a late start on it," Regi told the men.

"Seems to me that we should try to work a little longer this afternoon," Charlie then told the men. "Is the water cooler and truck staying out here, or do you need to take it back to the house?" Charlie asked Regi.

"No. We are staying here. I thought we could all ride back at the end of the day," Regi told Charlie.

"That's great. We have water and a ride back tonight. Let's put forth the extra effort. Maybe we will be rewarded for our efforts," Charlie encouraged everyone.

Back to the fields they went, pulling cotton and filling bags. They were all in such a good mood compared to other days that they lost track of time. They were twenty minutes late in arriving back at the house for dinner.

Before they headed back, Ryan, who rarely spoke with anyone, approached Regi privately. "Hey Regi," he said. "I've been thinking. You said that EZ got in the truck first, right?"

"Yes, that's right," Regi agreed.

"Did he get into the truck first because he was trying to escape?"

Ryan asked.

"What?" Regi asked, surprised.

"Yes. I'm asking if EZ tried to escape."

"Can you keep a promise?" Regi then asked the young boy. "If you talk about this to anyone, I promise things will get difficult for you," Regi threatened.

"I'm asking if his collar went off, like he was told it would on a second attempt to escape. The snake venom may have saved his life. It could have caused blood clotting which may have stopped the collar reaction," Ryan explained.

"How do you know this kind of stuff?" Regi then asked.

"I spent some time in the science lab at school. One day a kid in my class asked our teacher about snake venom and what it does to blood. We all thought he was crazy, believing that none of us would ever be in a situation where we would get a snake bite. I remember the teacher saying that different snakes can cause different problems, but clotting was definitely an issue," Ryan told Regi.

Regi was trying to wrap his mind around Ryan's theory. Ryan was the youngest one out there, and he was thinking beyond his years. "Let me get this straight?" Regi continued. "You're saying that venom could possibly save us from dying from our choker collars because the venom would actually stop the blood from flowing, causing it to clot?"

"That's what I am saying," Ryan said.

"Dang, Ryan, that may be our only way out of here. It's risky, but may be something we should discuss with everyone later. We would have to figure out a way to get venom without everyone getting bit. Let's first see how EZ responds to the antivenom. Don't say a word to anyone in the meantime, okay?"

"I won't. I promise," Ryan agreed.

CHAPTER TWELVE

"Alvaro! What are you doing here?" Daniel Roberts asked when he saw Alvaro walk up to the house after his extraordinarily long day out in the field.

"You're asking me, what am I doing here? What are you and Amber doing here?" Alvaro asked in his response to Daniel. "I've been here a couple of months, I think," Alvaro said. "Actually, I don't even know what day it is anymore. One day seems just like another."

"Amber and I came to work," Daniel replied. "It sounds like a great opportunity so we decided to just go for it."

"What are you talking about?" Alvaro responded. "You must be confused."

"No, I don't think so," Daniel responded.

"It's like that ol' song my momma used to sing. I don't even know who sings it, but it's something about once you get there, you can't leave," Alvaro responded back. "Yea, we're stuck here."

"I don't know what you are talking about, but Amber and I signed a contract to work," Daniel responded back.

"Did ya even take a look at that ol' contract?" Alvaro said with a smirk on his face.

"You bet we did," Daniel gloated. "We both looked at the bottom line and our eyes 'bout popped out of our heads."

"Yea, I bet you did, kids. Cuz y'all gullible," Ralph snickered.

"There ain't a one of us who have seen any lick of dough around here. Uh, guys?"

"Not one lick," Frank muttered while Davon and Ryan shook their heads. "Y'all got suckered."

Amber, who had kept quiet this whole time, finally spoke up,

"Well, if it don't work out, we'll just leave," she said, not truly understanding the predicament she faced.

"Yea, I don't think that'll work out well for ya," Ralph laughed.

Without a chance for anyone to further explain, Nia shouted at them from inside the house. "Are you guys coming? Your food is going to get cold."

"Follow me," Alvaro said. "There are some rules around here that you must follow." After all the men had received a plate full of mash potatoes, hamburger gravy, and two rolls, Alvaro showed the newcomers the routine. They were both given a cup and told about their responsibilities. "Nia and Tonya are in charge of the kitchen," Alvaro told them. "You'll probably meet Tonya tomorrow when she gets back."

It had only been a day since EZ's snake bite when Amber and Daniel arrived. EZ was still recuperating and had no idea that his two classmates had arrived. After dinner, Nia took Amber to their room to show her where she would be bunking while Alvaro volunteered to show Daniel. When both were finished unpacking their one and only suitcase, they joined the others outside.

Nia didn't join the guys outside though. She needed to check on EZ to see how he was feeling. He had finally woken up, but was extremely weak. She brought some chicken noodle soup to him rather than the potatoes and gravy that everyone else received that night.

"How are you feeling, EZ?" Nia asked when she brought the soup to him.

"My head is spinnin a bit, and I'm so damn tired," EZ responded back as he lifted himself up with the pillows.

"Do you remember what happened?" Nia then asked.

"I thought I would get the f**k out of this place since we had some wheels, and the next thin I know is this f**kin snake is staring me in the eyes."

"How's your neck feeling?" Nia then asked.

"Oh yea, it hurts like a son of b**ch too," he responded.

"Try to eat your soup. If you're still hungry later, I can heat up some spaghetti or potatoes and gravy. I'll be back in a while to check on you again. You probably just need some rest right now," she said.

Back outside the men sat around intently listening to Amber and Daniel's story.

"How did you get them collars?" Ralph asked first before either of them had a chance to talk.

"They gave them to us," Daniel responded.

"They snapped right on when we put them on," Amber innocently stated.

"Who are they?" Charlie then asked.

"That's a good question," Amber responded. "I don't know if we ever heard their names.

"Well, start from the beginning then," Charlie said. "Maybe you'll think of it as you tell us how you got here."

"My friend and I were jet skiing on my birthday with some guys. The guy I was riding with took off up the beach. My friend was right behind us for the longest time, but after a half hour or so I realized that she wasn't with me. I got scared and asked the guy to turn around, but he told me he couldn't right then. He was planning to meet another friend before heading back. I didn't know what to do so he dropped me off at the Dania Beach Pier. I thought it would be easier for Malaika to pick me up than head back with the guy later," Amber shared.

"Did she pick you up then? Davon asked.

"I forgot that my phone was back down the beach with our stuff. I didn't take it with me because I didn't want it to get wet," Amber continued to explain. "So, I had no way of reaching her at that moment."

"But, fortunately for Amber," Daniel piped up, "I was there fishing with my cousin. I saw her get off the jet ski and was surprised that she was walking alone. My cousin stayed with my gear, and I ran down the pier to find her."

"What does this have to do with you coming here?" Charlie then asked, trying to connect the dots.

"Down by the end of the pier was some chick recruiting people to come here. Amber said she was going to be late for her job interview, and I had just quit my job so we stood there and listened to her spiel," Daniel explained.

"She told us that she would give us a five hundred dollar advance on the spot if we agreed to sign on the dotted line," Amber added. "There were some other people there too listening to her, but I think we may have been the only ones really interested in the program."

"So, you signed right there and then for the job?" Jaheem asked.

"Listen guys, there isn't a kid from Carol City who doesn't want a chance to leave. We are no exception," Amber told them.

"The chick gave us five hundred dollars right there and then, and another five hundred dollars when we met her to come here," Daniel continued explaining. "The only catch was that we were not allowed to know where we were headed. With an extra thousand bucks in our pockets, we didn't care. That kind of money may come easy for some of you, but not us."

For the next half hour the men interrogated Daniel and Amber with questions, trying to figure out who offered them this job. From their description, no one had any idea who the chick might be. There were no physical features that stood out on her that would make her memorable, especially when no one had a photo of her nor could they draw one.

They also talked about how they got here. "We took a bus up to St. Augustine where that dude, Henry, met us and drove us here," Daniel explained.

"Do you know how long you were with him? Or, what direction you were headed?" Charlie inquired.

"No, we never paid much attention to the road signs," Amber said. "But, Henry took a phone call and mentioned to the person calling that he would see him in the morning."

"Obviously, you headed north to St. Augustine, but did you continue north? Did you see a sunset or anything before you fell asleep?" Charlie asked. "You must have seen something that would give you some clue."

"I was really hungry by the time we got off the bus, so we stopped to get hamburgers at America's favorite fast food joint," Daniel told everyone. "I had a Big Mac, and boy was it good. We ate, listened to some music, and then I fell asleep. I was tired."

"Yeah, you fell asleep before I did, but I think I fell asleep about twenty minutes after you," Amber said to Daniel. "Henry didn't seem to be in a talkative mood, so I closed my eyes while listening to the music. When I woke up we were just down the road."

Regi sat back observing everyone and their reactions to Amber and Daniel. They hadn't even noticed him yet. Regi had Amber in class, and like many of the teachers, he had heard what Daniel did on prom night. He didn't want to be judgmental though. If the truth be told, he and Nia had started dating before her graduation.

Regi met Nia the year before when she came to prom with John as friends. She never told John that she gave her phone number to Regi. He didn't call her until the summer between her junior and senior year. Since he was so busy with basketball, they didn't even go out on their first date until after the state championship game. Of course, they would both go to the grave denying it. He knew he didn't have a chance when he stepped foot into the administration office back in the spring. At this point, it didn't even matter anymore. He was here, and Nia was with him.

"Charlie," he said, "I need to talk with you."

Everyone turned to look at Regi when he spoke. "Is that you, Mr. Taylor?" Amber asked, startled that he was here.

"Yes, it's me," he said as he and Charlie walked down past the tree. Regi didn't feel like he needed to give his student any explanation as to why he was here. As far as he was concerned, the less she knew the better. He had his own worries, and none of them involved her.

"I know it's getting late, and I'm ready for a good night's sleep so I will try to make this short," Regi began. "I have a theory. Actually, Ryan helped develop it."

"Spit it out, Son," Charlie said, anxious to hear what Regi had to say.

"EZ was also bleeding from the neck when he got bit. If venom from a snake bite creates clotting, it should do the same for bleeding from a neck collar. It stopped the bleeding from EZ's collar. If we can figure out a way to collect some venom, then we might be able to stage our own escape."

"Won't that be super risky?" Charlie asked.

"Every single day and every inch of field that we harvest, I think over and over again, what can we do to get out of this predicament? I have come up empty every single day for months now. I don't have any theories or ideas that will get any of us closer to home. We still don't know why we were targeted. And, I don't have the slightest idea how to collect snake venom, but if it prevented EZ from dying, then it might give us a chance to drive away in the truck or EZ's car."

"Your theory is interesting," Charlie admitted. "Will we need more antivenom as a precaution?"

"I don't know. That's the problem. I'm just a basketball player who teaches because it goes along with coaching. I'm the farthest thing from a science teacher. We only have two more vials of the antivenom which are under lock and key right now. We need to keep that a secret so Ralph and Frank don't try to steal it or do something crazy. I don't want anyone else to know either. I think we should only talk with Ryan and Jaheem."

"I agree. No matter what we decide, the plan must be perfect. We will only get one chance of escaping at the most," Charlie responded as they headed back towards the group.

Marble Rye and Jaheem had already headed back inside to their beds, but Ralph was outside waiting to spit another useless comment into thin air. "You ain't now keepin no secrets from us Regi, are ya boy?"

"Ralph, I'm telling you. That mouth of yours is going to get you into trouble one of these days. Regi didn't have anything important to say. If he did, he would have told everyone. We were just talking about the stripper schedule. We are going to take turns using it, and we were discussing how we could possibly add more fields without getting caught so that we would have less manual labor to do. That's all, Ralph," Charlie said as he patted Ralph on the shoulder. "Now I don't know about you, but I'm tired and heading to bed like everyone else."

"Shit. I was hopin you could give me some good 'ol gossip," Ralph replied.

"It's not like we have anything to gossip about around here, Ralph. I don't see any casinos, women, or cigar bars on the block, do you?"

The sun was just peaking above the horizon when all the men and Amber arrived in the field the next morning. The men weren't even sure if Amber would be joining them since she was the only woman, but Nia told her to go. Henry had not given any other orders to Nia, so she sent her. It would be good for her to see what she signed up to do.

Regi told Nia all about the contracts that both Amber and Daniel signed, but he wasn't sure if they were even telling the truth. His theory was that they may know more than they were saying because they were from Carol City. If they had been two other random people who didn't know each other and didn't attend the same high school that EZ and Alvaro attended or where Regi had taught, he might think differently. Regi was beginning to wonder if someone from the school was behind this charade.

Henry was waiting for everyone when they arrived that morning. He had been gone for several days and did not make routine trips to the fields as he had in previous weeks. "You'll be seeing me a lot this week," Henry began. "There are some heavy rains in the forecast at the end of the week, and we need to get this cotton baled and loaded onto trucks. We'll be working longer hours than usual."

"Does that mean we'll get some time off when the rain comes?" Frank asked.

"Yes, that's what it means," Henry replied. "I want Charlie, Regi, and Frank to run the cotton stripper from sun up until midnight each night. I want this field and the other one over there done by Friday."

Ralph was not happy that Regi got selected since he was still only in his mid twenties, and Ralph was almost twice his age. There wasn't a thing Regi could do about it. He had won the trust of Henry. Ralph knew if he complained things could get worse for him, so he chose to keep his mouth shut.

"And, if you don't already know, we have two new recruits, Daniel and Amber. Please teach them the ropes. If I don't like our progress, I might add two men to run a night shift on the stripper too. I'll let you know by tomorrow. Any questions?"

"Is there enough fuel for the stripper?" Charlie asked.

"Yes, the tank was filled late last night. It shouldn't be a problem," Henry answered, pointing over to the side of the road where the cross streets intersect. There stood a thousand gallon fuel holding tank.

"I have one question, Henry," Amber said as Henry began walking away. "I don't want to mess up my nails. I was wondering where I could buy some gloves?"

"Do you see anyone else wearing gloves right now?" Henry responded back to Amber.

"No," she said.

"Then I think you just answered your own question," he said.

"Don't worry about those pretty nails of yours. You have to get the technique down so your fingers don't hurt," Davon encouraged her. "You'll get the hang of it in a few days," he insisted.

By noon it was clear to everyone that Amber was slower than the men. She couldn't carry as much weight in her bag either so she made more trips to the cotton pile to unload her bag.

Henry didn't seem to care. He kept her right there working like the others. He left and returned with a trailer, hauling two forklifts after lunch. There were cotton bales everywhere in the fields that needed to be loaded.

"Amber," Henry called out, "do you know how to drive a car?" he asked.

"No," she said shyly. "I was going to."

Henry cut her off. "I didn't ask for excuses or reasons," he told the young lady. "I was going to give you a chance to drive a forklift, but I don't want to take any chances on you rolling it."

"I can learn," Amber said enthusiastically.

"Not on my time," Henry attacked back. "Ralph and Alvaro can drive them today. EZ will take over for Alvaro tomorrow when he's back. Everyone else will continue picking and putting the cotton into the piles."

"EZ, like in Elijah Jackson?" Danield asked. "He's here too?"

"Yep, that's him. He's been here almost as long as me," Alvaro told them.

"So, what is this?" Amber said, "A class reunion?"

"Trust me. You're gonna wish it were," Alvaro responded back.

"If EZ is here, where is he?" Daniel questioned.

"He got bit by a snake the other day," Alvaro told his friends. "It didn't kill him, but it came close."

"Poisonous snakes out in these fields?" Amber questioned.

"This one wasn't," Alvaro continued to explain. "He was down by a stream fixing a flat tire on the truck. A water moccasin got him. It was just a fluke thing, that's all," Alvaro said, trying to convince himself that there wouldn't be any more incidents involving a snake. He wasn't going to tell them about the one in the field a couple weeks earlier. Amber already seemed frightened, and he didn't want her to freak out.

"It sounds like he might be getting well enough to come back to work soon."

When they arrived back at the house after a very long day, EZ was waiting for everyone to have dinner. He looked pale and seemed weak, but wanted to talk with his new friends. He and Nia had already decided that he would be sleeping again by himself in hopes of getting another night of good sleep without the disturbance of the others in the room. Ralph was a snorer, and everyone was tired of the noise. Most of the men covered their heads under their pillows or blankets, and a few used a square of toilet tissue to make ear plugs each night.

"So, what's this? A high school reunion?" EZ said when he noticed Amber and Daniel. He had never said more than two words to them in high school, but tonight he was being all chatty with them.

"I said the same thing when we heard you were here," Amber said.

"Well, shit. I never would've spected to see y'all asses here," EZ continued.

"Same goes for you," Daniel stated back.

"Whatcha all do wrong?" EZ asked. "You guys were good kids in high school."

"We didn't do anything wrong," Amber clearly stated, emphasizing that she didn't appreciate the accusation.

"Why would ya be here then?" EZ question again.

"It was a great job opportunity," Daniel began to explain when Tonya called for everyone to come inside for dinner. Without going into further detail, the three of them walked towards the door along with the others.

"Taking a three day siesta?" Ralph asked Tonya when they walked into the kitchen.

"Mind your own business," Tonya snapped back. "Hardly was I on a siesta."

Tonight the men ate well. They had beef tacos with tomatoes and lettuce along with chips and cheese. Every one of them went to bed with a full belly. The morning would arrive sooner than anyone desired, so no one lingered after dinner. They ate and went straight to their rooms.

Talking was at a minimum that evening. Those who knew Daniel and Amber were more irritated than anything, knowing that they chose to be on the plantation.

CHAPTER THIRTEEN

It was dark. The southwestern sky that typically glared with brightness at four o'clock in the afternoon was nowhere to be seen. The streetlights were on, and the traffic signals continued their infinite sequence of slowing and stopping cars, yet there were very few vehicles on the roads now. The traffic lights in Miami that once swayed back and forth on wires, mounted above the traffic, had long ago changed to horizontal lights mounted on galvanized steel. The city had done everything in its power to prepare for tropical storms and hurricanes. Now it was time for residents to do their part.

Tropical Storm Cecelia had made her name known to all in South Florida. She sprung up overnight in the seas south of Cuba. The meteorologists and hurricane trackers agreed that the storm would head northeast towards the desolate region of Red Bay, near the northern tip of the Bahamas, and fade away into the Atlantic Ocean. It would only be a tropical storm, and it did not have a chance of becoming a hurricane.

They were wrong. Cecelia started to head towards the Bahamas away from Florida, but just twenty-four hours earlier it surprised the experts and most Floridians. The storm abruptly made a turn towards Miami. Not only did it change its course, but it also changed its intensity. The twenty-three-mile-an-hour wind gusts seen just the day before in Sagua La Grande, Cuba were now approaching one hundred and thirty miles an hour. This was on the verge of being a category four hurricane, one to fear. The estimated landfall was now set to hit Atlantic Heights, east of the Biscayne Bay, and then onto the mainland, a mere seven miles from Hialeah Flats.

Just six miles north of Hialeah Flats was the home of the Bramble family. Their house was old. Every house in Carol City was old. It had survived multiple storms and hurricanes in years past, but this hurricane was appearing to be the biggest one yet to hit directly in their path. The latest local news report that John heard on the radio indicated that several wind gusts over one hundred and fifty miles per hour had been recorded at the Miami airport. It had been three years since they headed to the Sarasota area to stay with Shanice's sister. Ten years prior, they had traveled all the way to Jacksonville to stay with Ebony's brother, Charlie. The days of going there were now over. It took them almost nineteen hours to make the six hour drive because the roads were so heavily traveled.

They knew they would be at high risk staying in their own home. An evacuation order had been given, leaving residents very few hours to prepare. Most people did not have time to grocery shop, prepare for the storm, and evacuate. The Brambles were no exception. John Sr. and Ebony spent the previous day boarding up their windows and loading a truck for John to deliver items to Hialeah Flats. Warren Laikin offered them the keys to a brand new apartment. After putting all the job site tools into an empty garage and securing the property, John Jr. spent the remainder of the day moving their family belongings.

"John," Warren had told Junior, "I know you have nowhere to go in this short time frame, so please take the keys to one of the apartments in the first building. You can take furniture or anything else that is important to you. I just have one stipulation."

"What's that?" John recalled asking.

"As you know we only have occupancy approved for building number one."

"Yes, I know that Mr. Laikin," John told his boss.

Ebony had made her first sale, and the new tenants were scheduled to move into their new residence the following week. Building number two was ready for tenants as well, but the fire marshall and city inspector cancelled their meeting scheduled for that day which would have given occupancy to that building as well. Building three was two weeks away from completion. Buildings four and five had just received their final window installations. That left buildings seven and eight which were still in their skeleton state. No windows or doors had been installed in either of those buildings. If the buildings met the hurricane ratings as expected, all the buildings should survive without any damage. Buildings seven and eight may be the exception. They were more likely to receive storm damage because the doors and windows had not been installed yet. There wasn't anything to stop the rain and winds from entering. The true test awaited.

"Whatever you do, you can not, under any circumstances, let any homeless people into an apartment," Warren declared.

"But this could be a deadly hurricane," John responded back to his boss.

"Yes, John, I know. There are shelters set up throughout the city for people without a place to go." Warren continued to explain. "I know you, John. You will take pity on them, and open an apartment for them."

"I would want them to do that for me. You just did it for me," John tried to reason.

"The difference is that I can trust you, John. Your family will move back home after the storm. If your house is too damaged to live in, then I know you can afford to live here. I know how much you and your mother make, and it is plenty for you to sign a lease, if needed. I just don't want you bunkering down in your house because I don't trust it will withstand this storm," he said.

"Mr. Laikin," John started to say.

"John. If a homeless person comes here, then others will hear about it. Once they are in an apartment, it could literally take months to get them evicted. Laws are laws. I don't write them, but I do have to follow them. If they choose not to leave after the hurricane, then I would be forced to legally evict them. It takes time and costs money. Don't let it happen."

"Okay," John said, knowing that his heart disagreed with the laws of the state.

"Make sure you pick an apartment that is big enough for your family, and one that you would choose yourself if you planned to live here," Warren told John before leaving the premises.

John and a handful of workers were ordered to secure the buildings. Most workers left immediately upon hearing the evacuation order to take care of their own homes and families. The men who didn't have families were the ones who stayed to help. When all the tools and machinery had been secured inside the garages, those men left as well.

John and his father parked their cars in garages beneath two second floor apartments, and John parked the company truck in a garage in the second building, not too far from their building. The family opted for a three bedroom apartment on the second floor overlooking the pool. They would have preferred a third floor apartment, but knew the steps would be too much for Shanice when the elevators stopped working. They were hopeful that the new shafts would withhold the exterior water, but they had heard too many stories over the years of friends being forced to use the staircase waiting for elevator shafts to be pumped dry after bad storms.

They brought their mattresses, two chairs, the kitchen table and chairs, the large screen television, and personal items. They decided that their sofa and other furniture were just too old to even bring to the apartment. Shanice and Ebony had organized the kitchen by the time Senior and Junior returned from their final run. They had brought their emergency hurricane bin which was full of necessary items in case the electricity went out. It also included a deck of cards, dominos, a puzzle, and a board game.

John and his dad changed into dry clothes to settle in for the evening. They loaded the washing machine for a quick spin hoping the power would last long enough for them to dry their clothes as well. It was the first time staying in the city that they had felt secure during a storm. They were better prepared than most people even without the use of their television to get the local news. Tonight they would solely rely on their cell phones for news and information.

Ebony and Shanice spent an hour in the new kitchen preparing tacos and fajitas. They made extra chicken knowing that hot meals might not be available in just a few short hours. They all sat around the dining table talking about the wind and the rain and how different this hurricane had been from the others. Ebony and Shanice were not quite done eating, but Senior and John had just finished their last bites when they heard an explosion out on the street. John ran to the bedroom window to see that a transformer had blown causing a nearby tree to topple down onto a car beneath it.

"Dad, come!" John yelled as he laced his work boots before running down the stairs. Senior followed behind as John tried to cover his face from the blowing wind and rain. The streets were already flooding as they made their way to the car. Every drop of rain felt like they were being bombarded with BB gun bullets. The men could see a driver was knocked unconscious, from either the airbag or the tree branch that shattered the front windshield. In the middle of the back seat was a baby strapped into a car seat crying at the top of his lungs. Next to the baby was a young girl about three years old. The airbags had worked so the men could not see if the baby or child were injured. They could only hear the baby cry. The girl was motionless and speechless.

They tried to open the doors, but the car was locked. "Stay here dad. I'll go get my hammer and knife," John shouted hoping his dad could hear amidst the strong winds. Junior took off as fast as he could to the garage where he had left his tools. He dialed 911 en route, shouting to the operator, but the signal was weak. John tried to explain the situation, but could not understand what the operator was saying in return. He finally hung up, putting his wet phone back into his front pocket. He quickly unlocked the garage door and ran back to the stranded car after getting some tools.

John Sr. had made every attempt to remove the branch from the windshield, but its weight was too heavy for him. He tried to calm the baby too, but the noise and confusion made it impossible. There were no other vehicles around, and every house and building nearby had been boarded up. If anyone was still around, they would not even be able to see that there was a stranded vehicle with a family trapped inside.

John opted to smash in the front passenger seat window. He decided that he didn't want to risk any glass shards hitting the baby. He suspected the airbags would block the baby and girl, but he didn't want to be responsible for additional cuts. He pounded the glass as hard as he could with the hammer, trying to get a grip on the wet handle. The rain was piercing his face so hard that he didn't know if it was glass pellets or simply the rain that striked his face. As quickly as he could, he opened the front door, cutting the airbag with his knife to deflate it. He then unlocked the other doors from the passenger side, and proceeded to rescue the girl.

"Are you okay?" John asked.

"I think so," the girl said in such a soft voice that John wasn't even sure if she had spoken. She was in shock.

"I'm going to take you upstairs to our apartment," John told her.

"Then I'm going to come back and get the rest of your family," he said, trying to comfort her. He picked her up, grabbed her backpack, and ran as fast as he could through the rain-filled streets.

"Dad," John shouted again. "I'm going to take the girl upstairs to the apartment. Mom and Gramma will know how to take care of her. I'll get back down here as soon as I can. Okay?"

"Go, John. I'll get the baby."

Senior unstrapped the car seat, grabbed the diaper bag and backpack next to it, and threw the baby's blanket over the child as the baby continued to scream. With the baby still strapped in his car seat, Senior sludged through the water as it continued to rise. The ankle deep flood was now nearing a foot. All the street lights on the other side of the street and six of the buildings in Hialeah Flats were now without lights. He was surprised to see that both buildings one and two still had electricity.

John raced up the stairs as fast as he could without tripping, and rushed into the apartment. Both his momma and gramma were waiting for him as they had been watching from above. "I think the baby is okay," he said, "But, I really don't know. Here is the girl."

Ebony and Shanice were confused. Standing in front of them was a frightened little girl. "What baby?" Shanice asked as John slipped back through the door.

Moments later, Senior arrived toting a crying baby and diaper bag beneath a soaking wet blanket. "Here Shanice," he said without saying another word. As quickly as he arrived, he raced back out the door.

Ebony hugged the little girl. "It will be okay," she said, trying to reassure her that everything would indeed be okay.

"Where's our daddy?" the girl asked.

"They are going to get him right now," Ebony said. "What's your name, honey?" she asked. She then grabbed a towel that was still in a box on the living room floor and wrapped it around the girl. "Here," she said, as she wiped the water dripping from the girl's wet hair. "I bet you have a pretty name," Ebony then said.

"I do," the girl finally responded back. "I'm Melody."

"Oh, that is a beautiful name," Ebony agreed. "I'm Mrs. Bramble. Does your brother have a beautiful name too?"

"He's Dion. I think my dad said he's named after some football player, but I don't know. I just call him baby Dion," the young girl explained in a soft whisper.

Immediately upon holding baby Dion in her arms, he stopped crying for Shanice. "I like his name too," Ebony told the child. "Do you like being a big sister?" Ebony then asked the girl, trying to distract her from the obvious fact that her father still wasn't there yet.

"Yes, it's usually fun. I know how to change his diaper," she told both women.

"Well, then you will have to show us," Ebony insisted. Melody immediately grabbed a diaper from the bag as Shanice placed the infant onto a towel on the living room floor. Melody then proceeded to give step by step instructions to the women on how to change a baby's diaper. The women were impressed and applauded Melody for changing the diaper so well.

Fifteen minutes had passed, and the women were getting concerned that the men were not back in the apartment yet. Their rescue attempt of the children's father was more tedious than they thought it might be.

"I can't get the driver door open," Senior told Junior. "The tree branch is in the way." He tried to move the branch, but the darkness of the night and the weight of the branch made it impossible for him to move it alone.

John rushed to the other side of the car, hoping they would be able to budge the branch out of the way. Together they pulled on the limb and nudged it further onto the hood of the car away from the driver door. Senior tried to open the car again, but the door still wouldn't open. "The lock must be jammed," he shouted.

Junior crawled into the back seat and squeezed his arm between the seat and door frame of the car, trying to reach for the lock. If he could manually unlock the door, he thought they could rescue the father. He was completely soaking wet by now and didn't think about the storm. His only concern was saving this man's life. He tried for several seconds before he was able to release the lock. Senior immediately opened the door as John jumped back onto his feet into the river of storm water.

Senior knew this wasn't the best way to rescue someone from a car, but the paramedics still had not arrived on the scene. "He probably has whiplash," Senior told his son. "We need to be very careful with his neck."

As gently as possible, they pulled the man from the front seat to find a lash on his face. The tree branch had crushed the window and penetrated the airbag. It had gouged him above the right eye. He didn't have any other signs of physical damage, except he was unconscious. He was breathing steadily for which both men were thankful.

"Let's get on each side of him," Senior said. "We can put his arms around our shoulders and carry him."

"No, Dad," John replied. I think it will jar his neck too much. I think I should just drag him from behind. His head can rest on my chest as I walk backwards. You can lead me, so I don't fall."

Without giving his dad a chance to respond, John held the young man under his arms so his head rested against his body. Slowly they walked back across the street sloshing through water with the wind and rain beating down. The man's dry clothes were soaking wet within seconds. They were all soaking wet, and the blood continued to flow down the man's face. It was harder to walk now without getting blown over. The man's feet and legs were dragging in the river as John carried him across the road towards their building.

"There's a curb, Son," Senior shouted out to John. "Be careful on the curb."

It was too late. The man screamed when John fell backwards into the rushing water. The movement awoke him as he slipped under the water on top of John. He immediately thought he was having a nightmare.

"Where am I?" he shouted.

"You were in a car accident," Senior shouted back so he could hear. "Your baby and girl are safe inside. We are taking you to them now."

"This is a river," the man yelled as he struggled to get back on his feet.

"The hurricane is here," Senior said.

"Hurricane?" the man questioned. Then he realized that the nightmare wasn't a dream after all. "Oh, yeah, the hurricane. I didn't think it would land for another two hours."

"Yes. It's here," Senior commented. "Let us help you up the stairs," Senior continued as he pointed to a staircase that was barely visible.

Junior stood up, embarrassed that he had fallen with the man in his arms. "How's your neck?" he asked. "We thought you might have gotten whiplashed."

"It hurts, but my head hurts worse," he responded, holding a bloody hand against his forehead.

As John turned to help the man again, he heard a large crack above his head. He immediately fell back down into the water, this time face first. He started choking on the salt water that gushed into his open mouth. An extremely large palm frond fell from above, hitting him in the back and on his head. John was carried ten feet away before a large planter stopped him from being pulled completely under the gushing water. The landscapers had placed several out in front of buildings one and two just three days earlier.

The man held onto Senior as he led him the few steps to the bottom of the staircase where he sat to wait for them. Senior carefully placed each foot on solid ground before taking the next step as he quickly tried to reach his son. The wind was blowing so strong that he could not stand up straight. He waded over to John as quickly as the river allowed. "John, John," he screamed. "Wake up," he said, slapping John on the face when he reached him.

Senior then grabbed his son, pulled him up out of the raging flood, and dragged him into the hallway of their building. He was lying on the wet concrete floor at the foot of the stairs. John was dazed.

"My head is spinning," John told his father. He tried to stand, but found that even that was too difficult to do. He slid down onto the wet cement.

Not fully realizing the severity of John's condition, Senior replied, "I'll be back, Son. I need to help this man get to our apartment."

Senior wrapped the young man's arm around his shoulder as he carefully walked him up the stairs. "Slowly," he said, hoping he would not stumble.

"Are my kids okay?" he then inquired.

"Yes, my mother and wife are taking care of them now," Senior told him. The climb up the stairs was burdensome. Senior was so thankful they had chosen a second floor apartment right now.

Ebony was expecting to see both her husband and son when she opened the door. Realizing she needed a chair for the man, she quickly pulled the kitchen chair out from the table. Senior walked through the door with him and sat him on the chair.

"Daddy," the young girl yelled as she ran up to him. The blood was still gushing down his face.

"I'll be fine, Melody," he said. "You go take care of your brother right now, while I get cleaned up. Okay?"

"Yes, daddy," Melody agreed as she walked back into the living room and sat on the floor next to her brother.

Ebony handed a paper towel to the man. "Try to get the blood to stop first, and then we will see what we need to do to get it bandaged up," she said.

Senior had again headed back downstairs to get Junior. "Take my shoulder," Senior told John, as he put John's arm around his shoulder. "Use the handrail. We can go slow, but we need to get inside."

Just after John began his ascent up, he felt nauseous. "I'm getting sick," he announced as he hurled his dinner over the handrail onto the wet concrete. "Give me a minute," he told his dad.

They stood patiently waiting for John to give the go ahead to move. Senior continued to hold onto his son as he leaned over the rail a second time to hurl again. The acid in his throat burned, and the taste in his mouth was bitter.

In the few short minutes that Senior had been gone, the waters had risen more. The street was a river, and debris was floating in it. Explosions could be heard frequently as windows shattered, signs fell, and transformers blew in the surrounding neighborhood. Senior looked for the car, but the blackness of the night and the wall of rain prevented him from even seeing it now. Winds continued to blow water into the hallways of each building.

Fortunately, each apartment building had been built anywhere from five to seven feet above street level for this very reason. The flood waters had not overtaken the first level apartments yet.

"Okay. I think I'm okay now," John told his dad.

Again, the two slowly took one step at a time up the staircase. Senior supported his son with every step until they made it into the apartment. Senior took him straight into the bathroom. "Can you get into the shower?" Senior then asked. "I'll be back to help in a few minutes."

"I think I'm okay now," John answered. John sat on the floor in front of the tub, unlacing his boots which now seemed to weigh ten pounds each.

Shanice, who was now holding the baby in her arms feeding a bottle to him, took one look into John's eyes when she walked into the bathroom and said, "John, you have a concussion."

John was tired and only cared about falling asleep.

"You have to try to stay awake," Shanice announced.

"My head hurts," John replied as his eyes drooped closed for a long second.

"Junior," she said louder this time, "Please stay awake." She then walked back into the kitchen. "John, get in there with your son. Don't let him fall asleep. He has a concussion."

Senior, who was sitting on the floor by the front door removing his wet shoes, immediately stood up and took two steps towards the bathroom. He then looked down at his wet shoes, picked them up, and took them too.

After burping the baby, Shanice put him back into his car seat, where his sister watched him. She then sat down on the dining chair to talk to their guest while Ebony fetched some clean shorts and t-shirt for him. "Your children are fine," she told the man. I found some formula in the diaper bag and fed the baby."

"I just want to sleep. My head hurts, and my body aches all over," the man told Shanice.

"Do you want to get cleaned up first?" Shanice asked.

"Sure," he replied.

He took off his wet shoes as well, and Shanice led him into the second bathroom where Ebony had laid out some clothes and a towel.

"Once you get cleaned up, I'll bandage your forehead," Ebony told the man.

The two women walked back into the living room to talk with Melody when Senior appeared, still dressed in soaking wet clothes.

"How's John?" Ebony inquired.

"He's not feeling well. He has a concussion. I helped him with a quick shower. He's changing now," Senior replied. "If you can help him into bed, Ebony, while I get cleaned up, I would appreciate it," he said.

Ebony then waited at the bathroom door for her son to walk out. He was walking slowly. "My head and back hurt Momma," he said. "I just want to sleep."

"Yes, dear, I know," she replied back, "but I'm not going to let you fall asleep just yet. I want to make sure you don't have any other serious injury. Can I get you a Sprite in the meantime?"

"Yes. That actually sounds good right now."

Just as Ebony opened the refrigerator door the lights flickered. Everyone thought the lights would go out for sure, but they didn't. They flickered a second time, but still remained on for the time. She then went into her bedroom to find her purse. "I found some Motrin," she said on her return into the living room. "I bet our house guest and John could use this right now," she said to Shanice.

Ebony returned a moment later with a can of Sprite and the painkiller. Sitting down on the edge of John's bed, she asked, "Can you tell me what happened out there?"

John proceeded to tell his mother the details of rescuing the man and what happened to him. After speaking with John for fifteen minutes and making sure he didn't have any broken bones, Ebony stood up from the side of his bed to leave the room.

"Get some rest, Son," she said as she was leaving. "We can talk more after the hurricane passes."

The storm was howling, and the noise was louder than any they had ever heard before. Senior found three extra blankets and two pillows that he placed on the floor in the living room where a sofa should have gone. "Here's a place for you to rest," he told their house guest who had finished showering and came back into the room to see his children. Melody grabbed a blanket and pillow and made a spot for herself next to her dad and her baby brother.

Ebony tried to ask their guest a few questions, but he clearly was still dazed from the events of the evening. She had done a nice job of fixing his cut. Their hurricane emergency kit also included a first aid kit with butterfly strips. Under normal circumstances stitches would have made a better option, but there was nothing normal about tonight. Three butterfly strips and a large bandage covered half of his forehead. Ebony was hopeful that little Dion would not grab the bandage and try to tear it off.

He checked on his boy whom Shanice had placed back in his car seat. "Melody," he said, "I'm going to be alright. I just need to sleep. We all need to sleep. Maybe one of these nice ladies can get a bedtime snack for you. And, don't forget to go potty before going to bed," he said as he kissed his little girl on the forehead. "Good night, honey," he said.

"Good night, Daddy," Melody responded as she hugged her papa.

In the meantime, Senior closed all of the shutters to provide a buffer in case any debris broke a window. He then walked around the apartment to see if there was any water leaking through the windows, ceiling, or walls. He was pleasantly surprised to see that everything was fine. He checked on Junior again.

It was only nine o'clock in the evening when John, their house guest, and baby Dion fell asleep. Shanice and Ebony were shocked that the baby could sleep in this storm. Shanice gave Melody some pretzels and milk for her bedtime snack. She then tucked the little girl into the blankets next to her daddy. She was asleep within five minutes too.

The Brambles decided that two of them should stay up together while the third one slept. They would rotate shifts to make sure everyone remained safe. Ebony and Senior took the first shift together. Shanice didn't realize how tired she was until she tucked the little girl down for the night.

"Be careful getting into bed tonight," Senior reminded his mother. "The bed is lower than normal since the mattress is on the floor and not on a bed frame."

"I will, Dear," she replied back to her son.

It took a bit longer for Shanice to fall asleep than John and the others. Her mind drifted as she thought of Laurelyn, Cheryl, Mary Lou, her sister, and their neighbor, Adeline DeWitt, who chose to stay in her own home. Shanice also wondered about the family who was staying with them tonight. *Would anyone be worrying about them and wondering why they did not arrive back home tonight?* she thought. At this point, they would have to wait until morning to see if phone service was still available. They would try to reach them later. She said a prayer.

Senior and Ebony decided the best way to stay awake, without making noise and awakening their guests, was to start on a new puzzle. They turned off the living room lights and turned on the contemporary chandelier that hung over the kitchen table. They sat across from each other at the table as they began with all the border pieces. Over the years they had begun a tradition that they called 'hurricane puzzles.' They always kept a new puzzle in their hurricane bin which they would build to occupy their time as they waited for the storms to pass. The puzzle that Ebony had chosen this time was a picture of Mount Rushmore. She had always wanted to travel there, but had never been able to make the trip.

A couple hours into their puzzle, Dion started crying. Surprisingly, his father did not wake up. Ebony immediately could smell the problem when she walked over to him. He needed a diaper change. She took him into the bathroom and changed his diaper. The crying stopped. The happy fellow did not fall asleep immediately. Ebony warmed up another bottle of formula and fed him again. This time around, he only drank half a bottle of milk before falling back asleep. All the memories of John came flooding back to her. She had held a few babies at church over the years, but this was the first time one had been in her home. This wasn't even her home, but it felt like home she thought. Just holding the precious little boy in her arms also made her tired. She placed him back into his car seat so he could sleep safely, and she told Senior that she needed to get some rest herself.

"I'm going to drink a Mountain Dew and keep working on this puzzle," Senior told his wife. "I just checked on John while you were changing Dion's diaper, and he is resting fine. I'll wake Momma up in a couple hours when I get too tired," he said.

"Good night, Dear," Ebony told her husband as she walked into the other bedroom.

Senior walked up to the window after Ebony left the room and lifted the shutter slightly to peek outside. It was pitch black. The rain pelted against the hurricane-proof window, and the wind continued to scream through the night. Senior felt surreal. The contrast from outside to inside was as different as night and day. He could hardly believe that the apartment was surviving the impact of this hurricane. He looked into the darkness thinking how different life could be living at this complex. He then walked back to the table where he spent the next two hours searching for pieces to the puzzle.

CHAPTER FOURTEEN

Nia didn't talk to Tonya for days when they first arrived on the plantation, but no one knew it. She was in the kitchen most of the time, and the men were in the fields. She always pretended to get along with her because she didn't want the men to know the truth, at least not now anyway. Tonya had betrayed her for a large sum of cash. When Tonya realized that she had been scammed too, she came begging for forgiveness.

Nia didn't want to forgive her. All those sermons she had heard over the years about forgiveness were haunting her. She often thought, "*How can I forgive a person who I thought was my friend?*" The struggle in her heart and mind were real. Tonya deliberately brought her to this place, except Tonya had no idea where this place was located. They drove north up I-95 to Jacksonville, so Tonya claims, where she delivered Nia to an unknown person. Nia wouldn't know because she was drugged like the others when they arrived. Tonya then drove home to her parents before heading off to her dream job, as was the deal with her new employer.

The only problem was that Tonya only made it around the block after visiting her parents. She stopped at the gas station to fill up her car when a stranger approached her from another pump once her tank was full. He told her to get back into the car. He would be driving with her in the passenger seat. He told her he had a concealed weapon and would use it, if necessary. Afraid, Tonya obeyed him. He told her every turn to make as she drove away. If she went over the speed limit or caused any ruckus at all, he would put an end to her.

When they reached a back road a few miles out of town, he had her pull over to sit in the back seat where he drugged her just like she drugged Nia. When she woke up, she was wearing a collar too. Yet, she was told that she had special privileges and that the collar was fake. She was supposed to wear it, pretending to be like everyone else in the group. The gullible Tonya wore the collar for months believing it was fake.

Thinking she was getting paid and that the collar was fake, Tonya took some liberties that she would later regret. About two hundred yards from the house stood an old barn. It was weathered. Everyone had been told to stay away from the barn. Above the large double sliding doors was a very faded sign. The white paint was almost gone, and the little that remained was faded. From the house, it was impossible to see the inscription. Tonya's curiosity got the best of her one day.

It was another warm and humid afternoon when Tonya decided she would wander up to the barn to get a closer look. She really wanted to go inside, but thought a tour of the barn might need to wait until later. She had repeatedly told Nia that she wanted to know why there was a sign above the barn doors. The ladies had already come back from the fields and were getting ready to prepare the evening meal. Prep time would be short today because they were making pasta. They had about a half hour to rest before they would need to begin their preparations.

"Nia," Tonya called from under the tree, "do you want to go with me to see the barn?"

"Are you crazy?" Nia responded back. "You might have privileges, but I don't have any," she insisted.

"Fine. I'll just have to check it out myself," she said as she jumped from the log she was sitting on and started strolling towards the red structure.

"I wouldn't do that," Nia shouted back, hoping Tonya would have a change of mind.

With every step closer, Tonya could envision what the barn must have looked like when it was new. She thought there must have been horse stables inside and maybe a few barn cats that lived within the walls. She also imagined the odor of horse manure and the smell of fresh hay. She pictured herself walking into the barn, saddling up her light brown horse, maybe it was a Quarter Horse or Arabian. She wasn't sure, but she envisioned it being brown with a few patches of white here and there. After mounting her horse, she saw herself riding through the fields with her hair blowing back away from her face. She would ride for hours, stop by a creek, let the horse snack on grasses or a delicious red apple or two, and then stroll back in time for dinner.

It had been a long time since Tonya let her mind run wild. She had even tuned out Nia as she called out multiple times suggesting that Tonya turn back. At that given moment in time, Tonya could only dream and speculate. She was determined to learn more about the old barn that seemed a world away.

As she got closer she could see the faded greyish white letters across the barn doors. The sign read "Impregnation Barn." "*Oh*," Tonya thought, "*this is a breeding stable. That makes sense. Back in the day this farm would have needed plow horses.*"

There was still no sign of her collar working. She knew she held special privileges, so maybe the collar was fake after all. At this very moment, Tonya didn't care about the collar. She was on a mission to find out more about the barn.

Tall grass grew all around the building, and dirt tracks could be seen leading into the double sliding barn doors. About fifty feet from the barn doors, the tracks faded into more tall grasses. The land had not been mowed in several years. Small wild flowers blossomed on top of the grasses and weeds.

Tonya stopped to smell some small purple flowers. "Ahhh," the smell of fresh flowers, she said to herself out loud. She continued to walk closer to the doors. A large lock hung on the sliding doors. She wiggled it hoping it would unlock, but the lock was firmly tight. She then headed down to the stable doors. One by one she tried to open each door. She couldn't settle for just looking at the barn. She now wanted to peek inside.

A bee flew around her head, and she quickly ducked trying to avoid its sting. She could smell the odor of years gone by as she continued to try each stable door. She had never lived in the country. She inhaled and exhaled slowly trying to convince her mind that the smells were sweet and sour at the same time. She even tried to recall if she had ever smelled manure before. She couldn't remember. She closed her eyes as she took a deep breath and slowly exhaled when she opened her eyes.

She walked slowly from door to door reaching for each knob as if a door would open and carry her into an enchanted story, one that only fairy tales told. She knew the likelihood of the last door being open was slim. She took one long breath before reaching for the knob and gently placing her hand on it. With her eyes still closed, the door suddenly opened, frightening her. There, standing in front of her, was Henry. He was not the fairy tale she had envisioned.

"So, your curiosity has gotten the best of you I see," Henry said as he pulled Tonya into the stable.

"I've been looking at this barn for a very long time wondering and dreaming about its history and what might be behind these closed doors," she said.

"Well, I'll give you a little tour then," Henry offered. "These are the stables," Henry said as he pointed down the row. All of the stables looked like any other horse stable to Tonya. What she didn't realize was that a ten foot high wall stood on the back side of each stable with a wood stable door. A person could see all the horses from one stable once inside the stall, but no one on the inside of the barn could see any of the horses without opening a stall door.

"I love the smell," Tonya said giggling. "It's romantic. You know I've never rolled around in the hay before," she said, trying to entice Henry.

"Let me show you the rest of the barn," Henry then said as he kissed Tonya on the neck. "I can be enticed in a few minutes."

"Let the tour begin," she said, smiling and clinging to his side.

Henry opened the door that led from the corner stable inside the inner barn. The shock on Tonya's face was unforgettable to Henry. He started laughing. "Not what you expected?" he said, knowing full well that she expected to see the remnants of an old barn.

To Tonya's surprise, the inside was new with modern features and furnishings. He walked around a waiting area and headed to an office. "This is my office," Henry told Tonya. There were monitors everywhere and other high tech equipment that she had no idea existed.

"What is this place?" Tonya asked hesitantly.

"The tour isn't over," Henry said. "Follow me."

He then took her to another room that was full of medical equipment and a hospital bed. "This is the surgery room."

"Is this a hospital?" Tonya then asked.

"No, not really," Henry said. "Just in case anyone is in need of help, we will be prepared," he said.

"Prepared for what?" Tonya then asked.

"You're asking too many questions, Tonya. Let me finish showing you around,"

The smile on Tonya's face had now diminished. She was confused and frightened. "Don't be afraid," Henry then said. "You're going to love the nursery."

"Why would I love the nursery?" Tonya then asked.

"Don't you want kids someday?" Henry asked.

"Yes, but I would never want to raise kids here. After I'm done with this job, I'm going back to Virginia. I want to be near my parents when I settle down and have a family," she said.

Tonya was shocked again when Henry walked into the nursery with her. It had everything imaginable, plus more. "Does the television work?" Tonya said when she spotted it.

"Oh, yes, it works," Henry replied. "But, it has limited shows," he added.

"I love the colors," she added. Tonya then walked over to the rocking chair and picked up a lemon-lime fuzzy pillow. Embroidered on it were two tiny footprints. She stood for a moment just squeezing the pillow.

Henry wasn't sure if Tonya planned to attack him with the pillow, or if the room itself had softened her heart. Either way, he chose to take a few steps back towards the door while she relished in her thoughts. When he realized he was safe from potential fingernail scratches, he escorted Tonya through the remainder of the barn revealing the bed-rooms, bathrooms, living room, and kitchen. He was nonchalant as he pointed out various features of each room.

Tonya, on the other hand, was becoming anxious. The man she called her boyfriend was acting as if this was a normal situation. There was nothing at all normal about the living conditions on the planta-tion nor about this barn, house, facade, or whatever name it was being given. "This would be a really cool house to live in, if we were married and raising a family," Tonya finally said. "Too bad it's located out here in the middle of nowhere."

"So, you like it after all?" Henry asked.

"Yes, but why the old exterior barn?" Tonya replied.

"That was the original barn on this property," Henry replied. "It just looks intriguing. You even said so yourself. You have been curious about this place for a long time," Henry said with a smile. "I have just one more room to show you."

"Is there a playroom or movie theatre?" Tonya asked, hoping that this house was truly just a house with some high tech features.

"No," Henry replied. "This," he said, walking into another room that had straps tied to the bedposts, "is the impregnation room."

"What?" Tonya gasped. "This is your bedroom."

For months, Henry and Tonya had been dating. Each night Henry would pick up Tonya from the house and drive her to Henry's house. The only rule was that she had to be blindfolded while driving so she could not tell the others where Henry lived.

"You've been tricking me all these nights, pretending to drive a couple miles away?" Tonya asked her boyfriend.

"I wasn't trying to trick you," Henry protested. "I just couldn't have everyone knowing where I live, and I told you that from the start."

"What are the straps on the bed?" Tonya then asked.

"Oh, those are new. I just put them up to make it more fun for us," he said, fibbing this time. He then approached her and started kissing her neck. "Let's have some fun. Come join me," he said as he laid down on the bed.

Tonya was really confused. She really liked Henry, but now she wasn't sure if she could trust him. "Why did you call this the impregnation room?" she then asked as she looked into his rich dark eyes.

"This is where you're going to get pregnant," he said

"No," Tonya screamed. The sound echoed loud off the concrete walls with the door closed. "I'm not ready to get pregnant now," she said.

"You can play along with me," Henry explained, "just like you have been doing for months. Or, I can strap you down. It's up to you."

"I don't want kids now," Tonya protested.

"Unfortunately, when you signed the contract, you agreed to becoming pregnant." Henry replied. "We're going to have a baby together."

"No, I didn't," Tonya screamed. "You can't do this to me."

"Yes, you did," Henry told her as he walked her over to the desk with a contract sitting on it. "This is your signature," he said, pointing to the contract. "We have already done all the DNA testing, and the experts believe that you and I will produce the healthiest and strongest kids among all the men here. Things could be worse, you could be having sex with one of the older men or even having one of their babies."

Tonya leaped off the bed to the ground crying. She then looked at the contract and saw her own signature with the paragraph highlighted that detailed the mother clause. She had never read through the contract. She was just so happy to get a high paying job that she signed it without reading any of it.

"I'll give you a few minutes to decide how you want to proceed," Henry then told her. "We know more about you than you might expect. We already know that the next few days is the best time for you to become pregnant. We are not going to waste any more time. I know you and I have been having fun, sneaking around acting like our relationship is a game, but now we need to get down to business."

Henry left the room as Tonya sat on the floor crying, still in shock of what she had done. "*I can't believe someone is trying to force me to have a child*," Tonya thought to herself. As she contemplated her options, she became numb to her reality. Just a half hour previously, she had wanted to make love with Henry in the horse stable. Now she sat in his lavishly decorated room, but she didn't know how she felt. "*I can't believe I signed a contract without reading it*," she repeated over and over again to herself.

Henry was gone about a half hour before he returned. "Just so you know," he said when he walked back in, "This room is the only room in the barn without cameras. No one will be watching us."

"Is that supposed to make me feel better?" Tonya asked.

"It should," Henry replied.

"This is wrong," Tonya stated.

"No, it's a business deal that you agreed to participate in," Henry stated calmly. "You've been having sex with me all along, and you even mentioned something the other night about our kids."

"Yeah, but we had been drinking. How do you even know if I can get pregnant?" Tonya asked.

"I don't," Henry replied. "Our medical team will be arriving here in a few weeks. If you do not get pregnant naturally as we would like, you will then have my sperm implanted."

"You've got to be kidding me?" she then asked.

"No, I'm not. I'm trying to make this fun for you. It can be done the easy way or the hard way," Henry reiterated.

"You're telling me that I have absolutely no choice at all?" she then asked.

"Besides the contract that you signed, you have been with me every night for months now. Would it be any different if you got pregnant without even knowing about it?" he asked. "I thought this is what you wanted."

"What I want is to get out of my contract," Tonya announced. "I'm an American. I can get out of this contract."

"I'm sorry, Tonya. It's too late. If you read further, you will see that you signed an addendum that states you can be released from your contract at any time during your first ninety days of employment. You have already been here for five months now. Besides, I think we'll have some really cute kids," Henry added, trying to cheer her up.

Tonya stood and walked over to Henry who was now standing by the bed. She began beating her fists on his broad chest, repeatedly saying "I hate you. I hate you. I hate you." Henry turned his head away and didn't respond for a moment. After she hit him a few times, he finally grabbed both of her wrists. "How could you do this to me?" she screamed.

"I didn't do this to you," Henry replied. "You agreed to this. I thought you were willingly seeing me all this time because you were in agreement. I'm just giving you the eefore I need to be showered and out the door," he added. "It's your choice. Straps or no straps?" he asked.

When Tonya didn't return from the barn, Nia knew something was up. She began the food prep without her. Garlic bread with pasta and meatballs were on the menu for tonight's meal. She continued to butter the bread when she heard those familiar boots walk down the hallway. It was no surprise to her when Henry stepped through the kitchen door. Tonya had left for the barn about forty-five minutes earlier.

"I'm guessing you have seen Tonya," Nia said when Henry approached her.

"Yes. She was snooping around the barn. I told her and everyone else that the barn is off limits," Henry said.

"Yes, I know. I even warned her to stay away, but she refused to listen to me. Is she okay?" Nia asked, hoping that her punishment would be minimal.

"She's fine," Henry said. "She won't be coming for dinner tonight though. I just wanted to let you know. There's no need for you to worry."

"Is she being punished?" Nia blurted out. "I'm sorry. I shouldn't have asked you that question," she stated immediately upon asking.

"It's okay," Henry said. "No, she's not being punished. She simply won't be around this evening."

"You felt obligated to tell me?" Nia then asked.

"No. I just don't want you to think that I'm the bad guy in this equation. I'm not. I'm just the ranch manager of sorts. Work needs done, and it's my responsibility to make sure it happens," Henry said.

Nia contemplated whether she should continue to ask questions, but realized her water was boiling for the pasta. "Thanks for letting me know," she said. "I really need to get the pasta cooked for dinner. There are a lot of hungry people depending on me right now."

"Yeah, right," Henry said as he walked out of the kitchen. He then turned around and poked his head back through the door, "Maybe you and Taylor can play cards with Tonya and me some night?"

"We'll see," Nia responded with a smile.

The questions were really rolling around in her mind right now. *Why was Henry so secretive? Where was Tonya? What's going on in that barn? Why did he refer to Regi as Taylor, instead of using his first name? And, most importantly, why is Henry being so nice to her when this place is set up like a cotton plantation?* Nia knew she would not learn any of those answers soon. She was hoping in time that the entire group could actually sit down together for hours on end to brainstorm every aspect of the journey to see what or who was the common denominator.

Nia was so wrapped up in her thoughts that she jumped a foot when Regi kissed her on the neck. She never heard him enter the room.

"You must be deep in thought," he commented when she jumped.

"You startled me. I never heard you coming," she responded. "I was just thinking about something. That's all. Please tell everyone that dinner will be ready in five minutes."

"You bet," Regi said. "We can talk about your day later. I hope it was good."

"Okay," she said, trying not to sound agitated or concerned. She needed time to calm down. She was glad she had the distraction of the dinner meal so she would not have to linger or talk with everyone right now.

Within a few minutes, the men filed through the door as they had so many times before. The first question out of someone's mouth each night was always the same. "What's for dinner?" But, tonight the question was different.

"Where's that pretty litta thing who helps ya out?" EZ said with the same cockiness he had when he first arrived.

"That pretty little thing has a name, EZ. Don't forget it," Nia snapped back.

"Oh, is someboda in a bad mood right now?" he retorted back.

Nia bit her lip. She had learned at church that sometimes it is better to keep your mouth shut. She didn't have to say anything to him, and she didn't. Charlie was next in line, standing in front of her, waiting for his food. "Would you like some meatballs?" she asked, ignoring EZ all together.

CHAPTER FIFTEEN

It was three in the morning, the storm was worse now than it had been earlier in the evening. The far side of the hurricane was now overhead. John Sr. stayed up until two-thirty in the morning when the eye of the storm passed over. He woke his mother who was restless and asked if she could take over. He was exhausted. He made his rounds and found everyone soundly asleep. The apartment was still intact without any signs of water damage.

"Ebony changed the baby's diaper around eleven," Senior shared with his momma. "She then fed him a half bottle of milk, so we are hoping he stays asleep all night."

"Let's hope so," Shanice agreed.

"I still didn't want to leave him unattended since we don't know if his father will hear him cry or if he is well enough to care for his son. He was unconscious for a long time. I would rather be safe than sorry," John assured his mother.

"I'm happy to take my turn," she said as she sat down at the table. "Besides, I love puzzles. You put a dent in this one already."

"Thanks, Momma," Senior said as he reached down to kiss her on the forehead.

"You bet, Dear," she said with a yawn.

For the next thirty minutes, Shanice placed one piece after another into its proper place when she heard the cry of her grandson.

"Gramma, Gramma," John called from his room. Shanice stood up from the kitchen table where she had continued to work on the puzzle when she heard her grandson call her name again.

"What is it?" she asked Junior when she walked into his room.

"I'm either delusional or hallucinating," he said.

"What are you talking about?" Shanice asked.

"I just got off the phone with Henry. Before that I spoke with MacKenzie, and I even spoke with Mrs. DeWitt," John told his gramma.

"What are you talking about?" Shanice asked again. "Your phone was ruined in the hurricane. It was drenched under the water, and it doesn't work any longer," she told him.

"But, I just talked with them," John assured his gramma as he held his broken phone in his hand. "I even know how everyone disappeared. You know, all the people who keep disappearing from South Florida?" John said.

"Yes," Shanice responded quietly.

"And, I know what happened to Uncle Charlie too," he continued to tell his gramma. I know because I orchestrated it all with a little help from some friends."

"Junior, you were hit in the head earlier tonight and have a concussion. Please try to go back to sleep, and we can talk about this tomorrow or in a few days after we get help for the guests staying with us."

"I can't sleep, Gramma," John continued. "My mind is churning. I know everything, and I can prove it," he said.

"John, do you know where you are right now?" Shanice asked.

"I'm in my bedroom," John responded.

"Is this your house?" Shanice then asked.

"Yes."

"What's happening right now?"

"I don't know. I was sleeping and then I woke up," John said. "But, I know I just talked with Henry, MacKenzie, and Mrs. DeWitt."

Shanice was trying to remain calm. "Are you thirsty?"

"Matter of fact, I am," John said.

"I'll get some water for you. Will that be okay?" she asked.

"That's fine, Gramma," John responded.

John didn't know why his gramma was asking so many questions. Of course, he knew his house and his own bedroom.

Shanice was back in a minute handing a bottle of water to her grandson. It was a private label bottle. John snatched two cases from the lobby storage when he realized they would be staying here. He didn't even realize that he was drinking from a bottle. At home he drank tap water every night.

After drinking half the bottle, Shanice asked John a few more questions. "Do you know what happened to you earlier in the evening?"

"I came home from work and ate tacos that you and Momma made," John responded.

"Did anything else happen?"

"No," John said.

Shanice wasn't sure if she should continue to talk or wait until morning to further discuss the events of the evening with John. His mind was working over time, and he had some ideas of his own that were not related to the hurricane at all.

"John, it's late right now. Try to fall back asleep. If you can't sleep, then maybe you can help me build a puzzle. I'm working on one of Mount Rushmore. Your momma and papa started it earlier in the evening."

"Okay," John said as he laid his head back down on the pillow.

Shanice walked back into the living room to check on Dion. She could see that his diaper was wet. She quietly changed his diaper on the living room floor in the shadow of the dining table light. He was such a good baby. He started to wake up when she pulled off the wet diaper, but quickly put his thumb in his mouth and fell back to sleep. Shanice strapped him back into his car seat to keep him safe.

Melody was stretched out on the floor next to her daddy, but didn't wake up either. Her papa was breathing calmly and smoothly without any signs of stress.

Shanice worked on the puzzle for fifteen more minutes, but couldn't concentrate. She was tired and couldn't stop thinking about John's revelation. She needed to talk with him after the storm passed. She needed to know exactly what he knew. She checked on everyone one more time and decided to go to bed herself. The wind was howling louder than anything she had ever heard before, and sirens were randomly screeching throughout the city all night long, but she didn't care at the moment. She was in a safe place with a roof that did not leak. She felt secure, a feeling she had never felt before during a hurricane.

Shanice thought she would fall asleep immediately again, once she put her head down on her extra soft pillow. She was wrong. She tossed and turned and listened to all the noises outside. Every minute a different sound could be heard; a tree cracking, metal banging against an object in its path, the rush of water, sirens and more sirens. The rain pelting against the windows was harsh too. As the minutes ticked by, so did Shanice's alertness. Her eyelids eventually succumbed to the beating of the rain against the window. She doesn't remember when she fell asleep, but she does recall when she woke up.

When Shanice looked at her watch, it was five minutes past eight. The crying of the baby that awoke her had now passed. "*Someone must be feeding the young boy,*" she thought. She walked over to the window to open the blind. The sky was bright, as the dawn rose from the darkness of the night. Gray clouds still hovered above as a very fine mist fell through the sky. The hurricane had passed, and just a remnant of its gust could be seen now. Within an hour or two, the blue skies of South Florida would prevail again. She could see a river of water below in the street. Debris was everywhere.

"Mrs. Bramble? Is that you?" the house guest asked, overflowing with excitement, when Shanice walked into the living room.

"Yes. Good morning," she said.

"It's me. Joey Sanderson. Do you remember me? I had you as my third grade teacher." Before Joey gave Shanice a chance to reply he continued, "People just call me Joe now though."

"Oh, yes, little Joey. I remember you. I haven't seen you in how many years?"

"Well. Let me think. I've been out of school for ten years now. Going back to third grade is another ten years. So, I guess that means it has been around twenty years."

"Wow. You are such a fine looking young man now," Shanice remarked.

"I can't believe your family is the one that rescued us," he said with thanksgiving.

"We didn't know who needed help. Junior and Senior both knew someone was in trouble, so they just went out to do whatever was necessary," Shanice explained. "I'm going to pull up a dining chair so I don't have to sit on that floor. You know how old these rickety bones are now. But first, let me get some coffee," she said. "Then I want to hear how you are feeling and why on earth you were out in that storm."

John was still sleeping, but Senior and Ebony were awake and in the kitchen. Senior was working on the puzzle, while Ebony took three boxes of cereal out of a cabinet. "We have Cheerios, Frosted Flakes, and Cocoa Puffs," she told everyone. "What can I get for you Miss Melody?" she asked the young girl who came running into the kitchen.

"May I please have some Cocoa Puffs?" Melody asked in the sweetest voice ever.

"You certainly may," Ebony responded back, as she poured cereal and milk into a plastic bowl. "You will just have to sit on the floor over there," Ebony said, as she pointed to an empty spot near the kitchen table.

"I'll get some when I am done feeding the baby," Joe told Ebony.

After everyone ate breakfast, John strolled out of his room, walking slowly. "Who are you guys?" he said, when he entered the room. Introductions were made a second time, and then John helped himself to a bowl of Cheerios. Everyone gathered in the living room.

"Let's start with you, Joe," Shanice said, after pulling up a chair into the living room. "Both you and Junior were injured last night, and we need to know if you need any additional medical help. I don't believe either of you are experiencing life threatening problems. If you are, it may be difficult to get help now."

"My head still hurts, but I think I'm okay now," Joe responded.

Ebony then grabbed a few ice cubes and placed them in a ziplock baggie. "This will help that goose egg go down," she said. The welt on Joe's forehead was large, but nothing Shanice and Ebony hadn't seen before.

Joe went on to explain that he had picked up his children from the sitter's house and was heading home. He had left work later than he wanted, but didn't realize the storm was already here.

"What do you do?" Shanice inquired.

"I'm an electrical engineer out at the airport," Joe proceeded to tell them. "I couldn't leave work sooner because we had to secure the airport before Cecelia arrived. Most workers stayed there, but I needed to get my kids."

"That's fantastic. I'm so proud of you," Shanice said with a smile gleaming across her face. "Couldn't your wife pick them up?" Shanice then asked.

"That's the glitch in our story," Joe said. He then got quiet so only a whisper could be heard. "I don't want Melody hearing this news. My wife left me two months ago."

"What?" Shanice questioned boldly. "Who does that kind of thing? It's one thing leaving your man, but it's downright wrong to leave your babies." Shanice then gasped. "Sorry. I guess I was speaking too loud."

Melody had finished her cereal and was searching her backpack for something. She wasn't paying attention to the adult conversation.

"It's okay Mrs. Bramble," Joe remarked. "Things were going great for us. I had a good job. She gave birth to our beautiful baby boy, and our baby girl was growing up to be the sweetest thing ever," he shared. "Four months after Dion was born, she sat down at the kitchen table one night after I came home from work and told me that she had packed her bags and would be leaving the next morning. She couldn't handle being a mom anymore. I was devastated."

"Was it postpartum depression?" Shanice asked.

"I don't think it was that. I told her we could get a counselor for her and any help she might need, but she refused any help at all. She said that she might come back later for the kids some day, but for now she just couldn't be their mother. She needed time and space."

"Wow. What a devastating blow," Shanice finally said, after a moment of silence. "I'm so sorry to hear this, but it looks like you have been managing quite well. You should be proud of yourself."

"Thanks, Mrs. Bramble. It's been difficult, but I figured out a plan that's been working."

"So," Ebony said as quietly as she could. "If it's been two months why on earth haven't you told Melody yet? I'm not trying to pry into your business, but that just seems like an important detail she needs to know."

"I tried to tell her several times," Joe answered. "She gets really quiet and doesn't want to talk about it."

"Do you have any idea where she is living now?" Shanice then asked in the quietest voice possible.

Joe looked at Melody. She had grabbed a book from her bag along with her doll and sat on the floor beneath the kitchen table. She was reading to her doll, and the table was their pretend house. "Yes, I do. The kids' grandmother has been wonderful to me and them. She's been very active in their lives and has done everything possible to talk sense back into her daughter. She told me a couple weeks ago that she's living in the guest house of some really rich man she met in South Beach. I think he's an investor and wanted somebody to live on his property because he travels frequently. She runs errands for him, and he pays for her lodging and food."

"Wow! That sounds like a good deal for her," Shanice said. "Maybe the time away will provide the healing she needs to return home."

"We are all hoping so," Joe agreed. "In the meantime, Melody knows that her momma took a new job and won't be able to see her for a while."

Instead of continuing this conversation which could have led to much speculation, both ladies turned their attention to John for a few minutes. They wanted to know more about Joe's situation, but didn't feel they could continue to ask their new friend about it.

John took some more Motrin when he woke up, but still had a headache. He also had a lump on his head, but it wasn't as big as Joe's. "I'll be fine," he said. "I just need to take it easy today. I'm still tired."

"Both of you need to let us know if there is anything at all you might need," Ebony said. "We are here to help." Both John and Joe nodded in agreement.

While everyone was talking, John, Sr. had stepped outside. The early drizzle that lingered had now blown away, opening up the blue skies of South Florida again. John walked down the staircase to the landing and entrance of their building. The streets were flooded, and debris cluttered the flowing water as it passed by. John looked over to see that Joe's abandoned car was halfway submerged. Senior had learned years ago that rising waters continue after the hurricanes. He knew that they would be stranded here for a few days.

He then walked down the hallway to the opposite side of the building. High water, debris, and devastation were everywhere he looked. He walked back upstairs to report his findings to the family.

"I have some good news to report," Senior said when he re-entered the living room. "We are all here today and alive."

"Amen," Shanice said immediately, before John had time to say anything else.

John continued, "Unfortunately, it looks like Joe's car has been totalled. We should try to rescue anything out of it that is salvageable before the waters continue to rise."

"What do you mean?" Joe asked.

"Don't you recall what happened last night?" Senior asked.

"I remember driving along, and then the next thing I remember is you helping me up the stairs," Joe stated.

Senior proceeded to tell John about the events of the previous evening and how he had been knocked unconscious for a long time while they tried to rescue him. Joe had no recollection of the evening.

"Let's hope you are fine now," Ebony assured the young man. "Maybe you and John can go downstairs and retrieve any belongings that didn't get wet."

Senior and Joe put their wet shoes back on and headed down together to navigate their options. Ebony followed behind, but stood at the building's entrance to watch from afar. The men carefully took one small step at a time holding onto each other as they waded through the rushing water. A few times they stopped to let debris flow pass them before moving closer to the car.

Joe unleashed the trunk latch from the driver's side, and they opened the trunk. Senior was surprised to see that Joe had prepared himself somewhat too. He had two clear plastic containers in the trunk. One was full of diapers and formula. The other contained John's computer, a file, a few personal items, and some snacks. Joe collected a few more things that he had stashed in his console and threw them into his plastic bin. Senior opted to carry the lighter one with diapers, and Joe grabbed the heavier one.

Together they wrestled their way back through the river that engulfed them in every direction. Every step was difficult as they put one foot in front of the other, trying to maintain their balance. They were fortunate, Senior thought, that Hialeah Flats had been built on slightly higher ground. He knew they would be okay.

When they entered the apartment, Senior had another thought. Looking straight at John, he said, "Son, how is it that we have power, and none of the other buildings do?"

"That's simple," John stated, as he sipped on his soda. "I hooked up a generator to buildings one and two. Since we are the only apartment open, I hooked it directly to our power source. I put one in the other building so I could open the garage door to get the company truck. Matter of fact, we probably need to put more gasoline in the generators too."

"Clever, Son. Clever. I was so busy getting our house ready that it never occured to me to buy gas for a generator."

CHAPTER SIXTEEN

It had been three months since the rains from Hurricane Cecelia trampled parts of Florida and tore through the Southeastern United States as tropical rains. No one on the plantation even knew that the hurricane had made landfall in northern Miami just east of Carol City where most of them had previously lived. They just knew that the rains came and didn't stop for five days straight.

Rains had delayed the plantation workers on numerous occasions in the past, an hour here or a few hours there, but this was the first time that rains had delayed them for five consecutive days. After working double shifts preparing the bundles of cotton, the men slept much of their down time trying to recuperate from the difficult manual labor and the lack of sleep. Nia and Tonya even delayed their breakfast schedule on those rainy days so everyone could sleep an extra two hours each morning.

During those lazy days, the younger adults stuck together trying to figure out the connection they had with each other besides school. Alvaro, Davon, EZ, Daniel, and Amber talked about their enemies, but none could pinpoint just one person. There were a few guys from school that they thought could be possible candidates, but Daniel and Davon had no connections with those guys at all. Most names were weed dealers. Davon decided he was there by association. Since he was friends with Nia through church, he thought maybe it was a church connection, but everyone laughed at his idea. He even mentioned John Bramble, but they agreed that he was the last person on their lists. He would never conjure up a plan as significant as this. And, even if he had, he certainly didn't have the cash to back it.

If Charlie had been around to hear this conversation, it may have ended differently. He avoided these discussions because he swindled people out of their money in his younger days when he owned a used car lot. He did whatever he could to make an extra buck off a person.

Even if he knew a car needed some mechanical work, he would still sell it for top dollar. He was shameless. He didn't pay any attention to the younger 'boys,' as he called them, because he was too busy trying to grow his own tobacco plants. He had discovered a few tobacco plants down past the watering tree.

Charlie had been smoking cigars for twenty-five years. He took a real interest in rolling his own after he had been on several excursions to the Dominican Republic, specifically to learn more about the tobacco process. He spent hours walking through the fields and watching as workers meticulously rolled the fillers, bound them, and wrapped them with their final exterior leaf. He could even envision his own design, his logo, that would seal the deal on each cigar.

Charlie had studied videos online of all the varieties of cigars too. He tested many, but his choice over the years had been Ashton. He had been a guest of the Fuente family in the Dominican and savored their mild classical cigar. Until recently, he had only dreamed of smoking another one of them again. Now he was imagining his own brand. His best guess was that he was cultivating a Connecticut plant, but only time would tell when he could fully taste it, determine its sweetness, and smell the aroma.

He calculated that he would be able to roll one dozen cigars this season after he waited several months for the leaves to properly dry. The 'boys' had only been interested in weed, so they took no interest in Charlie's hobby. "I'm going to make a lasting crop out of this," he told Reggie one day. "I know how to harvest the seeds for more plants, and with this rich soil I might be onto something bigger."

Reggie wasn't interested in tobacco either, but he didn't want to dampen Charlie's spirits. He simply encouraged Charlie to keep growing the plants, if it made him happy.

Ralph and Frank were the only two who cared about Charlie's hobby. They begged Henry for cigs on many occasions. Once in a while, he would give them each a pack, but they had to pay for it.

"Don't be wasting those cigs," Henry would say. "Next time, they just might come at a higher price." The men were always willing to do extra chores for their smokes, but not Charlie. He wasn't going to plead to anyone.

Ryan didn't hang with the kids his age. He didn't like the fact that they still called him Marble Rye. He spent most of his time with Regi and Jaheem. Together, they rolled cotton into basketballs, using vines to secure the cotton.

Reggie then wove together some vines that were growing on a tree near the house and made a hoop. They found a large branch that had fallen from a tree during the storm, and buried the base of it into a hole that they dug with a broken shovel they found in the field. Then they collected stones from the fields, and placed them into the hole to help ground the pole so it wouldn't jar loose once they filled it with mud. With their newly created net, they had a hoop that was only an inch shy of regulation height, according to Reggie. The three shot baskets whenever they had a few minutes to spare.

The mornings and nights were colder now, and daylight was less. The weather had turned while the men were completing the harvesting of the last fields. Fall had arrived, and they were more than ready to say goodbye to the cold. They bellied close to the fires at night, cursing the cooler air. Yet, just a few short weeks prior, they had cursed the heat of the sun as well. None of them, except Ryan and Tonya, had ever experienced a fall outside of South Florida. They were not used to the colder temperatures at all. Henry bought each of them a pair of jeans, sweatpants, and a sweatshirt, but they even complained that they needed more layers.

After picking all of the cotton, mowing the stalks, and preparing the fields for the next harvest season, everyone thought their plantation life would finally come to an end. They were wrong. The very next morning a truck arrived, loaded with lumber, concrete block, and other building supplies.

"Who's that with Henry?" Ralph whispered to EZ when Henry and a young lady, likely in her mid twenties, walked through the kitchen door.

"This is our newest recruit," Henry shared with everyone who had already arrived for breakfast

"Recruit?" Ralph snickered loud enough that all could hear.

"Hey Ralph?" Henry inquired. "Did you misunderstand what I just said?"

"No, I don't think so boss," Ralph said, as he looked down towards the floor, keeping his eyes hidden from view.

"I didn't think you misunderstood," Henry replied back. "If you did, please let me know. I'll be happy to take you outside to explain myself." Henry had already learned that some of these men tried to push his buttons. On several occasions, the men were forced to do extra work before their dinners were served. Ralph was one of those men. Henry refused to put up with smart remarks from anyone.

"As I was saying, before I was rudely interrupted," Henry continued, "This is Leah Sanderson. Leah is here to help in any way possible. Once the babies arrive, she'll be caring for them while their mothers are working."

By now everyone had already entered the kitchen, and the men looked at one another when they heard the news. Their heads bobbled, and their eyes twitched. Ralph stood silent, afraid to say anything at all. EZ then raised his hand slowly into the air, as if he were still in elementary school.

"I think I misunderstood," EZ stated, using the most proper English he had ever spoken in his life.

As everyone set their eyes upon Henry who was standing near the door, both Tonya and Nia looked at one another. Standing only inches apart behind the island, prepared to serve the men their breakfast, they simultaneously said to one another, "You're pregnant?" Tonya had been hiding her pregnancy from Nia.

"Unlike Ralph, who was being a smartass, I think you are truly making a valid statement, EZ" Henry explained, while emphasizing his jab against Ralph. "Yes, I did say, 'babies,' in case anyone did not hear me properly. Both Tonya and Nia are pregnant."

This certainly wasn't the way Tonya or Nia wanted their private affairs to be broadcast, but it was too late.

Stunned by the information, Ralph reacted again without thinking first. "How did that even happen?" Ralph asked.

"Well, Mr. Smartass," Henry chuckled. "I don't think I need to explain to you, or anyone for that matter, how babies are conceived." Every man in the room laughed. "You're the oldest one here, aren't you Ralph? Henry inquired, although he knew the answer.

"Yes," Ralph responded.

"Well, I would have hoped by now that you would have figured it out too. It's hard for me to believe that a man of your age is still a virgin." This time the men roared even louder with laughter.

Ralph grabbed the plate of food that Nia was holding in her hands and abruptly walked out of the kitchen.

Henry then turned to Leah and spoke directly to her. "If you can't tell already, I don't put up with crap from anyone. If you want to embarrass yourself, then ask all the questions you want. But, remember, if you ask without thinking first, it's likely that you may embarrass yourself too."

Henry then looked back at everyone else who was still standing in the kitchen waiting to be served their meals. "Any more questions?"

Every one of the men had questions, but Ralph made their decisions easy. It was better for them to keep their mouths closed for now.

When no one else had anything to say, Henry continued. "Now for the real reason I'm here. Today we are going to embark on several new projects. Some of you will be building an exterior shower house for the men. It will keep you warmer during the colder months to be indoors rather than outdoors. Two of you will be building a chicken coop. And, the remainder will be constructing a fence for cattle and pigs that will be arriving soon. We will be raising our own Angus cattle and dairy cows, along with some pigs and chickens. Once these projects are done, we will tackle a larger project together as an entire group. Now, does anyone have any questions?"

Davon spoke up. "Are you assigning us to groups, or is that something we need to decide ourselves?"

"Good question, Davon," Henry replied. "If Ralph had stuck around, I would be letting him know that he will be the group leader on the bath house project. He has the most construction experience of any one of you. Frank, Davon, and Daniel will be joining him. Charlie will lead a group in building the fence. Jaheem, Alvaro, EZ, and Amber will join him. The final group will only be Regi and Ryan. Regi will be in charge of building the chicken coop. I'll be back in an hour. Make sure you are ready to work when I arrive."

"Excuse me," Leah then said. "What group would you like me to join?"

"You're coming with me right now," he said. "Grab a plate of scrambled eggs and bacon. Alvaro, you can come too. Grab a plate as well."

Leah sat in the front seat and ate her breakfast while Alvaro jumped in the back seat. "Finish up quickly," Henry said, after giving them a few minutes to eat. "I need to blindfold you so you don't know where we are going," he told the new arrival and Alvaro. "And, to answer your question about which group you will belong to, Leah, I think I will have you help with the bath house."

Alvaro didn't say a word the entire time he sat in the back seat. He was nervous. He had followed all the rules and worked hard in the fields. He didn't know what to think of this excursion. It was a chilly morning, yet he could feel the sweat drip down his face.

"Why didn't you tell me you were pregnant?" Regi asked Nia after everyone finished eating and had left the room.

"Because I didn't know until just now when Henry announced it," Nia explained. "I thought I might be, but I didn't know for sure."

"How would Henry know then? You haven't been seeing him behind my back, have you?" Regi raged, letting his mind wander far from the truth.

"No, Regi," Nia said. "Just calm down."

"So, I'm going to be a dad?" he asked.

"Yes, I guess you are, and I'm going to be a mom," Nia sighed.

"So, how does Henry know that you are pregnant?" Regi asked again.

"Tonya wasn't feeling well a while back, and then I haven't been feeling well either. I finally asked Henry if I could take a pregnancy test. He didn't have a pregnancy test, so he gave me a jar to use. He must have gotten the results back."

Regi's frown had now turned to a gleam in his eyes and a smile that grew across his face. "I can't believe we are going to be parents," Regi said, as he hugged Nia.

"I can," Nia said after a moment. "You ran out of condoms months ago."

"Yeah, I know, but we were being careful. I'll be right back," Regi then said, as he hustled out of the kitchen.

Nia then turned to Tonya who had been cleaning the dishes. "And, you weren't going to say anything to me?" she asked.

"I was told I couldn't say anything to you," Tonya explained. "I'm already four and a half months along."

"No way," Nia replied. "You hide it well. Is Henry the father?"

"Of course he is," Tonya replied back. "Remember the day I went across the field to the barn?"

"How could I forget? Henry stopped over to tell me that you were safe, but would not be coming back that night," Nia explained. "I never said anything to you because you were like a clam the next day when you returned. You never said a word to me either. You acted as if everything was alright, but I knew something had happened."

"Promise me that you won't say anything to anyone, including Regi?" Tonya asked. "I mean no one."

"Okay, I promise," Nia responded.

"You must act surprised when Henry tells you what is inside that barn. It's not what you think. Okay?"

"Yes, okay," Nia replied a second time.

"There's a small clinic or delivery room, a nursery, and even an impregnation room. The barn is a facade. There is a very modern house inside that barn. That's where Henry lives."

"You must be kidding?" Nia then asked.

"Kidding about what?" Regi said as he returned, almost skipping into the room.

"Nothing important," Tonya piped in. "What makes you so chipper right now?"

Without even responding to Tonya, Regi grabbed Nia by the hands and went down on one knee. "Nia," he said, "I know this isn't what you expected. And, it's certainly not what I anticipated a year ago. I know we don't have any idea what tomorrow will even bring, but will you be my wife?"

Nia was shocked. Regi placed a yellow gold band with a tiny diamond on her ring finger. "Where on earth did you even get this ring?"

she asked.

"I was going to ask you to marry me before I left for Niceville, but then you decided you didn't want to go with me. That's when you were working at the store with Tonya. I never had time to return the ring, so I kept it all this time."

"Wow," Nia replied. "I had no idea you wanted to marry me back then. I thought you were still mad because you got fired for dating me," she said.

"I was mad," Regi recalled. "I have no idea who shared our little secret. You never told John, did you?"

"No. I was afraid he wouldn't be my friend if I told him that I was secretly dating you. He and I had been through a lot together, and I wasn't willing to lose his friendship yet," Nia explained.

Tonya had continued to clean the kitchen the entire time that Nia and Regi talked.

"Are you going to answer the boy?" She finally hollered at Nia.

"Yes. I'll marry you," Nia said, as she hugged Regi. "Maybe we won't have to snoop around pretending that we aren't even dating." Nia was tired of hiding her relationship with Regi. She hid it from everyone at home, except her mother, and now she had been hiding it from everyone here. Nia wasn't even sure if she truly loved Regi or not, but she thought it was the best option at this point.

"Yeah, that would be nice," Regi admitted. "Obviously, they know you've been with somebody. I'll talk to Henry to let him know our plans."

After Regi left the kitchen, Nia turned to Tonya. "We need to talk," she said.

"Fine," Tonya replied, "but let me see that ring first."

The wide yellow gold band was frosted gold with a square diamond, about a half carat, inlaid into the band. The outside edge of the band tapered down so that the bottom edge was about half the width as the upper edge.

"You're so lucky," Tonya spouted. "I think Henry might like to marry me, but he is afraid to even ask me because of the contract he has with whoever is behind this thing."

"So, Henry is the father?" Nia asked, knowing that he was the most likely candidate.

"Yes, but I didn't have a choice," Tonya confided. "I was told that if I didn't get pregnant naturally that I would be impregnated with his sperm."

"Whoa. Whoa. Whoa," Nia stopped in her tracks. "What are you talking about?"

"The little secret I've been keeping is actually a big secret," Tonya said. "I think Amber and this new chick who just came might get impregnated by men they don't even like."

"What?" Nia asked.

"The plan is to impregnate all the women here. You and I have been fortunate to have boyfriends who actually like us," she said. "Don't you dare say a word to anyone. We could both get in a lot of trouble." Tonya ordered.

"What exactly is this place?" Nia asked.

"I'm not sure, but it appears to me that they have brought back a modern way of slavery. There's more to the story than Henry will tell me. Supposedly, everyone signed a contract to be here of their own free will. I remember signing my contract. I just never read it. Their goal is to continue to populate this land for a long time. As long as the collars keep working, there is nothing that can truly stop them."

"Do you think Henry is taking Alvaro and Leah to that room now?" Nia then asked.

"I have no idea, but it wouldn't surprise me," Tonya responded.

"What really happened to you on that day you went to the barn?" Nia asked Tonya.

"I'm not going to talk about it," Tonya replied. "Not now. You just have to realize that there is more to every story than people think."

Nia immediately felt sick to her stomach. She wasn't sure if it was morning sickness or sickness from hearing what may be the truth from Tonya. Either way, she rushed off to the bathroom.

CHAPTER SEVENTEEN

John and Joe slept most of the day following the hurricane. Their heads hurt, and their bodies were weak. John, Sr. decided there was no rush for them to risk their lives maneuvering through high waters, downed power lines, and the filth of the after-storm just to find their homes uninhabitable. They were safe, the men were resting, and they were far better off than most people at the moment.

"Do you want to go on a little hike right now?" Ebony asked Melody. The little girl had been restless, cooped inside with only a few books and toys that she had stashed in her backpack the day before.

"I thought you said that we couldn't go down on the streets because they are flooded," Melody responded.

"You are right. That's what I said, but we aren't going on the streets."

"Yes. I want to go then. I just don't want to get my shoes wet," Melody said, as if she were a grownup.

Ebony, Senior, and Melody left the apartment while Shanice watched baby Dion. They quietly shut the front door hoping not to awake anyone. The stench of the storm lurked in the humid air. It was a salty stench that they were not used to smelling.

"Which way do you want to go?" Senior asked Melody, as he pointed in opposite directions to both of the staircases at the end of the hall. She started skipping down the long walkway towards the far staircase. "We'll be going up," Senior announced to make sure she understood.

Melody waited for the couple to arrive at the staircase before she began her ascent. "One, two, three, four," Melody said, as she walked up each stairway.

"Are you counting the stairs?" Senior asked the child.

"I am," she said.

When she reached twenty, she was stuck. "Maybe we should all count," Ebony recommended. As they walked from one end of the building to the other and from floor to floor, they all counted the stairs.

They were up to forty when they reached the top floor.

Senior and Ebony were in shock when they gaped across the street and field from the fourth floor view. They couldn't see any dry land for miles. Roofs had been torn off of houses everywhere they looked. Many of the trees in the empty lot next to their building had been toppled by the high winds as well.

"Wow. This is going to take months to clean up," Senior told his wife. They were happy that sweet little Melody was too short to see over the railing. They were not sure how she would have reacted to the mess scattered before them.

The three stopped at each floor to view the mess from every view-point. Melody paid no attention to the discussions that were quietly spoken by the Brambles. She was still trying to count. She had never made it past twenty before, and now she was learning to count to thirty. Ebony had explained how to start on twenty-one, and then go to twenty-two. "You add a twenty before each number as you repeat numbers one through nine," she had told her. "When you get to the thirties, you simply say thirty before each number; twenty-one, thirty-one, forty-one."

When they arrived back at the apartment about twenty minutes later, Ebony asked Melody if she had any sidewalk chalk in her backpack. "You could play hopscotch out here," she said.

The little girl frowned in disappointment. "No. I don't have any," she replied.

"You might be in luck," Senior said. "I think I might have seen some in your papa's plastic bin. Stay here, and I'll be right back."

Moments later, Senior was back outside the apartment carrying a box of sidewalk chalk in assorted colors. "Let's set up the court down the hall here," he said, as he walked ten yards past their apartment door.

"What's your favorite color, Dear?" Ebony asked. "Just choose the color you want for us to make the squares and numbers."

Melody pulled a dark purple out of the carton. "I like this color," she said, handing the chalk to Mrs. Bramble.

"Okay. That's a perfect color to use. When we are done, you can color in the numbers and put flowers or anything else on the squares that you want. You can design them any way you like. Does it sound like fun to you?" Ebony asked.

"Oh, yes!" Melody shouted.

Ebony was startled by the whisper of her cell phone ring. She didn't even realize that she had placed it in her pocket on their walk. "It's Warren," she told Senior. Ebony walked down the stairs to the first floor so she could speak without Melody overhearing their conversation.

"Ebony," Warren said, "I have been trying to reach John all morning, but he hasn't answered his phone. Is everything all right?"

"Yes. Everything is fine now," Ebony told her boss. "John's phone is broken, so you'll only be able to reach him using my phone for now," she said.

"Are you guys safe?" he then asked.

"The apartments were wonderful. We didn't have any problems at all. The streets are still flooded below, but this building withstood the storm. John hasn't had a chance to survey the property and other buildings yet."

Ebony went on to explain the events of last night. She also assured Warren that the family were their guests at this point, and that John did not open another apartment for them. She told him about the damage she saw from neighboring streets when they went to the fourth floor of this building. She also told him that there didn't appear to be any damage in the courtyard other than a lot of leaves, fronds, and twigs in the pool. John had drained the pool as much as he possibly could prior to the storm arriving, allowing the storm waters to fill back into the pool rather than overflowing from it. "I'm sure we won't have any problem filling this apartment complex immediately," she said, after seeing how much damage surrounded them.

"We will likely have a waiting list," Warren said. "We won't be able to show any apartments until the city gives approval again," he said. "Hopefully, that will be soon once electricity is up and running again."

"How's your family and residence?" Ebony then asked.

"We are safe. We had some large trees fall into the corner of the house, damaging one of the upper bedrooms. Other than that, we had minimal flooding compared to other places around town. Fortunately, I can get a crew to fix it immediately."

"If John is feeling better tomorrow, we will check out each building to confirm the damages. We aren't sure about the buildings without windows, but all the others seem fine from a distance. I will send you photos too," Ebony assured the developer.

"Well, don't go out until the waters have subsided. And, let me know when you get a chance to check out your own home," Warren said.

"Regardless of what happens to our house, I have a feeling we might want to move here permanently," Ebony told him. "It was the first time ever that we encountered a hurricane and felt safe inside. Senior even checked all the windows periodically to make sure nothing was leaking. This place was built to withstand these Florida storms."

"That's wonderful news," Warren said. "I'm in no rush for you to make a decision. Let me know when the time is right."

"We will," she said. "I'll have John call you tomorrow too."

Ebony returned upstairs with a few pebbles she found while talking on the phone with Waren. "Your artwork is beautiful," she told the young girl. "Here are some pebbles for you too," she told her. "You'll need these to play the game. Once you are done with all the art and coloring, I will show you how to play hopscotch."

Melody thanked Ebony for the stones and continued coloring. She loved the sidewalk chalk.

While Ebony was talking with Melody, Senior went downstairs to the garages. He wasn't sure if the seals on the garage doors were tight enough to have withstood this storm. The parking lot sloped away from the garages for better drainage. When he opened the side entrance door to his garage, enough light shone through that he could see it was dry. There was a little moisture in the concrete near the large garage door, but Senior had expected to find water in the garage too. He was relieved that his car survived the storm.

Senior then walked over to the garage where Junior had parked his car. Again, enough light came through the entrance door that he was able to see inside. The seal on this garage door wasn't as tight as Senior's garage. The concrete was wet three feet into the garage. Fortunately, it did not affect the car either. It passed the test as well.

Six days later, Joe signed a contract to live at Hialeah Flats. Senior and Junior had taken him to his apartment, only to find that most of the first floor apartments in his complex had been flooded. He only had two months remaining on his lease. Since there weren't enough empty apartments in the complex for all residents whose homes had been damaged, the landlord agreed to terminate Joe's lease early knowing it was unlikely he would be able to move back in prior to the end of his agreement.

Joe and his wife, Leah, had planned to buy a house when their lease expired. Since that would not be happening, Joe didn't have to look elsewhere for housing. He loved the amenities at Hialeah Flats. Its location was perfect for him, providing easy access to the airport. Joe selected the apartment next to the Brambles. It was identical to theirs, allowing each child to have his and her own room. He also liked the ease of not having to carry groceries up an additional flight of stairs, even if there was an available elevator.

Most of Joe's furniture was ruined. The only room that did not get completely destroyed was the nursery. The door had been shut, and in Joe's rush to leave, he dropped a basket of towels in front of the door. He's not sure how that was enough to stop the water, but only the floor itself was damp inside the room. With the use of the company truck, they were able to move all of Joe's salvageable items to one of the garages, while waiting approval of the city to allow move-ins after the power was restored.

Ebony's first contract was with an airline pilot. He chose the penthouse on the fourth floor because of its spacious room and view. Most importantly, he also liked the convenience of its proximity to the airport. The ease of signing new tenants would only escalate now as families all over the city needed housing.

The city had not yet approved the occupancy of the other buildings yet. That would be delayed several weeks as they scrambled to confirm the safety of existing buildings and residences that had been damaged by the hurricane. The Sanderson family continued to live with the Brambles during that time.

The drive back to the Brambles' neighborhood was heart-rending. Many of the side streets were still filled with clutter, making it difficult to travel. On numerous occasions, John and his father stopped the truck to remove a branch or object from their path. The low-lying areas were still under water as well. Major devastation was everywhere. They were located in the middle of a war zone. Most of their neighbors were not back from staying with families or at shelters yet. The few who were back stood outside their homes, crying with one another.

Part of the Bramble roof had blown off, causing water damage throughout the kitchen and bathroom. With an uneven floor, the water made a path from the kitchen through the living room towards the front door where it left the carpet wet and mildewed. The stench was almost unbearable. It was easy to see that their decision to relocate to Hialeah Flats was made for them. Cecelia had spoken. Every house in their neighborhood, except one, was damaged. After crying with some of the neighbors, Ebony began loading the truck with some of the things that she wanted to keep. Senior thought most of it was too worn and old to even keep. He wasn't emotionally attached to any of it.

"Junior," Shanice called out to her grandson after he loaded a box into the truck.

"Yes, Gramma. What do you want?"

I haven't heard from Adeline. Will you walk across the street with me to check on her?"

Wet furniture, garbage, roof shingles, and miscellaneous junk lined their street. "Gramma," Junior stated, as they walked across the street, "Mrs. DeWitt's house doesn't have any garbage out in front, other than the lawn rubbish. Isn't that kind of strange?" he asked.

"Well, maybe her house is built better than the rest of ours," Shanice responded.

"Maybe you're right, Gramma, but even if you are right, it still looks crappy from the outside," Junior remarked.

"Be nice," Shanice remarked as they walked up to her front door.

Junior knocked on the front door when they arrived. He would have rung the doorbell, but knew the power was still out in this neighborhood. It wasn't scheduled to return for another twenty-four hours. He knocked a second time when no one answered the door after a few moments. It took several minutes, but Adeline DeWitt finally made an appearance.

"Well, hello, Shanice and Junior," she said. "I wasn't expecting to see you today."

Junior stood dumbfounded. He had known Mrs. DeWitt his entire life. She was the grouchy old lady who lived across the street. She wore old, outdated clothes and looked like she was eighty from the time he could remember. Today, she was dressed in a nice outfit, with her hair styled, and makeup applied. Junior did not recognize her. She looked twenty years younger than he thought she should be.

"Oh, how beautiful you look today," Shanice said when she greeted her friend. "You haven't looked this smashing in a long time."

"Why, thank you, Shanice," Adeline said with some spunk in her voice.

"We just came to check on you to make sure you survived the hurricane alright," Shanice explained.

In that short fifteen second greeting, John was mystified. The older woman, whom John had watched from across the street his entire life, now looked younger and fashionable when just days previous a hurricane struck the heart of their neighborhood. *"Why would she be dressed up, makeup applied, and ready to attend some important event when everyone else was trying to salvage every last bit of their homes and belongings?"* he thought. Even though her house was old and tattered, John did not see any ramifications of the storm to her property.

"I didn't have any problems with the hurricane," Mrs. DeWitt told them. "Why don't you step inside for some ice tea?" she then asked.

"Maybe later," John said, "We have a lot of cleanup to do."

Shanice then looked at her grandson with that look he didn't like to see. "Junior," she said, "Where are your manners? When a neighbor invites you inside for some ice tea, you kindly accept."

"My apologies," John quickly uttered. "I thought my parents needed my help right now."

"Apologies accepted, young man," Mrs. DeWitt said, as she ushered them into her home.

For the second time in two minutes, Junior stood dumbfounded.

"I've been meaning to talk to you, John," Mrs. DeWitt continued. Through the small front sitting room was another door. "Follow me," she said.

Looking inside the house from the front door, which John had done many times over the years, Mrs. DeWitt's house looked like all the other houses on the street. It was old and run down. The window draperies were white as if they had come straight from an old farmhouse. The living room sofa was a faded floral design, dating back to the sixties. The carpet was so old that not even a puppy would get in trouble for making a mess. But, what looked like an old, rundown house, was a sophisticated bunker. Junior could not believe what he was witnessing. The artwork over the sofa was actually a television monitor, framed to look like a photograph.

"We'll be glad to," Shanice said, as she nudged her grandson to walk.

The walls were steel, the doors were steel, the door jams were steel, and the ceiling rafters were steel. The house was a facade for a technically advanced hurricane-proof bunker of sorts. It looked as if another structure was built inside the house itself. *"How could this be?"* John thought to himself. He never remembered seeing any truck deliver supplies to this place. Other than UPS, FedEx, or US Postal Service, John didn't ever recall any visitors stopping to see Mrs. DeWitt, ever. As far as he knew, his gramma was her only friend.

They walked up a half step into another room. This was the kitchen of sorts. A large twelve foot table filled the room with four chairs on each side.

"I have strawberry lemonade, peach iced tea, or green tea," Adeline told her guests.

"Green tea for me, please," Shanice said.

John was still looking around, trying to capture every bit of detail in his mind. "Lemonade, please," he said, as politely as possible.

"Please sit down. I'll be right back."

John sat across from his gramma at the far end of the table. Adeline then opened another door and walked into a refrigerated room. She returned with three glasses full of each beverage, and placed them according to where each was sitting. "I'll be right back with some ice," she added, as she walked into the freezer which was half the size of the first room. She returned with a stainless steel ice bucket full of ice. Shanice and John added a few cubes to their drinks.

After they each sipped their beverage, Mrs. DeWitt pressed a button on a remote that was sitting on the table, and two of the walls retracted.

Four fifty-inch monitors hung from the walls on each side of the table. She then pulled a keyboard out from beneath the table where she was sitting and typed for a brief moment.

"This isn't what you expected to find here, John," she said, as she pulled a video up on the monitors. "I'm sure you have a lot of questions jumping around in that brilliant mind of yours too."

"Who are you?" John asked, trying to be respectful.

"I'll get to that later," Adeline responded.

Everyone who disappeared was now in view on the monitors. Each one was leaning against a wall in a room void of furniture, eating sandwiches and chips.

John stood up and walked up to one of the monitors to get a closer look. "Is this a live stream?" he asked.

"I won't keep you long, John," Mrs. DeWitt said. "Yes, it is. It's real-time."

"There's Uncle Charlie," John then stated when he saw his uncle on the monitor.

"Yes. That is your uncle," Mrs. DeWitt confirmed.

John turned away from the screen to look at the women. "What's going on here?" he asked, with a power in his voice that his gramma had never heard before. It wasn't the pleasant, happy voice that his gramma was used to hearing. It was a low and irritated voice.

Mrs. DeWitt began to speak again. "Do you remember the paper you wrote in high school, *Another Negro for My Plantation?*" she asked. "I'm sure you remember it." Adeline did not give John a chance to respond. "You detailed what you would do if you could right the wrongs of everyone who had hurt you and your family members, but then you failed to turn it in because you thought the consequences for doing so might be presumptuously negative."

John turned around looking at his gramma and his neighbor. "How did you know about that paper?" John immediately asked. "I didn't tell anyone at all about it."

His gramma looked away for a brief moment, but didn't say a word.

Adeline ignored John's question. "You wanted to kidnap these people, place them on a plantation, and let them work to experience what real slavery was truly like. You wanted them to realize that there are consequences for their actions and decisions. Their choices affect others around them, not just themselves. You wanted them to experience the hardship of years gone by so they could see first hand how far the African-American community has advanced. You wanted them to see that they have no excuse in blaming others, or in blaming society for their laziness or their inability to perform. You wanted them to learn that they need to be responsible young adults and older adults as well. Most importantly, you wanted them to stop playing the race card. You wanted them to stand on their own two feet, work their tails off for something they believe in or something they have skill in doing, and make it to the top without lying, cheating, or stealing their way to get there. You wanted them to become productive members of society. You wanted them to become heroes in their own way."

"You even gave them a list of other African-Americans who came before them who greatly impacted American culture for all people, not just African-Americans. I believe you included Ruby Bridges, Fred Hampton, Medgar Evers, Oprah, Denzel Washington, Sojourner Truth, James Baldwin, Serena Williams, Aretha Franklin, and Kobe Bryant, just to name a few. Your list was much, much longer because it was almost impossible for you to put a limit on the successes of African-Americans in our society."

John slowly shook his head up and down as she called off the names of American heroes. He recalled others on his list too that Mrs. DeWitt did not mention. His list was nearly a thousand names long, including Shanice Bramble.

"How did you get my paper?" John asked again.

"Your plan was flawlessly orchestrated," Mrs. DeWitt continued. "What you didn't know was that your grandmother found that paper in the trash and read it. And, you didn't know that there is more to me than appears at first glance. If you did, you would have added my name to your list. That's all you need to know for now. Go make the world a better place. Make a difference with the hurricane cleanup efforts. More importantly, keep being you. If you continue to be who your grandmother and I think you can be, you'll be adding your own name to that list someday too."

John was angry. He turned around and looked at the monitors again.

"That's EZ and Mr. Taylor," John said as he pointed to both men on the screens. "And, there's Alvaro." He then pointed to two other people. "You even have Nia and Davon there," John said, as he turned towards both women again. "I think you are wrong. I think I need to know more now, not later," he demanded.

"In time," Shanice said.

"No, I don't want to wait," John insisted. "That was my paper. I know every detail of what I expected to happen to each one of them, if I had followed through with the plan. John then turned towards Mrs. DeWitt. He looked her straight in the eye. "Are you telling me that every detail of each plan came to fruition?"

"Yes, but only you can finish the story," Adeline told the young man.

Shanice stood up, took her grandson by the arm and walked towards the front door. When they walked outside, the heat and moisture of the humid air reminded them that they were still in South Florida. Shanice then turned towards her friend and said, "Thank you for the nice visit, Adeline."

You're welcome, Shanice. Please come again."

John remained speechless as he slowly walked down the sidewalk to the end of the driveway and across the street. His mind was in overdrive, as he recalled the details of that long and deliberately written paper.

Halfway across the street, he finally spoke. "Who is she, Gramma? And, why would you ever give her my paper?"

Shanice was a wise woman. She knew it was best to minimize her conversation now. "You'll understand someday," she said.

"You better believe we are going to talk again." John was angry. He was confused, and he had many unanswered questions now. "I don't know who Mrs. DeWitt is. But, I do know she has power, Gramma. And, I'm not just talking about electricity that is flowing through her house right now when no one else in the neighborhood has it yet."

Shanice was not used to seeing this side of her grandson. She had not seen him this angry ever before. "In time, you will understand," she said. "Let's get back to help your folks, okay?"

CHAPTER EIGHTEEN

"Wake up, wake up, y' dudes," EZ shouted one morning. "It's snowin outside." He was so excited to see snow for the first time in his life that he forgot he even needed to use the washhouse.

"EZ," Ralph shouted back, "Shut up and go back to bed. We can see the snow in an hour when we need to be awake."

Breakfast was routinely served at eight o'clock now that daylight appeared later in the day. The men could sleep one hour longer each morning during the winter months without being scolded. EZ was not so fortunate this morning as he woke up at the crack of dawn. The days of staying up all night and sleeping the day away were over for him.

Davon, Alvaro, and Daniel also jumped out of bed when they heard the news. They scrambled as quickly as possible to put on layers of clothes, socks, and shoes. They ran outside just as the sun was rising. For five minutes their heads were tilted towards the gray smothering clouds that hung high above with their mouths opened wide, trying to catch any flake they could with their tongues. The large flakes fell effortlessly to the ground making their outdoors seem magical.

The two inches of snow that already covered the ground was cold and wet to the feel of their feet, but they didn't care. They ran through the side yard making tracks in the snow. When Davon's shoelace came untied, he stopped for a brief moment to tie it. That's when the snowball fight began. He had become the perfect target for Alvaro.

The young men could not have asked for better packing snow. It was the most perfect packing snow ever. They hid behind trees and logs, trying to escape the wrath of each snowball that came their way. Before too much time had passed, Regi, Jaheem, and Ryan appeared. Being a school teacher, Regi decided they should have teams. He had always been competitive. They needed an even number to make it fair though. All of the guys had their backs turned to the door, trying to agree to the rules of the game when Nia, Tonya, Leah, and Amber appeared. The guys were arguing over the rules and never saw the ladies come outside.

As quietly as possible the ladies packed several snowballs each and attacked the guys. They weren't interested in the rules of an official game. They just wanted to join in the fun. Their attack surprised the guys, and everyone started throwing snowballs at whoever was the easiest target to hit. There was continuous laughing and smiling for over an hour as the group continued to play in the snow. Never before had any of them experienced this much fun on the plantation.

Before long the older men appeared as well. The sun was up, and the snow was glistening off the branches of the trees. Across the field, it was twinkling in the sunlight as it continued to rise above the horizon. It was beautiful. Grouchy Ralph stood by the doorway of the house observing all the fun and laughter. For the first time in years, he actually cracked a smile. He had forgotten that a smile could be good for the soul.

"Let's make snow angels," Amber shouted when she was tired of being chased by another snowball.

"What's a snow angel?" Jaheem asked.

"I really don't know," Amber admitted. "I vaguely remember reading about one in a book when I was a kid."

Tonya knew all about snow angels. "I'll show you," Tonya piped in. "I used to make them every winter when I was a kid," she told the group.

Before long, they were all trying to make the perfect snow formation of themselves on the ground. The snow was still coming down heavily. In the first sixty minutes that they had been outside playing, another inch covered the ground.

"Ralph and Frank," Charlie called out. "Let's get a fire started. Everyone will need to get their clothes dried after making the snow angels," he said. "Plus, this old man is cold."

The men walked over to the wood pile and pulled some dry logs out from beneath the top layers that were not covered with snow. They grabbed some dried twigs and leaves to fuel the spark. Within a few minutes, a fire was roaring.

"The only thing we are missing now is hot chocolate," Tonya told the group.

"Maybe you ought to get that lil chef bod of yours into da kitchen to make sum," EZ sassed.

"Are you trying to piss me off, EZ, or just be funny?" Tonya asked in return. "Cuz, if you're trying to be funny, you failed. If you are trying to piss me off, then you almost succeeded."

"I'm just razzin' you," he confirmed.

Tonya wasn't going to take any heat from the guys. "This is the deal," she continued. "If y'all want hot cocoa, then EZ can make it for you. I can teach him."

Everyone spoke simultaneously, agreeing with Tonya that EZ should have the honors of making hot chocolate for everyone.

"Ya don't have any of those packets that you just pour into a cup of water?" EZ asked. "Cuz, I ain't likin the idea of havin to make anythin that can't be microwaved."

"You opened that mouth of yours, EZ," Charlie reminded him, "And, now you are going to make all of us hot cocoa."

Jaheem then walked up to EZ and stood tall above him. "Scoot into the kitchen, or you'll be seeing more of me," he warned him.

EZ and Tonya went off into the kitchen while everyone else scampered off to find their mugs. Within five minutes, EZ returned to where everyone had huddled around the fire, carrying a large pot of hot cocoa. Regi threw an iron grate over the flames so EZ could set the pot down to warm the chocolate milk.

"I done a good job, didn't I?" EZ asked after he took a sip of his hot chocolate.

"Not bad," Davon agreed.

"It's the best I've ever tasted," Jaheem stated.

"Yeah, it probably is, Jaheem. Cuz you probably ain't never drank any of this before," Ralph chimed.

It was still snowing outside, but everyone embraced the moment. Nia and Leah had gone back inside to slice onions and potatoes. They divided the portions evenly for separate helpings. Leah tore off individual sheets of aluminum foil in which Nia placed the helpings. They finished by adding five strips of bacon onto the potatoes and onions before folding the foil tightly to seal it. When they were finished they took a tray full of the foil packets outside and placed them directly into the coals. While Nia and Leah were preparing the potatoes, Tonya and Amber collected and cleaned fresh-laid eggs. They came back outside to the fire about ten minutes later with a pot full of scrambled eggs which Amber placed next to the remaining hot chocolate. This would be the first time ever that any of these men would eat a hobo dinner for breakfast.

A few weeks had passed since that snowfall. Something magical happened that day. It was the first time that a few of them ever felt like a family. Others felt contentment and purpose in their lives for the first time in years while the hardened hearts of a few began to soften. The polar vortex snowfall that reached the south that day changed these people for the better.

Everyone felt a sense of pride, too. In addition to harvesting the cotton, the men and gals had built a shower house, constructed a fence and chicken coop, and they had jointly worked together to build rows of greenhouses covering an acre of land. When they were finished with those projects, they also held a barn raising. The barn wasn't large like the one across the field from the house. This one was in the fields across the street from the house where the cattle were grazing. It allowed for easier storage of feed and grain for the animals.

Everyone had learned to do every chore on the plantation. They were divided into groups with chore rotations changing weekly so that each person could learn a new skill. No one complained either. They were glad that they were not bent over ten hours a day picking cotton.

Alvaro was paired with Frank. Davon was coupled with Ralph. Jaheem had the advantage or disadvantage, depending on one's view, of working alongside Leah, until Tonya's baby was born. Amber was disappointed that she was partnered with EZ, but she kept the disappointment to herself. Regi and Daniel worked together, leaving Charlie and Ryan as the final pair. Nia and Tonya remained in the kitchen until Leah would take over for Tonya in the short-term.

The farm animals needed to be fed, and the cows needed to be milked each day. The chickens multiplied quickly with eggs being laid and incubated, while other chickens laid eggs to be used in the kitchen.

Unplowed fields were being uprooted to prepare for new plantings and a vegetable garden. Additional farm equipment had been brought to the plantation, and some fruit trees were even planted on the property. The plantation was becoming a workable farm.

Charlie had even received permission to grow an acre or so of tobacco plants. The seeds were super small, but he managed to collect enough from his flowers to start seedlings in the greenhouse which he would later transfer to a field.

"Ryan," Charlie said one afternoon after their chores were finished, "Do you want to learn how to roll tobacco leaves?"

"Sure, I guess so," he said. "I have nothing better to do right now."

"The leaves are dry now. I don't want Ralph or Frank to help. I don't trust them. They might steal some of my tobacco leaves. I did all the work, so they will have to trade for them or do a chore or two for me if they want to enjoy one. It will be different next year once we plant the field and have a lot more to roll."

"Whatever you say, Boss," Charlie said to the older man.

"I'm not your boss. Henry is," Charlie reminded him.

"Yea, I know, but you and Regi are the smartest. So, I try to listen to you. Maybe I'll learn something one of these days."

"You already are," Charlie said. "You have never seen tobacco leaves rolled before."

"You're right about that," Ryan agreed.

"You're pretty smart yourself," Charlie then admitted to Ryan. "I was intrigued by your idea about the snake venom and antivenom."

"Yeah, I initially thought it could work," Ryan told Charlie. "The problem is getting the right kind of snake. I don't know enough about snakes to find the right kind. The stream is way too far down the road for anyone to walk without getting zapped, so we cannot even try to get a water moccasin."

Charlie agreed that no one really knew much about snakes. "My other concern was the guinea pig willing to try it out. I sure wouldn't want to be the person who died trying.

"You're right, Charlie," Ryan agreed. "I would have had to be the one, and I'm not so sure I want to die trying either."

This pair was the odd couple in the group. Charlie was one of the oldest, and Ryan was the youngest. Why they got paired together nobody will ever know. Whoever made the decision, made a good one. They both respected one another.

"Ahhh," Charlie said, as he opened the door of the barn. "Do you smell the sweet aroma of those leaves?"

"They do smell good," Ryan admitted, walking up to a table covered with leaves.

Charlie had found two plants that he cultivated and then removed the leaves to dry in the barn for several months. "We have to de-stem the leaves first," Charlie told Ryan, as he pointed to the center of one of the large leaves. Charlie showed Ryan how to carefully remove the large stem without tearing the leaf. "Can you help me with this?" he asked.

"It's better than listening to EZ and Ralph make up stories back at the campfire," Ryan told Charlie.

The men had cut down several old trees in the fall and were now using them for firewood on the cold days after their chores were completed. Today was one of those days when they could rest for a couple hours before the dinner meal.

"For sure," Charlie told him. "I like to talk, but those guys don't ever stop talking," Charlie chuckled. "Plus, they talk about things that aren't important."

"Even when no one else is out by the fire, Ralph will tell a story to himself," Ryan joked, causing Charlie to laugh some more.

Charlie and Ryan worked for three days stripping the leaves from their stems. Each day they were getting closer and closer to the end result.

"Are you going to try one?" Charlie asked Ryan after they began the process of rolling the fillers. They had sorted all the leaves by size and color. The long anticipated day of rolling tobacco leaves had now arrived. Charlie was excited. He knew the days of smoking a cigar were near.

"I don't know," Ryan answered. "I have never smoked anything ever," he told his mentor. "I'm not sure if I want to start either," he said.

"It's just a cigar," Charlie reminded the twenty year old.

"Yeah, but cancer is cancer," Ryan told Charlie. "My mom died of it. I don't care what I die from, but I don't want it to be cancer."

Charlie wasn't expecting such a deep conversation. He thought every kid wanted to smoke and drink. "Hey, I'm sorry kid," Charlie said. "I didn't know."

"Don't worry about it," Ryan told him. "Nobody else knows either. It's one of those things I don't ever talk about. I don't have anyone to talk to about it."

"Well, I won't ask again," Charlie promised Ryan.

As they continued rolling, Ryan was deep in thought. Charlie was afraid to say anything else to him at the moment. He wasn't sure if Ryan was remembering his mother, or if he had triggered some other thoughts in that young mind of his.

While Charlie waited for Ryan to speak again, he took his cup and added some water to a little bit of gum powder to make some cigar glue. Henry had bought the type Charlie had asked for when he agreed to let him experiment with cigar making. When the consistency was just right, Charlie sealed the binder to the filler. His first cigar was almost done.

When Ryan still didn't say anything, Charlie went back to his teaching mode. "We don't need much glue," he said. "This is only enough to keep the filler in place. Before gluing anything, I need to make sure we don't have any of the fillers wrapped too tightly either," he explained to the silent bystander. Charlie then pressed lightly against one of the cigars. "This one is perfect," he told Ryan. "Feel it yourself," he told him.

Ryan reached over and pressed softly against the cigar. "Now, touch this one," Charlie said, as he reached for another cigar. "This one is slightly tighter than the other one. Can you feel the difference?" he asked.

"Yes," Ryan finally said.

"In the factory, this one probably would not pass inspection. But, it's one of our first ones, and I want to test it against the others so that we know for sure next time around," he explained. "Go ahead and glue the binder to the filler and set it aside."

Ryan did as Charlie told him.

"It will probably take us a couple more days to roll all of the leaves," Charlie said. "I'm going to teach both you and me how to become professional torcedors."

"What?" Ryan asked, not fully understanding if Charlie was speaking English or Spanish.

"A torcedor," Charlie said very slowly. "A professional cigar roller," Charlie then reached over and patted Ryan on the shoulder.

"You know something?" Ryan said rhetorically. "You're not so bad. You are different than I thought you would be."

"What do you mean?" Charlie asked.

"When I was working at the deli, an older woman called me out one day. I made a foolish comment and said that 'African-Americans are all alike.' Ebony looked me straight in the eyes and said, 'Don't you ever say that again, young man. You are completely wrong. I don't know why you would ever think that, let alone say it.' She was really angry at me, and to be honest I didn't even realize why she was so upset. I think I understand now."

Charlie stopped rolling his cigar before it was even finished. "Did you say Ebony?" he asked.

"Yeah, what's the big deal? I worked with several older women. Ebony was one of the ladies who worked at the deli in Carol City with me."

"Do you remember Ebony's last name?" Charlie asked.

"No, I don't think I knew anyone's last name. Why?"

"What did she look like?" Charlie again questioned Ryan.

"I don't know. She was a black woman, probably in her fifties. She had short curly hair."

"Your description describes millions of black women all over the country, Kid," Charlie said. "Do you know anything at all about her?"

"She lives in Carol City, close enough that she would walk home from work each day," Ryan reported.

"Did she say anything about her family to you?" Charlie inquired.

"Do you think you know this lady or something?" Ryan asked. "She has a son. I think he's a year or two older than me. She's married, I really don't know much about her."

"Do you remember her son's name by chance?" Charlie then asked.

"No."

"Could it be John?" Charlie then asked.

"I really don't remember," Ryan explained.

"How about Junior?"

A light went off in the back of Ryan's memory bank. "Yeah, I think that's it," Ryan recalled. "He came in one day to get some cheese and meat for lunch. She introduced me to him."

"That's my sister," Charlie said.

"No way."

"Ebony Bramble. My nephew is John. He must have gone to school with EZ and some of the guys. I bet they offended him in some way."

"Let me get this straight. You're saying that you think they are behind this thing?"

"I'm not from Carol City, and I don't know any of you guys. I grew up in South Florida, but I never lived in Carol City. I may have sold a bad car to someone years ago, but they would never know each and every one of the guys who are here. Her family is the only connection at this point. Think about it."

"So, I say something negative once about the African-American race, and I end up on this plantation?" Ryan asked.

"I don't know," Charlie said. "But, I agree with her. You can never make the assumption that all black people or African-Americans are the same. Just look at the guys here, and how different everyone is from one another. How would you like it if I said that all mixed people or white people, if that's how you think of yourself, are the same? You would probably mock me and say that I am stupid."

"I wasn't thinking. Something was said that I didn't like, and I overreacted. If that's what this is all about. What on earth..."

Charlie did not let Ryan finish his sentence. "There is no way you just 'overreacted' once," Charlie said to Ryan, as he looked firmly into his deep brown eyes. "You have a vendetta with black men, don't you?" he asked. "Maybe someone who happens to be African-American did something to you. Maybe you are prejudiced. Saying one smart remark wouldn't land you on a cotton plantation, now would it?" the older man inquired of the youngster.

Ryan folded his arms and placed his left hand across his face. "Don't be mad at me."

"Kid, I'm living on this plantation now with you and a dozen or so of others who do not want to be here. I think all of our problems are bigger than me being mad at you because you were foolish." He then paused, "Just be honest with me."

Ryan looked away. He didn't want to meet the eyes of an African-American as he spoke the truth. "You're right," he said.

"Look at me, Ryan," Charlie insisted.

Ryan looked up from the tobacco leaves which he had been staring at since he began the conversation. "I do have a vendetta against African-Amercans. I haven't liked them since the time I was seven. My dad was African-American, and my mom white. My dad used to hit her. When I was old enough, or so I thought as a seven year old, I began to jump in the way to protect my mom. That's when he started pushing me around and calling me names. When I was nine or ten, he started punching me when he was drinking. He always apologized just in time to repeat it when he got drunk again. My cousins never liked me because they considered me to be a white boy. African-Americans at school didn't like me because I wasn't black enough. I never fit in anywhere.

"That explains it," Charlie said.

"Then one night, it was late, both my mom and I were already sleeping when we heard a loud knock on the door. We both thought my drunk dad was back home ready to attack. I actually grabbed a frying pan from the kitchen before my mom and I answered the door. I was going to be prepared this time. The knock was harder the second time, and we were scared. My mom asked, 'Who is it?' before opening the door. We were shocked to hear a woman's voice say, 'It's the sheriff. Can we talk to you?' "

"I can imagine a few different things were running through your mind at that moment," Charlie commented. "How old were you at the time?"

"I was twelve," Ryan told him. "My mom unlatched the dead bolt to see two officers. A man and woman from the county sheriff were standing there. 'Are you Joyce Smith?' the gentleman asked my mom. Of course, she told them, 'yes.' 'We regret to inform you that your husband has been killed in an automobile accident.' I was thinking, '*Praise Jesus!*'"

"I bet you were," Charlie half chuckled.

" 'From the looks of that frying pan in your hands,' the male officer said, 'I bet you both have seen enough.' I told them that we were tired of being punching bags every time my dad got mad. 'It's over now,' the lady responded."

Charlie was anxious to hear what happened. He wanted to get back to rolling cigars.

"Sure enough, my dad was drunk. He drove through the safety bar at a railroad crossing. The train clipped the back of his car which sent it flying through the air, spinning multiple times, before the car landed about fifty yards away. He died on the scene."

"I feel for you, kid, but you can't hate every black man because of this," he insisted. "I'm a good guy for the most part. I've been treating you fairly," he said, trying to convince Ryan that not all black men or African-Americans were bad.

"I know," Ryan said, "But, you must have done something to offend your sister or you wouldn't be here either," Ryan said, not expecting Charlie to give him an honest answer.

"To tell you the truth, I did do something to offend her," Charlie said. "If I tell you, you can't say a word to anyone. We need to do some more searching before we go out and accuse my sister and her family of wrongdoing."

"I won't say a word to anyone, not even Regi," Ryan told Charlie.

"You need to snoop around and suggest to the young guys that maybe John is behind this thing. Bring up stuff about high school and ask dumb questions jokingly that might get EZ or Alvaro or Daniel or any of them to answer you. I'll ask the older men and Regi to see what they have to say. But, keep it a secret for now."

"Okay, but are you going to tell me what beef you had with your sister?"

"I was stupid and foolish and greedy. I stole some money from her, and she hasn't spoken with me in years," Charlie explained.

"Yeah, you're right," Ryan said. "You were stupid and foolish. Who steals money from family?"

"You stole money from your sister?" a voice from behind questioned Charlie.

Charlie and Ryan turned around from the table to see Henry standing in the doorway.

"How long have you been standing there?" Charlie asked.

"Long enough to hear that you stole money from your sister. I came by to see how your project is coming along?"

Charlie showed Henry the cigars and the leaves that still needed rolled. "We still need to finish rolling some and put the wrappers on all of them." Charlie told Henry.

"I want to try one when they are finished," Henry said.

"I know. I plan to give a couple of them to you," Charlie told him. "I have the seedlings ready too. I think I have enough for an acre or more."

"Well, if this idea of yours works, you just might have a side business that keeps you out of the cotton fields," Henry said. "There's a lot of money to be made in the cigar business. We can dedicate some land for this too."

"It's going to work," Charlie reassured Henry.

"So, how much did you steal from your sister?" Henry then asked, changing the subject back to the previous discussion.

"Enough," Charlie answered.

"Enough to buy another car dealership or even to buy that 1962 Rolls Royce Ghost that was missing from your collection? Or, maybe enough to purchase a 1967 Aston Martin DBS Superleggera that you had been eyeing for years?"

Ryan had stepped back away from the table and away from both of the men. He wasn't sure where this conversation was leading, and he wanted to get out of harm's way if needed. He looked at Henry, then Charlie, and Henry again.

Charlie did not take his eyes off of Henry, nor did he answer Henry's questions.

Henry started to walk away. When he reached the barn door, he stopped and turned around. "By the way," Henry said after a brief moment of silence, "Your sister doesn't know anything about this plantation."

"For someone who doesn't know anything about this plantation," Charlie thought, *"Henry sure does know a lot about the money that was stolen*

from her."

Charlie didn't even hear the dinner bell ring. He was in a daze.

"Charlie," Ryan said, "The bell. We need to go now."

CHAPTER NINETEEN

Five days later, Charlie placed the final wrapper on his last cigar. He was anxious for Henry to arrive at the fire. They would be celebrating his victory of producing his first cigar. The others had been warned that only Charlie, Ryan and Regi were allowed at the fire once Henry arrived.

The men were mostly talking about why they should be allowed to stay and enjoy a cigar with Charlie. Ryan sat quietly for a few minutes observing everyone as they chatted and reasoned. His heart was heavy. He had never spoken with anyone about his father's death until the day he spoke with Charlie. He stood up and stood silently until everyone stopped talking.

"I have something to say to you guys," Ryan announced. "As some of you have reminded me occasionally, I seem more white than black."

"You jus figurin that out?," EZ teased.

"I owe all black men an apology," he continued.

"What for?" Ralph blurted out. "You ain't done nothing to hurt any of us. We've been the ones ragging you."

"I used to hate all black men," Ryan explained. "I didn't care if they were African-Americans or who they were. If they had dark skin, I hated them. Then I met you guys. I don't know why I am here. Just like you guys don't know why you are here either. But, I've learned a lesson or two. I was blaming your entire race for my dad not liking me. My dad was African-American. He used to beat the crap out of my mom, and then me when I got older and stood up for her. My cousins called me 'White Rye' because I wasn't black enough for them. I began to resent them too. I didn't fit in with any group at school either. I wasn't black enough or I was too tan. I held a grudge against the African-American community because they, specifically my dad, caused me the most pain. I was wrong. I thought all African-Americans were like him."

"Now that I am older, I know that alcoholism is a disease. A deadly disease. I guess, if there is any lesson he taught me, it would be not to be like him. One drink may just be one too many. You guys aren't so bad though. Yeah, we all have our flaws, but you guys worked your tails off, and we actually produced a large crop of cotton this past year. And, now we have worked together to create a self-sustaining farm with animals and all. So, thank you for teaching me that African-American men are not all alike. I don't know what's going to happen down the road with any of us, but I know that I will always call you my friends."

Charlie looked over at Ryan when he sat back down and smiled.

"Dang, that took some guts," Davon said.

"Thanks man," EZ said.

"You're not so bad yourself," Frank uttered.

"I just needed to get that off my chest," Ryan told everyone after they had thanked him for being so honest.

Standing under the tree on the far side of the house stood Henry. He had heard every word of Ryan's speech. He didn't want to interrupt him, so he waited patiently until Ryan was done. No one saw him standing there. After everyone was done talking to Ryan, Henry approached the group.

"Hey guys," Henry said when he approached the firepit. "Sorry to break up your party, but I have some business to discuss." Everyone stood up and left without complaining. They were still fearful of their collars and didn't want to offend Henry or give him any reason to increase their chores.

Charlie had made a cigar box which he had held tight in his hands the entire time Ryan was speaking. Charlie stood up and walked over to Henry who was now sitting on the log that Alvaro had just vacated. He opened the box in front of him. Five cigars lined the box. The other eight cigars that he had made were in hiding. Charlie hid them so they could continue to age without being stolen.

"You may choose whichever one you want," Charlie told Henry.

"Is one better than the other?" Henry asked.

"These four are all rolled about the same. If there are any differences, they would be so slight that only an expert would be able to tell the difference. This last one is rolled a little tighter than the first four."

Henry reached in and selected the fourth one at the far end of the box.

He then asked Ryan and Regi if they would like a cigar. Regi held his hand up and waved it back and forth to indicate that he did not want to try one. Charlie was surprised that he had declined. Regi had been an athlete his entire life. He had never smoked. He wasn't so sure he would choose cigars if he ever decided to pick up the bad habit. He had preached to his students on multiple occasions the ill effects of smoking. He didn't want his former students to think less of him now, if he lit up

Ryan, on the other hand, picked the cigar at the opposite end of the box from the one Henry had chosen. He rolled it through his fingertips as he had done when he was rolling them. He played with the cigar, but chose not to light it when Charlie pulled a twig out of the fire which he would use to light the cigars.

"I want this cigar," Ryan had told Charlie. "But, I'm not going to smoke it tonight."

"Are you sure?" Charlie asked again.

"I'm sure."

Ryan watched intensely as Charlie taught Henry how to light his first cigar. It took several attempts, but Henry finally got his lit. He coughed. Charlie chuckled. After they both were enjoying their first smokes, Charlie explained the actual process of smoking a cigar. It was very different from smoking a cigarette.

"You don't want to get it too hot, or let it cool down too much either," Charlie explained. "There is a perfect temperature needed to burn a cigar with perfection." Henry did exactly what Charlie told him to do while Ryan looked on, studying the process. If he ever chose to start smoking, he wanted to make sure he understood its purpose and how to savor the flavor.

After explaining the physical act of smoking, Charlie provided a history lesson on the types of cigars made in America, the process, and the economic value of the varying types.

"How does this cigar compare to the ones you have smoked before?" Henry asked.

"It's hard to explain the differences since you have never smoked a cigar before," Charlie began. "Since I haven't smoked in all these months, it's a ten on a scale of one to ten," Charlie teased.

All four men laughed.

"Seriously, though," Charlie continued. "It's as equal to any American made cigar that I have smoked in recent years. It's different than any I have ever smoked, but I am thoroughly enjoying it. The flavor is unique, and I have never smelled an aroma quite like this one. It has a sweetness to it. This one hasn't aged thoroughly yet so it's not as good as the expensive ones I have previously purchased in the Dominican Republic, but in time I can get a crop that is superior to any American grown leaf. This soil is rich and perfect for tobacco plants."

"I don't know the exact numbers, but there are no more than fifty or so cigar factories left in America today. Back in the late 1800's, there were nearly 42,000 factories in America alone. I know times have changed, but I am convinced with all the land here that we can continue to enlarge the crop fields each year on this plantation and yield a profitable cigar," Charlie explained, trying to convince Henry that the profits could be staggeringly high.

For two and a half hours, the four men sat on the logs around the fire pit, learning every detail of cigar making. Henry asked questions about the costs and profit margins. Regi talked about logistics. He wanted to know how many people were needed to roll the cigars, and the plans to market and deliver the product. Charlie explained in detail what he observed at the tobacco farms he had visited in the Dominican Republic. Henry was convinced that marketing would be the easy part. They could hire a marketing firm to handle that aspect.

Charlie shared details about his auto dealerships and what he had done previously with marketing. "Obviously, we are only selling one specific item, but the cash value can be enormous," Charlie again explained.

Charlie and Henry did most of the talking while Regi and Ryan listened. After listening for a very long time, Ryan finally spoke. "I only have two questions," he said. "It seems to me, based on the time it took us to roll a dozen cigars, that we don't even have enough people to physically do the necessary labor in the fields or in the factory. Wouldn't it be better to sell the tobacco leaves themselves to a business and simply be a supplier of raw materials instead?"

"I've thought of it," Charlie said, as he tried to look deeply into the eyes of Henry as the light of the fire reflected off his pupils. "That's a question for Henry. We need more people for sure. I have no idea what the plans are for us here. I don't know how long we will be here. I don't know if any others will join us. And, I don't know if we will ever leave. The only thing that I know is that I love cigars, and right now the only way for me to smoke them is to grow the tobacco myself and roll them."

The friendly chatter that carried on throughout the evening came to an abrupt end. Charlie continued to look into the eyes of Henry, hoping he could read his soul and force an answer from him. Regi was shocked that Charlie had taken this casual 'business' meeting and turned it into a personal inquiry. Henry had told everyone from day one that those specific questions were off limits. He would not be able to answer any of them, so please don't ask. Henry had even warned everyone that he would penalize anyone who asked.

"Charlie," Regi began to say when he was interrupted by Henry after what seemed like a minute of complete silence, except that of the crackling wood.

"It's okay, Regi," Henry said before Regi could speak another word. "I don't have those answers, Charlie," Henry said, as he continued to look back at Charlie in the darkness of the night.

"But, you could get them," Charlie boldly stated.

"Don't get too cocky," Henry warned. "I admire your hard work and eagerness to create something positive out of what you think is less than an ideal situation. You have considered every aspect of this venture. Your proven track record for success in the auto industry also helps your cause. Don't push it. I've given you an acre for your next round."

Regi could tell that Henry was uncomfortable with Charlie's direct attack. It was a backhanded insult. Regi agreed that those questions had never been answered, but he felt that Henry had finally opened up to them, and he was thrilled that Henry was even willing to give an acre for this project. That acre could easily be used for cotton instead. Wisely, Regi changed the subject. Looking at Ryan, he said, "What's your other question, Ryan?"

Ryan yawned and rubbed his eyes with the palm of his hands. He then yawned a second time. "I was just wondering if you have considered a name for your cigar?"

Henry chuckled as he stood to leave. "That's a question for another day, Kid," he said to Ryan. "It's a good question though."

To the surprise of Ryan Smith, he was able to celebrate his twenty-first birthday with his grandmother. Most guys his age would have preferred an ice-cold brew or two at the local nightclub or bar with their friends. The only problem was that Ryan didn't have any friends. He had been so judgmental to the people around him, that he turned everyone away. His only real friends were someplace north of Carol City, miles away. He actually missed the plantation. His grandmother wouldn't even remember the celebration. There were days when she didn't even remember her grandson.

Ryan didn't whine or complain that his grandmother's condition had worsened while he was away. He was thrilled that he could now care for her and provide the assistance she needed to endure her last days. He was honored to help her. His mother had always told him that "it's a privilege to help a grandparent, not a burden." He never forgot.

A couple days after Ryan returned to his grandmother's home, a neighbor spotted him and reported him to the police. The very next day the police arrived on his doorstep for questioning. This would have been the perfect opportunity for him to reflect on his whereabouts in recent months. Yet, he didn't. He had no proof. No one would have believed his crazy story.

"Can you show us some identification?" an officer had asked.

"Yes, but why do I need to show you some identification?" Ryan had asked. "I haven't done anything wrong," he answered.

"You're a missing person," the officer had explained.

"No. I'm not missing. I live here with my grandmother," Ryan had told the man in blue.

"Apparently, some people thought you were missing when the others down here disappeared," the officer continued to explain.

Ryan showed the cop his driver license, proof of his residency.

"So, you have not been missing?" a lady officer then asked.

"No. I'm not missing," Ryan assured them.

"Is there a reason you didn't dispel the rumors when there was a search for you?" the man continued..

"I never saw the news and didn't know anyone thought I was missing," Ryan told the officers. "Did my grandmother report me missing?" Ryan asked, not knowing if she had reported him missing.

"I don't know," the lady officer replied. She then walked back to the cruiser to check the report on the computer. When she returned she told Ryan that a person by the name of Cheryl Waggler had reported him missing.

"Oh, that's the neighbor," Ryan told the officers.

"She claims that your grandmother was ill and wouldn't be able to identify you."

"Really?" Ryan asked. He then opened the front door wide enough so that the officers could see his grandmother sitting in her chair in the front room. "Do you know who I am?" Ryan asked her.

"Absolutely. You are my grandson, Ryan Smith, and you have a special birthday coming up in a few days," she had told them.

The officer looked down at Ryan's driver license to see that his twenty-first birthday was indeed approaching.

"You're right. I do," Ryan said, nodding in agreement with his grandma. "Have I been missing?" Ryan then asked her. He was hoping and praying that she would answer correctly. She had good days and bad days, but so far this had been a good day for her. Ryan wasn't sure what would pop out of her memory bank.

"No, does someone think you are missing?" she had asked.

"The neighbor thought I was missing," he explained. Ryan then closed the door enough that she could not hear the rest of their conversation. "I don't know why the neighbor would report me missing. She's always been a little nosy," he added, hoping the officers would believe his sincerity. "Thanks for checking on me though."

"Sorry for the confusion. We will make sure the report gets updated," the officer kindly told him as they both turned to leave.

Three months had passed since that event and Ryan's return home. Ryan was now sitting on the back of a large yacht at the Miami Yacht Club. Even if he had never gone to the plantation, he still would not have believed that he would be sitting on such a large vessel in Miami. That was something for the movies, not for real life. He chatted with his boss for a few minutes, then patiently waited for his next interviewee. He would be conducting interviews all day long.

When the potential employee arrived, Ryan explained the details of the position and gave the candidate a chance to share his story. Then Ryan began asking specific questions. "Are you willing to relocate?" he asked the young man sitting with a lemonade in the back of the yacht with him.

"Yes."

"And, you understand that this job is a 24/7 position, where you will be living in a bunk house with other men?"

"Yes, I understand," the young male stated.

"I want to confirm that you realize that you will not be seeing your family during the length of your tenure? This job is in a remote location, far from the hustle of city living?"

"Yes, I understand," he stated again.

"And, you realize that you will not have access to modern luxuries, including cell phone usage or the internet?" the young interviewer asked the candidate.

"Yes, I get it," the candidate said in frustration. "I know. I'm going to work my ass off for a long ten months or so. I'm likely going to cuss and scream and ask myself, '*What the hell did I get myself into?*' But, when I'm done the jingle in my pocket is going to be worth all my misery."

"It's kind of like that," Ryan reassured the candidate. "It's a little more complex, but are you willing to learn how to cultivate cotton and tobacco crops?"

"Your explanation was very precise and clear. I get it. I'll be rolling cigars too," the young man told Ryan.

Ryan stood up and walked inside the cabin for a brief minute.

"I would like to offer him a position," he told his boss. "He looks strong and eager," Ryan said. "Plus, anyone willing to come down to the yacht club for an interview on a yacht is either desperate or fearless."

Ryan's boss was in unison and agreed that this man could make a good employee. Ryan promptly returned carrying a contract.

"Okay. If you don't have any other questions, I would like to offer you a position that will begin in two weeks. You will have to sign this contract before you can begin work," Ryan told him, as he gave him a set of papers stapled together. Ten pages of finely printed ink, covering both sides of the paper, had been given to the potential employee.

"You've got to be kidding, if you think I'm going to read a contract that long," the young man told Ryan.

"I'm advising you to read it first," Ryan told the guy who was a year older than Ryan.

"No. I'm in," he said, as he took a blue ballpoint pen and signed his name, Jonathan Steeple, to the final page. "Can I invite some of my friends to come down tomorrow to meet you?" he then asked. "They will probably be interested in making this kind of money too."

"Sure. We are looking for some additional workers as well," Ryan told Jon. "Just write their names down here on this paper so I know who might be coming." Ryan then placed a blank sheet of lined note-book paper in front of Jon. He scribbled four names. Jon then took his phone out of his pocket and provided their phone numbers as well.

"Here, you can even call them if you want," Jon told Ryan.

"I'll let you tell them about Dulce Acre Cigars," Ryan told his latest recruit. He was glad for the phone numbers. He would use them to pull up background information on all of Jon's friends.

Jon nodded his head in agreement and then walked down the ramp of the yacht. On his way down, he turned and shouted, "I'll see you tomorrow," as he continued to walk down the pier.

After Jon had left, Ryan turned to MacKenzie, who stepped out of the air-conditioned cabin. She had observed and heard every word of the interview. "How did I do?" Ryan asked.

"Not bad. The moment I heard that you acknowledged your mistake and had apologized to the group, I had a feeling that you would be an asset to the team."

"Thanks," Ryan told her. "I'm still in awe of the brilliance of the plan. Never in a million years could I have dreamed something like this."

"It wasn't something anyone had planned to do. It just happened," Mac reassured him.

"My only hope," Ryan continued, "is that you let me come with you when the others learn the truth. I would love to see their faces and hear their responses to your explanation. EZ is going to cuss everyone out, then he will want to hug you as if you have been best friends your entire lives."

"You're probably right. That sounds like EZ," Mac agreed. "When the time is right, I'll let you know."

"Okay," Ryan said. "Here comes my next interviewee. Three down and twenty-one to go."

CHAPTER TWENTY

The hurricane relief efforts in South Florida were massive. John made it his mission to rebuild his neighborhood. This took almost two years. He continued to work for Laikin Construction, but he also started his own construction company that built single-family housing only. They received federal funds for low-income families and hurricane relief funds to change the face of his neighborhood. Warren guided John through each phase of the construction projects to assure his success.

Sixty percent of the homes in his neighborhood were so severely damaged that he literally had them torn completely down. His childhood home included. The others needed partial teardowns, and very few had all their roofs intact. Mrs. DeWitt's fort, as John now called it, was the only house that did not need repair. She, however, hired John to modernize the exterior. She didn't want her place to look dilapidated with all the new home construction in the neighborhood.

To simplify the construction process, Warren's architectural team designed five house plans that the home owners could choose. Three of the five had the same foundation plan. They offered ten different options for exterior and interior finishes. There were just enough variations that the neighborhood did not look like a cookie-cutter hood which pleased all the neighbors.

The Bramble home was the first to be constructed. It was then used as a model home, and John's home office. With John's fifteen hours-a-day work schedule, he often found himself sleeping there rather than the apartment. His parents were not sure if they would move back into the new home after John was done using it as a model, or if they would sell it for a nice profit. They were enjoying the ease of apartment dwelling, as well as the resort-style salt water pool that they frequently used.

John made numerous attempts to talk with Mrs. DeWitt, but the timing was never right. Either contractors were nearby, preventing the needed privacy he desired for his discussion, or she was off to another meeting or two. She continued the fabulous upkeep of her flower beds throughout the entire construction phase. John had warned everyone to be careful not to destroy any of her plants.

Unlike the other projects that were coming to completion according to the construction timeframe that John had established, Adeline DeWitt gave John a written timeline of her expectations. She had given him two months to complete the work. He reviewed the information she had given him and debated internally whether he should agree to the terms. He had some questions for her, but decided she was not the person he wanted to debate. Instead, he jotted some notes down on her outline and agreed to the terms. John learned from that experience that men work harder when coffee and breakfast are served to them each morning. They were eager to show up at the job site on time, increasing their available hours to work.

After John's team completed Mrs. DeWitt's house, they only had two more houses to finish in John's neighborhood. John was sitting at his desk one evening finishing up some paperwork when he heard a knock on the door.

"Junior, are you in there?" a familiar voice called out to him through the front door.

It was Mrs. DeWitt. She wasn't young and beautiful looking like she had been on that day almost two years ago. Instead, she was the old Mrs. DeWitt that John had known growing up.

"Hi, Mrs. DeWitt," John responded on seeing the neighbor walk into the model home. "I've been meaning to talk to you," he said.

"Yes. I know, and I have been avoiding you," she wittingly remarked. "Be here tomorrow at seven sharp. Pack your bags. We are going on a road trip."

"What?" John asked.

"You heard me," she boldly responded.

"I have meetings with contractors first thing," he said.

"Not anymore," she continued. "Your work here is done."

"You really think that I am going to let you tell me how to run my business?" John asked.

"John, I know you haven't forgotten your visit to my home," she remarked in a monotone voice.

"How could I forget? I didn't speak to my gramma for two weeks because I was so upset," John confessed. "I don't know what I would have done if the hurricane hadn't hit. I've worked non-stop ever since."

"Do you think Warren Laikin is going to let your business fall to threads? Do you?" she then asked. "Just let him know you need to leave town on unexpected business."

John needed answers, and Adeline knew he needed answers. She could tell he was pondering the consequences for his abrupt departure.

"John," Adeline continued. "Your parents are already on a ten-day cruise. They don't even need to know that you have left. You simply lock the front door of the apartment and walk out with your bags. Shanice is coming. Warren will cover your business affairs. It's really that simple."

"But," John started to say."

"Be here tomorrow at seven," Adeline DeWitt demanded, then turned and walked out into the warm night air.

John stood silently in the hallway. He wanted to scream, but he wanted answers more. He dialed Warren Laikin's number.

"Hello, John," Warren said, as he answered the phone. "I was just going to call you."

"Really?" John inquired.

"Yes, I know you are finishing up the last two homes in your neighborhood right now. We have a new project that will begin in two weeks. This would be the perfect time for you to take a much needed break. I can wrap up the houses for you. They are on autopilot now anyway," he explained, without John even requesting his help.

"You don't mind?" John asked.

"Not at all. All my foremen are up to speed on their assignments, and I can oversee the completion of yours," he insisted.

"I have a nine o'clock with Beatrice Shallow. She's ready to begin installations," John informed Warren. Beatrice was the window treatment supplier that Warren had been using for the past thirty years. "She's planning to come here to the house. Marcus Rubbens will be coming at eleven. He wants to confirm the landscaping budgets for both homes."

"Well, that doesn't sound too difficult," Warren assured John. All the men working on John's crews had worked previously on Warren's as well. "I'll give you a shout if there is anything that comes up. Please text me the key code to the model home so I can enter when I come tomorrow."

Before the men even said "Goodbye," John had texted the code to Warren.

Shanice's suitcase was sitting at the front door when John arrived back at the apartment a little before nine. "Your dinner is in the refrigerator on a plate," she said when he walked in

"Thanks, Gramma," he replied. "So, you knew about this trip and didn't tell me?" he asked.

"Yes," she replied. "I knew you wouldn't agree to go until the houses in the neighborhood were finished, but the time is right for us to make the trip now," she explained.

John took his plate of pasta and meatballs and placed it in the microwave to be heated. He also grabbed cold ice tea from the refrigerator and poured a glass. After taking a large gulp, he stood by the counter waiting for the buzzer to beep. With a warm plate in hand, he sat down on the barstool to eat.

"To make things a little easier for you," his gramma said, "I washed all of your clothes and folded them. They are sitting on your bed."

"Thanks, Gramma."

"I also bought you a suitcase since you didn't own one," she continued. "It's in your room as well."

"Any other surprises?" John sarcastically asked, thinking his gramma had already done enough for him in one day.

She responded quickly, "Matter of fact, yes," she said. "I asked Joe to pick up a dozen donuts for me on his way home from the airport so we won't have to go out of our way to stop first thing in the morning."

"Did you get my favorite?" John asked.

"Of course, I did," Shanice responded, "plus a variety of others too."

"I guess there isn't anything you forget, is there?" John asked, as he was finishing his dinner.

"No, Junior. I've been traveling for many years. I know exactly what is needed for each and every trip."

"The spaghetti was perfect. Thanks for having it ready for me," John told his gramma as he put his plate into the dishwasher. I have some packing to do."

"I'm heading off to bed now myself," Shanice told him. "I will be ready to leave by six-forty. If I don't hear you up by six fifteen, I will wake you. If for some reason, you don't hear me, please wake me as well."

"Good night, Gramma."

The morning came much too early for John. After packing his suitcase, he spent much of the night reviewing every detail of the paper he had written five years previously. He reread it three times and made some notes that he tucked away in his phone. He then emailed a copy of the paper to himself, so he could retrieve it on his phone for future reference. He was restless and had a difficult time sleeping.

They arrived at the Bramble home, now being called the model home, exactly at six fifty-five in the morning. "Am I driving?" John asked his gramma. "If not, I would like to park in the garage," he told her.

John was confused because he thought he would be the one escorting his gramma and Mrs. DeWitt. Parked in Mrs. DeWitt's driveway, however, was a black Cadillac Escalade. It was identical to the one that belonged to Warren Laikin.

"No, Junior, you won't need to drive today," his gramma said. "But, please grab both of our suitcases and take them across the street to the SUV."

"Who is that?" John asked.

"Oh, you will see in just a moment," she replied.

After pulling into the garage, John took both suitcases out of the trunk and wheeled them down the driveway with his gramma by his side. He looked back to confirm that the garage door had closed completely before he crossed the street. He then looked at the license plate on the SUV.

"This is Mr. Laikin's Cadillac," John reported to his gramma. "How can he be going if he is meeting with our contractors today?"

"Warren will not be joining us today, my dear," Shanice responded back. The moment she said that, Mac opened the car door and proceeded to walk to the back of the vehicle.

"Hello Mrs. Bramble and John," she excitedly said. "You can put the suitcases in the back trunk area," she instructed.

Adeline DeWitt, dressed in casual clothes, walked out of her front door. A silk scarf covered her head and most of her face, not allowing her to be recognized by anyone on the street, should a neighbor drive by this early. This was the glamorous Adeline DeWitt today, not the elderly neighbor Mrs. DeWitt.

John assisted in loading her suitcase to the back trunk as well.

"You may sit in the front seat with MacKenzie," Mrs. DeWitt told Junior. "I would like to sit back here in the back with your gramma for awhile."

John didn't ask any questions. He slid into the front passenger seat as instructed.

"I'm surprised to see you today," he told Mac when they were pulling out of the driveway.

"I bet you are," she responded back.

John had confided in MacKenzie on several occasions when he first learned that the people mentioned in his paper had disappeared. He did not tell her anything about their stories and never directly identified the people involved. He simply had set up a hypothetical situation in which he asked her what she would do if someone had found a paper that she had written and acted upon it. He was vague, not providing any hints or evidence of the situation at hand.

She had told him that the possibility of something like that ever happening was so remote that she would not be concerned. She didn't think it was even possible. Yet, here she sat next to him now, driving him to some unknown place. He thought to himself, *"I should rephrase my thoughts. I know exactly where I am going. I'm going to an extremely large plantation, likely in one of the Carolinas."* Either Mac was not aware of the situation at the time, or she played ignorant to its reality hoping that John would not find out that she was aware of the scheme.

John knew that MacKenzie's involvement should be the least of his concerns at this point in time. He was along for the ride and apparently a big piece of the puzzle. "Would anyone like to tell me where we are headed?" he finally asked. They had passed the on-ramp to I-95 heading north, so he was confused. "I thought we were headed to one of the Carolinas."

"We are," Shanice told him. "We have one more surprise for you."

"I suppose I have to wait and see what that is as well, right?" he asked, trying to contain his emotions.

Mac turned the corner, went down a block, and then turned the corner again into a gated community. She punched in the four digit code needed to enter the guest entrance. She went three more blocks before turning down another street and pulling into the driveway of a home that had a large fenced-in backyard.

"We are here to pick up the border collie you spoke about in your paper," Shanice told him.

"Do you remember the name you gave him?" Mac asked.

"I remember his name," John replied, "It's Oreo."

Shanice didn't realize that John had spent much of the night reviewing his paper. Of course, he knew the dog's name. John never had a dog growing up, but he had read that they are very therapeutic. He felt a dog would be beneficial on the plantation.

At this point in the trip, John had not discussed anything about the people working for him. He would soon be learning that Henry was actually finishing up his final year of veterinary school. One day he would take over his father's practice. Getting experience with large farm animals would only help his resume. He had been around dogs his entire life, so he would welcome this new little guy.

MacKenzie jumped out of the vehicle and walked to the back to open the tailgate when a man in his mid-thirties walked out the front door with a young pup. "This is Oreo," Mac explained when John got out of the vehicle. The cutest black pup with a white line down the center of his nose ran up to them, wagging his tail.

The man extended his hand to John as MacKenzie introduced him. "This is our dog trainer, Mike Littleton," she said. "Fortunately for us, Mike has already done all the hard work."

"Oh, yeah?" John questioned.

"Yes, I have," Mike affirmed.

Mike proceeded to show them all the things the three month old pup had learned. Both Shanice and Adeline even stepped out of the vehicle to watch the dog demonstrate his skills. Oreo could sit, stand, halt, and fetch on command. Mike also explained that Oreo could corral animals too. Border collies love to do that job naturally, so it would be easy for him to corral cows, horses, goats, and sheep. "I probably don't even need to tell you that Oreo is completely potty trained as well."

He then exchanged his phone number with John and provided all the instructions for feeding, along with a six month supply of food. "When you are done with this food, it will be time to phase him into dog food that is better suited for his age. Don't hesitate to call if you need anything at all," he had told the group. Mike placed the crate that he had carried outside into the truck while John loaded the dog's supplies.

The pup barked for a few minutes as they pulled away, then settled down into his cozy blanket in the crate. They were two hours into the trip before he made another sound.

"Our estimated time of arrival is six o'clock," Mac piped in.

"Well, we might need to make an extra stop or two for this old lady, but we'll get there," Shanice chuckled.

After finishing his second maple iced glazed donut with creme filling, John was ready to tackle the questions and directions needed for this mission. He knew what his long term goals had been when he originally wrote his paper, but he wasn't sure if Adeline DeWitt or his grandmother were still following his idea. He had questions for them, but he also thought he could provide some answers as well.

"Before we get started," John began, "I really need to know who I am dealing with now. My paper was originally an ideology that I thought could change the social and economical face of African-Americans living in America today. Changing that face would also change politics as we know them. It was never meant as a trial and error experiment because I never thought it could be implemented. It takes power and money to deliver a plan of this magnitude. I have neither." John then turned to Mrs. DeWitt, looking her straight in the eyes and said, "Adeline DeWitt, who are you?"

"Have you ever heard anyone say that there is power behind power?"

Adeline replied. "There are ghosts that pull the shoestrings, tighten the waistband, and determine the course of history."

"I think I understand what you are saying," John answered.

"I'm glad you do, John, because I don't," Mac replied.

"I am that ghost. I am the unheard power that lies beneath the political framework that we call Washington. I control the Board of Directors of the Federal Reserve. I control the puppets that the American people call politicians."

"You mean that Alan Greenspan, Ben Bernanke, and Janet Yellen were determined by your influence?" John asked. "Even though they cross political divides, you hand selected them?"

"Yes, John," she answered.

"So, why have you lived across the street from us all my life, looking like an old grumpy woman? Then one day, which just happens to be a few days after South Florida is hit with one of its worst hurricanes ever recorded, you appear dressed in your best outfit, make-up brilliantly applied, and looking twenty years younger?" John continued.

"Shanice and I had planned to tell you what had taken place at that time. You became very angry with us, and we knew that you needed time to process the little information that you had at that moment. The timing of the hurricane was bad for us, but it actually was perfect for you because you were able to launch a new business which greatly benefited the lower income families in our neighborhood," Adeline explained.

"You were going to tell me back then the truth about the missing people?" John asked.

"Yes, we were, Junior," Shanice replied. "I sensed at that very moment that our timing was off. You were too occupied with relief efforts. We were trying to adhere to a schedule, but the storm changed the course of that plan."

"Mrs. DeWitt," John continued, "You were never an old lady living across the street from me? Were you?"

"No. I needed a place to work that was not conspicuous, and I needed a disguise that would convince all neighbors that a little old woman lived there. It worked, didn't it?" she said.

"You fooled me," John told her.

"She fooled me too," Mac told John.

"Let me try to connect the dots," John said. "What is your birth name? It can't be Adeline DeWitt?"

"You're right. It's not. It was Sherline Thompson."

"That's my gramma's." John started to speak, but stopped in mid-sentence. "No," he said.

"Yes," both women said in unison.

"Adeline is my sister, John," Shanice explained. "We are actually fraternal twins. Unlike me, Adeline has a brilliant mind. She could speak seven languages by the time she was eight. She scored a perfect score on every test that she has ever taken. She completed college at the age of sixteen, and the government recruited her to the Central Intelligence Agency by the time she was eighteen. When she reached the age of twenty-seven she was basically running the country."

"No one would have believed me or any government official that I was the perfect protege child," Adeline said. "I was black. I was a kid. And, I was a girl. I came up with a plan to be disguised forever. And, it worked. I continue to work behind the scenes for the government, directing all crucial decisions, and guiding this country. I have multiple names and multiple disguises. The one problem that remains is the great divide between African-Americans and white Americans. Your paper addressed the issues head on, and you are the only person who has devised a plan that would break down barriers and help bridge this gap. They need to have faith in themselves," Adeline shared.

"Why are you just now telling me that you are my gramma's twin?" John asked. "Do my parents even know?"

"I had never intended to tell any of you," Adeline continued to explain. "When I read your paper, I realized that your brain functions in a manner similar to mine. I don't want you to get involved in politics, but I want to help groom you as the next leader of our family. You can do wonders beyond your wildest dreams. I couldn't stand by without helping a cause that is greater than any of us."

"Son," Shanice said to her grandson, "it was complicated."

"What about you, MacKenzie? Did you know about Adeline DeWitt?"

"I found out prior to the hurricane. Adeline is my grandmother.

"That makes us cousins then?" John asked. "And, if we are cousins, that makes Warren Laikin my uncle," John continued.

"No. Warren is technically your second cousin," Shanice corrected.

"Isn't that cool?" MacKenzie piped in. "I had no idea until my dad and Adeline talked with me after the hurricane.

"You didn't know she was your grandmother?" John questioned "How can that be?"

"Well," Mac started to say, "I've always known her as my grandmother, not as Adeline. She's Gramma Laikin to me. She never disguised herself when she came over, so when I saw Mrs. DeWitt out and about in her yard, it never occurred to me that she could be my grandmother because she doesn't even look like the grandmother I'm used to seeing. She's my dad's mother."

"Wait!" John said loudly. "Did you adopt Warren or is he a rare example of a white child being born to a black mother?" he asked Adeline directly. "You know, it actually happens more frequently than people ever used to believe. But, I suppose back in your day without computers and the internet, it was considered a very strange possibility."

"I was too busy with my career to marry. My life was way too complicated to have children of my own. But, I saw how happy Shanice was when she and your grandpa raised your daddy. I wanted to be like her, but didn't want the responsibility of being a wife and mother. I foolishly made a decision one evening, which I'm not proud of, but I slept with a friend of a politician. I was young and lonely, even though I had everything going for me with my career. I still kept it hush-hush when I found out that I was pregnant. Your gramma is the only person I told initially. I took a chance and had the child at home, preventing any media frenzy. Of course, I had no idea I would give birth to a white baby. Thank goodness I had that child at home. Only your gramma, a midwife, and nurse were present."

"You should have seen the shock on my face when I saw that baby," Shanice said. "My tongue was so tied that I couldn't even spit the words out of my mouth when I handed Adeline her baby."

"Your gramma helped me quite a bit, and I hired a full-time, live-in nanny who helped raise him. Warren's nanny was a marine who retired from active duty early, due to an injury. He was perfect for Warren."

"Did anyone, including the father, even know that he was your child?" John inquired.

"During his grade school years, parents knew he was my child, although they didn't see me often. I went by the name of Adriana Laikin at the time. Most people thought I had adopted him, but I never corrected any of them. They wouldn't have believed me anyway. I never told his father."

"This is all so crazy," John stated. "And, my parents don't know any of this?" he asked again.

"They know the young me, Adriana Laikin. They don't know that Shanice and I are sisters. Your papa and Warren actually played with one another growing up. They didn't see each other for quite a few years when I sent Warren off to a military academy in Indiana. He then joined the airforce where he served for eight years. When he was done serving, Warren decided to become a builder and developer.

"That explains why he has taken such an interest in me," John replied. "You don't want to take after your father in the family business?" John asked MacKenzie.

"Not really, John," she answered. "I'd rather be involved in marketing and public relations. That's more up my alley anyway," she said. "I'm a people-person, not a builder," she said.

"So, you didn't know about my paper until your gramma dragged you into it?" John inquired.

"No. You hinted around earlier, but I didn't put two and two together until now. I helped in the strategic planning to make sure everyone got to their destination, but I had no idea you were behind this idea," Mac confirmed.

"If you followed my outline perfectly, we must be at the place where I reveal to everyone the fruits of their labor, correct?" John asked.

"That's correct," Shanice agreed. "Let's finish what we started."

"I'm not sure eight hours will be enough time," John said as they continued their trek up the highway. "I have a lot of questions, and I imagine I have a lot of answers too."

CHAPTER TWENTY-ONE

Six babies were born on the plantation beginning with the birth of twins, Jamal and Jeremiah, to Henry and Tonya. Once the couple found out that they were expecting twins, Henry agreed to marry Tonya, but it wasn't until Tonya proposed to him.

Tonya spent most of her days resting in the last trimester of her pregnancy. She was jealous that Regi had proposed to Nia, and although she wasn't thrilled about getting married or raising children on a plantation, she realized that Henry was her best option. She knew that it would be very difficult raising two kids alone. He was kind and considerate, and he didn't treat her as a subordinate, like he did the others. He treated her with respect after that night when she wandered over to the barn without permission.

It had been a perfect day. The humidity was gone, and it wasn't too hot. Charlie had stood in front of the big oak tree behind the house with the old barn in the background to wed both Henry and Tonya and Regi and Nia. There were no fancy dresses, no church bells, nor musical preludes. It was the most simplistic wedding ever. The ladies wore sundresses, and the men wore their nicest shorts and polo shirts. Tonya and Nia both picked white and yellow wildflowers just minutes before the wedding from a nearby field to hold as their bouquets.

"Tonya, do you take Henry to be your lawful wedded husband?" Charlie had asked. He repeated the same phrase to each of them, reversing the names and titles. When they all said their "I do," he pronounced them husband and wife. Henry had secured legal marriage licenses for each of them too.

Henry had one surprise for the entire group after the wedding. He had planned a wedding reception. Earlier that morning, he had picked up a small wedding cake for each of them and catered food. Only Amber and Leah knew about the reception. They were responsible for the kitchen that day. He couldn't have a reception without champagne and alcohol. It was the first beer most of them had in months. Only Regi had been allowed to join Henry for a beer before. It was a day of celebration, and everyone forgot for a moment that they were on the plantation.

Nia gave birth to Christian Taylor, whom they called Chris. When their baby was only a few months old, Nia found out that she was expecting again. They were excited to learn that a little girl would be joining their family. Without the help of the internet, they narrowed their names down to a few and eventually chose the name Cristiana. They planned to call her Tiana. She was born just on time, at eleven fifty-five in the evening, to officially share her birthdate with her paternal grandmother. Regi was absolutely thrilled.

Alvaro wasn't ready to be a father, but he continued to flirt with Amber while she was dating Daniel. She was gullible and liked the added attention.

"Alvaro," Daniel had said one day, "I'm really tired of you flirting with my girl."

"What are you going to do about it?" he said in return. "It's not like there are a lot of other available chicks around here."

"It doesn't matter. She's off limits," Daniel had warned.

Three days later, when they had been standing in line to get their lunches, Alvaro winked at Amber who had been helping in the kitchen that day. Daniel saw the wink.

"I warned you," he said. With a single blow, lunches went flying as the other men scattered to get out of the way. A brawl had broken out between the two men. Daniel was taller and stronger than Alvaro, but Alvaro had quick punches and was faster than Daniel.

Alavaro received a lash over his right eye, and the juice began to cloud his vision, but not before Daniel's tastebuds were tarnished with a bitter, gruesome taste from a bloody nose. The young men didn't stop fighting. It was a real live boxing ring smack in the middle of the table-less dining room.

Some of the men were cheering for Alavaro, while others hollered for Daniel. The two-minute brawl seemed to last thirty minutes. The men danced in circles around the floor trying to land a hook. When enough time had passed and both men seemed to have exhausted their tanks,

Charlie shouted, "One more round."

Neither were up for it, but neither wanted to bow down. They were fighting over a woman, believing that they actually had control over who she might date. How wrong they would be.

With all his remaining strength, Daniel tucked his head low and ran into Alvaro, slamming him into the wall to end the fight. Alvaro slid down the wall, breathless. Without looking back, Daniel slowly walked out of the room to clean up. Amber then came out from hiding behind the island and handed a wet washcloth to Alvaro who sat motionless on the floor, leaning against the wall. She tossed the cloth down onto his hand and walked away. She refused to speak to either of them for over a week.

Eventually Amber returned to Daniel, believing he was the father of her child. When Isabella Roberts was born, she had a striking resemblance to Alvaro. The bickering and arguing between the two men began again.

"There's one simple remedy," Henry had told all of them. "You are having a DNA test done."

Amber had agreed that was the only way to find out the actual father. A full week passed before Henry returned with results, and Daniel continued to treat baby Isabella as though he was her father.

Everyone had just finished eating dinner when Henry walked into the mess hall. "I need to see Amber, Daniel, and Alvaro outside now," he had said. "Everyone else remained inside." Once they were all outside, EZ snuck down the hallway to be the scout. Everyone else waited patiently to hear the news.

"Whatever happens, Daniel and Alvaro, please don't fight again," Amber had begged. "One of you will be disappointed."

"Matter of fact, not only will you two act like mature adults," Henry had warned, "I better not hear of any bickering and arguing from either of you. If I do, you won't see your pillow at night. I'll work you harder than any oxen or cattle. This is a truce. Do you understand men?"

They both nodded their heads in agreement. Henry had already relocated Daniel to a different work assignment to keep the two men apart from each other during the day. There was very little time that they would be together now.

Henry had no idea whose name he would find on the test when he opened up the envelope. He looked it over, and then said as gently as possible, "Isabella's father is Alvaro."

"No," Daniel had screamed at the top of his lungs, making the entire plantation aware of his defeat. He was angry and mad. He sulked for several days before he confronted Amber again.

"I'm not going back to Alvaro," she had told him. "He's funny and good-looking and all, but he's too immature for me."

"So, you want me to raise his kid?" Daniel had asked. "Cuz, it's not happening. He can raise his own damn kid. I don't want anything to do with her. You better change her name to Hernandez on her birth certificate."

"I don't need to change it," Amber had told Daniel.

"Why not?" he had inquired.

"Because I never put a last name down on it," she said. That made Daniel even more upset that she knew there was a likely possibility that Alvaro was the father.

"We're done," Daniel had told her.

It would be four more weeks before they spoke again. The plantation didn't stop because of their quarrel either. It was continuing to grow. Life went on despite their struggles.

Three months after Isabella came into the world, Josephina Goldman was born. She was another spitting image of her father. She raised the newborn count to six. Leah cared for the babies when their mommas were working. No one understood why she didn't get pregnant since the other three women had in a very short period of time.

Nobody knew Leah was married. Henry protected her marriage vows, allowing her only to see the men during meal times. He knew some of the other men were jealous that they could not be with a woman. He did not want to jeopardize her for the sake of some crazy hormones. She was so exhausted on most nights that she fell asleep with ease. A message had been sent to Joe, explaining that Leah was in rehabilitation and that she hoped to return someday. He needed to be patient with her. That was the hope Joe needed to stand by and wait.

With the addition of married couples and newborn babies, sleeping quarters changed as well. Regi and Nia moved into the barn, taking a guest room at the far end near the north stable. By now everyone knew the nursery was housed there, but none of them knew that the stables led into modern furnished bedrooms. That was a secret they were all forced to keep. They all thought the rooms were old windowless stables.

Leah also received a room to keep her away from the men. She was beautiful, and all the single men wished she was available. When she first arrived, she flirted right back until she received a warning that she had better stop. She was never given a reason, but she feared her collar would be activated if she didn't cooperate.

With the addition of new arrivals, several people were given additional responsibilities. Charlie was responsible for the entire tobacco crop. The first acre had been so successful that one hundred additional acres were added the following year. He was also in charge of the men's barracks, the new housing unit, which was built to accommodate the new employees. Charlie found himself so busy with his responsibilities that he rarely had to do manual labor any longer

He had a new system in place to cultivate the large crop too.

Regi was overseeing the cotton production and the newcomers who were working in his fields. The original crew had been given less strenuous jobs as they added more strippers and farm equipment to the plantation.

Jaheem was given the responsibility of caring for their livestock and chickens and for weeding the vegetable garden. He had learned at an early age that certain herbs and spices were essential to the strengthening of one's immune system. He had always had an interest in being a horticulturist, but made some wrong decisions in high school that led him away from pursuing a college education.

In his down hours, he helped drive a stripper or other farm equipment as needed. He also developed a health-kick routine with a few of the newcomers. Pushups, situps, and sprints became a regular part of his day. He wanted to stay fit, as if working on the plantation was not hard enough work by itself.

Amber was the only one who did not appreciate her role. She was conflicted with too many emotional setbacks that weakened her judgment. She was still dealing with the aftermath of her daughter's father being someone different than she had hoped. They added twelve bunks to the ladies' bedroom in the house, making it cramped. Even though she was one of the younger women on the plantation, she was in charge of assigning chores to the women each week. With added bodies, the house wasn't staying as clean as it had been before. She didn't like this job because it took her away from her daughter when she would otherwise have some free time.

Despite the challenges and changes that had emerged over the twenty-four months that Amber had been present, she was still fighting the urge to find companionship in the wrong places. After her blow up with both Alvaro and Daniel, she sought out Davon. It probably would have worked except she had a short temper. The lack of sleep and hormonal imbalance from breast feeding her baby was enough to light her fuse.

To this day, no one really knows exactly what Davon did or said to deserve her treatment, but everyone saw it one night when she slapped him across the face and stormed out of the kitchen.

That opened the gates for both Alvaro and Daniel to move back in. When she found out that she was pregnant for the second time, she decided she would name her boy Anthony even though she did not know the child's last name. Henry wasn't happy with her because he would need to issue a paternity test for the second time. If they had only stuck to the original plan of determining parents in advance, this problem would not have been an issue. Henry never heard who stopped it. All he knew was that the original plan for the impregnation barn had been altered.

After Henry heard the news, he called the three men and Amber to a private meeting. "Listen," he said to them all, "Nursing mothers and pregnant women can be very emotional. It's a part of life. That doesn't mean you should take advantage of one when the opportunity arises. You guys were all foolish. And, Amber, I won't even tell you what I would like to say. Again, you all have created conflict that should not be. There won't be any fights this time around. No arguing. No throwing punches. When the baby is born and the father is identified, I will call all of you together again to announce the daddy. In the meantime, stay out of trouble."

"Are you kidding us, Amber?" Daniel had said. "You told me that you weren't seeing anyone else."

"I wasn't, but then…" she started to say.

"Don't say anything, Amber," Alvaro piped in. "It doesn't matter what you say now. It's too late."

The three guys walked away shaking their heads. Davon kicked a pebble on the dirt road, and Daniel reached down to pick one up to throw at a nearby tree. They were angry and in disbelief that Amber was pregnant again. More shockingly, they were surprised to hear that they were all candidates for fatherhood.

"Well, I hope it's not my kid," Alvaro said, surprising the other two.

"Are you kidding?" Daniel asked.

"I mean, I love my daughter, but she takes away from my free time. I don't have time to shoot basketballs anymore or even chew on a piece of grass around the firepit. When I'm not working, sleeping, or eating, I'm with her."

"Yeah, duh, you idiot," Daniel responded back. "That's what parenting is all about. You didn't think about that before you pulled that twig of yours out of your pants?" Daniel said.

Daniel should have stepped away before he made that comment. Before he had time to duck, he was lying on the dirt road with an eye that would be swollen shut in no time. He could feel the blood rush to that part of his head while he grabbed his face in pain. He just stayed there on the ground while Alvaro continued to walk. He didn't even try to fight back. Davon stopped to make sure Daniel wasn't badly hurt.

"Oh, that's going to be a bruiser. There's no hiding it from Henry either," Davon assured.

"Shut up, Davon."

Daniel laid there for a few minutes longer. The fight had ended before it really got started. Daniel got in the last word, but Alvaro got in both the first and last punch. After Alvaro was further down the road, Daniel stood up and brushed the dirt and pebbles off his knees and hands.

"Was it worth it?" Davon asked, after Daniel rose to his feet.

"Oh yeah," Daniel said. He then went straight to the kitchen to get a bag of peas for his swollen eye.

That evening, as everyone was eating goulash and garlic bread, Henry stopped by to call a meeting for the original thirteen. He gave instructions to all of the new hirees and sent them off to tend cattle, collect chicken eggs, and do some other chores. He chose two women to head to the nursery where they would be watching the children for the evening.

"What's up boss?" EZ had asked after everyone else had left.

"We have some visitors on the plantation tonight," Henry stated.

"What?" both Ralph and Davon asked simultaneously.

"They will be here shortly," Henry continued. "I have six folding lawn chairs that I want you guys to set up on one side of the firepit for our guests. They are in the back of my truck. Move the logs that you use as seats out of the way so that you can set the chairs up on one side. Place the logs that you move to the other side of the pit so everyone can have a seat. They will be here in forty minutes. Ladies, please make sure your babies are fed if they need it. As you know, Lottie and Shanta will be watching all the kids while you are here."

"Is there anything else we need to know or do right now?" Charlie asked.

"No, that's all for now," he said.

The men grabbed the new folding chairs from Henry's truck before Henry pulled away, kicking up dust from the road as he headed off. As the ladies walked back to the nursery to make sure their children were fed and diapers changed, they questioned one another.

"What do you think this is all about?" Nia asked Tonya.

"I don't know," Tonya said. "Henry didn't tell me a thing. I didn't even know that we had company. Did you hear anyone come into the house?"

"Not a sound," Nia replied.

"I didn't either," Tonya noted.

"Maybe they aren't staying here," Nia suggested. "It's not like there are a lot of extra rooms out here."

"Maybe not, but there doesn't appear to be any hotels in the vicinity either," Tonya noted.

After the men rearranged the firepit seating, they each chose a log. They were trying to figure out who would be here and why. After all this time, they would be having guests. They speculated and speculated trying to figure out the meaning of this meeting. The longer they waited the more nervous they became. EZ and Alvaro ran over to the water hose to splash some water in their faces. They needed to calm down and cool down.

After thirty minutes had passed, the women appeared from one of the stable doors, walking through the tall grass down towards the fire pit. Just as the women arrived, they could see in the distance a puff of dust lift in the air, followed by a second cloud of dust.

"They're here," EZ said, stating the obvious.

Henry's truck was leading the way as a black SUV followed behind.

Daniel walked back into the kitchen to throw his third bag of peas into the freezer. He then placed his baseball cap low on his forehead before walking out to the fire pit, hoping that the shadow of his hat would hide his swollen eye.

CHAPTER TWENTY-TWO

MacKenzie pulled the Cadillac beside Henry's truck. Everyone got out of the SUV to stretch their legs while they waited for Henry to talk to the group first. Mac and John went straight to the back to let Oreo out of his pen. His tail was wagging faster than the wings of a hummingbird when Mac put a dish of water down beside him. After taking a long drink, the pup wandered over to the tree to mark his spot and then came straight back to them.

It was hard to ignore the comments being made from afar. Some of them were excited to see a puppy, while others were upset to see John. Adeline conveyed a few last minute thoughts after John and Mac discussed whether or not they should put a leash on Oreo.

"He'll listen to me," Mac remarked. She walked away and then called for him. "Oreo, come."

The pup obeyed immediately and came to the feet of MacKenzie.

"Okay. Maybe you should bring the leash with you in case one of the guys scares him."

Once they were done discussing the dog, Adeline spoke up. "Be careful," she said, "Some might be aggressive or say a few heated things to us, but we need to keep our cool. Never should you fuel a fire with more fuel when you are trying to suffocate it."

"I understand," John affirmed. "We need to stick to the game plan."

The men's anxiety levels had risen to an all-time high. They were ready to meet their enemy, or so they thought. "Everyone sit down now," Henry told the group. "I want you to know that your collars still work, and I can activate them in a split second. Don't make me do it. We have two rules right now," he continued. "Stay seated at all times and keep your mouths shut for now."

He then turned around and walked towards the group, showcasing the gun that he packed that day. He wanted everyone to know that he meant business, in case anyone decided to retaliate before listening.

The visitors walked up to the chairs and quietly sat down. Oreo sat down next to MacKenzie. Murmurs could be heard as they approached the group. Charlie kept shaking his head. EZ was jumping out of his seat, trying to stay seated was difficult for him.

Henry walked over to his folding chair and stood by it as he began the introductions. "This is Shanice Bramble, John Bramble, MacKenzie Laikin, and Adeline DeWitt," Henry announced, as he pointed each of them out. "I'm sure you know some of them."

EZ screeched unintentionally when he heard Mrs. DeWitt's name. "That's Mrs. DeWitt?" EZ said quietly to Alvaro, who was sitting next to him. Both guys dropped their jaws staring at her. *This couldn't be the same Mrs. DeWitt who lived in their neighborhood,* they both thought. She looked much younger than they remembered.

Charlie was squirming on his log. You could almost see the steam coming from his head too, but he did everything in his power to remain quiet.

Henry sat down next to Adeline in the empty chair when John stood up. He walked behind his chair, using it as a podium of sorts.

"Before I get started," he said, "let me remind you that I don't want anyone talking or asking questions now. I am going to talk for a very long time, and you are going to listen with your mouths closed. If I hear one single word come out of any of your mouths, unless I directly ask you a question, you will feel your collar at work."

John thought he would spook everyone into believing that he was a mean person and would trigger a collar, if needed. It took a lot of concentration for John to remain stern. He didn't want anyone attacking them physically out of rage and anger. In his heart, he knew they had every right to be angry and project that anger physically.

"By the way, this is Oreo," John said as he reached down to pet the top of the puppy's head. "He will likely become one of your best friends. He's planning to stay. As you can imagine, we didn't come simply to drop off this dog. We are here today to provide an explanation and answer the many questions you have been wondering for months. I'm going to start at the very beginning. I hope it makes sense once you hear the entire story. Please be patient with us."

John took a swallow of water from his water bottle before he continued. "Quite a few years ago, I wrote a paper in high school about an ideology I envisioned. I never turned that paper in, but these ladies here with me, my gramma and neighbor, managed to get their hands on it. I had no idea at the time they had even read it. They were intrigued by my concepts and wholeheartedly believed my plan was flawless. The motion began to place my concepts into action. I'm sure many of you are surprised that I would even consider writing a paper that involved the kidnapping of each of you, let alone get away with it. Everyone, except Leah, was identified in my paper. Each of you did something specifically to me or my family to hurt or offend us. It wasn't just about what you did or say, though. It was about the lifestyle that you had chosen to live."

Charlie nodded his head in agreement. He and Ryan had discussed a long time ago that the Brambles might be the ones behind this charade. He knew he offended his sister and was guilty of John's accusation. Several others shook their heads too. Davon knew exactly what he had done to his former best friend. Amber looked at Daniel with guilt written all over her face too.

John continued, meticulously speaking with intent and clarity, not leaving out any detail. "You see, I was tired of your behavior and that of the African-American population living in America today. It has been a continuous game of blame, laziness, and self-pity. I learned from my grandmother, Shanice, and my parents at a very young age that I need to be held accountable for my words and actions. Only I am to be blamed for my behavior. As I looked around my neighborhood, school, community, and even family, all I could see was hatred in this world. Everyone thought someone else was to be blamed for their misfortunes, attitudes, and recklessness."

John stared at everyone sitting in front of him, trying to read their reactions and emotions right then. He could tell that the older men understood completely what he was saying. Some of the younger guys still needed to hear the truth. John continued to talk, hoping he was making sense.

"You are all here for a specific reason. You have all been too busy cheating your way through life. You think you are better than others. You believe that you can go through life blaming others for everything.

This is the twenty-first century. It's not the eighteen hundreds. Yet, you believe that the color of your skin makes you a victim. You believe you're a victim of your great, great, great grandparents' generation."

"Oh, how foolish of you all. No black American had the right to vote back in the early days of this great nation. No black American could sit at a restaurant of his or her choice. No black American could attend a school with white Americans. No black American could use the same restroom as a white American. No black American could own his own business or property. Black Americans had self, family, and music. They were some of the hardest workers alive."

"They built this nation with their own sweat, blood, and tears. Yet, young blood came along and diminished their history, their efforts to unite as one nation, and their courage to free their names from African-American, Blacks, and Negros to simply Americans. We should be proud of our heritage, embrace it, and learn from it. Being an American isn't based on the color of your skin. Many African-Americans believe it justifies breaking the laws and encouraging a divide so that there is a distinction between White Americans, Black Americans, African-Americans, Asian Americans, and any other title you want to place before the word American."

John stopped for a moment and took a swallow of water from his Hialeah Flats water bottle again. "Let me continue. Do you understand that today is a different era? African-Americans can vote, own any business they desire, shop anywhere they desire, and they can eat wherever they please. There is no segregation any longer. Yet, you still want the world to pity you. You still want the world to give you special rights. You still want the world to feel sorry for you because of something that happened over a hundred years ago. You think it's fun to play the race card. Why not get an innocent person in trouble because you can?"

"The problem with this mindset is simple. When a generation of people deny the truth and start believing in these kinds of lies, then they become the scoffer, unable to distinguish between right and wrong. They become the enabler of their worst enemies." John paused for a moment before repeating himself. "They become the enabler of their worst enemies...themselves."

John then walked closer to the men, looking at them face to face.

He walked in front of each person as he continued to talk. "You act as if your rights have been infringed upon. You act as if you are living in bondage. Those who came before you would run from you if they saw the way you treat others. Some are lazy and ignorant, believing freebies are actually free. You are liars and thieves. Some of you continue to live in poverty because you don't want to work hard. Some like to destroy the lives of others by being drug dealers. Some of you like to walk around town with your pants down to your knees thinking everyone wants to see your ass. Some just think they are better than others so they go around disrespecting people. You have all offended me and those I love. More importantly, some have offended yourselves because you have denied yourselves the freedom to live independent of others. You choose to be a burden on our society or cause a burden on others."

After directing specific comments to certain individuals, John stepped back towards his chair again. "To teach each of you a lesson, I devised a plan to make it feel like you were truly living in the Antebellum South era. I wanted you to experience real oppression, so that you could better understand what slavery meant. My hope was that you wouldn't walk away from this place, where my ideology could develop, with the same attitudes you previously held. I was hoping you would all feel guilty of your wrongdoings and that you would repent of your bad habits."

"I would have hoped by now that each of you had time to reflect on your lives; the successes you may have had and the disappointments you have caused or played a part in. I'm sure none of you considered yourself a model American. I'm sure some have still kept secrets hidden deep in their souls, not wishing the others to hear about their selfish ways. Let me remind you that I'm not perfect either. I have made plenty of mistakes in my lifetime. The difference is that I have owned up to my mistakes and still am owning up to them now."

"In my paper, I allowed the first person who realized his error or sought forgiveness an opportunity to leave. Ryan Smith did exactly that. You weren't even the people he had truly offended, but he apologized anyway for his behavior and actions. He believed all black men, African-Americans included, were low-class jerks. He hated them all, until you guys taught him a lesson or two."

The men broke their silence momentarily by clapping for Ryan. Then Regi, who was used to being in front of the classroom, raised his hand slightly.

"I'm a long way from being finished, but I'll answer just one question, Mr. Taylor," John said.

"How do we know that Ryan is safe when we have no proof?" Regi responded.

"You have to trust us. The words you will hear today from all of us are true," John answered. "In time, you will see proof that the words we are sharing now are valid."

Regi was probably hoping for a more concrete response, but he accepted it for now. He had no other choice.

John continued again, "This is the United States of America, one nation under God. It's not two nations divided. You need to respect all people. You must stop blaming people for the color of their skin, for their beliefs, for their choice of political views, or for their desire to better themselves. You need to accept all people for being unique and different, regardless of their nationality or race."

"Blame yourself first when something goes wrong. See what changes you can make to correct a problem. Find a way to better yourself properly and legally. Don't cheat, steal, or lie. Don't destroy individuals and families by selling drugs to deepen your pocket. Own up to your behavior so that you can be respected by all. Most importantly, realize that every single action you take will impact somebody else. Sometimes the impact will be small, but sometimes it will be enormous. Sometimes it can save a life. And, in some cases it might end a life. No action ever stops with just one person. It's the Cause & Effect Theory. I learned that in Mr. Taylor's class." John pointed to Regi and everyone chuckled. Regi smiled.

John briefly sat down on his chair. No one dared speak. For the first time ever, they all agreed on something. They all knew they needed to remain silent. They all knew that John was in the driver's seat right now. He was calling the shots. He was demanding their attention. And, he was demanding their respect. John took another sip of water and stood up again and walked behind his chair.

"Let me further explain some details." John knew his next topic of speech would warrant some reaction from each of the men. He was bracing for the worst. "Every single person here signed a contract, agreeing to be here," John said.

Charlie, Ralph, Frank, and Davon all opened their mouths at the same time, and said, "No, I didn't." EZ, using his own choice of vocabulary, said, "Uh, ah." Daniel and Amber knew they had signed contracts, and Leah was in agreement as well.

Henry immediately stood to his feet. "Men, please don't force me to use restraint. Please keep your thoughts to yourselves."

"Yes, everyone signed a contract," Mrs. DeWitt said, "I kindly made a copy of the original for each one of you to have, if you don't believe us. The problem is that not a single one read his or her contract."

Charlie sat across from John biting his tongue. He kept shaking his head back and forth to indicate that he did not sign a contract.

"Let me take my Uncle Charlie, for example," John said, as he pointed to Charlie.

"You probably all know by now that my uncle owns multiple car dealerships in Jacksonville and throughout northern Florida. He signs contracts daily as people buy cars from him and sell cars to him. When I was young, he kept a model car on his bookshelf at home. Every time my family went to visit him, he would say to me, 'Junior, I'm going to own one of these cars someday.' It was a 1962 Rolls Royce Ghost." John looked back at Charlie again. "Isn't this true?" he asked.

"Yes. That's what I used to tell John," he said.

"Do you now own a 1962 Rolls Royce Ghost?" John asked.

"Yes. I do," Charlie admitted.

"Charlie wanted that car for a very long time," John told the group. "He also wanted another expensive and rare car, a 1967 Aston Martin DBS Superleggera. Not too long before Charlie arrived here, he purchased that car too. Isn't that right, Charlie?"

Charlie again admitted to the entire group that John was correct. "Yes, I purchased both of those cars together at the same time from the same person."

John chuckled. "You see, Charlie signed a contract to purchase those two vehicles as a package deal. He thought he was getting a steal on the purchase because the money exchanged was a lot less than the market value of both of those cars. Isn't that right, Charlie?"

"Yes, John. That's true again," he said.

John continued to share the story. "On the second to last page of his purchase agreement was a clause, stating that he would accept a reduced rate if he lived and worked on this plantation for a minimum of two years."

Adeline immediately rose from her chair when John was finished presenting this piece of information. She handed a copy of Charlie's contract to him, with the clause highlighted in yellow ink for his review. The copied contract was even notarized by Charlie's own notary, verifying its authenticity.

"What?" Charlie quickly asked, when he saw the highlighted area.

"Not only did Charlie not read his contract, but he failed to listen to the seller who told him that he would need to agree to an additional clause to purchase the vehicles. In his attempt to secure the deal, he failed to read the contract even when he was warned that the purchase was not simply of monetary value," John explained. "Did the seller not ask you twice if you read the clause?" John then asked his uncle.

"Yes," Charlie said, as he let out a sigh of frustration. "I told him I read the clause, but I never did. I was so busy making plans to drive my new car that I never read it."

"Shit," EZ said.

Everyone else sat silently as they tried to recall any contracts that they had previously signed. With soft moans and various facial expressions, the visitors could tell that everyone, except Frank and Ralph, remembered signing some type of contract.

"I don't believe any of this bullshit," Ralph then said, as he stood up from his log. Before Henry had time to reach for his cell phone, Adeline had already zapped Ralph's collar with a low voltage zap. She had been holding her cell phone in her hand the entire time. Ralph stumbled and immediately sat down grabbing his collar. "Damn it. These collars do work," he said.

"Ralph, that is your last warning," Henry told him. "It's getting late, and we are going to let you ponder everything you have heard so far. We will meet again here in the morning," Henry continued to tell the original plantation workers. "There is a lot more information to share, some very important information that you won't want to miss. It's too late to share everything now. Let me warn you that we will not tolerate any misbehavior or retaliation. If you choose to believe us, then you will find it rewarding in the end. Ladies, you can be dismissed now to take care of your babies before it gets much later. Men, I'm giving you one hour to have lights out. Everyone meet back here after breakfast."

John, Shanice, Adeline, and MacKenzie walked back to the SUV without saying a word. John helped little Oreo back into his crate. With car doors closed, they felt confident to speak freely.

"I think that went fairly well," Mac said, as she drove off down the road.

"They definitely have some things to think about tonight," Shanice agreed.

They drove back to Henry's place where Mac drove the Cadillac into a hidden bunker and garage. There was an entirely hidden part of the barn that only Henry had seen before. It housed seven bedrooms with private baths, a kitchen, great room, computer room, laundry room, and a workout room. The team would sleep well tonight.

Before heading to bed, Adeline checked all the monitors again to see that everyone was in their proper places. She then locked the doors from the outside of each of the residences, preventing anyone from walking outside during the night. She didn't trust that Ralph wouldn't try to lead a revolt. Both she and Henry were on high alert for any movement from any of them.

Ralph didn't have the energy to fight at the moment. He fell asleep with blood dried in streaks down his neck. No one even tried to locate their guests or find out where they were staying for the evening. They fell asleep like they had so many nights before, wondering what would happen next.

CHAPTER TWENTY-THREE

The next morning both Ralph and Frank woke up before anyone else for the first time ever. Their typical mornings were lazier than the others. They needed a jolt of caffeine which they had not had since they arrived. Henry did not trust anyone with hot coffee when they first came. He didn't want anyone to throw it on him or anyone else in frustration or anger. He never heard anyone complain that they were missing their morning coffee, so he never gave it to them. It saved him a lot of money.

"Hey, EZ," Ralph said, "It's time for that pretty face of yours to wake up."

Frank stood next to Ralph and laughed. "How do you like being awakened in the morning?" Frank sneered.

"Leave me alone, ya f**n mothas," EZ responded with his head buried in his pillow. EZ had made an effort to clean up his language, but being asleep the men had caught him off guard.

"Not today," Ralph said. "We have to be up and ready to learn our fate. Don't you want to hear about your future?" he teased.

"I was already dreamin about it, and bro ya woke me before I could finish it," he said.

"Yeah, yeah, yeah," Frank said.

"I was. I was sleeping with this hot chick and just as she turned over to look at me, you idiots woke me up. I couldn't even see who she was," EZ complained.

By now, all the men had awakened from the talking and laughing. They all heard EZ's recollection of his dream. The entire room broke out in laughter.

"That's right, kid," Ralph continued. "You only get it in a dream."

The room laughed again. EZ then jumped out of bed, pulled his shorts and t-shirt on and ran down to the shower house. He didn't like it when people laughed at him. He was much better at giving out a joke, than receiving one.

An hour later, all the men and women gathered by the firepit for a second time. Henry had given orders to the remaining crew and sent them off into the fields, the nursery, or kitchen. They wouldn't be back until lunch.

When the SUV rolled up for the second time, the men knew what to expect. The three ladies and John stepped out of the truck and came back to the seats they had sat on the night before. Adeline still held a folder in her hand with everyone's contracts, along with her cell phone which was already in 'ready' mode.

Oreo walked around each of the logs, sniffing with curiosity. He stopped on occasion to allow someone to pet him. Shanice noticed immediately that the puppy brought smiles to the men's faces. That was a good sign. Upon command, he immediately returned to Mac when she called for him.

"Good morning, everyone," John said, as he began the meeting. "I am going to continue in the same spot we left off last night. I'm sure you all had time to think about the contracts that you had signed."

Ralph and Frank still shook their heads, indicating that they did not recall any contracts, but they were willing to listen.

"Ralph," John said. "Let's start with you since you don't seem to believe you signed any contract."

"But, I didn't," he said

"That little secret of yours needs to come out of the closet now," John said

"I was a real jerk." Ralph looked around at everyone because he was too embarrassed to admit his wrongdoing. "Do these guys have to know?" he asked.

"No, but I want them to know the truth," John admitted, as he pointed to the scars on his leg. "You know the rest of the story. I'm sure you aren't proud of yourself for what you did to me, are you?"

"I gave John those scars," Ralph told everyone. "I had been drinking, like I had every night, and I wasn't in a good mood when I showed up for work one morning. I took a nail gun to John."

"Man, you are crazy," EZ said, forgetting that he needed to keep his thoughts to himself. Fortunately, no one objected to his comments because they all agreed with him.

"What's the rest of the story?" John asked.

"I knew I would get fired from my job, so I took off and drove around a while before hitting up the local bar until I couldn't drink any more. I took off down the road. I don't even remember where I was headed or anything else about that night, until I found myself submerged under water in my car. Some man dove in and rescued me from the car. I likely would have drowned, but I was too drunk to even know it at the time. I must have passed out because I don't remember much else."

"That man was me," Henry proceeded to tell Ralph and the group.

"Seriously?" Ralph asked.

"Yes," Henry responded.

"I've been here all this time, and you never told me?" he inquired.

"Why should I?" Henry asked back. "It wouldn't have mattered until now. I was following you, and you didn't even know it. You were driving like a mad man. I couldn't believe that you drove yourself right off the bridge. Any other time of day, the whole world would have seen you, but for ten minutes or so there wasn't a car around. Even after I rescued you, there were still no cars around. That's when I realized that I could leave with you without getting noticed, I took the chance."

"I kept you out of jail. The next day when you were sober, I gave you the option of turning yourself into law enforcement where they could prove you were drinking and driving. Instead, you chose to work on this plantation for a couple of years."

Adeline gave Ralph a copy of his signed contract.

"Dang, I don't remember any of this," Ralph concluded. "Thanks for keeping me outta the slammer. Yeah, this place definitely beats a lock up."

Henry just nodded.

"All along I thought I had been kidnapped.

"Frank, you're next," John continued. "How many jobs have you held in the past thirty years?

"I don't know," Frank said. "Who keeps track of something like that?

"We do," John said, without hesitating. "You have held eighty-three jobs in the last thirty years. That means, on average, you have held almost three jobs every year. Your average length of stay at any one job has been eighteen days. That means you work only around fifty days each year. There have been ten thousand nine hundred and fifty days in the past thirty years. You have been employed one thousand four hundred and ninety-four days. That is only thirteen percent of your time which equals just over four years of employment out of the past thirty years. You have been dependent upon government assistance the rest of the time. Do you honestly believe the government has the obligation to pay for your living expenses?"

"I kept trying, but those jobs were all shitty," Frank responded.

"You mean to say that working as a tile installer, roofer, security officer, maintenance repairman, welder, landscaper, retail clerk, gas station attendant, and dry cleaner were all horrible jobs?" John asked. "Not to mention nine other suitable positions that you held at one point in time."

"I didn't like them," Frank admitted.

"That gave you the right to take your frustrations out on my father and a number of other people you used to work alongside?" John asked.

"No, but I was always tired of everyone else getting the promotions or better jobs," he explained.

"Why didn't you change, then?" John continued. "Only you can make yourself better, not anyone else." Frank did not respond, so John asked another question. "Do you know how many days you have been working here on the plantation?"

"No. I gave up counting a long time ago," he said. "I can't even tell you what day of the week it is."

"You have been working on the plantation for seven hundred and seventy-nine days now. Congratulations. That is the most days you have ever worked for anyone."

"I never considered that before," Frank said. "I should feel proud of myself, I suppose."

"Actually, you should feel proud of yourself. You have learned a lot of skills that you never knew you had either," John agreed. "Do you like being a responsible adult?"

Frank had never considered any of these questions before. John could tell that Frank was trying to process the questions and provide solid answers to all them. "I like seeing the progress that we have made over the last two years. It has been interesting to see how cotton is produced."

"Do you like being homeless?" John then asked. "Or, do you prefer having a roof over your head?"

Again, Frank did not answer John's questions immediately. He was embarrassed and proud all at the same time. He was getting emotional because he knew that the plantation had been the best thing for him. "As you know, you were homeless for many of those years, and just three months prior to coming to the plantation you signed a contract for housing," John reminded him.

Adeline rose from her seat again and handed Frank his contract. "Warren Laikin, MacKenzie's father, offered you a place to stay in one of his rental properties with conditions of employment. He gave you three months to find permanent employment and if you didn't, you agreed to work for him in an undisclosed location. This plantation is that undisclosed location," Adeline said.

"I thought this was just my rental agreement," Frank insisted.

"Now, Frank, you honestly believed that Mr. Laikin would let you stay in an apartment without the ability to pay your rent? He explained to you that your work history was weak and that you had a history of failing to pay your rent. You were living on the streets at the time he gave you the apartment, correct?" John continued.

"Yes, but I didn't know that this was a legal contract."

"Frank, we all know that no one can lease an apartment without a legal contract. You are making excuses. This is exactly what I am talking about. You need to take responsibility for your actions. Man up to the fact that you failed to provide for yourself," John bluntly told the older man.

Shanice had been silent so far. "I am just curious," she said. "Do you like having food to eat everyday, not having to prepare it yourself? Do you like being here?"

"When you showed up last night, I still thought this was a game, a bunch of BS," Frank admitted. "Now, I am beginning to understand your point. I definitely like a bed that is mine, and it's nice coming in from the fields with meals that are already prepared. I can honestly say that I like being here."

"I'm glad to hear that Frank," John said. "Once you hear the rest of the story, you might even like it more. For those of you who are not convinced yet, you will have an opportunity to change your mind too."

"Who wants to be next? How about your stories, Regi and Nia?" John asked.

"John," Regi began, "Our story is simple. Instead of you standing in front of us, embarrassing us, I would like to speak first, if that's okay with you."

"Sure, go right ahead," John told his former teacher.

"I fell in love with your best friend. Everyone knows that you and Nia were close in high school. I actually think she went out with me because you didn't ask her yourself. I wasn't planning on dating a student, but it happened. As you know, I lost my job over it. Although I hated being here at first, I actually think this was the best thing for me and, well, my family too. It has taught me some lessons, and it has forced me to be a responsible young man. I have learned that basketball isn't everything in life. Although I miss it immensely, I found a way to improvise. With the additional recruits on the plantation now, I am also teaching which I love to do. It's a different kind of teaching, definitely more hands on, but it's still teaching."

Nia then looked straight into John's eyes, making sure she didn't look around at anyone else. She knew she owed him an apology. "I'm sorry, John," she began. "Regi is right. I really wanted to date you, but you never asked me out. I refused to go to Niceville with him. I actually broke it off because I was hoping you and I could get together and start seeing each other."

"That doesn't explain all the other guys you dated," John rebutted.

"I was trying to make you jealous, but that didn't work either," she said.

"Why didn't you say anything to me?" John asked. "I thought you only wanted to be friends."

"I guess I was young and afraid," Nia told him. "I was afraid of rejection. You seemed to have your act together. You were strong and unpersuaded by outside influences. I was weaker than you. I'm sorry. I hope you will forgive both of us," she said.

"I'm not there yet," John admitted. "But, I'll get there. You really messed with my feelings, and honestly I had compressed them until now when I saw you two together."

Shanice knew this was a moment that was too personal now for John. She needed to intervene before he broke down. "Nia," she began to say, "I think you." Shanice couldn't even finish her sentence.

The sound of an engine roared so loud just above them that it interrupted her thought. It seemed that the noise came out of nowhere.

Before they could continue the conversations, they saw a small plane blow by overhead. It was much closer than it needed to be, but it got everyone's attention. No one had seen a plane low in the sky the entire time they had been on the plantation. The only planes any of them had seen were thirty thousand feet in the sky.

"Look, it's going to land," EZ shouted. "It's circling."

All the guys stood up and went around the south side of the house to get a better look.

Henry shouted loud for everyone to hear, "Don't do anything stupid, and don't run towards the plane when it lands."

MacKenzie laughed. "You would think they had never seen a plane before," she told Shanice. Mac then reached down to pick up Oreo. "Last thing we need is for Oreo to be spooked by all this noise."

The runway was the long flat road that the men had walked along every day going back and forth from the fields. It was flat, straight, and went on for miles. All the other workers from the fields stopped what they were doing to watch the plane land. It circled a third time to make sure everyone would stay out of its way. About a mile or so down the road it touched down, and the pilot gradually slowed the plane down to taxi it up to the house.

"What's going on?" John asked his gramma.

"Oh, just another surprise," she said.

Once the plane came to a complete stop, the pilot, Ryan, and a third passenger took off their headphones and opened the door to get out.

"No way," EZ shouted. "It's Ryan."

No one could believe it. Ryan jumped down out of the plane and was standing thirty yards in front of them without a collar.

"Hey man, it's great to see you," Jaheem said, as he gave Ryan a hug.

"What brought your *ss back here?" EZ asked jokingly. "Man, it's good'a see ya. I neva knew I even mist ya."

One by one they each gave a greeting to Ryan. They were thrilled to see him.

"You guys might not believe me, but I miss this place. Mostly, I miss all of you," Ryan told his friends.

"Yeah, you're right, we don't believe that bullsh*," EZ said, joking around again.

"Look at you. No collar!" Jaheem exclaimed.

"Yeah, that's right. I guess that apology I gave all of you earned me some brownie points," Ryan said.

"Why didn't you tell the cops about this place?" Ralph then asked.

"I'm not sure that conversation would have gone over well for me," Ryan admitted. "What was I to say, 'I was kidnapped, but I don't know who did it, nor do I know where I was taken. And, by the way, I'm home now. I haven't been harmed?' They wouldn't have believed me because I had no proof."

"Couldn't you have shown them your collar?" Davon asked.

"What collar?" Ryan asked. "I didn't have one when I returned."

"Let's all go and sit back down," Henry ordered the crew. "And guys, grab three more chairs out of my truck, please," he told them. Davon, Jaheem, and EZ hustled over to the truck to get additional chairs.

While Ryan was chatting with his buddies, Warren and Jonathan spoke with Adeline, Shanice, and John to see how things were going. John was as surprised to see Warren as the men were to see Ryan.

"We haven't told them the punch line yet," Adeline told her son.

"John is simply revealing the flaws that brought them here. He still has more to go. Surprisingly, the men are taking it much better than I anticipated."

"That's good," Warren agreed. "They are going to be shocked when they hear the rest of the news."

"We will see how upset they are with us when that happens," Shanice chuckled.

Once the group was sitting back down and Warren had secured the plane to prevent anyone from trying to sneak off in it, he joined everyone else.

"This is Warren Laikin and Jonathan Trieger," Henry told everyone. "Warren is MacKenzie's father, and Mr. Trieger is legal counsel."

Charlie, who had been quiet the entire day, politely raised his finger to suggest that he had a question to ask.

"Do you have a question or concern, Charlie?" John asked.

"Yes, matter of fact, I do," he said, as politely as possible.

"I'm just wondering why you guys think it's important that you have legal counsel with you today?" he asked sincerely. "It can't be cheap to fly in the professional," he stated.

"Of course, leave it up to my uncle to inquire," John said.

"Thanks for asking. We thought some of you might think that you have grounds to send us to jail for taking you against your known will or keeping you here against your will. Let me tell you right now that you won't get anywhere in court with your accusations. We will explain further after we conclude with each individual account."

"I know some straightforward shooters too, John," his uncle snarled, believing that his attorneys could win a case.

"I don't think you will be needing any of them," Jonathan replied.

John stood up again, like he had before, once everyone was sitting back down in their seats. "Regi," he said, "Does this answer your question about Ryan?"

"I hope so because if it doesn't, then he has a twin that he never told any of us about," Regi replied.

"I'm sure you still have more questions that need answers, and we will get to those. This is a process that takes time," John told Regi.

He then began to recap for Jaheem the numerous times that Jaheem had bullied him throughout elementary and middle school because he was physically strong in stature. Jaheem towered over everyone at that age, and for the most part he still towers over people today.

He had punched John in the face for stealing a basketball during recess while playing basketball in fifth grade, he picked on him in gym class for years, and teased him for not being as athletic as himself. John also reminded him that he was the decoy that lured John away from his locker for a few seconds when he turned his back, allowing weed to be planted in it by EZ.

"I remember the day vividly when you laughed at me when the dog sniffed my locker. That cost me straight A's for my entire high school career. If I had not been suspended for something that I had not done, I never would have received zeros on the days I wasn't allowed to attend school. I know it wasn't a big deal to you and certainly less of a deal for your ex-buddy EZ. It was a huge deal to me though. "

"I forgot all about that," Jaheem responded. "Dang. I guess I wasn't so cool back then, was I?"

"Yeah, not so," John agreed.

"Elijah Jackson. Does anyone ever call you Elijah anymore?" John asked the neighborhood boy who grew up down the street from him. "Come stand next to me." John pointed to the empty grass where he was standing.

EZ stood up and walked over to John, who proceeded to put his arm around the shoulders of the boy he had known his entire life. "Elijah and I have known each other our entire lives. By now you would think that we would get along, laugh about stupid things we did as boys, or reminisce about the trouble we caused. Not with this guy. Elijah was trouble from day one. Weren't you, Elijah?"

EZ shifted his weight. He was uneasy standing next to John who was solid in structure, unlike EZ who was skinny and lean. John took his arm down from EZ's shoulders. "Yeah, I've heard that before."

"Elijah wasn't about doing friendly pranks to people he liked. He was a mean kid. As much as his mom tried to avoid the stories about his uncle, Elijah's cousins talked. He heard story after story, thinking he was invincible too. How old were you when you decided you wanted to be like your Uncle Kenny? For those of you who might not have heard about Uncle Kenny, he was Kenneth Cole as in "Boodie," the gangster, rapper, mobster, who blew up Carol City."

EZ scratched his lower jaw line and opened his mouth as if he was going to yawn. "I think I was four or five. I thought being a bad *ss would be cool."

"How did that pan out for you, Elijah?"John continued.

"I waz in troubla alot, but it wazn't so bad," he claimed.

"Would you prefer to be in prison right now?"

"I haven't done anythin bad enough to land me there," EZ claimed.

"I could press charges against you for destroying my property with that loud, boisterous car of yours," Mrs. DeWitt stated.

"I'm friends with several judges in our county, and the surveillance footage I have of you spray painting the roof of Hialeah Flats to the words of your uncle's song would land you in a cell," Mr. Laikin said. "It's all the evidence I need. Plus, John retrieved one can of spray paint that you failed to pick up once it rolled off the roof. It has your fingerprints on it."

Shanice didn't want to be left out of this conversation. She had always gotten along with Elijah, but knew he had continued to make bad choices throughout high school and beyond. She decided to speak.

"I have always liked your spunk, Elijah. You were the friendliest kid in the neighborhood. You had confidence that so many young people don't have. However, the older you got, the worse the stories about you became. We could press charges as well, Elijah. The note attached to that big rock you threw through our front window is in your handwriting. I actually have the notes of each of my students who wrote a letter to me on the last day of each school year. I found yours when we were digging through the boxes after the hurricane. Your handwriting did not improve much, and it certainly was you who sent that rock flying."

The men and ladies looked around at one another puzzled when Shanice mentioned a hurricane. They had not been privy to any information or news for over two years.

Adeline handed her sister a note that she pulled from the folder. *"Dear Mrs. Bramble,"* Shanice read. *"Thank you for being my third grade teacher. I'll see you around. Elijah."* Adeline also pulled out the note attached to the rock. They were practically identical in appearance.

"Wow! My handwriting didn't improve, did it?" he said, implicating himself.

"I'm sure we could convince Davon to testify against you too for selling drugs," John stated.

"That stuff wasn't so bad," EZ admitted. "Nobody got hurt. All of that coulda landed me in the block?"

Jonathan Trieger decided he would voice his legal opinion. "All of those incidents could land you in prison. If each sentence were to run consecutively, that means one after another, you could be facing up to twenty years behind bars. And, how do you even know that no one got hurt. Drugs destroy lives and families. It sounds to me, from what I have heard, that they almost destroyed you too."

"Shit. I had no idea."

"Well, fortunately for you, none of us have pressed charges. We were hoping to see improvement in your behavior once you spent some time here," John continued.

"My gramma just mentioned a hurricane. The reason it has taken us so long to come visit you is for that reason. Hurricane Cecelia touched down just north of Biscayne Bay and ripped through Carol City. It destroyed much of South Florida, but the people there are resilient. They came together and rebuilt much of it. I personally took on our neighborhood. The homes most of you left don't look the same any more. The entire city and Miami has changed. We can share about it at a later time."

"A hurricane ripped up Carol City?" EZ asked.

"Yes," Shaniced answered. "We will talk more about it later, Elijah. We still have a lot to discuss now"

"I will add just one thing," Mac stated. "I personally spent my spare time tracking down all of your family members. They are all alive and well. We will pass out photos to each of you of your family members which you can keep that were taken within the last two months."

"Now, back to you Elijah. I'm sure you are wondering what contract you signed," John said, putting his arm around EZ again.

"Yeah, you're right bout that," he said.

"You made a deal with your new stepfather. Do you remember the deal?" John asked.

"I promised him that I wouldn't burn the house down when they were gone on their honeymoon," EZ teased.

"You don't remember the contract that you signed?" John then asked.

"I rememba signin somethin, but I was high most of the time back then," EZ shared. "I don't have a clue what it was. There's no way on earth I would of been readin anythin back then."

Mrs. DeWitt handed EZ's contract to John, who then held it up so they both could see the highlighted area. "You made a verbal agreement with your stepdad, Jarod Jarvis, which you did not keep. He told us that when he and your mom came looking for you. Verbal contracts can still be valid in court, but that's not the one I am referencing now. The contract you signed was between you and Mrs. DeWitt herself."

EZ stepped away from John so he could get a better look at Adeline DeWitt. "This can't be da same Mrs. DeWitt from our hood," EZ said, looking at her again. "I mean she ain't look the same to me up close now. No offense, but ya look a lot younga and nica now."

"No offense taken," Adline responded with a smile. She wasn't about to say anything else to him about her appearance.

"Let's take a look at this contract, Elijah," John said, as Elijah walked back over to John so he could read the contract silently as John read it out loud. "It says right here," John said, as he pointed to the high-lighted area for EZ.

"I accept the terms that you, Adeline DeWitt, will not press charges against me for destroying your personal property, which I have seen the evidence which proves that I am guilty of such a charge, if I agree to the following:

1. I will not destroy anyone else's property in this neighborhood.

2. I will not drive around this neighborhood blasting my music from my car so loud that the houses shake.

3. I will not hold any parties at my house without the consent of my mother.

4. If I fail to observe any of the above conditions, I agree to spend time at an unknown rehabilitation site, located outside of Florida."

"Is this your signature?" John asked EZ. "You signed it using your full name, Elijah Jackson."

EZ looked at the signature, and he confessed that it was his signature.

"Let's review this contract. We already know that you did not keep your word for the first agreement. You just admitted that you threw a rock through our front window," John said.

He then asked Alvaro a question. "Be honest with me Alvaro. Have you ever heard EZ roaming the streets from a mile away?"

"We all know the answer to that question. Absolutely!"

"So, it looks like you did not keep your word for the second request. Can anyone give me any insight into the third part? I already know that you were not given permission to hold a party while your mother was away on her honeymoon. She told me that herself."

Both Henry and MacKenzie began to laugh. "You probably heard the noise of his party down at your place," Mac told John. "Henry and I showed up around midnight on the Friday evening after his mother and her husband left town. There must have been thirty or more people there. EZ didn't even know we were there. It was really easy to lure him away."

"You lured me away?" EZ asked MacKenzie.

"Actually it was Henry. You were so wasted that you actually handed Henry your car keys. He drove your car the entire way back, and I stayed back in Miami."

"But, you put a gun to my head," EZ told everyone.

"That's where you are wrong again," Henry chuckled. "We actually arrived on the plantation in the early evening, but you were still out of it. You must have been using LSD because you crashed. After everyone went to bed, I drove you over here in your car and carried you to your cot."

"You're tellin me that no one put a gun to ma head?" EZ asked.

"Nope. I think you must have made up that lie because you didn't know how you got here. You felt you needed some excuse to tell the others," Henry said.

Shanice then tried to explain the effects of lying continuously. "Lying is contagious," she said. "When people lie frequently, they begin to believe the lies are real. In their minds, the lies become their reality. In this case, you probably told the story enough to everyone here, that you began to believe your own story. No one ever questioned you about the story, so it became true to you so to speak."

EZ didn't even have a response to Henry or Shanice. He knew he had been lying to people for years. This time he was caught. "How's my momma, and that Jarod dude?" he asked.

"They are both doing well," John affirmed. "They really like their new place too. My team built them a new home at the same address your old home stood because most of it was destroyed during the storm."

"They didn't get hurt or anything, did they?" EZ inquired.

"No. Your mother told me that she and Jarod went to his brother's house. I think it's someplace in Arkansas, if I remember correctly," Shanice told Elijah.

"Do they miss me?"

"Yes and no," John began. "Your mom misses you, but she doesn't miss the drugs and trouble you always seemed to find."

"I actually spoke with her recently," Mrs. DeWitt spoke up. "I told her that a friend of mine heard that you might be out of state in one of the Carolinas. I would let her know if I learned anything more. I wasn't going to share anything else until after I came to see for myself."

"So, we are in the Carolinas?" EZ asked.

"Six of you owe me money," Charlie declared. Everyone laughed.

"Only if we are in North Carolina," EZ said.

"If we are in South Carolina, then six of you owe me the money," Regi confirmed.

Jaheem thought he would continue the conversation for just a brief moment longer. "If we are not in Georgia, then two of you owe me some loot," he added.

"Okay everyone," John said. "It sounds like you did some betting with each other. We are in South Carolina, if it makes you feel any better. You can figure out who owes who money over lunch. For now, we will take a break and reconvene in two hours."

CHAPTER TWENTY-FOUR

While the field workers were heading back to the house from their duties and the group dismissed for lunch, Warren called John aside. Before anyone realized it, dust covered the road as John and Warren took off in Warren's plane.

"I thought you would want to see all of our property," Warren told John.

"This is amazing," John told Warren. "You know, I have never been in a plane before."

"Oh, I know. I had wanted to take you up many times, but our situation was more complex than I realized. I had to be patient with my mother because too much was at stake."

"I get it now," John said, as he listened intently through his headphones. "I can't believe you are my uncle."

"I'm not. Technically, I am your second cousin. Your dad and I are cousins."

"Does he even know that?"

"He should. We used to play together as kids. To be honest, I don't know. Who knows what he was told when we were young. I didn't see him for years after I joined the service."

"Well, we need to make sure my parents are told the truth. There may have been some misinformation communicated years ago."

"Deal," Warren agreed.

Shortly after take-off, John spotted a large white house east of the barn. "What's that place?" he asked.

"That's the old plantation house that belonged to the original plantation owners. The house has been boarded up for years. It needs some updating and remodeling. A project for later," Warren explained.

John was in awe of the beauty of the land. Even though it was miles of flat, undeveloped land, the rich soil was beckoning cultivation. It looked amazing from his bird's eye view.

"Do we own anything beyond the river, way over there?" John asked while he pointed in the distance.

Warren maneuvered the plane and headed in the direction that John had pointed to hover along the river. "The original group owns the property that where the house physically stands. The old barn which is a front to our house, is on my property. The new barn is actually across the street and that property belongs to you. All the acres that have been farmed to date belong to the group. In essence, you own a thousand acres west of the road. The group owns the land north and south of their house, and I own ten thousand acres east of their house, all the way to this river. The white house you spotted a few minutes ago is located on my property."

"Let me get this straight," John responded. "I own everything west until the property reaches that old state road. Just beyond that is the highway. The river boards not only east where your property ends, but also north. And, the south border of all the joint properties belongs to the national park. It's dense, and there will never be any building there."

"That's as simple as it gets, John."

"Legally, they have all been working on their own property and living in their jointly owned home. Is that right?"

"Yes," Warren confirmed. He flew low for a long time so John could get a better look at the property. When they were done going from north to south and west to east, Warren then headed southeast towards the ocean. "We have some time to kill before we need to get back, so I thought I would let you see the ocean from this view."

"It's really that blue?" John asked as they neared a wildlife preserve.

"It is," Warren said. "Most of this land here is protected. It's not ideal for building, but has spectacular wildlife. We can head up towards Myrtle Beach so you can see what it looks like from the air too."

As they headed up the coast, the land was rather barren. Slowly small dots became larger, and John could see buildings. "All those tall buildings along the coast are hotels and condos," Warren told his partner. "A lot of people like Myrtle Beach, but I honestly prefer South Beach and countless other Florida beaches better."

"I just never expected to be flying today. Can we take my parents up sometime?" John inquired.

"Absolutely, there are going to be some changes in this family now. We still have to keep things hush-hush for Adeline's sake, but life is only going to get better for all of us."

"Thanks, Warren. I can't thank you enough for believing in me and teaching me that diligence and hard work pays off."

"It's been a privilege to be involved in your life," Warren said, as he turned and smiled at John. "We are about twenty-five minutes from landing. Your grandmother plans to meet us at the plane with our lunches. I told them we would be gone for most of the lunch break."

"I've enjoyed every minute of this flight," John explained. "I should get my pilot license. Would I be able to use your plane on occasion?"

"We probably could work something out, but first you must log the necessary hours before we can even discuss that. I'll get you hooked up with my buddy, Jarod Reynolds, who is a flight instructor."

"Thanks."

"You are welcome."

The twenty-five minutes flew by quickly and before John realized it, Warren was giving him instructions about their landing. John noticed some dark clouds to the west, and before he had a chance to ask Warren about them, wind caught the plane and jerked him to the side, hitting his shoulder against the door.

"Sorry about that, John. We hit a thermal, like an air pocket." Warren then showed John the small burst of clouds on the radar. "We will likely get another jolt or two before we land. You can hold on to that grab bar, if you like."

John reached up and held the bar just as the plane jumped in the air again. They could see the runway straight ahead. It was the long dirt road that they had observed for miles when Warren showed him the property just an hour earlier.

"I'm feeling a little queasy now," John remarked, as they hit another turbulence.

"We'll be on the ground in just a minute. You should be fine."

"This reminds me of the way I felt when I got that concussion in high school."

"Good news for you then," Warren began to chuckle. "You'll be feeling fine in fifteen minutes, unlike a concussion that can last a week or so."

John's stomach wasn't feeling well at all.

"Look straight ahead at the runway. Hang on just a minute longer," Warren insisted.

John did everything he could to stop the upheaval of his insides. "I need fresh air."

"Just a few more seconds while I bring the plane to a stop. You'll be fine soon."

Warren was right. Fifteen minutes later, John sat in the back seat of Warren's Cadillac drinking a lemon-lime soft drink, munching on chocolate chip cookies, and eating a turkey croissant sandwich. He was feeling much better now.

The windshield wipers were flapping back and forth as they waited for the storm to pass. They had landed just in time to beat the storm. Warren had told Henry that the meeting would be delayed thirty minutes as they waited for the weather to clear. As Warren and John sat in the SUV eating their lunch, Henry walked the ladies over to the new barn before the downpour to give them a tour of the facilities.

"This is so cool," MacKenzie said as she began petting one of the dairy cows. Most of the cows were still out in the field, but three had wandered back into the barn. Oreo, who was following Mac around, was sniffing, afraid to get too close to the cow.

"We like to keep this a free-roaming farm," Henry explained. "Since we only need to produce enough milk for those living here, we treat these cows like pets, rather than stock."

"Does that mean this big gal has a name?" MacKenzie asked.

"You bet she does," Henry said, laughing. "This is Aunt Clara."

"She's an aunt?" Shanice asked.

"See that cow over by the fence?" Henry said, as he pointed to a lonely cow munching on something as the rain fell down on her. "She was paired up with that bull which is over there in the pen." Henry then pointed to a large pen that housed a bull. "We call it 'naturally serviced' in the industry," Henry explained. "The momma cow had one calf, making this cow an aunt. She's next in line to see Mr. Bruce, the bull. It will be a couple weeks before that takes place."

After learning a few lessons about farm animals, the ladies walked back over to the large barn door and waited just a few more minutes for the rain to stop. Five minutes later, the skies opened up to a sun-filled glow that quickly dried out the wetness left by the rain.

Henry gathered those who were inside the house. It was time for the meeting to reconvene. They were all anxious to hear the remaining stories to see what fate would bring.

"**A**lvaro," John called out when they gathered again. "I was just reminded of the feeling I had years ago when I went flying just now. On our way back down, just before the storm hit, the plane hit a few pockets of turbulent air. My stomach jumped, and my head started to spin a bit. It felt the same as when you gave me a swirly back in high school. Do you remember?"

"We were just messin' with you," Alvaro responded.

"Well, Alvaro, when you and your friends pick someone up, hold him upside down so his head is jammed into a locker room toilet, flush it, and walk away laughing, that is assault. I ended up with a concussion. I sat there for about a half an hour, waiting for everyone to leave the building. I was embarrassed, and I felt like crap. I missed going out for pizza with my friends after the game, and I felt sick all weekend. I didn't do anything for several days. Matter of fact, Johnny, the older janitor who worked at the school, found me there. He was walking his final rounds of the building checking to make sure no one was left inside before leaving for the evening when he found me. He didn't say a word. He knew exactly what had happened. He had seen it before. He stood me up and put his arm around my shoulder and walked me to his car. He then gave me a ride home."

"Man, I didn't know," Alvaro protested.

"What?" John asked. "You didn't know you gave me a swirly. You bullied me. You harassed me, and then you walked away. You didn't know that you did those things?"

"That's not what I meant. I didn't know that I hurt you."

"Oh, so that makes bullying, harassing, and mocking someone okay if you don't physically hurt them?"

Alvaro was silent.

"I didn't think so," John continued. "I know that I am not the only one that you did that too either. There were several other band members that you chose to pick on. It was always you and your posse of bullies."

Alvaro looked down towards the dirt. He couldn't make eye contact with John.

"You were the star tight end of the football team. That full ride scholarship to the University of Florida has done some good, hasn't it? You were given a free ticket. Not only a ticket out of the hood, but a chance to get a college education. You know that is something that many athletes work their entire lives to achieve, but never receive."

Alvaro remained silent, and John continued to talk.

"Now, I don't like to start rumors, but MacKenzie told me that even your mother didn't like the person you were becoming in college."

"That's what she told me directly," MacKenzie acknowledged. "Is that true, Alvaro?"

Alvaro finally looked up. "Yes, it's true. I was partying, drinking, and using drugs while I was on the football team. It started with just a little bit of marijuana after the games. It took away the pain from all the tackles. And, then I was offered growth hormones, thinking it would be beneficial. Rarely did anyone get drug tested. I didn't think it would happen to me. It did, and I was suspended, as you probably all heard. I told my mom that I didn't care about the scholarship or school. I was there just to play football. If they were going to take that away from me, then there was no point in going to school at all. She begged me to get my act together, but I wouldn't listen."

"How do you feel now?" John probed.

"I've been drug free the entire time I've been here. I don't miss the weird feeling in my head at all." Alvaro then flexed his arm. "As you can see, I really don't even need the growth hormones. Manual labor does the trick too."

All the guys sitting around Alvaro chuckled. They all knew that they were physically stronger now than they were when they first arrived. John waited a moment, hoping Alvaro would apologize.

"Do you have anything else to say?"

"What?" Alvaro asked.

"Haven't you learned by now that apologies are always necessary when someone wrongs another person? It doesn't matter if time stands still or if years have passed. When a person does something to harm someone physically, verbally, or emotionally, then it is his or her responsibility to apologize. It's that simple. So, when you are ready and have thought long and hard about your actions, then we can talk."

Alvaro still sat motionless, looking towards the ground. He apparently had never been taught that valuable lesson in life. "Look at me, Alvaro," John finally said. "You can't bully your way through life like you have done in the past. Your physical skills and strengths should be used as an asset to help you, not hinder you. My guess is that you have hurt a lot of others along the way that I don't even know about. This is a good time to search your soul to see how you can change. Strength may make you a stronger person, but it doesn't make you a better person."

Alvaro still didn't say a word as he looked down into the mud puddle inches from his foot. John gave him time to talk, but when he remained silent John continued on to the next person. He wasn't going to wait all day for Alvaro's apology.

"Tonya," John said, "we all know that you signed a contract to work. What happened along the way?"

"I was offered a job, and I didn't do anything wrong, so I thought." Tonya then looked towards Nia, but Nia at that moment refused to look at Tonya. "I actually became good friends with Nia. We hung out socially, but in the end I was deceptive. I was using her. I thought I would profit from her mistake. I just needed to trick her into coming with me. I tried multiple times to get her into my car, but my plan always backfired. Eventually, I pretended to pull a gun on her when we were at the beach. It was my last attempt to get her to come before I left town for my new job. I was never supposed to get emotionally attached and become friends. I'm really sorry, Nia."

Nia wasn't sure what to stay at that moment, but Regi had a question. "Do you mean to tell us that you were being paid to bring Nia here?"

"Not exactly. I had been offered this job as a cook, but at the last minute I was getting cold feet. I asked Nia to come with me, but she turned me down."

MacKenzie had been quiet for most of the discussions, but now was her turn to talk. "Just like I hired Henry, I decided to hire a cook as well. After talking with Adeline and Shanice, we decided it would be better to get a younger person who could better handle the dynamics of living in a remote area easier."

"What most of you don't know about Tonya is that she had taken some culinary classes, but decided to drop out of culinary school. She thought this job would give her a chance to see if she really liked being in a kitchen all day. Unlike a high-pressured restaurant position, this would be laid back and entail a variety of meals for breakfast, lunch, and dinner. She knew that she would have to wear the collar like everyone else. I didn't give her details about it, but said that was one of the conditions. I even gave it to her the morning she met Nia at the beach. She told me that she was going to be in the area, so I met her for the delivery. That would save me a trip up here, and Henry would know she's the one when she arrived wearing the collar. She was planning to visit her parents first and then meet up with Henry. Why don't you tell everyone what happened next?" Mac suggested.

"At the last moment, I decided that I could trick everyone and send Nia in my place. I would get a direct deposit to my bank account each week. Henry didn't know who I was so if Nia showed up, he wouldn't know the difference. It would be easy money in my pocket. As far as I knew, MacKenzie would never be coming here. So, when Nia left to use the restroom, I quickly paid a college guy sitting at the bar one hundred dollars for a roofie. I figured he or his friends would have one since they had been flirting with girls at the beach all day. I took a gamble, and it worked. I then pretended to have a gun and forced Nia to walk to my car. I had slipped the roofie into some bottled water which she drank on the way to my car. Once she was there, she fell asleep, and I slipped the collar around her neck."

"You have got to be kidding me?" Nia bursted out. She started to charge towards Tonya, but Jaheem stood in her way and grabbed her before she could reach Tonya.

"Nia, stop," Regi begged as he and Jaheem walked her away from the circle. "We can stand in the back for now and listen to everything else being told."

"I hate you," Nia yelled. She knew that Tonya had betrayed her, but this was the first time she had heard some of these details.

MacKenzie then spoke up again. "The problem was that I had been eying Nia all day and happened to notice Tonya practically pushing Nia towards her car. I ran down the beach to where they were headed, but was too late in arriving. I didn't realize that Nia had been given a roofie until I saw her collapse into the back seat and watched Tonya put the collar around Nia's neck. I couldn't follow her because I didn't have my car. It was still several blocks down the street."

"Our plan to get Nia up here was different than this one," Henry inserted. "When Mac and I realized what was happening, we went along with her scheme just so she would think she was off the hook with her contract. It was actually quite clever, but we weren't going to let her walk away without righting her wrong either. When we learned that Tonya lied to her parents and told them that she was coming here when her real plan was only to check on Nia and leave, we interfered with her plans. We picked her up at a gas station and decided to give her a taste of her own medicine."

"It's amazing that you two even get along," John stated after he heard this story for the first time.

"We didn't," Nia told everyone. "I didn't speak with her for the first two months we were here. The only thing that kept us civil were these dang collars. We feared them more than we feared ourselves."

"I'm sorry," Tonya told Nia.

"Well, now that I know the truth, it's going to be a long time before I can ever trust you again."

There was a moment of awkward silence.

"We'll be talking more about those collars soon, but first I want to finish our briefings," John told the group.

John walked up to Daniel and lifted the brim of his hat. "Interesting," he said quietly, then he pulled Daniel's hat back down to cover his eye.

John was eager to hear that story, but decided it was best to wait and ask about it privately. "Both Daniel and Amber know why they are here." They both nodded their heads in unison agreeing with John's statement. From what they had observed over the past two days, they knew their story would be airing their dirty laundry soon. In light of what everyone else had done, they were hopeful that they wouldn't be judged too severely by anyone.

John continued. "Both Daniel and Amber signed contracts to be here. I'm trying to figure out a nice way to say this," he continued. He then stopped talking briefly as thoughts rolled around in his head. "It was the Monday following our senior prom at school. All of you who went to high school with us will recall that Monday well. I became the laughing stock at the high school, not because I had done something wrong. It was because I chose not to participate in a non-scholastic activity after prom. Both Daniel and Amber engaged in that activity and mocked me later."

Alvaro and EZ chuckled. They remembered vividly that day and what they had said to promote the mocking among the students.

"Just for the record, I am glad I did not participate. From what I hear, Amber, you still haven't learned any lessons in loyalty, commitment, or faithfulness. I am glad I chose to walk away."

Although she was a bit embarrassed, Amber was still immature and foolish. Instead of accepting the situation for what it was, she had to speak her mind. "At least I've been having fun the past two years," she responded.

Of course, John was much smarter and wiser than Amber. "Yes, I am sure you have been having fun," he commented. "I bet both of your children's fathers are pleased."

Nobody said a word after that harsh statement. They all knew it was true. John made the decision to move forward with the next recruits.

"That leaves us with Davon and Leah," John continued. "Davon used to be my best friend. We confided in each other. We went to church together. We prayed together. We participated in youth group activities together. He was like a brother to me. All of our wonderful memories together came crashing down in ten minutes on a particularly hot July Saturday afternoon."

John proceeded to take off his shirt in front of everyone. He turned around slowly, listening to the gasps he heard from those who were seeing his scars for the first time ever. They were battle scars, ones that would tell a story for a lifetime. The scars on his chest and back were ugly. He then walked up to Davon and reached down and grabbed his hand. He took his former friend's hand and touched the deepest scars with the tips of Davon's fingers. He wanted him to feel the roughness of his skin to remind him that his once perfect teenage body was no longer flawless. It looked like he had been to battle. It looked like he had been attacked by scavengers.

After Davon touched John's skin and as John was walking back to his chair, he immediately stood up and ran about twenty yards away. He grabbed his stomach, bent over, and threw up his lunch onto the grass two feet from a nearby tree. He fell to his knees, and heaved a second time.

Shanice had known Davon for many years. He used to come to the house often, and he spent many Sundays eating her home-cooked meals during the potlucks at church. She knew he was her grandson's best friend, the one who made an extremely poor decision to set John up to take the fall for his shortcomings. Shanice couldn't imagine John forgiving him, when she herself had a difficult time doing so.

As Shanice approached the young man, he was weeping like a baby. She stood a few feet from him watching the tears stream down his tender dark cheeks. It wasn't until that moment that Shanice knew that she also needed to forgive Davon. John couldn't come here and say all the things he had said to everyone without there being forgiveness for all involved. She was the one who painstakingly cared for John back to health after he was released from the hospital.

Everyone was still watching Shanice and Davon from their seats, but they didn't say a word. They watched in anticipation. Shanice surprised them when she got down on her worn knees next to Davon. She placed her arm around his shoulders and whispered quietly into his ear. No one but Davon could hear the words she spoke. "Son," she began, "I believe you and John have some talking to do right now. I want you to know that I had no intentions of forgiving you until just now when I saw your reaction. I'm not sure what John will do, but I am forgiving you for what you did to my grandson. I hope you can be part of our family's lives again someday."

Davon didn't get up, but stayed on his knees facing the field. When

Shanice tried to stand without any support, she struggled. She then placed her hands on the back of Davon's shoulders to push herself to her feet. When Davon realized what was happening, he turned and stood up holding onto her arms to prevent her from falling. He then looked Gramma Bramble in the eyes and said, "Thank you."

Shanice quietly walked over to John and whispered something in his ear. John walked away from the group and headed towards Davon. They both walked across the grass to the front of the house where the dirt road led to nowhere, or so it seemed. The men walked side by side down the road for almost an hour.

Shanice, still standing in front of everyone, let out a sigh of relief. *"This has been a long time coming,"* she thought. She never knew if this day would actually ever arrive. She didn't want to go into details with those who didn't know the full story. She figured Elijah would share with them later, since he was aware of the situation.

"I'm not going to stand here and talk with you about what just took place," Shanice began. "Most of you probably already know. I am going to share with you the story of a young third grader that I had in my class many years ago. His name is Joey. He was one of the sweetest boys that I ever taught. He paid attention in class, followed instruction, was respectful of others, and tried his very best. When he didn't understand something, he would politely raise his hand and ask a question to clarify his doubts. He was always trying to help other classmates, and he refused to do poorly on a test. He was a smart young fella."

As Shanice told her story, she looked around at all the men sitting in the group, but she refused to look at Leah. She didn't want to give Leah the chance to speak without completing her story. She did notice, out of the corner of her eye, that Leah had become frigid in her seat.

"That young Joey grew up and became Joe. He worked two jobs as he struggled to make ends meet. He wasn't going to give up on his dream of becoming an electrical engineer. He took class after class, studied hard, and eventually received a four-year degree in electrical engineering."

It was at that moment that Leah knew that her Joe was the same Joey being discussed. She tried to hide her gasp with a cough. Shanice continued to speak.

"He married a beautiful woman, and together they had a beautiful young daughter, Melody, who is as bright as her father. A couple years ago, the couple was blessed with a son, Dion. The little baby isn't so little anymore, though. He's a funny toddler who loves to laugh. His sister, who can read really well at her young age, even tries to teach him how to read. Unfortunately, the children's mother decided being a mom wasn't satisfying enough for her, and she chose to leave their family."

"That's just down right stupid," EZ said, before realizing that he shouldn't have spoken. "I'm sorry, Mrs. Bramble. I shoulda kept that thought to myself."

Shanice continued again. "The beautiful young mother tried to run from her problems. It's possible that she had postpartum depression like many young mothers after giving birth to a child, but that's something we will never know. This particular mother found herself trapped between her own selfish desires and the responsibility of adulthood. After quitting several jobs that were completely unfulfilling to her, she accepted a position caring for babies. Who would have thought?"

A few of the men chuckled when they heard this part of the story, but no one spoke, and no one guessed that it was Leah that Shanice was speaking about.

"What this young mother doesn't know is this," Shanice said, as she turned to look at Leah for the first time. "Your husband and children were rescued by John, my grandson, and his father during Hurricane Cecelia. It ripped through Carol City like you wouldn't believe. Their car was hit by a falling tree when Joe was heading home during the storm. Fortunately, Joe recovered from his concussion, and neither of your children were hurt."

Leah sat there with her mouth opened wide, as shock filled every inch of her body.

"Joe still works out at the airport. He's had a promotion since you have last seen him, and your children are growing like weeds. There isn't anything they would like more than to see their mother and wife again."

"Really?" Leah shouted through the tears. "I can see them again?" she asked, as she stood up to hug Shanice.

"Yes, Dear, you can," Shanice assured her.

The guys couldn't believe that Leah was married. They had tried to flirt with her on numerous occasions, which led Henry to the "off-limits" mandate that he held for her.

"You never once told us that you had children," Tonya remarked.

"I was too embarrassed to tell you."

Adeline then took a photo out of her packet of information and handed a picture of the Sanderson family to Leah. "This picture was taken two days ago," she told the young woman. "Joe knows that we are hoping to bring you home with us, if that's alright with you."

"Yes, definitely, yes!" Leah shouted. "I can't believe I'm going to be able to see them again. I thought we were all stuck here for a while. I honestly don't remember when my contract even expires."

Warren had patiently waited before he said a thing. He then asked Leah, "Are you ready to be your kids' mother again? We need to know that you truly are ready for that responsibility again. I've heard that you are doing a great job with the babies and young ones here."

"Oh, yes. I am so ready. All the days that I've been caring for the little ones, I just dream about Melody and Dion. I can't believe I was so foolish to leave in the first place. How did you know that I would have a change of heart after taking care of babies who weren't my own?"

"We didn't," Shanice said. "We were hoping that we could find some good in that broken heart of yours and take a bad situation and give it some hope. I don't think it was by coincidence that my family stumbled upon your husband during the storm. I think the good Lord was watching over all of you and put us at the right place at the right time."

CHAPTER TWENTY-FIVE

"Those guys are a bunch of liars," Frank stated loudly so all the living creatures on either side of the dirt road could hear him. He had placed all of his belongings, which consisted of three t-shirts, a sweatshirt, two pairs of shorts, one pair of sweatpants, a pair of jeans, a pillow, sheet, blanket, three pairs of socks, tattered tennis shoes, some dollar store flip-flops, a tooth brush with a newly opened tube of toothpaste, his metal cup, and his signed contract into his pillowcase and was clutching it back and forth between each hand, as it laid heavy against his back. Nia had also given him some peanut butter and jelly sandwiches, crackers, and some water before he set out on his journey. "I don't believe any of them. They're a bunch of liars."

Frank had been walking down the dirt road for nearly three hours already. The sun was still high enough in the sky to provide all the daylight he needed to make his trek. Unfortunately, the dirt road would not lead him off of the plantation anytime soon. He was hot and tired and had already gone through much of his water. He could only go in two directions when he left the house, if he were to stay on the road. He chose to walk in the opposite direction of the fields they had worked because he knew there was nothing for miles in that direction. He had passed the stream that Jaheem, Regi, and EZ had told the group about when the truck had a flat tire. He still had most of his water with him at that time, so he didn't think to fill his water jug.

He continued to walk with sweat dripping down his forehead into his eyes. He stopped for a moment to wipe his face on his pillow case. *"I've been dreaming of the day my collar would come off,"* he thought. "I can't believe no one came with me," he muttered out loud. "What are the guys thinking? I'm free at last." He really had wanted Ralph to join him, but Ralph refused. Initially, Frank believed every word John said. Once his collar came off he was overwhelmed with confusion, believing that his freedom could be snatched from him a second time just as it had been before.

After John, Warren, the attorney, and the ladies had made their peace, Frank stormed off. He had three days to consider his decision and had decided prior to hearing the rest of the story that he was tired of working on the plantation. He had made up his mind to leave, hoping that would be the best option for him. He didn't even listen to all the details because he simply wanted to leave.

"Where do you plan to go?" Ralph had asked him. "It's not like you have a family or any relatives to see."

Even Oreo tried to convince Frank to stay. He followed Frank down the road for a half mile, corralling him in an effort to get Frank to turn back. When Frank refused, Oreo returned to the sound of Mac's whistle.

Now Frank kept pondering Ralph's question over and over again in his mind. "He's right. I have zero family. Nobody even cares about me. This was the closest thing to family that I've had in years. But, there is still something compelling about being your own boss one hundred percent of the time," Frank told himself.

The stars were bright, and the sky was big. It was always big on the plantation because there were very few trees around. Overgrown fields were on both sides of him, and when he looked straight ahead the road led to the horizon. He looked around again at the overgrown fields. He knew the bugs and potential snakes could be bad if he walked through the tall weeds. He didn't want to do that, so he decided to stick with the dirt road. The sun was setting in the field to his left, so he knew he was traveling north.

He continued to walk aimlessly. The perk in his walk was no longer there. It had left him hours ago. He was tired and was now debating with himself. Maybe he would feel different in the morning after a good night's sleep, he thought.

"I guess this spot is as good as any," he vocalized loudly, as he sat down on the dirt road. He pulled out his remaining sandwich and ate it slowly. When he was done, he rinsed his sticky fingers with a little bit of water and drank a big swig. "Should I keep walking under the moonlit sky?" he asked himself. He could hear the crickets and katydids in the fields around him. He had once thought the green bush crickets were grasshoppers, but Regi had pointed out to everybody one day that the large green insects in their fields were actually katydids. Regi had explained that cicadas actually sing during the day, and the crickets come out at night.

He placed his pillow on the ground and pulled out his blanket to sleep on top of it until he got cold. "*I guess my blanket and pillow are going to get dirty,*" he thought again. He laid down, looking up into the night sky. He found the Big Dipper and then the Little Dipper, but he didn't know any of the other constellations. "*I wish I knew more about stars.*"

"*Where should I go?*" he thought. "*I don't have any family, so no one has even missed me. I can go anywhere. Maybe I should continue north where the summer days aren't so miserable.*" As he laid quietly, thinking of his freedom and his plans, he drifted in and out of sleep. "Oh, this is uncomfortable," he said out loud for the second time, when he rolled over. "I wish I had my bed right now." He tossed and turned throughout the night.

When he finally woke, the stars were not as bright in the sky. He figured it was probably four or five in the morning, but decided he should continue his hike while the sun was still down. He wouldn't be falling back to sleep now anyway. His hips were sore from sleeping on the hard ground, and his muscles were now stiff.

"To another day of freedom," he said, as he jolted his water jug up above his head, only to realize that it was now almost empty. "There must be another stream or more water somewhere near me," he hoped. He walked in the stillness of the night for probably an hour when his stomach started to growl. The sky was getting brighter, but the sun still had not risen yet. He looked around in every direction. The road still beckoned him, even though he could see no end in sight. He then recalled the words that Henry had spoken months earlier, "Some of you might think you can just walk out of here. I'm telling you right now that this place is bigger than you can ever imagine. There's no easy walk out of here."

Frank searched his pillow case again. "Did I already eat all the sandwiches?" he asked himself. In the darkness of his bag, he fumbled through his t-shirts and socks until he found a package of Ritz crackers.

"Oh, geez. Crap." He looked in both directions again. His mind was torn. *"Lies or freedom?"* he argued with himself. He stood dazed, looking to the north for a minute, then to the south, and then back to the north again. "What should I do?" he screamed as loud as he could, but no one was around to hear him. As he was pondering his options, he turned to the east and watched as the sun rose just above the horizon.

Fourteen hours earlier, John had whispered into MacKenzie's ear before addressing the group again. "Say a prayer for me," he whispered, "I'm not sure everyone is going to believe us."

"Good morning," John addressed his attentive audience that day, as they met to hear the details about the plantation itself. Everyone had gathered outside again for their final day of meetings. "Now that you all know why you are here and you have all been given a copy of your signed contract, we want to explain some specifics about this arrangement. You may not agree with everything that has happened or will continue to happen, but this is the arrangement that has been made, and each of you will be given a choice later today that decides your future."

"I am going to start with the land itself. Warren took me up in his plane yesterday to get a bird's eye view of the land. I own a thousand acres across the street from the house where the new barn is located." John pointed to the new barn to make sure that they all knew which barn he was referencing. He then pointed to the old barn, which everyone still believed was the old barn, except for the married couples and Leah. They still had been sworn to secrecy not to say a word about its interior. "The old barn belongs to Mr. Laikin.

"Yes. I own it along with ten thousand acres that run parallel to this property, all the way to the river," Warren said.

"That's a lot of land," Charlie said.

"Yes, it is, Charlie," Warren agreed, as he smiled.

"All of you, including Ryan, own this house, the bunk houses, the shower house, the smaller barn, and the chicken coops," Warren continued. "In total you jointly own another thousand acres."

"You're shittin us," Frank sassed when he heard the news.

"No, Frank, he's not," Jonathan Trieger announced. "I have all the documents here to show you and to prove to you that you are rightly titled to this land. If any of you had read your signed contracts, which I doubt any of you have done yet, you would see that you signed off to some additional stipulations. We are going to review those now with you."

"As it stands today, not only do you own this land, but you also are stakeholders in the cotton venture that you began. Over the past couple of years, you have each profited forty-two thousand eight hundred and fifty-seven dollars, after all expenses have been paid and distributed. In addition, twenty percent of all your profits have been given to three charities."

"The Carol City Poverty Relief Organization was established after Hurricane Cecelia to help low-income families recuperate from losses due to hurricanes, illness, loss of jobs, and a number of other misfortunes. We felt many of you would appreciate this type of organization since many have walked down similar paths. The Cancer Society of Florida is another charity in which you are contributing. This was chosen in honor of the loved ones whom some of you have lost to cancer. The third charity is the Florida Scholarship Fund which allows children of all ages to receive funding for education, athletic endeavors, and personal enrichment programs such as summer camps. The purpose of this is to help ensure success for all children facing restraints that prevent them from bettering themselves."

"Wow," Jaheem said, shocked that this much effort was put in place to help each of them advance to a better place in life.

"You guys care that much about each of us?" Ralph asked.

"When I first wrote the paper, I didn't," John admitted, "but these two ladies, my gramma and my neighbor believed we could not only fix a problem, but set a standard in place to help generations to come. They have diligently been working on this for the past four years."

"All the land that has been farmed so far, which is a fraction of the property owned, belongs to you. John and I will both be adding our properties into the mix to generate several businesses that will blow your socks off. We will continue the cotton business and Charlie's tobacco venture. In the 1800s, there were over forty-four thousand tobacco plantations in the United States. Today, there are less than fifty tobacco manufacturers remaining. With Charlie's knowledge and success of his first crop, we should be able to become the largest supplier in the United States within the next seven years," Warren explained.

"You guys are insane," EZ stated. "I mean that in a good way too," he added. "So, I got myself a real job now, huh?"

"Yes, Elijah, and it even gets better," John shared. "Mrs. DeWitt's and Mr. Laikin's teams of business experts and legal counsel have established a logistical plan which includes everything imaginable to make this a success. We don't want to hire people just to hire people. We want to transform lives, making people accountable for their actions. This isn't going to be done in spite to harm anyone, but to help them. When recruits first come, they will be living under the same conditions that you already encountered. We want people to walk away from here with a new understanding of life, a new set of values, and money in their pockets."

"Right now, people working for minimum wage can't get ahead because the cost of living is too expensive. You probably all thought you were working for free, but the reality is that we set up bank accounts for each of you, and there is money in them. And, Charlie, your car dealerships are running on automatic pilot, so you haven't lost one dime on any revenue from them either," Jonathan added. "I will explain to you privately what is happening with them."

"I definitely want to talk about that sooner than later," Charlie confirmed.

"We plan to give you a general overview right now of our plan. Then, as a team, we want to speak with each of you privately to discuss what your potential roles can be. By sunset tomorrow, we will need an answer from each of you to accept or decline your offer."

"Wait, wait, wait," Regi said in a disturbing way. "I am confused."

"Go ahead," Adeline said.

"If we own the property as you have indicated, and the business is ours already, why do we even need your consent to move forward with plans?"

"I'll answer this question," Jonathan said with enthusiasm. "Currently, all fourteen of you own the property which we spoke about previously and the property which you have been cultivating for the past two seasons. The cotton business itself is a separate identity that currently leases the land from which you have cultivated the cotton. This business, like all businesses, is set up with a Board of Directors. We are the Board of Directors. We currently sell your finished product."

"Technically, you guys could choose as a group not to sell your cotton to us. There is nothing we can do legally to force you to sign the new agreements which we are proposing. Of course, if you choose not to work with us, we would take our existing properties on both sides of you and continue our plans because they will be generating millions of dollars in revenue. And, it's very likely that we would try to buy the land of anyone who doesn't want to participate and give them a cash offer too great for them to refuse. This in return would diminish your property and your competition would likely succeed in limiting your ability to perform at the highest level possible."

"Basically, what you are saying is that money and power take precedent right now?"

"Not exactly, what I am saying is that there are legal parameters in which businesses must operate. We are operating under those parameters and legitimately giving each of you an opportunity of a lifetime. Not only have we tried to correct some disturbing behavior patterns, but we also have provided a way for you to make a living that is solely dependent on your own leadership."

Regi continued his questioning. "If, for example, I want to go back to teaching and coaching basketball, I can do that, and I will still receive a percentage of profit from the business?"

Warren spoke next. "Regi, you can choose to make whatever decision you feel is best for your family. The profit in the business is based on you working for the company. If you choose to leave, you will not receive any stipend for work not performed. There are several options. You can receive fees from leasing your land back to the business. You could choose to lease your land to this group, or to anyone else for that matter. If you choose to lease it to someone else it may be difficult because there is no infrastructure within the current property."

"None of the roads on this twelve thousand acre plot belong to the fourteen of you. Your property is surrounded by our property, which greatly limits your option to build roads out. This main dirt road actually belongs to John. You could also choose to sell your property to anyone of your choice. Or, you could choose to do nothing at all. I guess there is another option as well. You could choose to build a house on your seventy-one acres. Even if you choose to do nothing with the land, there are still property taxes that must be paid annually. That is not a small sum for a property of this magnitude."

"I get it. Thanks for the explanation."

"You know, Mr. Taylor," John continued. "There is actually something else that could be much more rewarding for you in this scenario. You could homeschool a bunch of troubled youth here on the plantation who have natural athletic skills and create your own basketball team. Do you realize the headlines you would make if you could win a state championship having those boys learn valuable life lessons here, while going to school, and becoming stellar athletes? I'm sure you and Jaheem could establish an incredible program."

"I guess I've been looking back at the wasted days I spent here early on, rather than the future that still lies ahead."

Jaheem looked over at Regi. "Maybe he has a point."

"In my opinion," Ralph muttered, "I think you first played God by judging and punishing us for the things we did to you all that you didn't like. Not that we didn't deserve punishment. You just took matters into your own hands and hid it behind the law."

"What's your point?" Warren asked, not giving Ralph a chance to answer. "If we were punishing you, we would not have set you up for success. I still think your best option is here rather than behind bars."

"Maybe, but at least we would have had a chance for probation instead of jail time."

"And, you believe the prison system is a better option?" Henry inquired. "I can't imagine anyone preferring that as a first option, let alone the strain it causes on society."

Ralph pondered for a moment. "No, I don't," he answered. "I just have a mean streak in me, and wanted to vent."

Trying to be respectful, Warren continued. "You have a valid opinion, Ralph. However, with the exception of Charlie, none of you would have had an opportunity like this to make millions. This story is not just about the money either. This is about making lifestyle changes. This is about accountability. This is about reform."

Shanice spoke again. "My dear, Elijah," she began. "Be honest with me. Do you think you would still be alive today if you had stayed back in Carol City?"

He thought about it for a moment. "Probably not."

"We know there were some drug lords after you, and you will never need to worry about them ever again."

"I was in much deeper than I shoulda been," he admitted.

"You guys can say all you want," Jonathan piped in again. "The bottom line is that attorneys and prosecutors love people who are less polished or educated. They make a pretty penny off of the ignorance of people. I know for a fact that this plantation did all of you some good."

Adeline then stood up. "Before we move on and talk details," she said, "we want to release you of your current obligations. But, I have to warn you. If anyone chooses to steal a vehicle, plane, or do anything else to harm any of us, there will be immediate retribution. Within two minutes of that plane taking off, it would disintegrate in midair. It wouldn't be the first plane I have blown up, and likely won't be the last. As far as the vehicles are concerned, I'll let you drive a half mile down the road before detonating a bomb to explode in them. That's far enough away to keep any of the debris from harming anyone else."

"Shit. Who are ya Mrs. DeWitt?" EZ asked.

She didn't bother to answer Elijah's question. She took a quick look at her phone and began talking again. "Now that I have made myself clear to each of you," she said, "I want you to take off your collars."

They looked at one another in disbelief. They didn't think this would be happening now. Immediately, their demeanors changed and smiles returned to their faces. There was a slight clicking sound, and all thirteen collars were unlatched.

"It feels good, doesn't it?" Ryan asked his friends.

Each one took his or her collar off and rubbed their necks. They were free at last. Henry walked around to each of them and collected the collars as they spoke to one another in relief.

"I can't believe it," Alvaro stated. "I'm so used to this thing that I feel naked without it." The men laughed.

"Can't I keep mine for a souvenir?" EZ asked.

"Not today," Adeline told the neighbor boy. "That is one expensive souvenir that you can't afford to keep."

"Come on guys, let's go," Frank said, as he tried to get anyone to leave with him. "I'm out of here. Freedom at last."

"Frank," Ralph said, "We still need to hear the details. Besides, where do you plan to go?"

"I'm going to walk to the nearest gas station and hitch a ride," Frank said.

"Seriously, Frank," Ralph tried to reason with his friend, "There ain't no nearest gas station. You know where we keep gas for the farm equipment."

Henry then tried to reason with Frank. "You already admitted that you liked having your own bed to sleep on each night and home cooked meals every day. Why would you give those up now, especially since you have an invested interest in this place?"

"It's just too good to be true. This is like some story or movie that you see in the theater. This can't be real."

"Hey, Frank," Ryan said, as he approached Frank. "I'm telling you the truth. This is not fake. I've already seen the money in my bank account, and you'll be seeing yours soon too. This is, by far, your best option. You've been thrown a lot of curveballs in life, and you have chosen to duck and take your eye off the ball. You don't want to take your eye off this curveball. It's going to be a homerun for sure, if you choose to take it."

"Cute analogy, kid, but I'm not buying any of this. I'll be off of this plantation in twenty-four hours. Best of luck."

"Yeah, you too," Ryan told Frank, as he reached over to hug him.

"Thanks for being my friend, Ralph. You're the only friend I've ever had. I'm going to miss you, but I'll know where to find you. Take care."

"Hey man," Ralph responded. "You don't need to hug me. I know you'll be back within twenty-four hours. It's going to take you a lot longer than twenty-four hours to find your way out of here."

While the men were saying their final goodbyes to Frank, Nia had quickly gone into the kitchen and made some sandwiches for Frank.

"Here," she said, as she handed him some sandwiches and crackers.

"If I had known you would be leaving us so soon, I would have tried to put a care package together, but this is all I could find on short notice."

"Thanks, Nia. This should tie me over until I get to a gas station."

As everyone waved goodbye to Frank, the betting began.

"He'll be back by nightfall," Regi insisted.

"No, I think he'll return at sunrise," Charlie began.

"I think you are both wrong," Ralph stated. "He'll be back in four hours. He's too lazy to walk any further than that."

"Don't you think you should go after him by sunset?" Tonya asked her husband.

"Nope," Henry replied. "There's nowhere for him to go except down a long, dusty road. He'll run out of food and water, and he'll be back tomorrow. Just wait and see."

The rest of the day was spent reviewing the details of the business, job roles, and plans to reunite family members. Everyone had a specific skill set that would be utilized in the business. Some of the group would be staying on the plantation while others would be working from home offices in South Florida.

With the exception of Frank and Daniel, everyone had signed new contracts indicating their role within the business ventures. Daniel was undecided if he wanted to stay, depending upon the birth of Amber's child. They agreed to wait until after the baby was born to determine the role Daniel would play in the business.

Shanice and Adeline pulled Charlie aside after Jonathan had spoken with him. "We have some bad news for you," Shanice told him. Adeline then pulled some photos out of her folder and handed them to Charlie.

"When did this happen?" he asked.

"Exactly one week after your disappearance," Shanice recalled.

"Anna phoned Ebony right away, acting as if she was concerned about you. The truth is that she was elated when you disappeared. That gave her the alibi she needed to move on."

"What about the kids?" Charlie asked.

Both of his children had been out of college for a couple of years and living on their own. "Bryce wouldn't talk to Anna for several months after she told him that she was leaving you. Brianna had told Bryce that she had suspected something was going on, but never could prove anything. We believe they will be happy to see you again."

"I sure do miss them," Charlie said. "I suspected that Anna was having an affair too, but I was too busy working to confront her."

"Fortunately," Adeline added, "You did a great job in securing your business assets. Since Anna left you, prior to the legal limits of missing persons being met, she is not privy to any of your business accounts. We have written up a new will for you that Jonathan can review with you appointing both Bryce and Brianna as your sole recipients. In addition, as of today, your debt to Ebony has been paid in full, including interest."

"Thank you. Jonathan mentioned that he wanted to review some more things with me after I spoke with you. I guess this is what he was talking about."

"It is," Adeline admitted.

"Eboy is not aware of any of this. I am hopeful she will be forgiving," Shanice added.

"Yes, I really messed up. Greed got the best of me."

"It sure did," Shanice agreed. "but those days are gone now."

"I learned a lesson or two. I can't tell you how excited I am to be launching a tobacco business. Don't get me wrong. I love cars, but there's something exciting about the cigar industry."

"Knowing your success with your dealerships, I'm sure you will do just fine in the tobacco business," Shanice said.

The team continued to talk with each person individually, answering questions and concerns. The evening ended on a peaceful note. Everyone was smiling and enjoying themselves. Charlie had pulled out a cigar for each of them. Shanice and Adeline declined the offer along with Regi and Nia. Ryan, who still wasn't sure he wanted to try one, took a few puffs. Charlie even gave him a really good one to try, along with the first one that Ryan had ever made.

"Wow. There's such a difference in taste," Ryan said, expecting both cigars to be alike.

"I told you there would be a difference," Charlie chuckled.

"I don't know if I'll be able to sleep tonight," Jaheem told everyone as he puffed away. "It feels like Christmas Eve when I was a kid. I was so anxious for the morning to come that I couldn't sleep."

His friends laughed.

"To new beginnings," Alvaro shouted.

"To friendship," Ryan stated.

Many of them stayed up longer than they had planned, but when morning arrived they were still full of smiles.

"This is the beginning of a new chapter," Davon told everyone in the room when they were first waking up. "I just hope I don't blow it again."

"Most of us probably feel that same way," Jaheem said. "I definitely was foolish in high school, and I sure hope I never go back to my old ways."

Today was the beginning of a new day for each of them. Some would be heading home, and others would be staying to oversee the new workers who were on board now. They had a plan, and almost everyone was eager to see where it would lead.

After breakfast, Charlie and Leah climbed into the private plane with Warren, Jonathan, Shanice, and Adeline. Neither Charlie nor Leah had expected to be leaving the plantation via aircraft. Ryan and Jaheem walked out to the plane with them to wish them well. Nia and Regi also came out with their children to watch the plane take off.

Charlie had already notified his children, and they were planning to meet him for lunch at a restaurant near the airport in Jacksonville. It would be a quick stop for Charlie to see his children before they headed back to Miami where Charlie could talk with his sister, and Leah could reunite with her children and husband.

MacKenzie and John were taking Ryan, Elijah, and Davon back with them in the Cadillac. The others would be coming at a later time. A schedule had been established, and everyone had agreed to the terms.

"Look," Charlie pointed to everyone in the plane after they had taken off. Beneath the plane, several miles from the house, they could see Frank walking down the road towards the house. "What time is it?"

"It's five minutes after eleven," Shanice stated.

"I guess we all lost that bet," Charlie said.

"Speak for yourself, Charlie." Adeline told the small group. "Warren, you owe me a thousand dollars."

Everyone on the plane laughed.

Frank stopped and watched until the plane flew out of sight. Thirty minutes later he knew everything would be just fine. While sweat dripped off his stringy hair onto his forehead and into his eyes, he could barely see something approaching down the road. His feet were aching as he dragged one foot in front of the other. His hunger pains were long gone, and his mouth and throat were parched beyond anything he had ever experienced before. He slowly kept walking. Despite his physical agony, he finally saw a glimpse of hope. Oreo was running down the dirt road to greet him, carrying a bottle of water in his mouth.

ABOUT THE AUTHOR

Andre Linoge is a black man of courage, dignity, and strength. Although life has not treated him as equally as some might prefer, Linoge does not hold that against anyone. He is a realist who knows that good conduct goes a long way in life. Believing in oneself and staying true to healthy moral principles matter to him.

He does not look at a closed door as a lost opportunity. Instead, he sees a closed door as a learning tool that leads to a better view. Sometimes that view may be from another opened door, sometimes it might be from a small window tucked away in an old alley, and sometimes it might simply be a crack in a wall. No matter the place from which that view is seen, it is a picture of hope, opportunity, and perspective. No one can take that view away from you, nor change the fact that you saw the view. It is always a part of one's soul, which cannot be erased. Using the experience to gain a better understanding is key in moving forward.

Andre Linoge loves to learn. He believes learning is essential to living a happy life. Instead of complaining about the things he cannot control, he believes in changing the negative things in his life that he can control.